DETEST-A-

TENTACLE

2.0

DEADLY DEPTHS

Lee Gabel

Frankenscript Press
Box 717, #105 - 1497 Admirals Road
Victoria, BC, Canada   V9A 2P8

Tentacle 2.0

Cover illustration and design by Lee Gabel

Cover images supplied by DepositPhotos

Body font (ITC Galliard Pro) by International Typeface Corporation
Folios, heads, and caps (Zapf Humanist 601) by Bitstream Inc.

ISBN 978-1-9991856-9-5 (ebook)
ISBN 978-1-7387436-9-8 (paperback)
ISBN 978-1-998869-00-8 (hardcover)

Want to join Lee's Reader Group or find out more about Lee and the books he writes? Please go to: LeeGabel.com/links or visit his bookshop at: Bookshop.LeeGabel.com

TENTACLE 2.0

DEADLY DEPTHS

Friendship takes many forms.
Sometimes you need to let go to find it.

Rite of Passage

When Sam cracked open his eyes, they had already adjusted to the darkness, like a pirate switching an eye patch to descend below deck. But his visual advantage did nothing to help him orient himself. Varied points of dim light peppered his field of view.

Stars? How long have I been out?

It must have been the strong malodor that had pulled Sam from unconsciousness. The humid air here carried a pungent scent of seaweed, rot, and oxidizing metal, and left an oily sheen on his skin. It took energy to breathe.

He rubbed his eyelids in hopes that his vision would improve and offer more clues, but his hands came away gritty and his eyes burned. It felt like someone had thrown sand in his face. The more he blinked, the more his eyes protested.

Sam winced and licked his dry lips.

Salty. And so thirsty.

Relief came only when he kept his eyes closed. He pictured the last good thing he could remember before blacking out: a cloudless dawn sky.

He swallowed hard and his parched throat clicked. Once the burning in his eyes had faded, he opened them again and craned his neck to scan his unfamiliar surroundings. Pain immediately shot through his neck and shoulders like he was the recipient of some cruel voodoo doll curse, which was a definite possibility considering what he had already done during this trip. If only he had a do-over.

Flashbacks of the oppressive sinkhole at Mar-a-Verde and the bloodthirsty acidbacks flooded his mind, pushing out the image of a perfect summer morning. Could there be acidbacks here, too? What about rats? Or spiders? Panic welled up, fueled by the oppressive miasma of death and decay. Sam barely managed to stifle a scream. He focused on the points of light above and around him, which seemed just a little bit brighter now. Their positions shifted even with the subtle movements of his head.

They're not stars.

The occasional sound of dripping water kept odd but regular time in this mysterious place and helped him get his panic in check. His breathing calmed and he began a systematic check of his body from where he lay.

Sam wiggled his toes on both bare feet and heard small splashes. He raised his right foot up and detected the change of water to air on his skin and the tickle of drips finding their way back down the soles of his feet to their source. He began to prop himself up on his elbows when a different, searing pain from his abdomen took his breath away. He fought against spasms that made the pain worse and laid back once again, breathing through clenched teeth.

Sam ran the fingers of his left hand over his shirt, just above the waistband of his shorts. The fabric felt warm and sticky to the touch. Held in front of his face, he could see nothing except the void made by his hand against the backdrop of random pinholes. He didn't need to see it to know what it was. Sam brought his hand close to his nose, then tasted a fingertip, confirming his suspicions.

Blood.

He gently peeled back the hem of the shirt and exposed his skin to the air and whatever else that might be watching him. It did not take long for his fingertips to find the source of the pain and blood. A gash about six inches long crossed the left side of his abdomen. There was no way to know how deep the cut went without probing it. The last thing he wanted was the pain to cause him to pass out again.

Sam's problems multiplied. He couldn't move easily. He had no idea where he was or how to get out. And he had no food or water.

No water.

That meant he'd be dead in three days, or less depending on how long he had been unconscious.

Some Hawaiian holiday this turned out to be.

FOUR DAYS EARLIER, staff, students, and family had packed the Washbrook High School auditorium to capacity. Staff had just finished their congratulatory speeches and begun calling up students to the stage to accept their graduation diplomas.

Sam pulled out his phone and opened his text messages. Ever since his parole officially ended, he had spent a lot of time assimilating modern society and technology. But one aspect he could never grasp was the ever-changing abbreviations used in text messages. Instead, he spelled everything out. It was slower, and most younger people found the messages rude, but at least there was no confusion on his side.

His last text to O'Connor, held captive in a blue speech bubble, stared back at him. "Where are you?" Just like when he checked fifteen minutes ago, there was no response, not even those infuriating three little dots that showed when someone was typing.

Sam shoved his phone back into his pocket. "Dammit, O'Connor." A parent sitting in the next seat gave him a wary eye.

Sam discovered long ago that O'Connor was a wild card and

he had prepared for it. He had taken an aisle seat at the back of the auditorium to stow his suitcase and allow easy escape and re-entry from the adjoining hallway.

A steady stream of students were crossing the stage in alphabetical order, their faces filled with nervous, happy energy. They had already reached "H". Soon, it would be—

"Jack Johnson." Principal Durant, dressed in a sharp pant suit, directed her gaze to the opposite side of the stage as Jack walked confidently to accept his diploma.

Cheers erupted from a section of the audience. Sam meant to clap but O'Connor's uncertain arrival kept him distracted and on edge. He checked his phone again. No new messages.

Sam scanned the audience. "Jesus Christ," he said as he stood up. Several audience members shushed him with disapproving looks. "Sorry," he said as he bolted for the exit.

He peered up and down the empty hallway outside the auditorium, his hands on his hips. He could hear names echoing from the auditorium doors. Sam stepped back, leaned against the wall, and rubbed his face, now covered with a sheen of anxious sweat. "Fuck me…"

"Thought you'd never ask. When and where?"

Sam looked up to find O'Connor standing several feet away, grinning and flashing her eyebrows at him. At her feet was a single well-traveled suitcase perched on its wheels. She wore leather work boots, cargo pants and an almost-white button-up shirt with the Detest-A-Pest logo embroidered on it. Clamped between her jaws was her signature smoldering cigar stub. At least she wasn't wearing a hazmat suit.

"Don't start." Sam pointed at her emphatically. "I told you we should've taken the same flight."

O'Connor turned on her best bedroom eyes. "Are you fingering me, Sam?"

"Ugh." Sam shook his head, exasperated, and waved his hand

toward the auditorium entrance. "Hurry up or you'll miss Brad." Sam eyed the cigar. "And put that out."

"Don't get your fucking panties in a twist." O'Connor plucked the cigar from her mouth and rubbed the lit end against the tread of her right boot. She left a pile of ash behind as she stuck the cigar back between her jaws.

"Come on! You're going to miss him." Sam waved O'Connor into the auditorium and led her to his aisle seat, parking her suitcase next to his.

"Stop fuckin' fussing." O'Connor pushed Sam away and sat down. She looked at the parent next to her. "How's it hanging, toots?" Before they could respond, O'Connor spotted Bradley waiting in the wings at the side of the stage.

O'Connor stood up clapping and cheering, loud enough to overpower the names announced by Durant. "Alright! Brad-ley! Brad-ley! Brad-ley!"

The audience turned toward O'Connor's boisterous outburst, some yelling at her to be quiet.

"Please." Principal Durant leaned into the microphone. "You in the back, please keep your voice down."

O'Connor waved her off. "Eat me. I saved all your asses last year, remember?" She cupped her hands around her mouth. "Brad! The Bradmeister! Rad Brad!"

Durant cut her losses when she saw who was up next and announced the next name. "Bradley Shaw."

Sam knew O'Connor was beyond his control, so he tuned her out and focused on applauding his son's accomplishment, a wide smile on his face.

"That's my boy!" O'Connor jumped up from her seat and pushed past Sam, trudging quickly toward the stage.

Sam made a half-hearted attempt to stop her, then shrugged and continued clapping. "Just don't embarrass him," he said to himself.

O'Connor hoisted herself up on the edge of the stage, swung her right leg up, and rolled the rest of the way.

Bradley had stopped his progress to center stage, black graduation gown swaying around his feet. "O'Connor?"

He watched with surprised amusement as she stood to face him, holding out open arms.

"Gimme some sugar!" O'Connor wrapped Bradley with a tight bear hug and rocked backward, lifting him off his feet.

Sam shook his head and laughed quietly to himself. "Always the showboat."

O'Connor released Bradley and stepped over to Principal Durant. She recoiled at O'Connor's approach. "What? I'm not gonna bite you… unless you want me to."

Durant furrowed her brow and frowned just as O'Connor grabbed the microphone.

She pointed at Bradley. "Give it up for Bradley fuckin' Shaw! Man of the fuckin' hour." O'Connor dropped the microphone, hooked her arm around Bradley's neck, and led him off stage, encouraged by hoots and hollers from his classmates. He grabbed his diploma from Durant as he walked by, sharing a brief handshake.

"Thanks," Bradley said to Durant. "And sorry." He motioned at O'Connor pulling him across the rest of the stage and down the side stairs. Durant returned a pained smile and nodded before picking up the microphone and continuing the ceremony.

"Let's blow this popsicle stand."

"It's awesome that you're here… I can't believe it actually, but I can't leave yet," Bradley said.

"Sure you can. Come on. Sam's waiting."

"O'Connor." Bradley grabbed her shoulders with both hands. "Listen to me." He hugged her and whispered in her ear. "Thanks, but I want to sit here with my friends. Plus Trillian is up soon." He stepped back. "Okay? See you when it's over."

O'Connor hadn't expected to be overruled by a teenager, but

she recovered quickly. "Damn straight." She nodded and pointed back at Bradley as she walked casually back to her seat. "Bradley fuckin' Shaw in da house!"

Instead of disdain like when O'Connor had first piped up, the audience broke into applause. She bowed and returned to her seat.

Sam grinned at her. "Even when it's not about you, it's always about you."

O'Connor shrugged. "What can I say. When you got it, you got it. And I got it."

"Trillian Stark," Principal Durant announced. Claps and cheers rose up from the audience.

Trillian strutted across the stage, her bright orange and closely cropped hair practically lighting the way.

Sam placed a hand on O'Connor's shoulder and shook his head. "Once is enough."

O'Connor stood, clapping. "Okay, *dad*." She grabbed her cigar stub with one hand and placed her index finger and thumb of her other hand between her lips and blew. A shrill whistle blasted across the auditorium. "Trillian for the win! You go, girl!"

Sam clapped enthusiastically. "You're too much."

"Au contraire," O'Connor said between whistles. "I'm never enough!"

"I think the audience would disagree."

O'Connor managed to keep her voice down for the rest of the ceremony and Sam was quick to pull her out of the auditorium when it finished twenty minutes later.

"Your friend sure likes the sound of her own voice."

Sam turned to find his ex-wife looking at him warmly. He glanced up the hallway to where O'Connor was busying herself reading one of the many bulletin boards scattered around the school. Out of earshot, a good thing.

"Claire." Sam pushed his and O'Connor's suitcases aside and

gave her a hug. Their bodies still fit nicely together, even after their separation so many years ago.

"My… *our* son is all grown up." Claire pulled away. "We did a good job."

"*You* did a good job. I had nothing to do with it."

"The last couple of years have meant a lot to him, Sam. You've really stepped up," Claire said.

Sam opened his mouth to respond, then balked.

"Take the compliment. I don't give them out lightly."

Sam nodded. "Thank you."

"Mom! Dad!" Bradley hustled down the hallway toward Sam and Claire, with Jack and Trillian following close behind. He hugged Sam. "If O'Connor was here, I was hoping you'd be too."

"I wouldn't miss it. Congratulations, son."

Jack spotted O'Connor in the crowded hallway and dragged Trillian over to her. "What you did was epic! Why didn't you do that for me?"

"Sam made me late."

"Fuck you. Did not," Sam said from behind the group. "She didn't listen to me and had to take a different flight."

"I got here, didn't I?" O'Connor gave Sam a playful sneer. "So, can it, Mr. Maxipad."

Claire gave Sam a curious eye. "Mr… *Maxipad?*"

"I… I used a maxipad as a bandage once," Sam stammered. "Never mind. I'll tell you later."

"That's actually a good idea," Trillian said. "I mean that's *literally* the reason maxipads exist."

"Who asked you, *tangerine?*" O'Connor scrutinized Trillian's short orange hair. "You cut that yourself?"

Trillian stepped up to O'Connor. The graffiti-covered Doc Martens poking out from under her gown gave her an extra inch over O'Connor and she used it to her advantage. "As a matter of fact, yeah. Saves me a shit-ton of money."

O'Connor spotted Sam glowering at her and took the hint. She nodded at Trillian. "Smart."

Looking to diffuse the tension, Claire stepped past Sam and addressed the group. "Anyone hungry?"

Jack pointed at O'Connor with both hands, grinning ear to ear. "Taco Siempre?"

"Abso-fucking-lutely." O'Connor pulled Jack into a headlock and gave him a noogie. "I'm buying."

Sam grabbed the suitcases as the rest of the group navigated their way around other mingling families in the hallway and headed for the school's main entrance.

Sam glanced at Jack and Trillian. "Where are your parents? They're invited too."

Jack and Trillian shared a knowing glance and shrugged in unison. "My folks are in Germany. A river cruise this time. And Trillian's are—"

"My foster parents don't give a shit," Trillian said. "But that doesn't matter." She grabbed Bradley's hand and interlocked her fingers with his. "I consider you guys my family now."

Fifteen minutes later, Claire pulled her red Nissan Leaf into the parking lot of Taco Siempre. Jack's orange Honda Civic was already there and the three teens were sitting on the hood of the car laughing at the unfolding scene. Their graduation regalia lay piled in the back seat of the little car.

"Took you long enough," Jack said.

O'Connor rolled her eyes. "*Tell* me about it."

"Would you rather have *walked?*" Claire locked the Leaf and tossed the keys in her purse.

Sam watched the two women bristle at each other, ready to jump in and put out any fire that developed.

"No," O'Connor said. "Thank you for driving."

Sam pulled O'Connor aside. "That was remarkably civil of you."

"Yeah, well... Don't expect me to make it a habit." O'Connor pushed by him and led the group through the front doors. There was one booth left inside the small restaurant. For six people, it would be a tight squeeze. "Claire? Could you grab a table?"

Claire spun on her heels and headed toward the booth.

"Wait."

Claire paused and faced O'Connor again, an annoyed expectation on her face.

"What do you want to eat?"

"Just a diet Coke."

O'Connor stared. "A diet Coke? That's it?"

"That's what I said." Claire sneered and headed back to the booth. "You should check those hearing aid batteries."

Jack leaned toward Bradley and lowered his voice. "I don't think your mom likes O'Connor."

Overhearing, Trillian answered for Bradley. "What was your first clue?"

Sam had watched the entire exchange. "Are we going to have a problem?"

"Not while we're here." O'Connor glanced at Claire, who was sitting at the booth close to the window, then back at Sam. "Thank Christ we leave tomorrow."

"I thought you two were cool, from last time," Sam said. "She hasn't forgotten about your trip to the morgue together."

"Shit. Forgot about that. It's been a while and we've been busy."

"Just keep it civil, okay? I'll have a beef burrito and a coffee." Sam strolled over to the booth and slid onto the red melamine bench seat next to Claire. "Sorry about O'Connor. She takes a little getting used to."

"Yeah. I know," Claire said. "I'm not exactly easy, either."

Sam smiled. "Well, she's trying to be good. Trust me on that."

Claire gazed at the traffic on Glenoaks Boulevard.

Sam squeezed her hand gently. "It's good to see you."

She smiled pensively. "You, too." Claire squeezed back and pulled her hand away.

"Sorry."

"Don't be. You're here for Brad and that's all that matters to me."

Bradley and Trillian scooted onto the bench seat across from Sam and Claire holding trays with drinks.

"Mom, you got a diet Coke. Dad, a coffee. Trill, you got an Orange Crush, right?"

Trillian nodded, grabbed her drink, and doled out the three drinks on her tray. "Mountain *Dookie* for you."

"Hey!" Bradley protested. "Try it before you diss it."

"I'm not touching that bilge-water."

Jack and O'Connor returned to the table and sat, O'Connor next to Sam.

"It'll be a few minutes, guys," Jack said.

Claire whispered casually into Sam's ear. "Did you plan on being a buffer between me and O'Connor?"

Sam smirked. "Maybe."

Claire touched Sam's knee lightly under the table.

"So, kids." O'Connor leaned forward, thrumming her fingers on the tabletop. "How's it feel to be free of school?"

"Fucking awesome." Immediately, Jack tried to backtrack. "Sorry, Mrs. Shaw."

Claire waved him off. "You're worried about swearing in front me *now*? Forget about it. You've earned it." She addressed the three teens. "What are your plans?"

"I don't know," Jack said. "I haven't really thought much about it. Maybe take a gap year? Start a business?"

"Huh." O'Connor leaned forward to glare at Claire. "I distinctly remember starting this conversation."

Before the two women could get into another verbal scuffle, the intercom interrupted the Mexican music playing from the speakers in the corners. "O'Connor. Order's up."

"Make yourself useful and get the food," Sam said.

O'Connor grumbled and slid out from the booth. She pointed at Jack. "You. On your feet. Help me with the order."

Jack mobilized at once, following O'Connor to the pickup counter.

Claire shifted her gaze to Trillian. "What about you?"

Trillian took a sip from her orange soda. "Oh, I don't know. Probably marry your son and have a couple of kids. Brad could get a job at the Food Fresh and we could rent a place near the school." She grabbed Bradley's arm and batted her eyelashes at him. "Sounds perfect, right?"

Bradley's face drained of color as he choked on a mouthful of Mountain Dew. "Um…"

Claire shared an amused look with Sam.

Trillian burst out laughing. "Got you good."

Bradley let out a breath of relief. "Well, it's not like I don't want to do those things… just not yet."

Trillian side-hugged Bradley. "Good answer."

Jack set a tray of food on the table. "What'd I miss?"

"Brad and I and getting married and having eight kids." Trillian tried to keep a straight face, but it was next to impossible.

"Eight?" Bradley's eyes bugged out. "I thought it was two."

"Anything can happen," Trillian said.

"Are you serious?" Jack's eyes darted back and forth between Bradley and Trillian.

"No. I'm kidding. But you should've seen Brad's face."

"I'm glad I amuse you," Bradley said.

O'Connor slid the second tray of food onto the table.

"I'm glad you amuse me, too." Trillian gave Bradley a quick kiss on the cheek. "Now let's eat."

"Hold on." O'Connor held onto her tray and placed a hand on Jack's. "What do you all think about Hawaii?"

The group exchanged looks across the table.

"Sounds like a nice place to visit," Bradley said.

"Except for the molten lava. Burning to a crisp would not make a good holiday. There's been a lot of that over there lately." Jack tried to unwrap his burrito and O'Connor smacked his hand.

"I've always wanted to tour the observatories on Mauna Kea," Trillian said.

"That would be cool." Jack leaned back. "Random fact. Mauna Kea is taller than the Titanic is deep."

Trillian raised a brow. "That *is* random."

"What would you say if I said I had plane tickets for everyone? Let's call it… a graduation gift."

The three teen's jaws dropped in unison as they looked at each other.

"You're joking," Trillian said.

Bradley shot a quick glance at Sam, but his face didn't give anything away.

"O'Connor doesn't joke about things like this," Sam said.

Trillian stared at O'Connor. "Shut up. Are you serious?"

Jack glanced at Trillian, then at O'Connor. He smiled and began to nod slowly. "I think she's serious, guys."

"No way." Trillian's eyes went wide. "*Are* you serious?"

"Come on, O'Connor," Sam said. "Quit the games."

"But I was enjoying it. Weren't you?"

Sam chuckled. "Yeah, I guess I was."

"So, we're going to Hawaii?" Bradley locked eyes with Sam. "For real?"

"I don't want to steal O'Connor's thunder, but… yeah. You're going to Hawaii—"

Trillian squealed and leaned over the table, pulling O'Connor into an awkward hug. "Thank you thank you!"

"Okay." O'Connor struggled to stay upright, almost pushing Trillian back. "Enough." She sat back down. "It's got to be okay with your parents."

"Mine are floating somewhere in Germany," Jack said.

"Face up or face down?" Bradley began to laugh.

"Dude, that's dark." Jack faced O'Connor. "Getting permission is a no-brainer."

"And like I said before…" Trillian shot a look at Claire. "My foster parents don't care what I do. I'll just tell them I'm going and they'll say, 'you're blocking the TV.' "

O'Connor glanced at Claire. "I've got a ticket for you, too."

"Me?" Claire showed genuine surprise. "Oh! You didn't have to do that. Thank you. But I'll never be able to get time off on such short notice."

O'Connor shrugged. "It's an open ticket. You can use it whenever you want."

Claire hesitated for a moment and considered the consequences of what she was going to do. Then she reached out and gave O'Connor's hand a light squeeze. "Thank you. Really."

O'Connor nodded. "Not a problem."

Sam leaned back to regard Claire, then O'Connor. "Is this what you call 'burying the hatchet'?"

O'Connor half-grinned. "Maybe." She dug into the trays and began handing out food. "Let's eat God's bounty before it's stone cold."

And they did.

CLAIRE OFFERED TO put up Sam and O'Connor for the night. Sam had experienced sharing a room with O'Connor during their trip to Mar-A-Verde, before it was reclaimed by the sea. Nothing had changed. O'Connor still slept like a rock and snored like a jackhammer. He moved to the couch in the living room to preserve his sanity, but his brain obsessed over the upcoming trip and made sleep an impossibility.

At the first hint of dawn, Sam gave up and hauled his suitcase to the front door. He pulled out his phone and the lock screen faded up with the time: 5:08 am. He folded the blanket that he had used during the night and placed it on the end of the couch.

He went to the kitchen and started brewing a carafe of coffee. "This should help wake people up." Sam paced the kitchen as hot water filtered through the coffee grounds and released a pleasant but strong aroma that could stir anyone from sleep.

Claire was first to the kitchen. "Hey."

Sam nodded at her. "Hey." He pulled open the wrong cupboard looking for mugs.

"Third one over," Claire said. "You sleep okay?"

"Not really." Sam pulled four mugs off the shelf. "You know I'm super anxious when there's multiple variables and schedules to keep."

"Variables like Brad and O'Connor?"

"Especially O'Connor."

"I remember," Claire smiled wistfully. "Some things don't change."

"Do I hear someone taking my name in vain?" O'Connor's voice echoed from the hallway.

"Nope," Sam said as O'Connor strolled into the kitchen. "Always with love." He glanced at her. "Coffee?"

"Does the Pope shit in the woods?"

Sam poured a coffee for O'Connor, Claire, then himself. He took a lingering first sip and felt relaxation flow through his body. "We have a nine-fifteen flight, so we should get moving."

O'Connor gulped some of her coffee and strolled out of the kitchen. "I'll get the kid up. Don't want to be an *uncontrollable variable*." She pounded on Bradley's door three times, then burst into his room.

"Get your ass out of bed." O'Connor's voice boomed and Sam swore he felt the house shake. "We leave in five." She returned to the kitchen, a satisfied grin on her face. "He's moving."

"You're very good at that," Claire said smirking.

"I've got a real talent with kids." O'Connor gulped her coffee.

The doorbell rang.

"You've got *something*." Sam set his coffee mug down and headed to the front door.

Trillian and Jack stood on the front stoop with their suitcases, trying hard not to show their excitement.

"Is it okay for me to park in the alley?" Jack rocked his suitcase back and forth. "I think there's enough room beside the garage. My car's small, but if there isn't room I'll park—"

Claire appeared behind Sam. "Go ahead, Jack. You'll be fine."

Sam took Trillian's suitcase and set it next to the door. He reached for Jack's, but he had already hopped down the steps and was halfway back to the Civic before he realized he was dragging his suitcase behind him.

"Shit." He shook his head, ran back to the stoop, and handed his suitcase to Sam.

"Just a little bit excited?" Sam winked at him.

"Just not totally awake yet." Jack ran back to the Civic and hopped in through the open driver's side window.

"Make it quick, Jack," Sam called out as he placed his suitcase next to Trillian's. "We got coffee, but we also got to go soon, like in ten minutes."

"On it!" Jack started the Civic and peeled out, making a U-turn in the middle of the street. He shot back past the house and turned into the alley.

"I'll take one of those coffees," Trillian said.

Claire waved her in and Sam followed them back to the kitchen. Bradley had just finished stirring sugar into his coffee as Trillian beckoned for it.

"Please, kind sir!"

Bradley handed her his mug and poured another for himself, emptying the carafe. He added sugar and was about to take a sip when Jack burst through the front door and into the kitchen.

"Hey dude, is that for me?"

Bradley gave him a sideways look. "Of course. I live to serve."

Jack took the mug gladly. "Thanks. You're a lifesaver."

"Hey, barista." Trillian nodded Bradley over and shared her coffee with him.

Sam's text message alert went off. He checked his phone. "Our ride is here, people. Grab your bags and saddle up."

Bradley ran back to his room.

"Get my bag while you're at it," O'Connor called back before gulping down the rest of her coffee.

Claire took everyone's mugs and placed them in the sink. "It was nice to have a full house again, even if it was for one night."

Sam hung back at the kitchen. "You can still come, you know."

Claire took Sam by his sturdy shoulders. "You know I can't." She wrapped her arms around him and gave him a brief fierce hug. "Be careful."

"It's a Hawaiian vacation," Sam said. "What could go wrong?"

Claire took a half step back. "Are you forgetting who's leading this charge?" She locked her gaze with Sam's.

"O'Connor," they said in unison, laughing.

"We may not be married anymore," Claire said, "but you're still important to me. So I'll say it again. Be careful."

Sam nodded. "I will. You have my word."

O'Connor bounded back through the front door. "What's the fucking holdup?" She saw Sam and Claire in a partial embrace. "Wait. Are you two…"

"No," Sam said. "Just saying goodbye."

"Uh, really?" O'Connor squinted doubt at him.

"Really." Sam stepped to the front door. "Where's my suitcase?"

"Already got it loaded. Come on."

O'Connor hopped down the front steps toward the waiting Nissan Pathfinder Armada.

Sam paused at the front door and looked back at Claire framed by the kitchen that he never knew, but should have. He should have been around for a lot of things, most of all for his wife and son. Regret and guilt flooded him. He offered a subdued wave and closed the door.

O'Connor stood waiting for him by the SUV, then pulled him aside. "It's for the best."

"What is?"

"Claire staying here," O'Connor said. "Less complications."

"What do you mean?"

O'Connor laughed and pulled open the passenger door. "Get your ass in the car. We got a plane to catch."

He saw that the front passenger seat had been reserved for him. Sam walked around the back of the Pathfinder to allow time to collect himself. O'Connor would freak out if she spotted tears.

Sam hopped into the SUV and buckled himself in. He peered out through the driver side window and saw that Claire had opened the front door and was standing on the front stoop, waving.

"Have a great time," she called out.

Jack leaned through the open window and waved enthusiastically. "We will!"

Sam waved again as the SUV pulled forward, sure that Claire would never see it. But O'Connor did.

She pulled herself forward from the back so she could whisper into Sam's ear. "Don't go and do something stupid."

"That's funny coming from you."

O'Connor grabbed a fistful of Sam's shirt, more serious than playful. "I mean it. We're on vacation. *Less* complications, remember?"

"Can I quote you on that?"

O'Connor held Sam in her silent serious gaze.

"Don't worry." Sam twisted in his seat to face O'Connor. "It's all water under the bridge."

O'Connor nodded, satisfied that Sam wasn't hiding anything, and let go of his shirt. "Better be." She sat back.

Bradley looked at O'Connor, then Sam. "Everything okay, Dad?"

"Abso-fucking-lutely." Sam twisted to look at everyone in the back seats. "Next stop, LAX."

Cheers erupted from the teens as the Pathfinder headed west on Sheldon Street. The driver navigated through the twisted knot of asphalt that tied Los Angeles together and soon merged onto San Diego Freeway, which took the group through the Sepulveda Pass and south to the Los Angeles International Airport.

The dawn traffic was light and made the trip effortless. Forty minutes later, the SUV rolled into the roundabout of 1 World Way and stopped in front of Terminal B. The driver popped the back hatch.

"Everyone out. Grab your stuff." Sam was preaching to the choir because everyone had already unbuckled and hopped out of the SUV as soon as the driver stopped and unlocked the doors.

Sam closed the back hatch and waved to the driver. "Our flight leaves at Gate 208. Everyone ready?" He surveyed the group. O'Connor rolled her eyes and sighed, ready to go but clearly bored. On the opposite side of the spectrum, Bradley, Trillian, and Jack practically vibrated with excitement. "Let's roll out."

With a little difficulty, O'Connor matched Sam's stride. "Slow the fuck down. We've got lots of time."

"I'll relax once we're through security."

"It'll be a piece of cake. Except for my leg," O'Connor said. "That always gets security's attention."

Sam chuckled. "At least we don't have weapons in our suitcases this time."

Trillian turned to Bradley and Jack. "Can you believe this is happening?"

"It's totally sick," Bradley said. "I can pretty much guarantee that no one in our graduating class is going to Hawaii right now."

"I was sad to miss the grad after-party, though. And the pancake breakfast," Jack said. Trillian and Bradley stopped in their tracks. He looked back at them and laughed. "What? I'm kidding!"

The group worked their way though security without issue, except for O'Connor and her leg of course. It didn't help speed things along when she told TSA officers that she kept her bowie knife in her prosthetic. The joke backfired and she had to send her leg through the X-ray machine. Sam managed to convince the officers not to fine her, but they confiscated her cigar stub.

"Jesus Christ, O'Connor." It took all Sam had to keep his cool. "Wasn't it you who was telling me about keeping this vacation *uncomplicated?*"

"It was funny."

"Yeah. I can see you laughing from inside a jail cell as we leave you behind," Sam said. "Pretty damn funny."

"You're so dramatic." O'Connor pulled away from the group and headed up the escalator to Level 4, Departures. "You'll retell that story often. You watch."

Sam scowled and followed her.

Bradley leaned into Trillian and Jack and lowered his voice. "I say we keep to ourselves once we get there. These adults are creating too much drama."

"I second that," Trillian said. "Besides, we need to find Jack a girlfriend."

"But I have no time—"

"No time for a girlfriend, yeah, yeah." Bradley shook his head, grinning. "We've heard this before."

"But what about a temporary one, at least." Trillian looked at Jack over the rims of her sunglasses. "Would you go for that?"

Jack considered the idea. "That might work."

O'Connor crested the top of the escalator and did a one-eighty, blocking Sam.

"What are you doing?" Sam looked at her confused. "Move."

"Shit," O'Connor said with a sigh, and stepped aside, revealing Hope leaning against a support column. Her hair was a little shorter than it had been in the Bahamas, but she was still decked out in black: leather jacket, jeans, and Vans. Her black T-shirt featured Mickey Mouse sporting two middle fingers with the words "FUCK STRUNK" underneath. It was a far cry from the usual obscure punk rock band. Beside her sitting on rollers, sat the hot pink suitcase. It occurred to Sam that the suitcase had more stickers on it. The Bratz, My Little Pony, and Disney stickers were partially covered by other, newer ones, specifically "Mar-A-Verde SUCKS" and a large "ReLAX" centered in the fuselage of a plane icon.

"No complications, huh?" Sam shook his head and chuckled to himself.

"Yeah, I kind of forgot I invited her, last minute."

"No, you didn't forget."

"Well, shit, Sam," O'Connor said. "You're shacking up with her, so what does it matter?"

Sam gave O'Connor a light slap on the back. "Thanks."

Bradley gazed around Sam's shoulder to see why O'Connor was blocking the way. "Hope?" His eyes brightened as he hustled over and gave her a hug, much to the surprise of Trillian.

"Who's *that?*" Trillian's jealousy seeped through.

"No idea," Jack said. "But she looks kind of like you, except older."

"Shut up." Trillian narrowed her eyes at Jack, then at Hope and Bradley. He glanced back at her and waved her over.

"Hope, this is my girlfriend Trillian." Bradley slid his arm around Trillian's waist.

Trillian held out her hand. "Hi."

Hope returned a firm handshake, then cocked her head to one side. "Trillian… as in *Hitchhiker's Guide to the Galaxy?*"

"Yeah," Trillian said. "My fosters were a fucking laugh riot."

"And this is Jack, my best friend."

"Cool." Hope and Jack shook hands. "I hear you had some wild times with spiders last year."

"Damn straight," Jack said. "Built my own flame thrower."

"And almost incinerated yourself," Bradley said. "Why didn't you join in the fun?"

"Uh yeah, no." Hope grimaced. "I don't do spiders."

Sam poked his head into the conversation. "And where we're going, there won't be any spiders."

"Hey, Sam." Hope's voice softened as she stepped up and hugged him, more tightly and closely than she had with anyone else.

"Glad you could make it," Sam said quietly, his voice warm and close to her ear.

"I wouldn't miss it." Hope backed up and eyed Bradley. "I mean you only get to graduate high school once. And thanks to the generosity of O'Connor, we can all celebrate together."

O'Connor took a bow and attempted a Southern drawl reminiscent of Elvis Presley. "Thank you. Thank you very much. You're beautiful."

Sam pointed at Hope's suitcase. "I see you're still lugging the pink abomination."

"Yup." Hope kicked the side panel. "Still rolling and collecting memories."

"Look," O'Connor said. "I hate to break up this little trip down memory lane, but time's ticking. I didn't get up at oh-dark-hundred to stand around and yak."

"Right." Sam cleared his throat and led the way. "Let's get everyone checked in. Gate 208."

"Then food," Jack said.

"Then food," Sam nodded.

Jack looked around the main foyer as they walked through it. "They need a Taco Siempre here."

O'Connor snapped her fingers. "Yes. They do."

"But…" Bradley grinned at Jack. "Is mixing spicy food and a five hour flight really a good idea?"

"For me it is," Jack said.

"What about everyone else?" Bradley pinched his nostrils closed. "You can't open the window on a plane."

"Okay. TMI." Trillian grabbed Bradley's hand and tugged him along.

"Wait up!" Jack ran to catch them.

"What do you plan on doing while we're in Hawaii?" Hope watched Sam's face as he answered.

"As little as possible."

But life has a funny way of throwing curveballs when one least expects it.

SPOKES

PANDORA ROCKWELL PREFERRED Lanai to the other Hawaiian Islands. The small island west of Maui had a year round population of a few thousand people. Because most of the land was privately owned, those who made the effort to travel there were offered unrivaled privacy. That was a bonus, since Pandora was a self-made millionaire, soon to be billionaire if she played her cards right.

Pandora had built her company, Rockwell Simulations Inc., from the ground up. She had spent the past twenty-five years using cutting edge computer technology to analyze real-time atmospheric data. Everyone wanted to know what the weather would be like tomorrow or next week. And Pandora decided that her company would be the only system to deliver reliable results. There were many competitors, but none came close to Rockwell's accuracy.

During the past five years, Pandora had incorporated artificial intelligence into Rockwell's forecasting to further increase its range. Millions of AI calculations, based on current and past weather events, atmosphere dynamics, and particle physics, allowed weather predictions that were up to eighty percent correct over thirty days.

The world beat a path to her door. Television networks, radio stations, newspapers, airlines, and other companies that relied on accurate weather subscribed to her top-tier subscription service and made her rich. Her limitless access to money led to her becoming a sought-after angel investor. She was always looking for new opportunities.

But everything had a cost. For Pandora, she chose business deals over family life, and as a result had been divorced three times before she gave up on marriage. Her second marriage had produced a daughter, Maddilyn, which she considered the second best thing she had brought into this world. Lucky for her, Maddilyn didn't hate her like her ex-husbands did.

Maddilyn had wanted for nothing growing up. The latest toys, the best clothes, the most attentive nannies and tutors, nothing was out of reach. Now seventeen years old, the only thing she lacked were good friends who liked her for who she was as a person, and not just because her mom was loaded. She went with her mother to Lanai because Pandora swore it would be a "real vacation", and not business-related. Maddilyn liked new experiences. Anything could happen. "My life can't be predicted by a Rockwell simulation," she would often say.

Club Nihoʻgula was a small all-inclusive resort, hosting two dozen finely appointed two-bedroom cabins situated around a restaurant, pub, and gift shop. Located on the east coast of Lanai, the club faced an expansive but secluded cove. Rocky beach heads extended north and south where numerous shipwrecks littered the shores in shallow, mostly unmarked graves. On a clear day, the West Maui Mountains ten miles east could be seen poking through their cloud halos. The spectacular sunrises were worth getting up early for. Many small businesses contracted with the club to supply extra guest amenities, such as snorkeling and sight-seeing tours. The club was open year round, but the summer months were busiest for Club Nihoʻgula and its exclusive guests. Many were regulars, like Pandora, but this was the first time Maddilyn had gone with her.

Today marked the beginning of week two of their "real" vacation. Pandora and Maddilyn had claimed the two chaise lounges on the beach in front of their cabin. The essence of coconut tanning lotion hung heavy between the two of them.

"What are your plans for today, Maddi?" Pandora focused on her phone.

Maddilyn sighed and adjusted her Armani sunglasses on her nose. "Nothing."

"What about snorkeling?" Pandora gazed out into the cove. "Looks gorgeous out there. Maybe you'll find some treasure."

Maddilyn ignored the question. She adjusted her red bikini top, flipped herself face down on her chaise lounge, and turned her head to watch her mom through her sunglasses. All she wanted to do was work on her tan while listening to music or a book. Her current steamy romance series partially made up for the lack of available guys. But books and her imagination could only go so far.

Pandora reclined on her chaise lounge, a wide-brimmed sun hat and sunglasses shading her face, and a tropical-themed silk sarong covering up the bottom half of her white bikini. She focused intently on her phone with one hand and ran her fingers along the seams of her sarong with the other. Back and forth, back and forth.

To Maddilyn, it looked like Pandora was texting someone, but she couldn't be sure.

"That's not work, is it, Mom?"

Pandora set her phone down and focused on the cove. "Of course not. This a *real* vacation, remember?"

"If you say so." Maddilyn closed her eyes and let the warmth of the tropical sun lull her towards deep relaxation. It was only a minute or two before she could hear Pandora's fingers tapping on her phone again. It was the one thing that stopped Maddilyn from completely giving in to the summer heat.

Pandora casually glanced at her gold iWatch. "You know what would be nice?" She spoke loud enough for Maddilyn to hear. "A tall, cool Hawaiian iced tea. Would you be a dear and fetch one from Gus?"

Maddilyn cracked her eyes open and saw Pandora looking at her over the rims of her sunglasses. "Really, mom?"

Pandora kept her gaze on her watch as the corners of her mouth curved up in a subtle smile. "I'd be forever grateful, honey. You get yourself one, too."

That caught Maddilyn's attention. The drinking age in Hawaii was twenty-one. "Really?"

"Really," Pandora said, "but without all the *adult stuff* in it." She wiggled her fingers.

"Oh." Maddilyn pushed herself up, tied on her own red silk sarong, and trudged up the beach toward the bar. "I'm only here to be your servant," she said, thinking she was out of earshot.

"I heard that," Pandora called back. "Remember, you *chose* to come."

That was true. And honestly Maddilyn's life could be so much worse. Perhaps she could dig up a little more gratitude.

She could see Gus serving a guest at the bar. Gus was the easy-to-remember name he chose for guests, but his real name was Kanakamana. He had said it meant "powerful man." But Maddilyn couldn't keep the name in her head. All she heard was "Copacabana", a song by Barry Manilow that Pandora had overplayed so much that the track was burned permanently into Maddilyn's brain.

Powerful man, however, was apt. Tall and well built without being grossly chiseled, Gus's best feature was his bright smile. Tied for second was his dark, shaggy hair and the intricate Hawaiian tattoos that spanned his arms and chest. Unfortunately, he was at least twice her age, but that didn't stop Maddilyn from inserting his likeness into her romance novels. It made the books better.

She stepped up to the bar. Gus nodded at her and smiled as he finished with another guest.

God, his smile.

Maddilyn felt her knees weaken. She planted herself on one of the bamboo stools in front of the countertop.

"Maddi! What can I do for you?"

Steamy romance novel thoughts of what Gus could do for her flashed through her young mind, temporarily distracting her. "Uh, could I get two Hawaiian iced teas?"

He grabbed two tall glasses and gave her a sly grin as he filled each half full of ice. "Two?"

Maddilyn shrugged. "Well…"

"One adult version? One young adult version?"

She nodded and sighed, her shoulders deflating. "I can't wait to be twenty-one."

"Slow down," Gus said as he prepared the two drinks. "Enjoy your youth. You'll miss it when it's gone."

Maddilyn rested her head on her arm on the countertop, her eyes watching wave after wave curl onto the beach. "This place needs more guests my age."

"Agree. One hundred percent." Gus placed the two drinks beside her arm. Maddilyn sat up. "The young adult version has the red umbrella." He winked at her.

"Thanks, Gus."

"My pleasure, Maddi. Say hi to your mom for me."

"I will." Halfway back to their chaise lounges, Maddilyn knocked back half of her mom's Hawaiian iced tea, then filled it back up from hers. She'd never know the difference. Besides, it wasn't even noon. Who drinks before noon?

Near the shoreline, maybe thirty feet from where Pandora sat, a splash in the water caught Maddilyn's attention. It was different from the predictable waves that crashed on the shore. She squinted where she had first seen the disturbance and saw movement again. It looked almost like a dozen people were skipping stones, all at the same spot at the same time.

"What the…" Maddilyn's eyes went wide as saucers as she

watched something roll out of the surf, like a multi-blade propeller on its side, but soft and organically shaped. Whatever it was, the thing gained speed quickly and headed right for Pandora.

"Mom?"

The thing reached Pandora in a few seconds and latched onto her arm.

"MOM!" Maddilyn dropped the drinks and ran.

PANDORA'S PERIPHERAL VISION caught the creature's movement before she had a chance to set her phone down and react. A mass of slimy legs and a bulbous body wrapped itself around her left arm.

She screamed and tried to shake the creature off, but it clung to her more tightly. Then she felt intense pain, as if she was being burned and cut at the same time.

"Mom!" Pandora thought she heard Maddilyn's voice but wasn't sure if she imagined it or not. She tried to dig under the creature's legs with the fingers of her free hand, but it was like trying to grab strands of algae in a tide pool. The creature's leg kept slipping away until something pricked her finger. She pulled her right hand away and saw a cut on her index fingertip, like a paper cut, but deep enough to draw blood.

Then as quickly as it started, the creature bolted back toward the water and disappeared, leaving her left arm mottled with bloody cuts. The attack had lasted no more than thirty seconds.

Maddilyn arrived a second later. "Mom! Are you okay?" She wrapped her arms around her, then saw the blood. "Holy fuck!" She grabbed one of their beach towels and wrapped Pandora's left hand and forearm.

She looked back at the bar ready to yell for Gus, and realized he was already on his way, his phone to his ear.

"I've called medical." Gus crouched next to Pandora. He took off her sunglasses and peered into her eyes, checking both her pupils. "Mrs. Rockwell, I'd like to look at your arm. Will you let me do that?"

Pandora stared at him, through him, like he wasn't there.

"Grab the other towel and cover her up," Gus said to Maddilyn. "She might be in shock." He took her right hand and noticed a small amount of blood clotting on her index finger. "Mrs. Rockwell?"

Maddilyn unfolded another towel and spread it over Pandora, despite the noonday sunshine. "Is she going to be okay?"

As if on cue, Pandora's eyes cleared, and she smiled. "Gus. Why so formal? Call me Pandora."

"Okay." Gus gave Maddilyn a quick, reassuring look. "I think she's going to be okay." He returned his focus to Pandora. "Will you let me take a look at your arm?"

"Go ahead," Pandora said.

Gus unwrapped Pandora's left forearm slowly and carefully. "Let me know if you feel any pain and I'll stop."

Pandora nodded. "It doesn't hurt actually."

Gus worked the towel off, revealing the remnants of bloody cuts, but the bleeding had already stopped. He gently raised her arm to get a good look at the cuts, but most of them had closed up. "That's weird."

Maddilyn shot him a concerned eye. "What?"

"It looks like the cuts have mostly healed." Gus scrunched his brows in confusion. "Or the cuts weren't very deep to begin with."

"What would do something like this?" Pandora asked.

Gus shook his head. "I was serving someone. I didn't see the attack."

Pandora raised her forearm for a closer look at some of the healing cuts. "That thing was wrapped around my arm, like a snake." She looked at Maddilyn and Gus, baffled. "And it was slimy."

"Whatever it was, it took off just as I got to you," Maddilyn said. "It rolled, like a bike wheel, but without the tire. Know what I mean?"

"Yeah, but I don't know of anything that would move like that." Gus looked back at the bar. A couple of customers were standing waiting to be served. "I got to get back, but the medical staff will be here soon, a few minutes. I'd feel better if they checked you out."

"I'm not going anywhere." Pandora ran a gentle finger lightly over her forearm.

Gus jogged back to the bar. On the way he picked up the two glasses that had been filled with the Hawaiian iced teas from earlier.

"Thanks, Gus."

He gave them a thumbs up.

Maddilyn shifted her attention back to Pandora and her forearm. Something wasn't right. "Uh, Mom?"

Pandora looked at her, confused by Maddilyn's concern. Her forearm had almost completely healed. "What is it?"

"Where's your watch?"

Pandora glanced at her wrist, then down at the sand beside her chaise lounge. "Did it fall off?"

Maddilyn dropped to her knees and ran her hands through the warm sand. "It's not here."

"It's got to be there," Pandora said. "Check underneath."

"I checked already."

"Check again. That thing cost twenty grand."

Maddilyn rolled her eyes. "It's not like you can't buy another one." She sat on the edge of her chaise lounge and propped her chin up on her hand.

"That's not the point." Pandora slid off the chaise lounge and flipped it on its side. She ran her fingers across the first few inches of sand.

"Satisfied?"

"No." Pandora sat back on her heels and let out an exasperated sigh. "I'm fucking pissed."

"Twenty-K can get you a new watch but can't buy you a new arm," Maddilyn said. "Be thankful it wasn't permanently shredded."

Pandora glared at her and stood. She brushed the sand off her sarong and stormed off across the sand dune. "I'll be in the cabin."

"No shit," Maddilyn said to herself. She spotted Pandora's phone balancing on the edge of the upturned chaise lounge and grabbed it. "Missing something?" Maddilyn waved the phone in the air without looking back at her mother.

Pandora stomped back, grabbed her phone, and resumed her emphatic exit. The two medical staff had just rounded the bar, getting their directions from Gus.

"Over here." Pandora beckoned them to follow.

Maddilyn laid back onto her chaise lounge. "Gus got a thank you, but not me. God forbid she thanks *me*." She inserted her earbuds and pressed play on her current audiobook.

The central character's confident voice swept aside everything that had just happened and helped Maddilyn slip back into some steamy romance. She grinned, licked her lips, and closed her eyes behind her Armanis. "Hello, *Gus…*"

HOME BASE

THE DETEST-A-PEST CREW took up six of the eight seats in row 14 on the Hawaiian Airlines Airbus A330, four in the middle and two on the right. Jack let Bradley and Trillian take the two seats next to the window and took the aisle seat across from them. Sam, Hope, and O'Connor filled out the rest of the middle seats. O'Connor insisted on the other aisle seat so she could stretch out her prosthesis.

During the flight, Jack let it slip to a flight attendant that this was his first plane ride. The flight attendant presented him with a metal pin that read "First Timer Club" with the Hawaiian Airlines logo underneath.

The flight path over the Pacific Ocean didn't offer much to look at except clouds and water. After the in-flight brunch, Sam and Hope slept and O'Connor played games on her phone. The teenagers passed the time by watching a couple of in-flight movies. Their favorite was *Top Gun: Maverick*.

The cabin intercom woke Sam and Hope with an announcement of final approach to Honolulu. He stretched and leaned toward O'Connor. "So, where are we going?"

O'Connor gave him a look. "Bitch, *please*."

"Look, I know it's Hawaii, but where?"

Hope touched Sam's hand. "We land on O'ahu."

"I know *that*, but where are we *staying*?"

Hope shrugged, then both looked back at O'Connor. She had her arms crossed against her chest.

Noticing their stares, O'Connor closed her eyes and a satisfied smile appeared on her face. "You're going to have to wait and see."

Hope leaned over Sam and lowered her voice. "Seriously?" She gave O'Connor a light slap on her shoulder.

The cabin intercom buzzed on. "Aloha folks, we are now beginning our descent to Honolulu International Airport. Please return to your seats and fasten your seatbelts."

Jack leaned across the aisle. "Brad, can I switch seats with you? Just for the landing?"

Bradley faced Trillian next to him. "Do you mind?"

"Nope. I don't like watching landings anyway." She planted a quick kiss on his cheek.

Bradley scooted past Trillian, crossed the aisle, and took Jack's seat.

"Man, this is so cool." Jack wasted no time taking Bradley's spot. He planted his face against the window, taking photos and videos with his phone. "I'm slowly getting why my parents travel."

"Hate to break it to you, Jack," Trillian said, "but there's more to travel than watching the plane land."

"I know that… but still." Jack was like a kid in a candy store.

Bradley beckoned at Trillian. They both leaned into the aisle and he whispered into her ear, "We *have* to find him a girlfriend."

Trillian smiled and nodded. They kissed and leaned back into their seats.

Jack watched as the plane navigated parallel to the heavily populated south coast of Oʻahu. The high-rise buildings of Honolulu floated by, seeming so close at times that one could reach out and touch them.

O'Connor couldn't have picked a better spot for a holiday.

EVERYONE PULLED THEIR luggage from the overhead compartments and disembarked the plane. Upon entering the main terminal, a Hawaiian Airlines attendant pulled Jack aside.

"Wait, is there something wrong?"

The attendant laughed. "No, but you're a 'first timer.' " She tapped the button pinned to Jack's shirt. "That means you get an official Hawaiian Airlines welcome."

The rest of the group watched with amusement as the attendant reached into a plastic bin on the floor behind her desk and pulled out a lei made of a mixture of ginger and kika blossoms. She placed it around Jack's neck and kissed his cheek.

"Welcome to Hawaii." The attendant's smile radiated warmth.

Bradley raised his arms. "Finally!"

Jack rejoined the group and everyone walked into the main concourse. "What?"

"You finally got *lei'd*," Bradley said. "So, what was it like? Was she gentle?"

Jack shook his head and playfully raised his middle finger at him. "I don't kiss and tell."

"Respect." Trillian bumped fists with Jack then looked at Bradley. "Paying attention?"

"What?" Bradley said. "I don't kiss and tell either."

"Uh huh. Right." Trillian rolled her suitcase ahead of Bradley, enjoying making him squirm.

"I'd love to watch this mesmerizing teenage drama all day," O'Connor said, "but I want to be sipping Mai Tais on a beach before sunset."

Outside the terminal, a wall of heat hit them and made everyone except O'Connor wilt. She split off from the group.

Sam and Hope exchanged glances. "Where are you going?

Looks like taxis are over there." He pointed in the opposite direction.

"We want terminal three." O'Connor looked back at the group. "Come on. Paradise awaits." She continued to walk away from what seemed like the correct way to go.

Hope nudged Sam. "What does your ticket say?"

"O'Connor has the tickets, so we got no choice than to stick with her."

"Once a control freak, always a control freak," Hope said.

Sam and Hope course-corrected and the teens followed blindly.

O'Connor made a beeline for the Wiki-Wiki shuttle to Terminal 3. "Come on, peeps. Move your asses."

Everyone found seats and the shuttle lurched forward.

O'Connor rubbed her left knee. "Sure beats walking."

"I'm getting the feeling that we're not staying in Honolulu," Jack said as he watched the main airport shrink behind him.

"Then where are we…?" Bradley's words faded away.

Trillian sat and watched this new world fly by, unfazed by the change of plans.

Jack tapped on his phone. "Looks like terminal three is where—"

"Mokulele Airlines," Bradley said.

"Yeah. How'd you…"

Bradley motioned out the window. The Wiki-Wiki shuttle pulled up in front of a large beige hangar with both steps and a ramp leading to the entry. Above it were the words "Terminal 3 Mokulele" and the Mokulele Airlines logo.

"Alright." O'Connor cackled with glee. "We're almost there. Hold on to your butts."

The group followed O'Connor inside where they checked in. One at a time, an attendant weighed the entire group plus their luggage. Flight crew transported the luggage out onto the tarmac and loaded them into a waiting Cessna 208EX Grand Caravan.

A Mokulele Airlines pilot stepped out from behind the check-in counter and clapped her hands together. "Attention ladies and gentlemen," she said. "We've got your luggage loaded. Please follow me out to the runway."

The pilot began to walk and talk as she led the group out of the hangar to the awaiting Cessna. "Our flight time to Lanai will be just under an hour, so you'll have the afternoon to relax and unwind. Where are you staying?"

All eyes fell on O'Connor.

"Club Niho'gula," she said.

Immediately Jack began working his phone, digging up information. "Whoa. Look at this." He turned his phone to Bradley and Trillian, displaying an image of a secluded cove with a white sandy beach, crystal blue water and a cloudless sky. Both their jaws dropped.

"Shit, this place is posh," Jack said.

"Nothing but the best." O'Connor grinned, enjoying how the surprise destination was playing out.

Sam spotted the waiting Cessna on the runway. "Shit. Anyone having flashbacks of Mar-A-Verde?"

"What's Mar-A-Verde?" Bradley asked.

"Our last job," O'Connor said. "We almost died."

"What?" Bradley glared at Sam. "You never told me that part."

Sam shrugged. "It wasn't important."

"Are you serious, Dad?"

O'Connor laughed. "Cool your boots. The difference here is the runway isn't going to crumble into shark-infested water."

"Jesus." Bradley gave O'Connor a playful shove.

"That plane looks a little bigger, too," Hope said. "It's got a belly."

O'Connor clutched her gut and shook it. "Like me."

"That's the luggage compartment," the pilot said.

"Again, like me." O'Connor pulled an unlit cigar from her shirt pocket, bit the end off with her teeth, and clamped it between her jaws.

"Sorry, there's no smoking during the flight," the pilot said.

"Don't worry your pretty little head. I've got an *oral fixation,* if you know what I mean." O'Connor wrapped her lips around the cigar and flashed her eyebrows at her.

The pilot rolled with the innuendo. "If you light it, I'll throw you out of the plane myself."

"Jesus," O'Connor said. "Live a little."

"Not when I have passengers."

"She's all bark and no bite," Sam said to the pilot. "Trust me."

O'Connor exchanged a pointed glare with the pilot, then turned to Sam. "Way to throw me under the Cessna."

"Just get in the plane, oh fearless leader," Sam said. "I'm dying to see this resort."

"I can show you, Sam." Jack pulled out his phone.

"Never mind," Sam said. "We want to be surprised."

"Speak for yourself." Hope shaded Jack's phone with her hand to get a better look. "Nice." She whispered into Sam's ear, "You won't be disappointed."

The pilot stood next to the Cessna's open door, which doubled as stairs, and directed everyone inside with a flourish. "Pick your seat, except for the front row."

Sam and Hope climbed aboard and took the seats in the third row. On the interior wall beside each seat leather hung a wireless headset.

The pilot stopped O'Connor. "You sit up front."

"Why?" O'Connor scowled at her. "So you can keep your beady little eyes on me?"

"Smaller planes like this one require proper weight and balance distribution," the pilot said.

O'Connor stepped nose to nose with the pilot. "Are you fat-shaming me?"

The pilot stood her ground. "It's proper safety procedure."

A second pilot, already in the cockpit performing a preflight systems check, twisted in his seat. "Is there a problem?"

The first pilot shook her head without taking her eyes off O'Connor. "Nope. No problem, right ma'am?"

Bradley placed his hand on O'Connor's shoulder. "Focus on the Mai Tais," he whispered.

O'Connor backed down. "I need a fucking Mai Tai right now." She stepped into the plane and took one of the two seats in the front row, directly behind the cockpit. Jack took the seat across the narrow aisle from her.

"Great view of the dashboard." Jack took out his phone and began snapping photos.

Bradley and Trillian took the two seats in the second row and the fourth row remained vacant.

"Please take a moment and fasten your seat belts." The first pilot closed and locked the passenger door, then joined the second pilot through the front right side door. She crouch-walked along the center aisle and double-checked that the group was belted in, then returned to her seat and faced the group, avoiding O'Connor's stare.

"This Cessna is a single turboprop unpressurized airplane," the pilot said. "Because of this, the flight can be quite noisy. We recommend wearing the headsets by your seat to reduce the noise and to hear about points of interest during the fifty minute flight." She placed her own headset on, as did the rest of the group.

The pilot spoke into the microphone attached to her headset. "Thank you for flying Mokulele Airlines. Enjoy the flight."

The propeller kicked into action, vibrating everyone inside. Slowly the little plane rolled away from its terminal. The two pilots worked in tandem as they taxied into position and waited for clearance from the tower.

Bradley and Jack had their phones out capturing photos and video. Sam looked across the aisle to Hope and smiled. She extended her hand and he took it, leaning to kiss it once lightly.

O'Connor saw the gesture. "Get a room," she said but no one heard her over the sound of the engine.

Sam returned his gaze to the window. He was glad Claire had decided not to join the group. It would have been awkward.

The Cessna received its clearance and the pilot throttled up. Everyone sunk into the backs of their seats as the Cessna surged forward, accelerating down the runway. Sam gripped the armrest.

The nose of the plane tipped up and the vibration cut in half as soon as the wheels left the ground. Moments later, the plane banked to the left.

"We're now en-route to Lanai, seventy-three miles south-east of O'ahu," the pilot said. "To the left, just past the sprawling metropolis of Honolulu is Diamond Head Crater, formed about three-hundred thousand years ago after one massive volcanic eruption."

Jack, Bradley, and Sam took the opportunity to view the spectacle.

"For those on the right side, all you can see is ocean," the pilot continued, "but four-thousand five-hundred miles south is New Zealand with the Cook Islands in between."

The left side of the aircraft was the place to be. About halfway through the flight, the pilot pointed out Molokai, nicknamed "The Friendly Isle". Hawaii's fifth largest island, it was home to the highest sea cliffs in the world.

Despite her initial dust up with the pilot, watching the ocean drift by ten thousand feet below had a calming effect on O'Connor. She was about to drift off to sleep when Trillian tapped her shoulder and pointed out the window. The southern tip of Lanai was directly ahead.

"Attention everyone, we're on final approach to the island of Lanai, nicknamed 'The Pineapple Isle' and about half the land mass of Molokai," the pilot said. "Most of Lanai, ninety-eight percent, is owned by Larry Ellison, CEO of Oracle Corporation."

The pilot banked left, lined up to the single runway of Lanai Airport, and made a smooth and effortless landing. Pine trees surrounded the island's one aircraft terminal and felt like a coffee shop in comparison to the sprawling terminals on Oʻahu.

The first pilot parked the plane, hopped out, and opened the passenger door. The second pilot began unlocking the cargo hold and removing luggage.

Everyone disembarked, O'Connor making sure she was last out of the plane. She paused by the pilot and plucked the unlit cigar from her mouth.

"Look. We got off on the wrong foot." O'Connor thought of making a prosthetic joke but decided against it. "Thanks for your professionalism and for getting us safely to such a… flat and beautiful place."

The pilot nodded. "You're welcome. If this isn't your final stop, maybe we'll meet again."

"Maybe." O'Connor leaned in and lowered her voice. "If you let it slip that I was nice to you just now, I'll fuck you up." She winked at her.

"Noted."

O'Connor detected a subtle grin from the pilot. She gave her a nod of approval and extended her hand. "Good to see women in positions of power."

The pilot took O'Connor's hand, shared a firm handshake, then led the group to the small terminal.

The pilot directed the group to the one arrival gate. Orange traffic cones had been lined up to highlight the path of entry, as if there was any other choice.

Three small, connected buildings serviced arrivals, check-ins, and baggage claim, and the entire complex was powered by solar cells attached to the roof. There were virtually no amenities except for bathrooms, vending machines, a ZipZoom car rental kiosk, and a visitor information center.

Jack took in his surroundings. "Reminds me of a highway rest stop."

"Totally," Bradley said. "Except with more places to sit."

"Speaking of which..." Trillian hustled toward the main concourse. "Nature calls."

O'Connor nodded at Hope. "The girl's got the right idea." She quickened her pace. "Last one there gets to piss themselves."

Hope ran to catch up with O'Connor's head start, intent on beating her.

"I didn't need to go until they started talking about it." Bradley glanced at Jack, then both sprinted toward the concourse.

A benefit to an exceedingly small airport terminal is never getting lost. The entire complex could be explored by foot in a matter of minutes.

"And the cheese stands alone," Sam said to himself. "I'm going to go wait for our luggage... Great idea, Sam."

He walked to the main concourse and headed right to Baggage Claim. The three floor-level roll-up doors were shut but he could hear commotion behind them.

"Ahh! Much better." O'Connor left the women's bathroom and plucked the cigar from her mouth. "Can't say I drained the vein, but I made my bladder gladder." She cackled and gave Sam a playful punch in the shoulder.

Sam gave her a sideways look. "Thanks for the update."

The middle luggage door rolled open and the group's six suitcases sat lined up in a row. Sam began lifting the luggage out and onto the floor.

"At least we don't have to fight a crowd." Sam strained to lift O'Connor's suitcase. It was heaviest by far. "What the hell do you have in here?"

"Wouldn't *you* like to know." O'Connor tried to smile seductively. It didn't work.

"It was rhetorical."

Jack and Bradley rejoined the group, followed moments later by Hope and Trillian. Everyone looked relaxed and left Sam thinking that he should visit the bathroom too.

Jack pulled out his phone. "Should I call an Uber?"

"Nope," O'Connor said.

"Rent a car? There's a ZipZoom back there."

O'Connor shook her head.

Jack glanced at Bradley and Trillian. "We're not walking, are we?"

O'Connor rolled her suitcase toward the exit. "It's handled. Follow me."

"You know the drill." Sam ushered the rest of the group forward. "If O'Connor says she's got things handled, don't argue."

Everyone followed O'Connor out the side of the terminal where a silver Chevrolet passenger van sat waiting, a Club Niho'gula logo affixed on the side panel.

"All aboard, bitches!"

WITH LUGGAGE LOADED and everyone buckled in, the driver began the sixty-minute drive to Club Niho'gula. O'Connor took the front passenger seat.

Lines of pine trees followed the single lane highway in both directions. The rich red dirt that surrounded the plains and gentle hills of Lanai spilled onto the asphalt, giving it a rusty, weathered look, as if one had gone back in time. Some of the roads weren't even paved.

As they drove through Lanai City, some properties had the expected palm trees growing in the yard, but most featured tall pine trees.

"What's with the pine trees everywhere?" Jack asked. "I mean we're in Hawaii. I was expecting more palm trees."

"I know, right?" Trillian looked out the back window of the van. "If no one told me I was on a Hawaiian island right now, I swear I was in an episode of *Heartland*." She shifted her gaze to Bradley. "It looks like prairie land, doesn't it?"

"It does," Bradley said. "I think we just passed a stable."

In less than three minutes, the shuttle had passed through Lanai City and onto Keomuku Highway, where the road transitioned into a dusty one-lane road that accommodated both directions of traffic.

The shuttle passed a shooting range and more open fields where herds of horses lazily grazed on the surrounding grass. Then the highway reached a summit where it became immediately apparent they were all on an island.

Through a seemingly endless series of switchbacks carved into the ochre earth, the illusion of vast plains dropped away, revealing misty blue ocean and a never-ending cloudless sky.

"Whoa. Shit, what's that?" Jack pointed out the left side of the shuttle. A rusted hull of a ship sat beached out in the surf.

"That's Shipwreck Beach. It's forbidden." It was the first time the driver had spoken since leaving the airport.

"Forbidden?" For O'Connor, rules were meant to be broken. "Why?"

"Cursed," the driver said before falling silent again.

O'Connor glanced back at Sam, raised a curious brow, and grinned.

"No." Sam shook his head. "Don't get any ideas."

"Where's your sense of adventure? Live a little."

"Visiting a cursed shipwreck sounds like a complication, doesn't it?" Sam held O'Connor's gaze. "You said no complications."

"Come on. Maybe there's *sunken treasure*."

The driver cast a distrustful eye at O'Connor, then returned his attention to the road ahead.

"Nope," Sam said. "Relaxation is the goal here."

O'Connor straightened herself in her seat and crossed her arms against her chest in frustration.

Sam whispered into Hope's ear. "Now she's sulking."

"She'll get over it," Hope whispered back. "By the way… I'll help you relax."

Hope's breathy words melted in his ears. He turned to her and kissed her. "You're on."

"There it is!" Jack pointed forward at the gates of Club Niho'gula in the distance. Lanai's elusive palm trees and many more pine trees surrounded the club like a living fence, disguising the real fence made of bamboo and hardened clay. The pillars on both sides of the gate were a similar rust color to the dirt on the island and gas lanterns burned bright from the top. The gate itself stood twelve feet tall, made from a combination of bamboo trunks, pine latticework, and rope.

Jack sat back and sighed. "This is going to be awesome." All three teens bumped fists.

The shuttle rolled past the gates and parked under a large porte cochère in front of the main lobby.

"I was expecting it to be bigger," Bradley said. "Like the Four Seasons or something."

O'Connor looked back at the rest of the group. "Bigger's not always better, ain't that right, Sam?" She winked at him.

Sam shook his head. "Whatever you say." He was glad the day of travel was coming to an end.

"Being smaller means they focus on what's really important," O'Connor said. "You'll see."

Everyone hopped out of the shuttle. Their feet made little rusty puffs with every step. The driver helped Sam unload the back of the shuttle.

"Thanks for getting us here, bub." O'Connor presented her open hand. The driver regarded it like it was a strange and dangerous animal, then took it, sharing a brief and firm handshake. O'Connor had concealed several bills into her hand. The driver looked at the money as if it was infected with some kind of disease, then finally pocketed it as he watched the group roll their luggage into the lobby and out of sight.

"Cursed." The driver hopped back in the shuttle and parked it in its designated spot in the maintenance lot, out of sight from guests.

THE LOBBY'S WALLS were lined with several indoor palms and the large rooftop skylight bathed the entire area in warm natural light. Despite the palms, the air carried the sweet scent of pine.

After O'Connor checked in, she handed out the electronic cabin keys, one for everyone. "Follow me."

"Have you stayed here before?" Bradley asked.

O'Connor led the group across an intricate tiled floor that led to the courtyard and cabins behind. "A few times. But mostly I stayed on O'ahu, the north shore. For the surfing. You know, until I fed my leg to the sharks and that chapter of my life closed."

Trillian and Jack exchanged a grimace.

"Sorry." Bradley gulped. "Didn't mean to be a buzzkill."

"Don't worry about it." O'Connor said, speaking around her cigar. "What's eaten is eaten." She gave Bradley a playful shove that almost knocked him over.

The group walked through an open air lounge, past a small pool surrounded with chaise lounges, and to the promenade that followed the curve of the cove.

A bar and restaurant, gift shop, and a small marina anchored one side of the cove. In the opposite direction, twenty-four pine-and-bamboo cabins with thatched roofs dotted the lush green lawn. Each cabin had its own walkway that joined up with the promenade, ending with a little mailbox made of a large bamboo trunk.

Hope's eyes bugged out. "Holy crap, O'Connor. You weren't kidding. This place is *gorgeous*."

O'Connor nodded, a big grin on her face. "Fuckin'-A. The

Four Seasons is swish, but this place is just as good." She spread her arms out. "It hasn't changed a bit."

Hope scooted close to Sam and lowered her voice. "How much does this place cost?"

Sam shook his head. "No idea. She'd never tell me anyway."

"When were you last here?" Jack asked.

O'Connor dodged the question. "Let's get to our cabins." She charged forth down the promenade until she reached cabins 13 and 14. "We'll take thirteen, 'cause I don't believe in that hocus pocus superstitious bullshit."

"We?" Hope glanced at Sam.

"Looks like we're sharing a cabin," Sam said.

"Please let there be two bedrooms," Hope whispered to herself. She ascended the steps to a thatch-covered porch and waited until O'Connor had unlocked the door. Sam and Hope followed her in.

The cabin was divided in half, the front hosting a modest kitchenette, table and four chairs, sofa, and coffee table. Bedrooms on both sides divided the back half further, with a simple but elegant bathroom-shower combo in the middle separating the rooms.

Hope breathed a sigh of relief upon seeing the two rooms.

O'Connor noticed. "Yeah, I thought we should have our own love nests."

From the porch Sam watched Jack unlock the door to their cabin and lead the charge inside, followed by Bradley and Trillian.

Sam rolled his suitcase inside. "I'm assuming the cabin layouts are the same?"

O'Connor nodded. "There *will* be teen sex."

"I'm sure it's not the first time." Sam met Hope in the bedroom she chose.

Hope draped her arms around Sam's neck. "Is there going to be *adult* sex too?" she whispered.

"Count on it." Sam kissed her.

"Too bad the walls are paper-thin," O'Connor called out from either the bathroom or the other bedroom. Despite the clarity of her voice, it was difficult to know where she was.

Hope placed her mouth next to Sam's ear. "We got to be teenagers again."

Sam looked at her confused.

"Stealth fucking," she said grinning.

Sam smiled back, then hugged and kissed her.

"Get a room, for fuck's sake," O'Connor said from the doorway. "Oh... right." She roared with laughter and headed to the porch.

"Relaxing," Sam said, reassuring himself. "It's going to be relaxing."

"Uh huh." Hope ran her hand down over the crotch of Sam's jeans, then up to hook her finger on a belt loop and led him out of the room.

The teenagers were on the porch talking excitedly with O'Connor. Sam propped himself on the doorframe.

"How's the cabin?"

Trillian shot a self-conscious look at Bradley and Sam thought he saw her cheeks turn a delicate shade of pink.

"It's great." Bradley poked his head in Sam's cabin. "Looks the same."

"Two bedrooms," Sam said.

Bradley nodded, trying to avoid eye contact. "Yeah, two bedrooms."

"I can hear your mom now."

Bradley laughed nervously. "Yeah."

Jack glanced at his phone. "We should take a look around."

"Then eat," Sam said. "How about meeting us at the restaurant in an hour."

The three teens nodded, then ran down to the promenade, heading toward the marina.

Sam placed a hand on O'Connor's shoulder. "I can't thank you enough."

"I consider you guys family," O'Connor said. "How about you buy me a Mai Tai?"

Hope furrowed her brows. "Isn't this place all-inclusive?"

"Well, shit. Of course it is." O'Connor laughed. "You can order me one, then." She plucked her cigar from her mouth. "You think I'll be able to light this puppy here?"

Sam looked at the well-manicured grounds and the sandy beach beyond the promenade. He could have sworn he saw "No Smoking" signs on the way in. Everything felt clean and fresh, not a receptive environment for an everlasting cigar.

"You can try, but my money's on 'no,'" Sam said. "It's a filthy habit anyway."

"Go fuck your mother."

Sam laughed and hooked one arm around Hope, the other around O'Connor. "Let's get you that Mai Tai."

"Mai *Tais,* plural," O'Connor said.

The sun wouldn't be setting for another few hours, and the adults planned on making the most of it.

BRADLEY, TRILLIAN, AND JACK strolled along the beach that lined the private cove of Club Nihoʻgula. The sun hung low and would soon disappear behind the western side of Lanai.

Trillian had taken off her Doc Martens and shoved her socks inside. She held them in one hand, Bradley's hand in the other. The warm white sand flowed over her feet and between her toes with every step.

"You guys going to take off your shoes, too?"

Bradley shrugged. "Maybe."

Trillian leaned into Bradley's shoulder. "Feels super nice."

Jack tapped away on his phone, missing the conversation. He still wore his flower lei around his neck and his "First Timer" button.

Bradley nudged him. "What's so important that you need to be on your phone now?"

"Ha." Jack said without looking up from his handheld screen. "You should talk."

"Do you see me on my phone?"

Jack finally looked at them both. "I'm reading about the guy who owns this island. Larry Ellison, you know? Oracle? They mentioned him on the flight here."

"What about him?" Trillian gave a look of genuine interest.

"I don't know," Jack said. "I just find it amazing that a person could buy an island like this. I'm going to do that some day."

"Invent something everyone needs, make a billion dollars?" Bradley smiled at him.

"Something like that." Jack pocketed his phone. "Stranger things have happened. What about you guys? What's going to be your claim to fame in ten years?"

"Start a graphic design company, make a billion dollars," Bradley said.

Jack looked to Trillian for her answer. The weight of his stare, then Bradley's, compelled an answer.

"Marrying Brad and having twelve kids is going to take about ten years, I figure."

Bradley tried to laugh but it came out like a choke. "Twelve? Why does the number keep going up?"

"Because it makes you squirm." She tickled him.

"Seriously, though, Trill," Jack said. "What do you want to do?"

"Seriously? I don't know. Travel? Write? I've always just gone with the flow. Life of a foster kid, I guess. It's turned out okay so far."

The three teens reached the marina at the end of the beach. A set of concrete stairs led back up to a gift shop and the promenade, which joined with the pier that extended part way into the cove. Scattered tourists dotted the walkway. The opposite side of the pier hosted several jetties for snorkeling, sight-seeing excursions, and mooring facilities for a few large yachts.

At the top of the stairs, Bradley faced Trillian and Jack. "Should we head back?"

"Let's do the pier before the sun sets," Trillian said. "It's so different than Santa Monica."

Bradley focused on Jack.

"Yeah," Jack said. "Sounds—"

Something in the water, smooth, without fins or any defining features, breached the surface, rolled, and disappeared.

Jack's eyes widened as he looked past Bradley and Trillian, beyond the cove and towards the mountains of Maui.

"What?" Bradley looked out at the water.

"Did you see it?"

Trillian tried to follow Jack's gaze. "I don't see anything."

Jack pointed as accurately as he could, but whatever it was he had seen had disappeared. "It was right there, in the middle of the cove, maybe a bit further out."

Bradley and Trillian exchanged a glance. "Uh, what did it look like?"

"You've seen pictures of the Loch Ness Monster?" Jack looked at them, still wild-eyed. "It was like that." He pulled his phone out, tapped on the camera app, and aimed it out at the cove. "If only I had gotten pictures."

They waited for a several minutes before Bradley piped up. "Whatever you saw, I don't think it's coming back."

Jack nodded.

"Let's walk the pier, then head back to the restaurant." Trillian held out her hand for Bradley.

Jack held out a moment longer before following. The three of them had been walking only a few minutes when two women passed by, both wearing sarongs, one in a large sun hat, and one with a lei around her neck. As they came closer, it became clear that one of the women was younger than the other.

"Dude," Bradley whispered to Jack out of the side of his mouth. "Dude!"

"What?" Jack said, annoyed that his attention had been pulled away from the water of the cove.

"She's checking you out," Bradley said.

"The one in the lei," Trillian added.

Jack finally focused on the two women as they strolled past. The younger one wearing the lei pulled down her sunglasses to get a better look, but it was unclear if she was looking at him or all three of them.

"Howdy. Beautiful evening." Jack smiled as the two women passed without saying a word. He looked back at them and saw the younger one look back at him, her sunglasses shielding her eyes.

"Howdy?" Bradley stared, incredulous. "Smooth, dude. Real smooth."

"Well, she took a second look, didn't she?"

"Probably couldn't believe her ears," Bradley said. "Howdy." He laughed.

Jack brushed it off. "Whatever."

"It was the lei," Trillian said. "Appreciating nice flowers is a good character trait."

"Oh, really?" Bradley looked at her, smirking.

Trillian nodded. "Yup. Women love a good lei."

Bradley groaned at the pun.

"In that case, I'm going to wear this lei for as long as possible."

"How you going to do that?" Bradley asked.

"I don't know. Maybe I'll soak it in water overnight." Jack slipped into thinking mode. "I'll figure something out. I've decided I'd like my leis to last a long time." He grinned at Bradley.

"Okay, Mr. First Timer."

Jack realized the Hawaiian Airlines button had been in full view when he passed the two women earlier. "You think she was looking at my button?"

"She was looking at *something*," Trillian said.

They reached the end of the pier and stood for a moment to appreciate the view. Jack snapped a picture with his phone.

Trillian looked back at the restaurant and bar. "Anyone hungry yet?"

Jack's stomach growled, right on cue. "A hundred percent."

"I was hungry when we left," Bradley said.

The three teens headed back along the pier. They passed a snorkeling and excursion outfit. The sign above the door read "Palakiko Tours." The main building looked weathered and run down. A new coat of paint would have done the place a world of good. A teenage Polynesian girl worked outside the main building, coiling rope and securing two boats to the pier. She barely looked up from her work as Bradley, Trillian, and Jack passed by.

Jack smiled at her and waved. The girl returned a short glance and a curt wave. The long dark hair in front of her face worked like a shield.

"You got your eyes on *two* girls now?" Bradley looked at the girl briefly, then settled back on Jack.

"That one didn't see my 'First Timer' button either."

"Being a virgin isn't a bad thing, you know," Trillian said. "It's actually kind of cool."

"Who said anything about being a virgin?" Jack quickened his pace, then spun around to his friends. "Come on. There's burgers waiting with our names on them."

Bradley smirked at him. "Taking another look?"

Jack saw that the girl had paused her evening duties to study the threesome. "Shut up, dude." He turned again to keep his lead.

"You're bad," Trillian said.

"He knows I'm fucking with him." Bradley placed his hand in hers. "I'll always be his wingman."

They ran to catch up to Jack, their stomachs rumbling in anticipation. Neither of them saw the strange smooth creature break the surface of the water for a second time that night.

THE SUN DROPPED behind Club Nihoʻgula's main building, casting the pool area and bar in warm shade. Evenly spaced copper tiki torches added a flickering orange glow to the shade. O'Connor and Hope claimed one of the only tables left between the promenade and the pool. Sam stood at the bar.

Gus took a quick look at him. "You're new."

"Yeah," Sam said. "Arrived today."

Gus extended his hand. "I'm Gus. I'm the go-to bartender here at the club. Plus, I can get you anything you need."

"I'm Sam." The two men shared a solid handshake. Sam pointed back at his table. "The one with the cigar, that's O'Connor, and the other is Hope."

"She knows there's no smoking anywhere on the island, right?"

"Yeah, she knows," Sam said. "I like to think of it as an accessory, like a piece of jewelry."

Gus nodded. "What can I get you, Sam?"

"A Mai Tai, a Hawaiian Iced Tea, and a soda with lemon."

Gus gave Sam a subtle curious glance as he prepared the drinks.

"The soda's for me. Recovering alcoholic." When Gus didn't respond, Sam added, "Sorry, too much info."

"No worries. Got an uncle who drinks too much. It's tough." Gus placed three glasses on a tray and slid it toward Sam. "All in moderation, right? Or so they say."

"Something like that." Sam grabbed the tray and began the short walk to the table.

Hope sat back in her chair, admiring the cove and the rose-tinted clouds surrounding the distant peak of Maui's Puu Kukui reflecting the setting sun. "Why would anyone want to swim in a pool when they have *that?*" She motioned to the beach and crystal blue water.

"The pool ain't got no nasties in it that'll bite your leg off," O'Connor said. "That appeals to some people."

"Okay, I'll give you that."

"Oh, you'll *give* me that?" O'Connor rapped on her leg with a fist. "How kind. My leg thanks you."

Sam slid the tray onto the table. "O'Connor, your Mai Tai has arrived."

"First of many." O'Connor grabbed her drink and took a sip. "Damn. It doesn't get better than this."

Hope tasted her Hawaiian Iced Tea. "This is delicious. Want a taste?"

"It's just soda for me."

Hope placed her hand to her mouth. "Oh my God, I'm sorry. I forgot."

"It's fine." Sam held up his glass. "Here's to rest and relaxation."

They clinked glasses and drank. Three rounds later, O'Connor had absorbed all the energy in the vicinity, and amplified it with her voice.

She looked at Sam glassy-eyed. "Another round, Jeeves?"

"Is that all I am to you? A butler?" Over time Sam had learned to enjoy O'Connor's drunkenness. He looked at Hope.

"I'm good—" Hope belched and placed her hand on her mouth. "Oops."

Both O'Connor and Hope fell into hysterical laughter. Other guests had been giving them the eye for the past half hour. Sam shrugged, offered a lopsided grin, and tried his best to roll with the drunkenness.

A voice louder than O'Connor's rose up from the opposite

side of the lounge, across the pool. Guests in the lounge shifted their focus. A large woman with spiky blond hair and salt-crusted clothes had pulled another guest to the side as they left the restaurant.

From where Sam, Hope, and O'Connor sat, the woman's words were unintelligible, but carried a clear, angry tone.

The guest tried to get away but the woman pulled him closer. Sam spotted a ragged scar that spanned the woman's left forehead to her cheek, twisting her left eyelid in such a way that it didn't close completely when she blinked.

The woman shook the guest, then let them go with a push that almost knocked them over.

Sam continued to stare until the woman turned his head, feeling like they had locked gaze.

"You got some competition, O'Connor," Sam said as he averted his eyes. "On the loudness scale."

O'Connor and Hope turned to watch.

The woman walked to the closest table in the lounge, this time speaking clearly for everyone to hear. "Mind your own fucking business."

Two women dressed in bathing suits and sarongs approached the restaurant from the promenade, the older one taking the large woman aside just as she had done earlier. She spoke heated but subdued words.

"Get off me," the large woman said with a scowl.

The woman began tapping the older woman's shoulder with her finger as she continued to speak.

"Who the hell is that, and how do I get on her good side?" Hope said.

"I'll find out." Sam hopped out of his chair and strolled to the bar. He leaned toward Gus, who was also watching the drama unfold. "Who's the woman?"

"Which one?"

"The one with the sun hat."

"That's Pandora Rockwell. Owns Rockwell Simulations," Gus said. "She's with her daughter Maddilyn."

"And the asshat?"

"Nina Skulk. She runs specialized excursions." Gus shook his head. "Honestly, she's a cancer. They tried to ban her from the island, but guests actually *complained*. No idea why. My advice, that you *didn't* hear from me… steer clear of her. She's bad news."

Skulk looked like she was under pressure, from her spiky crew cut and a shirt and jeans one size too small that accentuated both her curves and muscles. The woman was ready to blow at the seams at any given moment.

Sam nodded and rapped a knuckle on the bar countertop. "Thanks, Gus." He rejoined Hope and O'Connor.

"Spill," Hope said.

"Later." Sam continued to watch the altercation from across the pool.

O'Connor stood abruptly, her chair sliding back. "Hey, idiot."

Sam covered his eyes. "Oh God, no…"

O'Connor yelled across to where Skulk stood. "Why don't you get the hell out of here and let these fine folks enjoy their evening?"

Even from their vantage point, Sam could see Skulk's face redden with rage. She turned to charge around the pool and address O'Connor, but Pandora caught Skulk's arm again and said something inaudible.

Skulk stepped forward, almost nose to nose with Pandora like she was going to challenge whatever it was that she said. Pandora stood her ground. After a few seconds, Skulk charged away toward the marina.

The guests in the lounge clapped and cheered, everyone except Pandora. Instead, she scrutinized O'Connor from across the pool before disappearing into the restaurant, with Maddilyn following close behind.

"Jesus," Sam said. "We're not even here one day and already you've made enemies."

"And friends. Look!" O'Connor raised her glass to the rest of the lounge guests. They raised their glasses in accord, clapping and cheering. She sat down. "This calls for another round."

"Or not," Sam said. "Look who just rolled in."

Bradley, Trillian, and Jack approached the table from the promenade.

"When do we eat?" Without a beat, Jack's stomach snarled in agreement.

"Holy shit." O'Connor tipped back on her chair. "Was that you?"

Jack grinned. "You don't mess with my stomach."

"Damn straight." O'Connor pushed back a little too hard and lost her balance. Bradley and Trillian caught her and her chair before it hit the floor.

"The ladies are living it up." Sam tilted an imaginary glass to his lips.

Hope smacked Sam on the shoulder. "I saw that. Careful, or you're sleeping on the floor."

"Or with *me!*" O'Connor laughed.

"Let's go." Sam led the rest of the group around the pool, through the opposite side of the lounge, and into the restaurant. As they went, other guests congratulated O'Connor for standing up to Skulk.

Bradley noticed the interactions. "What's going on?"

"Nothing, except O'Connor being O'Connor," Hope said. "Swelled head achievement unlocked."

The group entered the restaurant. The decor inside matched what they had seen in the lobby, but here there was an even mix of small palm and pine trees throughout. Many illuminated netted glass orbs designed to look like fishing floats lit the open dining area. They hung at varied heights and gave the room a warm glow.

The host eyed O'Connor and her cigar, then the rest of the gang. "That's six of you? And that cigar stays unlit?"

"The night's young, toots!" O'Connor flashed her eyes at the host.

"Sorry, but yeah." Sam nodded. "Yes to both."

The host snapped his fingers, made a quick hand gesture, and two bus staff pushed two empty tables together, resetting them for six people. "Follow me."

"Dude!" Bradley nudged Jack. "Dude, look!"

"Wha—" Jack spotted the two women they had passed on the pier earlier. "Holy shit," he said in a whisper.

"Go for it." Trillian smiled enthusiastically at him. "Make a move."

"Like what?"

"I don't know," Trillian said. "Say 'hi' or something. Quick."

Jack's lips had gone bone dry. They'd pass the women's table in seconds. He gave his lips a lick, opened his mouth to speak, but O'Connor's voice came out instead.

O'Connor stumbled and leaned over the table where Pandora and Maddilyn sat. "Nice work with that *asshole*. I would've kicked her to the floor too, but that's just me." She laughed in their faces and filled the air with boozy breath.

Bradley glanced at Trillian. "Asshole?" he mouthed.

Trillian shrugged.

Jack smiled at the younger woman. She met his eyes briefly, then looked away. He couldn't tell if it was disinterest, shyness, or boredom.

"Sorry for the intrusion, Ms. Rockwell," Sam said. "Enjoy your evening." He ushered O'Connor and the rest of the Detest-A-Pest crew after the host to their table.

Jack latched onto Sam. "You *know* her?"

"I know who she is, yes," Sam said.

"You got to tell me *everything*."

"Cool your boots." Sam sat. "Food first."

Jack took a seat that allowed him to see Maddilyn from across the restaurant.

A waiter approached the table. "Welcome to Ono. My name is Alana and I'll be your server tonight."

Before she could continue, O'Connor pushed her menu aside, unopened. "I know what I want. Calamari. And lots of it."

Alana's eyes widened for a moment, then she shook her head. "No no. Calamari is not available."

"What do you mean?" O'Connor balled her fists. "It's summer. There's the ocean. Get a net."

"I'm sorry," Alana said, "but all forms of cephalopods are revered here at Club Nihoʻgula."

"Cepha-what?" O'Connor began to raise her voice.

"Cephalopods," Alana said. "Squid, octopus, cuttlefish. To eat one would bring about a curse upon everyone here."

O'Connor stared at Alana, then leaned toward Hope. "This is a joke, right?"

"Don't think so," Hope said. "You've got to embrace local customs. This isn't New York."

"I don't have to embrace jack."

"Hey, leave me out of it," Jack joked.

O'Connor daggered Jack with her eyes and Jack took the hint, shielding himself with his menu.

Sam turned toward Alana. "I think we're going to need some time with the menu. But we'll have a Mai Tai, Hawaiian Iced Tea, soda with lemon, and whatever these guys want to drink." He motioned at the teens, then added, "nothing alcoholic, of course."

Bradley shook his head. "Dear old dad. Destroyer of fun."

Alana took the teenagers' drink orders. "I'll check on you in a few minutes." She excused herself to attend to other guests.

"Why the fuck are they preserving something so damn delicious?" O'Connor scowled. "Makes no sense."

Hope looked at her. "It doesn't have to make sense to you. We're on their turf."

"Their *turf* is still on American soil, honey."

Sam sighed. "Can we… not do this?"

Jack piped up and broke the tension. "Sam, tell us everything you know about *them*." He nodded toward Pandora and Maddilyn.

Sam shared the limited information he had learned from Gus about the Rockwells and Skulk. Jack pulled out his phone and began searching for anything he could find about the Rockwell family.

The table's drinks arrived and the group ordered their entrées. Bradley and Sam played it safe with Surf and Turf burgers while both Trillian and Jack branched out with the Lobster Risotto.

Hope had been hooked on lobster since their excursion to Mar-A-Verde last year. She ordered it even though it was imported to Hawaii.

Because O'Connor's coveted calamari was off the menu, she went with land animals instead, choosing Lanai Venison. Eating "Rudolph" went a long way in smoothing over O'Connor's animosity toward the universe.

"Ho ho ho-ly shit this is good." O'Connor had said mid-meal, laughing, her mouth filled with bloody rare meat. "Santa's going to get five stars."

With bellies full, the gang retired to their cabins. Sleepiness that only a full stomach can induce replaced the adrenaline of a day of travel.

Under the cover of darkness, no one noticed a boat halfway out into the cove.

DEFENDING TERRITORY

AT HALF PAST four in the morning, Lanai, Niho'gula Cove, and the rest of the Hawaiian Islands had just begun to wake up.

Morning Glory, a Grady-White Freedom 215, had sat anchored in the middle of the cove since midnight, positioned directly over the well-known wreck of the *Templeton,* a schooner that had run aground in 1808. With little wind, clear skies, and no moon, the conditions were perfect for night-time snorkeling. The only light came from the ones dotting the promenade, the stars above… and the underwater flashlight.

Larry Kirkland and Dennis Brink were not there to snorkel. They had rented the boat and scuba equipment the previous day in Maui and waited until nightfall to travel the ten miles west to Niho'gula Cove. They had agreed to alternate their dives until they had used up their tanks.

Dennis checked his watch again. This was Larry's third and final dive and he had been submerged for thirty-five minutes. It was illegal to use scuba equipment in the cove and as the first glow of the rising sun backlit the Maui mountains, Dennis itched to get moving. Their efforts had not been rewarded so far and he didn't want to add arrest to the list.

With nervous fingers Dennis thrummed his wetsuit, black with a double yellow pinstripe traveling the length of his arms, torso, and legs.

"Come on, Larry, you bastard. Move your ass." He glanced at his watch again. The face read "4:41am."

Dennis peered over the starboard side of the boat. The blue-green glow of Larry's flashlight below swept the rotting, fractured hull and the rocky bottom of the cove in wide arcs. He could see shadowy creatures propelling themselves around his body.

Twenty feet under the surface, Larry shone his headlamp on his pressure gauge. He had about ten minutes of air left. He had to wrap things up but decided to do one more pass over the sunken wreck.

He moved slowly over the crumpled wooden deck, swaying his metal detector back and forth. He barely noticed the octopuses that circled him just beyond his reach. But he was prepared. If they got too close, he had a spear in the other hand. That would do the trick.

Larry's pressure gauge flashed, showing two minutes of air remaining. Just as he reached the end of one side of the deck, his detector began to vibrate. He decided to give it one more minute. They had gone too far tonight to go home empty-handed.

He reduced his sweeping arcs until he was able to narrow down the spot that was triggering the detector. Larry fanned the sand away to reveal a single gold coin with a square hole in the center.

He grabbed the coin, hooked the detector to his belt, and headed to the surface. As he ascended, the octopuses began grazing his body and wrapping their tentacles around his legs and arms. He used the spear to stab some of the creatures, but there were too many. They seemed to come from everywhere all at once. With air running out. Larry's only choice was up and through the attacking octopuses.

Focusing on Larry's ascent, Dennis did not hear the man and woman board the *Morning Glory*. The man wrapped his dagger-tattooed arm across Dennis's chest and held a large knife across his throat with his other hand. His rich skin and dark hair with blond tips could barely be seen in the dawn light.

The woman stood in front of Dennis, a black bandana shrouding the lower half of her face, and a scar running through her left eyebrow.

"Where is it?" the woman said.

The man tightened his grip and Dennis felt the knife's blade digging into his neck. If this woman was anything like the man restraining him, he knew his chance at escape would be slim.

"Where's what?" Dennis's eyes darted back and forth in panic.

The woman struck the side of Dennis's head. "Don't play dumb. You know exactly what I'm talking about."

Larry surfaced at the stern of the boat, octopuses crawling all over his arms and legs. He held the coin up with one hand and pulled the regulator out of his mouth with the other. "Found one!"

"Larry! Get out of here! Get—" Before Dennis could get another word out, the man cut a deep gash across his throat, cutting off his voice instantly and flooding the front of his wetsuit with a gush of blood.

The woman grabbed Larry's extended hand and began to pull him onto the boat. But the writhing octopuses made her grasp slippery.

The man dropped Dennis to the deck and joined the effort, pulling Larry onto the boat by his scuba tank. The struggle became a tug-of-war between the man, woman, and the octopuses, too numerous to count, and Larry was the prize. Somehow, the octopuses kept a hold on Larry so strong that his wetsuit began to tear in spots, his blood collecting in the ripped neoprene.

The scuba tank slid off Larry's back and arms, sending the man onto his backside. The woman readjusted her grip as the man grabbed a rope and looped it around Larry's wrists.

The woman pried the gold coin from Larry's hand and let him go. "Finish him, Niko."

Niko secured a tight knot around Larry's wrists and looped the rope around Larry's neck, but then lost his grip. The octopuses won the war and dragged Larry back into the water. Niko grabbed the remaining rope and tied it to the hull of the *Morning Glory*.

"We got to sink it."

The woman was already back on their cabin cruiser, a Cutwater C-288 Coupe named *Wavy Jones*. She pulled her mask off, exposing the scar that spanned forehead to cheek.

Nina Skulk stood grinning at the gold coin in her hand. She pocketed it, fastened a second rope to a cleat on the *Wavy Jones,* and threw Niko the slack. "Sun's up. Make it fast."

Niko found a cleat on the bow of the *Morning Glory* and tied the rope to it. He cut the anchor and jumped back into the *Wavy Jones*. Skulk throttled up the dual Yamaha engines and towed the *Morning Glory* northeast toward Auau Channel.

The octopuses lost interest and released Larry as the convoy headed for open ocean. He spun and sputtered, grabbing a breath every time his face broke the water's surface. His wrists had turned a light shade of purple due to lack of circulation. If he couldn't free himself, his fate would lie at the bottom of the channel. After watching Dennis's murder, Larry was sure he'd be killed too.

Skulk cut the engines. Niko grabbed a rubber mallet, guided the *Morning Glory* to the port side, and jumped aboard. He stepped over Dennis's bloody, lifeless body.

"Hold it steady."

Skulk took up the slack until the two boats were side by side.

Niko zeroed in on the *Morning Glory's* submerged drain plug at the back of the transom. He raised the mallet and smashed the plug several times, breaking its seal with the hull.

"Gonna take a while," Niko said. "Give me the fish spear."

Skulk tossed a long-handled spear with two barbed points. Niko pulled the hatch in front of the transom and rammed the spear through the hull several times. Water gushed into the compartment. The stern had already lowered compared to the bow, showing that the boat was taking on water.

"Should be under in twenty minutes," Niko said.

"Not good enough." Skulk pulled a pistol from a holster on her belt and aimed at the bow section of the hull.

Niko held his arms up. "Wait. Too loud." He waded through puddles of Dennis's blood to the helm and opened two hatches under the console. Using the spear, he punctured the hull several more times on both the port and starboard sides. "Five minutes, tops. Good?"

Skulk holstered her pistol in agreement and started *Wavy Jones's* engines. Niko hopped aboard, untied the sinking *Morning Glory,* and tossed the slack rope into the aft deck of the sinking boat.

"Can I see?" Niko regarded Skulk warily in the early morning light. "The gold?"

As Skulk navigated the *Wavy Jones* back toward Nihoʻgula Cove, she pulled the coin from her pocket and held it up for Niko to see. The orange dawn sky reflected off the intricately engraved gold coin and through the square hole in the center.

Niko reached forward to touch the coin, but Skulk pulled it back and pocketed it. "The hole, square." He met Skulk's gaze and grinned. "*Templeton?*"

Skulk nodded. "Knew it was out there. And there's bound to be more where that came from."

As they entered the cove, Skulk throttled down the engines to a minimum and steered the cruiser toward the marina.

"We've got work to do." Skulk nailed Niko with serious eyes. "Investors to impress."

"And we split the take fifty-fifty?"

"Don't worry." Skulk returned her eyes to her approaching moorage, the corners of her mouth curling in a subtle grin. "You'll get your cut."

LARRY HELD HIS breath until his lungs burned. The last thing he wanted was to resurface and draw attention to himself, but he was close to drowning himself.

He kicked his fins and broke the surface, drawing a huge, replenishing breath. The *Wavy Jones* was already well on its way back to the cove.

Larry felt the rope tug on his wrists, now purple from constriction. He turned and saw the *Morning Glory* drifting and taking on water fast. The aft section was almost totally submerged. He estimated he had minutes left before he'd be pulled down with the boat.

He kicked his fins with all his strength and swam around to the cockpit. The dawn light made details hard to see, but the red cross decal on the port side of the cockpit stood out.

Larry pulled open the door and the first aid kit fell and bobbed in the water. His fingers were numb and almost unresponsive, but he forced his thumbs to unlatch the kit.

The contents of the first aid kit spilled out into the water around him, but he managed to stop the pair of scissors with his swollen hands. Maintaining balance in the sinking boat while wearing swim fins was a challenge. Manipulating scissors with fingers that didn't obey his commands made the feat next to impossible. He balanced the scissors on the dash of the boat and picked them up with his teeth.

His constant drool made the scissor handles slide unpredictably in his mouth, as he slipped the tip of the blades between his wrists. He couldn't cut the rope in the conventional sense, but maybe he could open the scissors and pry the rope loose.

He clenched his jaws with all his might on the metal thumb

loops, then felt a *crack*. Bits of molar crumbled into the back of his throat.

Larry gagged and involuntarily spat the tooth fragments out, losing grasp of the scissors at the same time. The scissors fell out of the coil of rope, slid off the dash and sunk like a stone before his eyes.

With his wrists still tightly bound, Larry had all but given up hope when the warm rising sun struck the back of his neck.

Heat. That was it.

He wrangled the empty kit's plastic case floating in the water beside him, propped one side of the case between his knees, and ran the rope between his wrists back and forth across the narrow edge of kit's leading side.

Back and forth.

Back and forth, as fast as he could manage.

There was no time to check for progress. Either the friction from the edge of the plastic case would cut the rope, or he would die trying. This was his only option. He couldn't swim back without his hands.

He sawed back and forth, back and forth.

With his muscles aching, Larry heard a *crack,* then a *snap*. One rope broke and that's all it took. The remaining loops coiled around his wrists slackened and fell away. He pushed off from the *Morning Glory* and watched it sink.

Almost at once his blood began circulating slowly through his freed wrists, and with it excruciating pain. But his hands were still useless to him, without any sense of touch or grip strength.

He hadn't noticed it before, but the torn holes in his wetsuit continued to bleed. Somehow the octopuses – *were they octopuses?* – that had held him earlier had breached his skin.

The small cuts were the least of his worries. Larry still had at least a mile to the cove, and his strength was almost at zero. Exhausted, he oriented himself and began the journey back to the cove, working against the current, the swim fins helping propel him more efficiently. He aimed for the side of the cove farthest from the marina where he could escape on foot unseen. As he swam, he formulated his story.

But everything is farther away than it seems, and when Larry entered the cove, he felt his energy drain from his body. Every stroke, every finned kick took increased effort.

He felt his body sinking into the water a little bit more with every passing second. Flipping onto his back, he took a large breath to keep his buoyancy as exhaustion overtook him.

Just before Larry blacked out, he felt something grip his arms. *Tentacles?*

He gave in, the fight in him gone.

FOLKLORE

BRADLEY AND TRILLIAN watched Jack finish off his third serving of breakfast, this time crepes with pineapple compote and whipped cream. The resort could have been a dump but if you threw in an all-you-can-eat buffet of any kind, Jack was all in.

Bradley eyed him with amusement. "You done? You're not going for another round, are you?"

Jack leaned back in his chair and placed his hands behind his head. His full belly stretched out his T-shirt and his partially wilted lei collected on top. "I'm seriously thinking about it."

Trillian shook her head and sighed. "Fill your boots. We're going to explore." She stood and extended her hand to Bradley.

"Later, man." Bradley grinned and flashed a middle finger at Jack. He followed Trillian away from the table and towards one of the many exits.

Outside on the promenade, they kissed, the morning sun warming both their faces.

"How long, do you think?"

Bradley smiled and made a quick mental calculation. "Thirty seconds max."

Not even ten seconds later, Bradley and Trillian heard quick footsteps approach from behind. Jack placed his arms around their necks and inserted himself between them.

"I figured two thousand calories to start the day was enough," Jack said. "Besides, I got to save some room for lunch."

"Stop talking about food." Trillian pointed at the Niho'gula Trading Post. "The gift shop requires our full attention now."

The three of them stepped inside and faced aisle after aisle of kitsch. As high end as Club Niho'gula was, the *Trading Post* felt like a giant step backward in time and quality. Then they saw the prices.

Bradley held up a T-shirt for Jack. "This has got your name written all over it. Only two hundred dollars." The front of the T-shirt read "I got lei'd in Lanai."

Trillian picked up an orange silk sarong with pineapples randomly scattered across the fabric and wrapped it around her shorts. "What about this? Only three hundred and fifty."

"You look awesome." Bradley picked up a tube of lip gloss. "But I can't even afford the orange-flavored Niho'gula-branded Lip Smackers. Fifty bucks."

"You're kidding." Trillian examined the tube, then placed it back on the display rack. "Shit. We are so out of our league."

"Tell me about it," Bradley said.

"Hey guys." Jack waved them to the back of the shop. "Look at this." He stood in front of an old picture on the wall depicting a massive octopus shredding the stern of a boat. "It's like that final scene in Jaws, when Quint gets eaten."

Jack took out his phone and snapped a picture of the old photograph. "They should make a movie like that."

"Already have," Trillian said. "A movie *and* a book. *20,000 Leagues Under the Sea* by Jules Verne. You should read more."

Jack smirked at her. "No time."

"It's real." The voice came from an older Hawaiian woman who was reclining in a hammock behind the cash register. She wore a T-shirt with a hand-drawn coconut bra illustration across the top and tie-dyed shorts. "It happened in the cove, late nineteenth century."

Bradley looked at her dubiously. "So you're saying someone

just happened to be here with camera equipment when the ship—"

"The *Templeton,*" the cashier said.

"When the *Templeton* was attacked and destroyed?"

The cashier shrugged. "That's what the history books say."

Jack leaned toward Bradley's ear and whispered, "I smell bullshit."

"Bullshit or not, that's what happened," the cashier said, grinning. "The legend of *Pepehi Waapa* goes back a couple hundred years, way before that photo was taken."

Trillian crouched in front of a display case of jewelry to get a good look at a silver bracelet in the shape of an octopus. Its long curling tentacles acted as the wrist band.

"You like that?" The cashier smiled at her. "It's from a local artist."

Trillian nodded. After seeing the price of nine hundred dollars, she stood again. "*Pepehi Waapa?*"

"Boat killer. That's literally what it means." The cashier regarded the teens with serious eyes. "It was named that right from the beginning. Makes you wonder why, huh?"

Bradley considered the detail. "I guess so."

The cashier stood and leaned on the counter next to the cash register. "You can buy a numbered print of the disaster. I still have a few in the back."

"I think we're okay," Bradley said.

"Well, see anything else you like?"

Trillian stole a quick peek back at the octopus bracelet. "Lots, but we—"

Bradley interrupted Trillian and continued. "We're here for a while. We'll be back."

"Don't take too long," the cashier said. "We don't have a lot of guests here, but they got deep pockets and love souvenirs."

Trillian followed Bradley and Jack to the entrance. "Oh hey, I love your shirt," she said to the cashier.

"It's much more comfortable than the real thing." The two women shared a laugh. "The name's Nora by the way," the cashier called back as the teenagers stepped back out into the mid-morning sunshine.

"Later, Nora." Trillian gave a thumbs up before rejoining the guys.

Bradley pulled Jack aside. "You didn't believe that crap about the boat attack, did you?"

Jack balked. "I need more information before I decide."

"Nora's just doing her job," Trillian said. "Selling stuff and talking to guests. I liked her."

Across the cove arose the shrill sound of a whistle. A small crowd had formed on the opposite side of the beach.

Jack squinted to discern more detail. "What's going on?"

The three teens looked at each other.

"I don't know," Bradley said, "but let's find out."

The three ran toward the commotion.

JACK, BRADLEY, AND TRILLIAN sprinted down the promenade and jumped over the steps to the beach. They could see Sam and Hope standing nearby, and a few other guests with their phones out. Two Club Niho'gula medical personnel crouched next to a diver at the water's edge, a stretcher close by.

"What's going on, Dad?"

Sam craned his neck to get a look at the unfolding scene. "We've only been here for a few minutes, but it looks like a diver was injured."

Trillian nudged Jack and motioned toward the opposite side of the gathering crowd. "Look. It's that girl."

Jack turned to see Maddilyn standing next to Pandora, both with their phones out. He caught Maddilyn's eye and offered a timid wave. She partially hid a smile behind her long blond hair and returned her attention to her phone.

"What was that?" Jack said, confused.

Trillian shrugged. "I don't know. Maybe she's playing hard to get. Maybe she wants you to pursue her."

Jack snorted. "I don't understand girls."

"Welcome to the club," Bradley said. Before Trillian could protest, he planted a kiss on her cheek.

Trillian smiled. "Good recovery."

Jack gave the crowd a cursory glance and pulled out his phone. Sam stopped him. "A little respect, hmm?"

Jack nodded contritely. "Where's O'Connor?"

At the water's edge, one medic spent most of their time keeping people away, but O'Connor was the exception. Most of the time she was an unstoppable force of nature.

O'Connor knelt beside one medic but directed her question to the injured diver. "What happened?"

"Ma'am, please step back." The attending medic signaled the other.

The medic working on crowd control placed a hand on O'Connor's shoulder.

She shook it off like it was white hot. "Take your fuckin' hands off me. I'm a paying guest here and I want answers." She tapped on her prosthetic leg. "I know all about shark attacks in Hawaii."

"This wasn't a shark attack," one of the medics said as they moved the diver onto the nearby stretcher. "The teeth marks aren't typical."

"If it wasn't sharks, then what did this?" O'Connor noted the diver's torn neoprene and purple hands.

The medics continued to dress the diver's wounds, wrapping his bloody forearms and hands in gauze.

The diver locked gaze with O'Connor for just a second, then looked away. "Fell off... boat. Swam..."

O'Connor gave the diver a look of distrust. "Bullshit. Why are your hands purple?"

"Ma'am, please." The medics wrapped the diver in a blanket, strapped him to the stretcher, and transported him across the beach.

O'Connor followed. "Where are you taking him?"

"Where do you think?" one medic shot back. "Mind your own business."

O'Connor stopped in her tracks and the remaining crowd gathered around her. The medics carried the diver through the resort, following a path that would cause the least amount of disruption, until all three were out of sight.

Sam stepped up behind her. "Everything okay?"

"No." O'Connor gnawed on her unlit cigar stub and squinted at the path the paramedics had taken. "That diver knows more than he's saying."

"He did almost drown," Sam said. "He's probably delirious."

"No. There's something else going on."

"Repeat after me. Rest and relaxation. Those are *your* words," Sam said. "Don't get any ideas."

O'Connor narrowed her eyes at him. "Who, me? Fuck no." She waved at Gus at the bar. "I need a Mai Tai."

"But it's not even noon."

"You got a point, Sam?" O'Connor trudged up the path from the promenade to the bar and settled herself on a barstool.

It was clear to Sam that the gears in O'Connor's head were turning and gaining speed. While he couldn't predict what kind of day lay ahead, he was certain that rest and relaxation wasn't on the schedule.

THE DOWNSIDE TO three helpings of breakfast was the sleepies. Jack had successfully fought them off so far but was losing the battle. The sofa and the coffee table he had his feet propped up on were too comfortable.

Bradley plopped himself on the opposite end of the sofa and pulled a stack of books from a narrow shelf under the table.

Trillian launched herself at the sofa between the two guys and snuggled into Bradley. "Whatcha reading?"

Bradley flipped through the stack of books. "Not sure yet. Help me pick something."

One by one, they sorted through the books: *The History of Lanai, Wildlife of the Hawaiian Islands, Polynesian Flora and Fauna.*

Trillian stopped Bradley on a book titled *Hawaiian Folklore.* "Winner winner chicken dinner."

Bradley opened the thin book, its laminated hard cover cracking as it bent. "Looks pretty old." He flipped to the copyright page. "Published in 1968."

"Look at the contents." Trillian advanced a page. "Mysterious legends, mysterious folklore, mysterious myths… I'm sensing a theme."

"How about mysterious *creatures?*" Bradley found the corresponding page and began reading. "Beware of the *Night Marchers.* Apparently if you look at them, you'll be pulled into the spirit world."

Trillian flipped a page. "Pele's a real hothead. The goddess of fire and volcanoes can take the form of a white-haired old woman. Ooo." She wiggled her fingers in mock terror. "Don't pick up *that* hitch hiker."

The top half of the next page featured an illustration strikingly similar to the photograph in the *Niho'gula Trading Post.* A tall, masted ship crumbled in pieces under the grasp of an octopus's many tentacles.

Bradley read the title. "*The Curse of Pepehi Waapa*." He exchanged a look with Trillian.

"The boat killer," they said in unison.

He skimmed the paragraph under the pen-and-ink illustration. "Here's the *Coles Notes* version. A giant octopus attacked the schooner *Templeton* during the night of June 16, 1808, four hundred feet from the western shore of Lanai. The entire crew were lost, including the *Templeton's* cargo, crates of gold coins from China. The channel between Lanai, Maui, and Molokai is well known to be a ship graveyard to this day and night travel is not recommended."

"Did someone say gold coins?" Jack rubbed sleep out of his eyes and leaned across Trillian to look.

Trillian handed the book to him and went back to snuggling Bradley.

"One thing's for sure. That photo back at the Trading Post is definitely a fake." Jack scrutinized the illustration. "It's probably staged."

"If that book's accurate, the shipwreck happened at night," Bradley said.

Jack nodded. "Bingo. Night photography in the 19th century was pretty rare."

"But it's all folklore," Trillian said. "Without proper records, it's anyone's guess. So, all of it could be possible."

"We should try and find the gold." Jack's eyes twinkled.

"Just think how many girls you could attract with all that gold," Bradley said. "Way more than the two you have on the hook now."

"Hey!" Trillian crossed her arms against her chest. "We're not all gold-diggers."

"Sorry, that came out wrong," Bradley said. "All I meant was that at a place like this, having money is an attractive quality."

Trillian scowled at him. She wasn't buying it.

"But if there's a giant octopus out there, we need weapons to defend ourselves." Jack grinned.

Bradley side-eyed him. "You're going to invent a special weapon, aren't you."

"You know me too well," Jack said.

"Money isn't as important as you think." Trillian stood and headed for the bedroom. "I mean I'm with *you,* aren't I?" She slammed the door closed.

"Dude. Burn!" Jack laughed.

Bradley sighed and pulled himself up. He knocked on the door softly. "Trill? I'm sorry. Can I come in?" He listened for a moment.

"Damage control," Jack said quietly.

Bradley nodded and entered the bedroom, closing the door softly behind him.

Jack shook his head. "I just don't get girls." He set the book down and brainstormed ways to defend himself against mystical sea creatures. A cool invention, especially a weapon, should impress anyone with a brain.

NO AIR MAN

AFTER BRADLEY AND TRILLIAN had worked things out, everyone headed to the restaurant for lunch. Their fresh, local fare was served surprisingly quickly, considering that other guests had occupied every other table in the restaurant.

"Don't overeat," O'Connor had said before the meal began, without explaining why. Now that everyone had finished eating, the reason became obvious.

O'Connor jammed her soggy cigar between her teeth. "How about we all go snorkeling?" She alternated her gaze across the table, from Sam, to Hope, then to the teenagers. "There's a shipwreck in the cove. Bet you didn't know that."

Bradley, Trillian, and Jack exchanged glances.

"No, we didn't." Bradley tried his best to look surprised.

O'Connor clapped her hands. "Then it's settled."

"It is?" Sam winked at Hope.

"There's an outfit at the marina that can take us in…" O'Connor looked at her phone. "Half an hour. So get your asses ready to get wet."

"You sure you want to do this?" Sam glanced at the others. "Have you forgotten about the diver this morning?"

"Nope. I'm sure it was nothing." O'Connor waved her hands to shoo everyone back to the cabins. "Now go suit up."

Forty-five minutes later, everyone had gathered outside Palakiko Tours except O'Connor. Sam, Bradley, and Jack wore relaxed swim trunks and T-shirts. Trillian wore a pair of black shorts over top of an orange one-piece bathing suit. Somewhat less modest, Hope had chosen a one-piece swimsuit that featured a short skirt covering the bottom, similar to the uniform of a figure skater.

Both Bradley and Jack had to fight the urge to stare at Hope, Bradley especially. After his earlier misstep with Trillian, he wanted to make sure there were no more misunderstandings today.

Bradley took Trillian's hand, kissed it, and smiled. "Did you get your swimsuit before or after you changed your hair color?"

"Before, actually." Trillian studied him, keenly aware of his reaction to Hope's swimsuit. "Do you like it?"

"I do." Bradley grinned and whispered in her ear. "You make me thirsty."

Trillian gave Bradley's hand a gentle squeeze.

"Where's O'Connor?" Jack asked. "I thought she was all gung-ho about this snorkeling."

Sam hooked a thumb back toward the promenade.

O'Connor hustled down the pier in a pair of overalls. She passed Nina Skulk on the way, and they exchanged daggered looks with each other. "Take a picture, numb-nuts," she yelled back.

"She's going to dive in *those?*" Jack shook his head in disbelief.

O'Connor joined the group, hands on her hips, breathing heavily. She had left her cigar behind. "What's up with that asshole?"

Hope looked back down the pier. "Who?"

"Whatever her name is. Skull-face."

"Skulk," Sam said. "She's bad news, remember? Avoid her."

"Screw that. She needs to avoid *me*. Now let's get this party started." O'Connor unzipped the overalls and revealed a one-piece swimsuit and shorts combo similar to Trillian. However, her prosthesis was different, hidden behind a purple, intricately connected lattice cover.

"Check this out." She unfastened the leg covering which resembled a space-age spider web and revealed a sleek, black and silver prosthesis and foot. "Made of titanium and carbon fiber. Virtually indestructible, corrosion-proof, and the 3D-printed covering is fuckin' fantastic."

"Looks great," Sam said. "I don't want to know what it cost."

"Like I'd tell you." O'Connor grinned and snapped the leg covering back on.

"Ready to get started?" The group turned to face a young Polynesian woman in front of Palakiko Tours. While they had been waiting for O'Connor, the young woman had laid out six sets of fins, masks, and snorkels. "My name is Kailani and I'll be escorting you out to the *Templeton* wreck site."

Bradley whispered to Jack, "That's her, dude. The chick you waved to last night."

"I know. Shut up." Jack surveyed the equipment laid out on the pier. He swallowed to moisten his suddenly dry mouth. "Where's the scuba tanks?"

"Scuba diving is against the law here," Kailani said. "It's too disruptive to the marine life."

"Oh." Jack crossed his arms, disappointed.

Kailani locked gaze with him. "You're welcome to sit this one out if you don't feel comfortable."

"No, I'm good. I've dived before."

"Has anyone else here dived or snorkeled before?"

The rest of the group shook their heads.

"Okay," Kailani said. "I'm going to take a moment to go over the equipment and give you some first time tips."

O'Connor shifted her weight back and forth. "How long is that going to take?"

"As long as it takes for you to understand me." She looked at O'Connor. "Ready?"

Kailani explained how to attach the fins for a proper fit and how the dry snorkels worked. She spent extra time with O'Connor to make sure she understood how to best attach her fin to her prosthetic foot.

"Most of the *Templeton* is found between ten and twenty feet below the surface. You'll need to hold your breath, so figure out how long you can hold it, and only stay under water for half that time. Stay relaxed." Kailani paused. "You will see lots of sea life, most likely octopuses. They are harmless and curious, and might touch you. But do not touch them or anything else, and absolutely *do not* take anything home with you."

Kailani looked at everyone in the group, one at a time, her eyes serious. "I'm going to repeat that last part. *Do not* take anything out of the water. We'll know."

O'Connor gave her a sideways glance. "How? How will you know?"

Kailani narrowed her eyes at her. "We have ways." She addressed the rest of the group. "Now if everyone's ready, let's get into the boat and get your fins on."

Palakiko Tours operated two excursion boats, named *Octopussy* and *Octopuppy,* both twenty-four foot Privateer Renegades. The boats sat on floating lift docks made of buoyant high-density polyethylene, giving them airtime and an opportunity to fix any exterior issues between excursions. Kailani led the group to the two rows of facing seats on the first boat.

Everyone managed to get their fins strapped on without issue, even O'Connor with her new high-tech swim leg.

"How do your masks feel? Put them on and make sure the seal is good and comfortable." Kailani watched the group try the masks. "Anything feel weird? Now's the time to swap things out if the mask isn't a good fit."

No one expressed discomfort.

Kailani untied the *Octopussy* from the lift dock and gave the boat a gentle shove. It slid backward into the water. "Alright. Make yourself comfortable." She stood at the center console and started the engine. A man stepped out from the main building and waved at her. Kailani gave him a thumbs up in return.

"Who's that, if you don't mind me asking?" Jack said.

"That's my dad, Lono." Kailani backed away from the pier. "We're business partners. He runs the other boat."

Jack nodded. "Cool."

"I get it. She's the pussy, he's the puppy," O'Connor whispered to Sam with a grin.

Sam shook his head subtly. "I do hope you'll keep that to yourself."

Kailani navigated out toward the middle of the cove. After clearing the end of the pier, she turned toward the group, one hand on the wheel, and pointed at Jack. "You've dived before and everyone else are newbies, right?"

Jack nodded and looked to the others, reaffirming his extra experience.

"I think you'll find snorkeling more enjoyable," Kailani said. "It's less complicated, that's for sure. If you're not comfortable swimming, we have some vests that will keep you floating."

O'Connor glanced self-consciously at the rest of the group, then adjusted the mask resting on her forehead.

Bradley leaned into Trillian's ear. "Maybe we'll find some treasure."

"We can't take it home anyway," Trillian said. "So, I kind of hope we don't. Besides, I thought *I* was your treasure."

"You're right." Bradley kissed her cheek.

With *Octopussy* situated close to the center of the cove, Kailani killed the engine and dropped a small anchor.

"A few tips. Breathe, relax, and float. Snorkeling is more about gliding than swimming. You should only have to use your fins. Keep your lips sealed around the snorkel mouthpiece. Like I said before, these snorkels have a valve that will keep water out." Kailani smiled as she talked. She clearly enjoyed her job. "If your mask fogs up, I can help clear it, or you can try a little spit. Last, but most important, have fun. We want you to have a great experience. Now let's get wet."

Sam gripped the edge of the boat. Hope stepped up beside him.

"How are you feeling about this?"

"I'm a little nervous," Sam said.

"I think we all are, except maybe Jack." She took his hand. "One thing I guarantee, there's no rats down there."

Sam nodded and watched the crystal blue water distort the wreck and the reef below.

One by one, the group adjusted their masks and eased themselves into the water.

O'Connor took Kailani aside. "I'll take one of those vests you were talking about."

"Sure thing." Kailani dug a vest out of a storage bin next to the console and handed it to O'Connor.

"Don't advertise it."

Kailani shrugged. "No judgment, but I don't think your friends will care."

O'Connor slipped the vest on and lowered herself into the water.

"How is everyone feeling? Okay?" One by one, Kailani looked for apprehension in the group and saw none. "Remember, you will see octopuses. That's a guarantee. They love this wreck. But they are harmless. Take your time and only do what feels comfortable to you. You can return to the boat for a rest any time. I'm not going anywhere."

Jack gave Kailani a thumbs up, and his lips curled into a smile around the mouthpiece of his snorkel. Everyone else followed Jack's lead and five more thumbs shot up.

Jack disappeared under the surface, wasting no time diving down to get a closer look at the wreck. The others floated close to the surface, getting used to their new activity.

Kailani kept one watchful eye on the group and one on her surroundings. A boat had just left the marina. It was a boat she recognized all too well: the *Wavy Jones*.

BEING UNDER THE ocean brought back Jack's memories of scuba diving three years ago in Cozumel with his parents. It was one of the only trips where they had traveled together.

Compared to Cozumel, the water in Niho'gula Cove seemed bluer and clearer. The schools of tangs and butterflyfishes were just as curious about him as he was of them, as they moved in synchronized directions around his body. But there were no octopuses in sight.

The wreck below stretched at least fifty feet in both directions. Most wooden surfaces were either covered in oysters, barnacles, or coral, and disguised the *Templeton's* exact resting shape. But it was clear even to the casual observer that the curved nature of the wreck meant that the schooner had been broken in multiple places.

The shattered remains of one mast was clearly visible jutting out of the cabin midway along the deck.

The need for air pulled Jack out of his reverie. He kicked his way up to the surface and took a much needed breath. He had no idea how long he was submerged, but Kailani did.

She leaned over the edge of the boat. "Jack, you were under for…" Kailani glanced at her watch. "Must've been just over a minute. That's a little long. I like to avoid doing CPR, especially on hot guys."

Hot guys?

Jack blinked at her through his mask. Did he hear that right? She thinks he's a *hot guy?*

"How about do a thirty-count, then come up for air?"

Jack nodded and gave her a thumbs up, a wide smile surrounding his snorkel mouthpiece.

He looked around and saw that everyone else was still hovering around the surface. With his heart thumping from excitement, he took a breath, submerged, and began a count to thirty.

This time Jack gave himself a goal: get close enough to the wreck to take a good look, with no touching of course.

He pumped his legs and fins, propelling him toward the middle of the wreck. A blanketing silence and a faint ringing in his ears replaced the ocean sounds at the surface.

As Jack reached the railing of the *Templeton's* deck, he inverted himself right-side up and kicked with his swim fins to stop his forward momentum. The current produced disturbed the sand, silt, and broken shells resting on the surfaces of the wreck, exposing something else. Something... shiny?

Before he could give this visual blip any further thought, Jack spotted dark movement out of the side lens of his mask. Because of the rubber seal, the mask blocked a lot of his peripheral vision. He turned his head and faced an octopus swimming straight at him.

The fast-approaching alien-like form sent a bolt of terror through his body. Panic displaced everything that Kailani had said about the harmless nature of octopuses.

Jack turned in the water and swam laterally along the deck toward the bow. Parts of the shipwreck appeared to morph into more octopuses, and the creatures swarmed him in a matter of seconds. Their cold, slippery tentacles slid over his legs and arms. But there was something more, almost like fingernails on his skin.

His lungs burned for air and adrenaline had his heart throbbing in his chest. Jack swam past the bow and broke free of his confusion. He was moving parallel to the ocean floor. But he needed to swim upward. He needed to surface at once.

He arched his body toward the refracting sunshine above and kicked as hard and fast as he could. The swarm of octopuses had vanished or returned to their hiding places. He didn't care. All he wanted was fresh, sweet air to fill his lungs.

Jack didn't think he'd make it, but he held on for one more

second. He shot out of the water and took in a large breath. After a moment, he gathered his bearings. The *Octopussy* was about sixty feet away. It was surprising and a bit scary how turned around he had gotten while fighting his terror.

He swam back to the boat and saw Kailani standing at the stern, her arms crossed.

"You didn't count to thirty, did you?"

Jack pulled out his snorkel mouthpiece, slid his mask onto his forehead, and grabbed the gunwale near the transom. "I lost count. The octopuses freaked the shit out of me. Came out of nowhere."

"Octopuses are masters of disguise," Kailani said. "They can change color and shape at will. You were probably looking right at them and didn't even know it." She gazed at him with unexpected admiration. "You must've been pretty deep to see them."

"Right at the deck," Jack said between breaths. "But I didn't touch anything, I swear."

"I believe you."

Jack closed his eyes, battling his exhaustion. "I think I need a spear or invent a weapon or something for next time." When he didn't hear a response from Kailani, he opened his eyes to see her smile had disappeared.

"Did I say something wrong?"

"Killing an octopus is *never* okay." Kailani stared at him, her dark eyes glistening with anger. "Promise me you'll *never* do that."

"Um, yeah. I promise," Jack said. "But I still might try inventing something, something I *won't* use, of course… is that okay?"

Kailani turned and busied herself with the bin of vests next to the console. "You better get out there and join your friends. You don't want to waste time."

Jack sighed. He had blown his chances with this girl. After he had regained his strength, he reset his snorkel and mask and swam out to where O'Connor and the others were.

"Count to thirty, Jack," Kailani called out to him. "I'm always watching."

She still cares.

Jack gave her a thumbs up and joined his friends. Maybe he still had a chance with Kailani, a slim chance. But he also knew that a new weapon was in his future.

AFTER AN HOUR and half in the water, Kailani signaled everyone back to the boat. She piloted the group the short distance back to the pier. Further out in the cove, Skulk maintained her suspicious watchful eye.

Kailani turned to address the group sitting behind her. "Did everyone have a good time?"

She was met with nods and thumbs up.

"Besides Jack," Kailani continued, "did anyone else see any octopuses?"

Bradley punched Jack lightly on the shoulder. "You didn't say you saw octopuses! All we saw was fish. Dozens of them."

"So many colors," Trillian said. "So graceful and beautiful."

O'Connor nudged Jack's swim fin with hers. "Spill it, Jack. What was your first time with octo-*pussy* like?"

"Ha ha." Jack sneered at O'Connor. "Freaked me out, to be honest."

"I think it was almost drowning that freaked you out the most." Kailani entered the marina and headed for the Palakiko Tours moorage.

"You free-dived?" Hope looked at him with surprise.

"Did you get to the wreck?" Bradley held Jack in an excited gaze.

Jack knew what Bradley was getting at and nodded, smirking.

"Jesus, Jack," Sam said. "If you're going to be stupid, we can forget the snorkeling completely."

"I was fine. Really."

"I'm responsible for your safety," Sam said. "You're not dying on my watch. Understand?"

"But I was—"

"You understand?"

Jack nodded, his grin melting away. "I won't do it again, no matter what I see."

"Wait." Bradley grabbed his shoulder. "*Did* you see something?" He gave Jack a focused stare.

Jack hesitated for a moment, remembering the shiny distraction on the deck of the *Templeton*. It could have been anything. He hadn't had a chance to get a closer look. "Nah. Just octopuses."

Kailani smiled to herself knowing that Jack would think twice before trying a stunt like that again. She revved the engines and the momentum of the boat carried it up and into the lift dock. She threw a rope onto the pier, hopped out of the boat, and tied it off. "You can leave your snorkeling gear there." She pointed to a couple of plastic bins beside the main boat house.

O'Connor slipped out of her vest and other equipment and retrieved her overalls. "We all want to go out again. How about this evening?"

"We don't do tours in the evening," Kailani said. "It gets too dark too quick. Lack of visibility is dangerous."

O'Connor stepped closer. "What about in an hour?"

"A group can do one excursion per day." Kailani began sorting through the equipment in the plastic bin. "It might not seem like it, but snorkeling…" She glanced at Jack. "And *diving* is hard on the body."

"What if I paid double? Triple?"

Kailani sighed. "Wanting to go out again is a real vote of confidence, but safety is our top priority. The answer is still no."

O'Connor was poised to argue but Sam placed his hand on her shoulder. They were like an old married couple and spoke with looks. O'Connor grumbled and backed down.

After the group had removed their fins, masks, and snorkels, Kailani pulled Jack aside.

"Look, I'm sorry for *throwing you under the boat* before, but you know, safety is super important to me." She held out her hand. "Friends?"

"Friends." Jack gave her a lopsided smile and shook her hand, even though he really wanted to hug her instead.

"How about I take you guys on a hike," Kailani said. "Teenagers only. Consider it a peace offering?"

Both Bradley and Trillian were quick to agree.

"Great." Kailani dragged the bin to the door leading into the main house. "I've got a few things to take care of. I'll meet you on the promenade in twenty minutes."

Everyone returned to their cabins. After Trillian and Jack changed into dry clothes, they found themselves waiting on the promenade for Bradley.

Trillian stood with her back resting on the promenade railing and crossed her arms against her chest. "What's taking him so long?"

Jack shrugged and faced the cove.

"Hey… Did you really almost drown?"

Jack avoided Trillian's gaze. "Yeah. I lost track of time when I was trying to get away from some octopuses. I think if I had been underwater for another second, I may have died. I was really far from the boat."

"Shit, Jack." Trillian fell silent for a moment. "Don't do that again, okay?"

Jack remained silent.

"Okay?" Trillian looked at Jack and found him focused on the cove.

"Yeah, okay." Jack said absently, then pointed. "You see that?"

Trillian turned to look out to the cove. "What?"

"There's something out there." Jack retrieved his phone, framed up whatever he was seeing, and snapped a picture. He displayed the picture and pinch-zoomed it.

"I don't see anything," Trillian said.

Jack looked up from his phone, his brows scrunched in confusion. "Shit, it's not there anymore. But look at this. What *is* that?" He held up his phone with the zoomed image on it. The object was black and curved in the water.

"Maybe an octopus is watching you," Trillian said with a grin. "Waiting…"

"Be serious."

Trillian shook her head. "Well, I don't know. Why is it that you're always the one to see weird things?"

Jack shrugged. "Lucky, I guess." He slipped his phone back into his pocket.

Bradley crossed the well-tended lawn toward them.

"What were you doing back there?" Trillian called out.

"Probably hand to gland combat," Jack said quietly with a snicker.

Trillian gave Jack a playful slap. "Gross. Shut up."

"What?" Bradley looked at the two of them. The mild confusion on his face faded fast. "The adults are heading to the bar. I gave them the deets." He slid his arm over Trillian's shoulder and glanced at Jack. "Your lei is wilting."

Jack picked up the string of flowers in his hands. A few petals fell off. "I know. But I want to make the most of it."

"Wait!" Trillian stared at Jack intently.

"What?"

"You left the 'First Timer' button back at the cabin!"

Jack gave her a sideways look. "Ha ha. Totally hilarious."

"What's hilarious?" Kailani approached the three of them, a knapsack slung over her shoulder.

"Uh, that I'm still wearing my lei."

Kailani touched a flower and more petals fell off. "I think it's dead."

"And there's nothing worse than a dead lei," Trillian said. Kailani laughed and the two girls bumped fists.

"It's not dead until I say it's dead."

"Come on," Kailani beckoned. "Follow me."

She led the three teenagers off the promenade toward the north end of the beach, opposite the marina. They passed Maddilyn stretched out on a chaise lounge.

At first it looked like Maddilyn was asleep, but she plucked out her ear buds and perked up as the group passed by, propping herself up on her elbows.

"Don't get sunburned, Maddi." Kailani squinted at the bright afternoon sky. "Perfect day for it."

Maddilyn watched the four teenagers continue on their hike, longing mixed with jealousy on her face.

Jack glanced back and gave Maddilyn a small wave. He was careful not to be too obvious so he could keep his options open. But what did he know? The world of girls was about as foreign to him as the wreck of the *Templeton*.

A paved path at the north end of the cove led away from the beach, but only for about a hundred feet. Kailani stepped over the slack chain barrier at the end.

"We're heading into uncharted territory," Kailani said. "Anyone who's got a problem with breaking a few rules can turn back now."

Bradley, Trillian, and Jack shrugged indifference at each other and followed Kailani onto the rocky bluffs that followed the north edge of the cove.

Jack quickened his pace to get closer to Kailani, passing Bradley and Trillian.

Bradley grinned and whispered to Trillian, but loud enough for Jack to hear. "He's making a move."

Jack glared at them, then met Kailani's stride. "Do you take guests out here often?"

"Not really," Kailani said. "Most guests that come here are boring adults."

Jacked looked back at Bradley and Trillian. "Hear that, guys? We're not boring."

"Wait. I didn't say *that*." Kailani kept a straight face for as long as possible, then grinned back at them. "Kidding. You guys seem cool."

Kailani stopped at the end of the bluffs. From where the group stood, the beaches of Lanai were in full view as they stretched northwest.

Jack placed his hands over his eyes to shield them from the sun, then pointed at a large brown object in the distance, the surf breaking around it in white crests. "What's that?"

"Good eye." Kailani slid her knapsack off her shoulders and unzipped it. She pulled out a pair of binoculars and handed them to Jack.

He zeroed in on the object. "Is that a... ship?"

"Yup," Kailani said. "The channel is filled with them. Some more visible than others."

Bradley poked Jack for a chance to look. "Can we check that one out?" He raised the binoculars and scanned the wreck, then handed them to Trillian.

"Not that one." Kailani found a smooth rock to sit on. "It's a protected heritage site. Illegal to explore." She dug into the knapsack, pulled out a few bags of snacks, and a six-pack of Big Swell IPA.

"Hope you like hoppy beer." She pried off four cans. "This is one of the best, and it's made right over there." Kailani pointed east across the channel at Maui.

Jack examined the snacks. The assortment included Hurricane

Popcorn, Ono Giant Shrimp Chips, and Taro Chips from Hawaiian Chip Company. "I've never tried taro chips before. What do they taste like?"

"By themselves, they don't taste like anything. But these are barbecue flavor." Kailani picked up the bag of shrimp chips. "This tastes exactly like what it sounds like. And this…" She pointed at the bag of popcorn. "This has bits of seaweed and mochi crunch."

"Rice crackers," Bradley said. "We got those back home."

"Right." Kailani began cracking the seals on the cans of beers, handing them in turn to the others. "Never have I ever…?"

Jack tilted his head and smiled at Bradley and Trillian, a look that said, "Interested?"

Bradley and Trillian exchanged glances and nodded. "Why the fuck not." He was about to sip from his beer when Kailani stopped him.

"Never have I ever seen a shark up close," she said, then took a swig. The other three sat and blinked.

"I'm glad O'Connor's not here," Bradley said. "She'd never stop talking. Did it attack you?"

"No." Kailani pulled open the bag of taro chips. "I was in a cage."

"Not for long, I hope." Jack took a taro chip and crunched it.

"No, but still freaky as shit." Kailani looked at Jack. "Your turn."

"Never have I ever held sunken treasure from the *Templeton* in my hands."

Kailani's eyes narrowed on him. "You got a one track mind, Jack. That's dangerous." No one took a sip.

Jack nudged Bradley. "Go, dude."

"Never have I ever seen *that* boat near the *Templeton*."

"Our beers are going to go flat at this rate," Trillian said.

"Maybe you guys *are* boring." Kailani sighed, glanced over her shoulder to the center of the cove, then took a long swig. "That's the *Wavy Jones,* captained by none other than Nina Skulk."

She sneered and slipped into Hawaiian. "*Maʻi ʻaʻai...* a cancer to this place. But a lot of the guests love her for some reason, so she stays."

"Never have I ever eaten snacks." Trillian grinned, drank half of her beer, then shuddered. She opened the shrimp chips and crammed a handful into her mouth. Everyone else drank too.

"I had to do something to save this game," Trillian said through shrimp crumbs.

Jack looked at Kailani. "What really happened to the *Templeton?*"

"Everyone thinks a great octopus destroyed the *Templeton,*" Kailani said.

"*Pepehi Waapa.*" Jack took another drink of his beer. "Sorry, I screwed up the game."

Kailani looked at Jack, impressed. "Whatever, but yeah. There's a whole industry selling that 'boat killer' bullshit. I believe that octopuses protect the cove, but sinking a ship..." She shook her head. "No way. That's fantasy."

"The legend says that the *Templeton* was filled with gold coins from China," Jack said.

"*Was* there treasure on the *Templeton?*" Bradley raised the binoculars to his eyes.

"How the hell should I know?" Kailani munched on a shrimp chip.

Bradley scanned the beach and marina through the binoculars. "If there *is* treasure, maybe the octopuses are guardians."

Kailani shook her head, then reconsidered. "Maybe, if only to keep greedy humans away. Greed doesn't occur in nature."

"It kind of does, actually," Jack said. "Look at monkeys."

"Okay, Britannica Boy, but not in octopuses." Kailani held up her beer. "Drink up."

Trillian nudged Bradley for the binoculars. She returned her focus on the *Wavy Jones*. "Hey guys. They've got a scuba diver on board… I can see the tank." She glanced at Kailani. "That's illegal, right."

Kailani nodded.

Bradley tried to take the binoculars, but Trillian avoided his grab and placed them to her eyes again. "And is that… that woman from the restaurant?"

Jack choked on a mouthful of beer. "Rockwell?"

"Let me see." Kailani threw her empty can into her knapsack and beckoned for the binoculars.

Trillian handed them to her.

"You're right." Kailani's jaws clenched in anger as the man in the wetsuit jumped into the water. "They're diving for *something*. Fucking ballsy to do it in broad daylight. They'll get away with it, too, because the management here are cowards. As for Rockwell…"

Through the lens of the binoculars, Kailani focused on the woman leaning against the console of the *Wavy Jones,* a sarong covering the bottom half of her white bikini and a white sun hat and sunglasses concealing her face.

"Looks like her, but I'm not completely sure." However, Pandora Rockwell was a regular guest at Club Niho'gula. Kailani had Rockwell's mannerisms memorized like the controls of her own boats, as the woman fiddled obsessively with the hem of her sarong. It didn't really matter what she wore.

Why was she with Skulk?

That was the real question.

NIKO PULLED ON a blue wetsuit with green stripes extending down his outer arms and legs and slipped on a bright yellow scuba tank.

"This is a bad idea," he said. "Bright yellow scuba gear in broad daylight?"

Skulk touched the handle of her pistol holstered at her side, just to remind herself that it was there. "Doesn't matter what color it is. I'm untouchable. Guests come to see *me,* and now we're close." She turned and grinned greedily at Pandora. "Isn't that right, Rockwell?"

Pandora pulled the wide brim of her sun hat down to shade her face. "But there's no need to draw undue attention."

"Exactly." Niko pointed at her. "She gets it."

"But I call the shots." Skulk crouched to Niko's level and lowered her voice. "If they found something, the *gravy train* stops. We need to get to it first."

Niko didn't need convincing. He knew Skulk would use her pistol without hesitation, even on him. He pulled on swim fins, a mask, and placed the regulator in his mouth. He grabbed a spear gun, stepped off the transom, and disappeared into the crystal water.

"You better find something soon," Pandora said.

"Or what?" Skulk closed the distance between them until she could feel the heat coming off Pandora's body.

"Or I'll find someone else."

The two women stared at each other, neither willing to back down. But Skulk knew she didn't hold all the cards.

"I've been more than cooperative," Pandora said, "despite your *crew's* incompetence and delays. I'll take it out of your share."

"I've gotten rid of the dead weight." As Skulk stepped back, a glint from the bluffs caught her eye. "But there's no need to worry. Niko does not disappoint."

"He better not."

Skulk picked up her binoculars and aimed at the glint. Within her magnified field of view, she saw a group of four teenagers sitting on the bluff, one looking straight back at her with binoculars of their own, an orange-haired girl she had seen before. And beside her was the Palakiko girl.

Kailani.

Without realizing it, Skulk bared her teeth. Pandora noticed. Part of what made her a successful businesswoman was noticing the insignificant details others missed.

"What's wrong?"

Skulk lowered the binoculars and faced her. "Nothing that can't be taken care of."

"Don't bullshit me." Pandora reached for the binoculars, but Skulk held them back, both struggling in a stalemate.

"The less you know, the better," Skulk said. "Don't want to cause *delays,* do you?"

Just as Pandora let the binoculars go, Niko splashed up onto the transom. He had discharged his spear gun and a coin sat gripped in one hand. Tentacles the same color as his wetsuit covered his arms and torso.

"Take the fucking thing!" He threw it at Skulk, the gold metal rolling across the deck toward the cabin.

A tentacle slithered over the stern and along the deck, following the coin as if it had eyes.

Pandora stepped back in horror, recalling her recent attack. "Octopus?"

Skulk pulled a knife from her belt, stepped on the tentacle, and severed it, the cut end continuing to writhe across the deck toward the coin. Returning the knife to her belt, she twisted her boot treads, shredding the rubbery flesh and stopping any further advance.

"Get the fuckers off me!" Niko had pulled himself onto the stern, but a large octopus still covered his back, its seven remaining legs wrapped and probing around him.

Skulk picked up a fishing spear and stabbed the octopus's main body several times. Intent on surviving, the octopus released Niko and focused on stopping the spear, its legs wrapping up the shaft and closing in on Skulk's hands.

She lifted the octopus off Niko's scuba tank and tossed the entire squirming mass, spear included, into the ocean. Panting, Niko pulled himself onto the deck and began removing his remaining gear.

Skulk scanned the deck, then narrowed her eyes at Pandora and held out her hand. "Rockwell, you have something that belongs to me."

"Most of it belongs to *me,*" Pandora shot back.

Skulk grabbed Pandora's wrist, gripping it tightly enough to make her hand turn a shade of purple. She yanked it, pulling Pandora close. "Not *yet.*"

Pandora pulled a gold coin out from under her sarong and handed it to Skulk. She glared at her, holding her wrist a moment longer before pushing her backward. Pandora stumbled but kept her balance.

Skulk held the coin up and examined it closely. It was an eighth of an inch thick, an inch and a half across, with a square hole in the center. Chinese symbols decorated both sides.

Pandora rubbed her wrist. "Can I at least get a closer look?"

Skulk nodded at Niko, who had peeled off the top half of his wetsuit. Small cuts lined his shoulders, biceps, and torso, some still weeping drops of blood. Niko stood and pulled the anchor.

Skulk snapped the coin into her hand and slipped it into her breast pocket. "At the presentation."

Pandora squared her up. "You better deliver. I didn't come here to leave with nothing."

Niko took control of the boat's console. The engines rumbled to life and he navigated the *Wavy Jones* back to the marina.

"We've just scratched the surface, Rockwell." And except for a few "teenage" details, everything was unfolding the way Skulk wanted it to.

TRILLIAN TOOK CONTROL of the binoculars and resumed her surveillance. "If it is Rockwell out there, she sure doesn't care about being recognized."

"It doesn't matter," Kailani said. "Skulk is connected. Plus, she always has a legit reason for being anywhere."

Jack opened the Hurricane Popcorn and grabbed a handful. "What do the rich like to do?" He alternated his gaze at the others as he tossed popcorn and mochi crunch into his mouth.

Bradley shrugged. "Spend lots of money?"

"Or what do the rich have in common?" Jack continued.

"They *have* lots of money?" Bradley drank from his beer. "What are you getting at?"

"We were talking about it just a second ago," Jack said. "That's a massive hint."

Kailani layered her arms on her knees and rested her head on them. "Greed."

Jack snapped his fingers. "Point to Britannica Girl. Rich people always want to get richer."

"I guess," Bradley said. "I'm not rich so I wouldn't know."

"So, if there *is* treasure out there…" Jack felt Kailani's angered glare on him. "It's just a thought experiment, Kai. Bear with me."

Kailani studied him for a moment, a subtle smile of amusement mixed with attraction on her face.

Jack continued. "If there's treasure out there and someone rich knew about it, maybe they'd want to keep it for themselves and get richer."

"But if you're talking about Rockwell, didn't you say she was worth mega-bucks?" Bradley locked eyes with his friend. "Why would she risk her reputation on something that's probably pocket change to her?"

"Maybe she collects shit like that," Trillian said from behind the binoculars. "Rich people collect weird shit."

Kailani squinted at the *Wavy Jones* out in the cove. "Now that I think about it, Skulk's boat *has* been out on the water every day for the past week."

"Anyway, thought experiment over." Jack grabbed more popcorn.

"Holy shit." Trillian jerked back, her face white. "She knows."

Jack looked to the others for clues. "Who does?"

"Skulk," Trillian said.

Bradley tried to grab the binoculars, but Kailani snatched them away first. In the magnified view, she saw the glint of Skulk's binoculars aimed right at her. She also detected a smile on her face.

Or was it more like a sneer?

The diver breached the surface and launched himself up onto the transom. At first Kailani thought his scuba tank was missing, but then she realized something was covering it. She couldn't tell what.

Then it *moved*.

A tentacle shot out toward the deck. Skulk pulled out a knife, the sharp edge reflecting the sun, and severed the writhing appendage.

Kailani dropped the binoculars into her pack and began cramming the snacks and remaining beers on top.

"We got to go, like, *now*," the urgency in her words clearly evident. "Give me your cans." She grabbed Jack's and Trillian's beer cans and emptied them onto the grass.

"Hey, I was going to finish that." Jack looked back at the *Wavy Jones* in the distance. "Wait, what did you see?"

Bradley sucked back the rest of his beer and handed Kailani the empty. She zipped up her knapsack and hoisted it onto her shoulders.

Jack found Kailani's eyes with his. "Kai, what did you see?"

"Skulk is *bad*," Kailani said. "Stay the fuck away from that bitch. Now let's go."

Bradley, Trillian, and Jack followed Kailani back along the edge of the cove toward the cabins and beach. They outpaced the path they had come, despite feeling the effects of their beers.

As they approached the north end of the beach, the group saw a gathering of people surrounding a figure lying prone at the water's edge.

"Not again," Jack said.

All four teenagers quickened their stride.

SAM AND HOPE watched O'Connor finish her fourth Mai Tai. The alcohol had taken the edge off her irritation with Kailani earlier in the day. In fact, alcohol tended to make O'Connor a little easier to be around.

"God, I love all-you-can-drink." O'Connor licked her lips.

"It was smart of you to get an all-inclusive package," Hope said. "You're getting your money's worth, that's for sure."

"You're darn tootin', toots."

Sam finished his soda with lemon, stood, and stretched. "Let's hit the beach."

"Hit the *head*, then the beach." O'Connor wobbled at her chair. Hope reached to help but O'Connor waved her off. "I can take a piss by myself, sweet cheeks."

Sam took Hope's hand in his and walked to the promenade. They stood facing the cove and watched the surf break over the white sand.

"I'm constantly amazed at what O'Connor can do with one leg," Hope said.

"She has two legs. It's just that half of one is made by NASA."

Hope poked Sam playfully. "You know what I mean."

Sam nodded. "I think she hides a lot behind that tough exterior. There must be pain behind it. No prosthetic is perfect." Sam drew in a deep breath of warm, sea air. "O'Connor complains a lot, but never about her leg."

Sam and Hope felt a warm hand on each of their shoulders as O'Connor squeezed herself between their bodies. Her unlit cigar was back, firmly clamped between her teeth.

"What're we talking about, love birds?"

"You, actually," Sam said.

"Your leg, to be specific," Hope added.

"You mean this old thing?" O'Connor had switched her swim leg with her usual workhorse, designed to look as close to a real leg as possible. She rapped on it affectionately with her knuckles. "Takes a licking but keeps on kicking."

"It was the North Shore, right?" Hope cringed. "I hope you don't mind—"

"I'd tell you to shut the fuck up if I did." O'Connor tweezed the cigar with her finger and thumb as if it was lit. "But yeah. North Shore on Oʻahu. Chun's Reef. I was no beginner, but no expert either. Just hitting my stride when that fucker took a big bite. The rest is… bionic."

Sam and Hope fell silent and watched the surf.

"Jesus. Don't get all emotional on me," O'Connor said. "My life took a turn, I adjusted. Not sure I'd be here with you guys if I hadn't been bitten by that tiger." She marched down to the beach, kicking white sand with each step. "I still love it here, so quit wallowing and come on!"

Hope looked at Sam. "You think she's hiding the pain now?"

"Maybe. But this place *is* like medicine." Sam inhaled the fresh air as he took in the cloudless sky, the blue water, and the groupings of palm and pine trees. "It's *not possible* to feel bad here."

Hope and Sam ran to catch up to O'Connor. Except for a handful of guests, they had the beach to themselves.

"We should make this a yearly trip," O'Connor said. "Better yet, secure a few contracts here and make it all a business expense."

"I think the kids might have other plans, but I'd be down for that." Sam nudged Hope. "How about you?"

"I don't know. I think I might go for my masters in zoology. I haven't decided." She gave Sam a quick, curious glance, then settled her gaze back on the beach ahead.

"That'd take you back to California," Sam said.

"I haven't had any other offers, so..."

Before Sam could respond, O'Connor trotted ahead. "What's gotten into her?" He followed.

"Maybe it was the Mai Tais," Hope said to herself. "Or maybe she didn't like our conversation." She swallowed her disappointment with Sam as best she could and went after them.

Sam caught up to O'Connor at the north end of the beach. She was standing in front of a diver, lying face-up where the surf met the rocky bluffs. The diver's pale and bloated face looked up at them like a grotesque apparition. A deep, burgundy gash ran across his neck, almost ear to ear.

"What the hell?" Sam shifted his eyes from O'Connor to the diver and back. "Is he dead?"

If O'Connor had been wearing sunglasses, she'd be looking over the frames at Sam. "Does he look alive to you?" She kicked the diver's arm, not hard but with enough force to move the limb. "Definitely dead."

"Jesus Christ, I can't believe you just did that."

O'Connor shrugged. "It's not like the guy's going to care now."

Hope strolled up behind Sam, then gasped, covering her mouth with her hand. "Oh my God. What happened?"

"Obviously someone offed him," O'Connor said. "That gash wasn't made by any sea creature."

"Remember that other diver?" Sam crouched but didn't get closer. "He had gashes all over his arms."

"It's the same," Hope said.

Both O'Connor and Sam turned to her, confused.

"The wetsuit. It's the same as the other guy," Hope repeated. "Black, the same yellow stripes along the sides…"

The memory clicked in O'Connor's head. "Well, fuck me sideways. Hope's right. And that means—"

"He was working with the other guy?"

Hope and O'Connor began ping-ponging theories.

"Someone didn't like what they were doing—"

"Or they were in the wrong place at the wrong time—"

"Someone—"

"Murdered them," Hope and O'Connor said in unison.

Sam stood. "But the other guy survived."

"I'd bet you a thousand dollars that wasn't part of the plan," O'Connor said.

"No one plans on getting their throat cut," Hope said.

Sam took out his phone and dialed.

"Who are you calling?"

He looked at O'Connor, surprised. "Who do you think? The front desk."

As Sam relayed details, O'Connor kneeled down to get a close look at the body. There were similar small cuts in the diver's neoprene wetsuit, especially on his legs, but far less in number than the previous diver.

"I'm surprised that sharks didn't eat him," she said. "Unless he—"

"Bled out somewhere else." Hope scanned the cove as if there was a potential clue hidden in plain sight.

Sam pocketed his phone. "Medical staff will be here in a few minutes. We're supposed to make sure no one touches the body." He shook his head and sighed. "This is the second time in less than twenty-four hours. You're like a magnet for trouble."

"More like a magnet for *adventure*." O'Connor laughed.

"If you keep showing up next to dead bodies," Hope said, "you might start looking like a suspect."

"You worry too much."

"Maybe you don't worry enough."

Five minutes later, two medical personnel ran to the beach carrying a stretcher and a folded plastic sheet. They recognized O'Connor at once.

"*You* found the body?" one medic said.

O'Connor nodded, and straightened her posture, clearly chuffed.

"The police are going to want to talk to you."

"I got nothing to hide." O'Connor motioned at Sam and Hope. "Plus, I've got witnesses."

The second medic crouched and scanned the body for any clues separate from the diver's sliced neck. "Did any of you touch the body?"

O'Connor glared at Sam before responding. "Nope. The first thing we did was call you."

The first medic positioned himself between the diver's body and O'Connor. "Get comfortable. We got to wait for police and an ambulance before we can do anything."

Sam tapped O'Connor's shoulder and pointed out several chaise lounges just below the promenade. "Let's take a load off."

During the hour it took for police and the ambulance to arrive, the Club Niho'gula medics propped their stretcher up vertically and stood on both sides like sentries, guarding the diver's body. They hid the diver and his badly mutilated neck from any curious onlookers under the sheet.

BRADLEY, TRILLIAN, JACK, AND KAILANI ran down the paved path to the beach and headed for the crowd. There was a man in a police uniform interviewing O'Connor and a woman crouched beside the body, peeking under a bright blue plastic sheet, and taking notes.

"We're always late to the party." Bradley said.

"I don't know." Trillian eyed the way the club medical personnel and ambulance paramedics were protecting the diver's body. "I'm not getting a party vibe."

Bradley made a beeline toward Sam. "What the hell happened this time?"

"No one knows exactly how, but a diver was killed." Sam ran his index finger across his neck. "Throat cut."

Bradley stepped toward the scene at the surf.

"Brad," Sam said. "They're not going to let you look."

"I know, but…" Bradley approached the paramedics anyway.

"Jesus." Trillian exchanged a worried glance with Jack and Kailani.

In response, Kailani narrowed her eyes toward the marina, just for a moment, but long enough for Trillian to notice.

"Do you know who did it?"

"I've got a pretty good idea," Kailani said. "If you had to guess—"

"Skulk?" Jack looked at the two girls.

"It's rare for anything bad to happen here," Kailani said, "but if it does, is a safe bet that Skulk is behind it."

"But two divers in one day." Trillian craned her head to get a view past the crowd and managed a brief glimpse of the side of the diver's body. "Same kind of wetsuit as before, too."

"Yeah," Sam said. "We noticed that too."

The island paramedics and the coroner remained tight-lipped and refused to let Bradley look at the diver, just as Sam had said they would. O'Connor stood several feet away, engaged in conversation with a police officer. Another man stood beside the officer, pointing the camera of his phone at O'Connor.

Bradley positioned himself behind the man recording video

so he could eavesdrop and gain some details. That plan derailed when the police officer concluded his interview, closed his note pad, and slipped it into the breast pocket of his shirt.

O'Connor turned to the man recording video. "Who the hell are you?"

"Harv Nakamura for the Lanai Daily," the man said.

"Just the paper?" O'Connor scanned the crowd. "Where's the TV cameras?"

"You're looking at it," Harv said. "I do double duty. Anything else you want to add to your story?"

"What do you mean *story*. This is the real deal." O'Connor looked behind and saw the paramedics unfolding a body bag in preparation for transporting the body.

"I mean anything you didn't tell the police?" Harv grinned slyly. "Anything that might be considered *a scoop*?"

"What's in it for me?" O'Connor grinned back at him, chomping on her cigar.

"Your two minutes of fame?"

"Don't you mean *fifteen*?"

Harv gave her a sideways look. "Where do you think you are? We got thirty miles of paved roads here and no traffic lights."

O'Connor shrugged.

"It's down to one minute now."

"Wait. There is something. But turn off your camera." O'Connor waited for Harv to comply, then stepped closer. "You weren't here this morning when the other diver washed ashore."

Harv's raised his brow. "Dead?"

O'Connor shook her head slowly. "Hospital." She sported a wide smile and took the cigar out of her mouth. "That enough of a *scoop* for you?"

Harv nodded. "Thanks." He pocketed his phone and headed toward the promenade.

"You owe me," O'Connor called.

Harv barely looked back and held up a brief thumbs up.

O'Connor jammed her cigar between her jaws, stepped up to Bradley, and hooked her arm around his neck. "You think he's good for it?"

"Yeah," Bradley said. "I think so."

The two of them joined the rest of the group. Kailani had stuck around too.

O'Connor sniffed. "Hold on a second. Am I smellin' beer?"

Bradley glared at O'Connor, whispering through clenched teeth for her to *shut up*. He extricated himself from O'Connor's hold and headed for the other teens.

"Brad." Sam's eyes held him in a serious gaze. "A word."

Hope pulled Sam close and lowered her voice. "Be nice. He's eighteen and on holiday."

"And he has my genes." Sam didn't need to say anything further. She nodded and kissed his cheek lightly.

Bradley swallowed hard and presented himself.

"Have you been drinking?"

"Yeah," Bradley said without hesitation. "Just one beer."

Kailani cleared her throat and stepped up. "It's my fault. I brought them on—"

Sam held up a hand and she fell silent. "But he could have said no." He took Bradley aside. "Look Brad, I can't stop you from drinking, but I hope you choose wisely. The drinking age in Hawaii is twenty-one. If you drink in public and you're caught, that goes on your permanent record. Then there's the fact that you're my son. You know where my relationship with alcohol got me."

Bradley nodded. "It won't happen again."

"That's not what I'm saying," Sam said. "Just make smart choices."

"Okay, Dad."

Sam patted Bradley on the back affectionately. "You hungry?"

"I could eat."

"Let's put this ugliness behind us." Sam beckoned the rest of the group. "We're headed to the restaurant. Anyone interested?"

"Does a frog bump his ass when he jumps?" O'Connor grinned.

Trillian sidled up to Bradley. "Did you get in shit?"

"Actually, no," Bradley said. "He was cool about it. I think he was more worried about me ending up like him."

"Wish I had a dad like that." Trillian rested her head on Bradley's shoulder and followed the adults to the restaurant.

Kailani stepped up onto the promenade. "Hey, sorry about getting Brad in trouble."

Jack shrugged. "I wouldn't worry about it. Sam's pretty cool."

"Okay. Well…" Kailani glanced at the restaurant, then back at the Palakiko boat house. "I got to go. My dad's gonna be wondering where I am." She paused then peeked past her long hair, her brown eyes settling on Jack's. "See you tomorrow?"

"Count on it," Jack said, a broad grin on his face.

"Okay." Kailani turned and headed toward the marina.

Jack swore he saw the beginnings of a smile before her hair obscured her face. He stood and watched her go, smitten.

"Hey, Romeo!"

Jack turned to see Bradley leaning against the side of the restaurant, flashing his eyebrows at him.

Jack raised his middle finger at him. "Just stop."

"Dude, you got to make a move," Bradley said. "It's obvious she's into you."

"Think so?"

"Totally. Just ask Trill. But right now, there's prime filets with our names on them."

The two of them headed into the restaurant to join the others.

KAILANI STRODE DOWN the promenade and headed up the pier toward the boat house. There was something about Jack that had captured her eye today, despite him endangering his life and his attitude toward octopuses. She found it difficult to stop thinking about him, until the usual realization dawned on her as it always did eventually.

He's a guest. Don't get invested.

"Something on your mind?"

The familiar voice sent a chill down Kailani's back.

Skulk stood leaning against a support for the pier. She lit a cigarette, the flame washing her face in an orange glow.

Kailani scowled at her and continued walking.

"What happened down there?"

Kailani faced Skulk and did her best to stare her down. "Where?"

"I think you know where." Skulk took a long drag on her cigarette.

"A dead diver."

"Hmm," Skulk said. "Too bad he didn't make it."

"Like you give a shit."

Skulk shook her head slowly, tsk-tsking her. "Such foul language from such a pretty face."

"Fuck you." Kailani resumed her walk to the boat house, her pace a little more urgent. From behind, she heard Skulk call to her.

"Be careful *tita*, the cove is unforgiving. There's a curse for those who betray its waters."

"You should talk," Kailani called back. "You're the one with scuba gear on your boat… and guns."

Skulk's eyes narrowed. She followed Kailani with her gaze until she reached the boat house.

Kailani stepped inside and locked the door behind her. She rested against the door and took a few calming breaths.

Cooking noises floated down from the kitchen upstairs. Smells of spiced hamburger, beef gravy, eggs, and rice mingled in the small space. Lono was preparing one of their favorite meals: Loco Moco.

Her stomach growled as she hustled up the back stairs, eager for the day to end. She paused at the landing between floors and peered out the porthole window at the rest of the marina. She could still see the orange glow of Skulk's cigarette and she was sure that Skulk could see her. The same shiver found the back of her neck again.

Kailani headed up the second flight of stairs, looking forward to sharing the details of her day with her dad, and maybe catch a football game on TV. But Skulk still held space in her head rent-free and she hated it.

SEEKERS

AS THE SECOND day of their holiday began, the effects of jet lag were beginning to wear off. The group, specifically the adults, were getting up earlier in the morning, eager to get the day started. The teenagers were teenagers and would sleep into late afternoon if allowed.

But O'Connor would have none of it. She rapped on the teenagers' cabin at seven in the morning, only after Sam convinced her to not wake them up at six.

Using her duplicate key card, she barged into the cabin. "Rise and shine, you filthy animals!" O'Connor banged on Jack's door, then Bradley's. "Put it in your pants and get dressed. The day's wasting."

Bradley opened his door a crack and poked his face out. "Is this necessary?"

"It is if you want to eat."

"We can eat whenever."

O'Connor plucked out her cigar and tapped Bradley's chest with her index finger. "Not on my watch. Come on. Restaurant in thirty minutes."

Bradley responded with a groggy nod and closed the bedroom door.

"Jack? What about you?"

"I'm up." Jack's voice filtered through his closed bedroom door.

Satisfied, O'Connor stomped out of the cabin and slammed the door behind her.

Twenty-five minutes later, Bradley, Trillian, and Jack rolled into the restaurant and took a seat around the table Sam and Hope had claimed. They already had steaming cups of coffee in front of them and a carafe nearby. The mingling smells of assorted breakfast dishes and hot coffee set their stomachs afire.

O'Connor was nowhere to be seen.

Trillian grabbed a mug and slid it toward Sam. "Coffee. Now. Or die."

Sam filled her mug as Bradley and Jack tapped their mugs close to Trillian's, anticipating the caffeinated kick.

"O'Connor's not here?" Bradley scooped two spoons of sugar into his coffee, stirred, and sipped.

"Not sure where she got to," Sam said.

"So, she threatens to hold back our meals if we don't get here by seven thirty, then fucks off herself?"

Trillian shot a look at Jack and held back a giggle.

Sam glanced around to see of any other guests heard Bradley's profanity. "Tone it down, Brad."

"Right. Tone it down. I'll get *right* on that." Bradley shook his head and drank more of his coffee.

Sam tossed the teenagers menus. "Take out your aggression by picking a nice big breakfast."

As the coffee took the edge off the early morning, O'Connor appeared behind the teenagers, then slapped her hands down on the table.

Bradley jumped and spilled some of his coffee. "Jesus, O'Connor. Mellow the fuck out." The words were out before he could stop them. He sent a contrite look at Sam and raised his mug to his lips.

Under O'Connor's hands was today's issue of the Lanai Daily. The bold headline across the top read, "Unexplained Death Baffles Police."

"This place needs our services." O'Connor pulled out a chair and sat across from Sam and the others.

"No. No." Sam sat forward, shaking his head. "Don't start, O'Connor. This is a holiday. Do I have to remind you—"

"I know what I said. But shit…" O'Connor slid the thin newspaper across the table. "Read this."

Everyone crowded around Sam and read the article, which included a small backgrounder on the *Pepehi Waapa* legend. Sam looked across the table and shrugged. "So? What's the big deal?"

"Come on, Sam." O'Connor sat back in surprise. "Those two divers. Same cuts on the arms, same wetsuit."

"Doesn't say anything about the wetsuits."

"But *we* know they were the same," Hope said.

"You're on *her* side now?" Sam sighed. "That diver's neck…" He shot a quick look at Bradley, Trillian, and Jack. "That wasn't made by some creature. And those cuts. What makes cuts like that?"

"I don't know, but we'll find out and deal with it," O'Connor said. "That's what we do."

Sam shook his head. "We're guests here. What we do is relax and have a good time."

"After we get rid of whatever the hell is attacking people here." O'Connor locked gaze with Sam. "Right?"

Sam said nothing and gulped his coffee.

"They might even comp the entire stay," O'Connor said. "Since I'm footing the bill, I'm gonna jump on anything that will save me some bucks."

Sam just stared at her. Hope and the three teenagers watched the spirited back and forth like a tie-breaking game of pickleball.

O'Connor squinted at him. "Or you going to go half on this little excursion?"

"You know I can't do that," Sam said.

"Then we are going to exterminate whatever is causing the problems."

Now that the caffeine had had a chance to work, Bradley felt more himself. "Sorry about earlier, Dad. You know, the swearing."

Sam rubbed his temples. "Sure, whatever."

"It might be fun," Bradley said. "We might even become heroes."

"Key word there is *might*."

A server approached their table. "Have you decided on breakfast this morning?" One at a time, everyone recited their selections.

After the server returned to the kitchen with their orders, Jack piped up. "I've got an idea for a new harpoon design. I won't be bothered by octopuses again."

"Wait." O'Connor leaned forward and plucked the cigar from her jaw. "Are you saying the creature we're up against is an octopus?"

"I'm saying that's what attacked me yesterday, at the *Templeton*."

Sam's serious eyes settled on Jack's. "When you nearly *drowned* yourself?"

"Yeah, but if I had a weapon, it wouldn't have taken so long to surface."

"Kailani says the octopuses here are harmless," Trillian said.

Jack crossed his arms against his chest. "No. If I hadn't fought back, I swear those things would have kept me underwater."

Trillian picked up her coffee mug. "So, what you're *really* saying is you don't believe her." She sipped. "She's going to be so pissed at you."

"Yeah, well what do *you* know about it?" Jack thrust his chair away from the table and stormed out of the restaurant.

"Okay," O'Connor said. "Who pissed in his cornflakes?"

Bradley motioned at Jack marching away. "He likes her. Kailani. Plus it's seven forty-five in the morning."

O'Connor let out and exasperated breath. "Teenage drama is such a waste of time. Go hit up Tinder and find a fuckbuddy. No strings. That's what I do."

"Ugh." Bradley shook his head in disgust. "Too much information."

"We're human, *Brad*," O'Connor said. "We're all sexual beings, *Brad*."

Hope watched Jack head toward the marina. "Is someone going to go get him? His breakfast is going to be here soon."

"Let him blow off some steam." Sam sent a disapproving look at Trillian. "We can wrap it up."

Trillian felt Sam's stare and turned away to see Jack in the distance. Guilt washed over her. She had some repair to do, but it would have to be after breakfast. Hunger took priority over everything.

But what if Kailani was wrong? What if the octopuses here *weren't* harmless?

As JACK HEADED towards the marina, he replayed the conversation he'd had with Trillian. Deep down, he knew she was right and he could have handled the situation better. But he couldn't silence his creative brain. If building a weapon for himself that would help him feel more secure diving around the *Templeton,* he would make sure it happened.

Jack's intent was never to kill, but to defend himself if he needed to. If Kailani couldn't deal with that, then that was her problem.

He strode past the pier, toward a section of the marina that he hadn't explored yet. He paused at a garbage can and rooted through its contents. He pulled out a single-use plastic bag and set it aside.

"Find anything interesting?"

Jack looked behind and saw Maddilyn in sunglasses, leaning against one of the pier supports and munching on half a mango.

She had sliced the fruit into cubes such that when she inverted the skin, the cubes separated for easy eating. She wasn't in a bikini today, but her jean shorts and T-shirt still made his heart skip a beat.

"I want to build my own harpoon gun," Jack said. "But it's going to different."

Maddilyn studied him curiously. At seven forty-five in the morning, Jack was the most interesting person around. "Why not buy one?"

Jack found a drawer slide at the bottom of the garbage can. He moved it back and forth, testing the bearings. It was a little stiff, but nothing that couldn't be salvaged with a little cleaning and grease.

"Because I'm an inventor and regular harpoon guns don't do what I want." Confidence resonated in Jack's voice. "That's how I'm going to make my millions."

"I'm Maddilyn by the way. Or Maddi." She pushed herself away from the support and strolled over to where Jack stood. "Want a bite?" She presented the last cubes of mango attached to the inverted skin.

"I'm good, thanks. I'm Jack."

She finished the mango, dropped the skin in the garbage can, and licked her lips. Maddilyn nodded at the drawer slide. "What's that part for, Jack?"

"Well, I need something long that slides back and forth really easy…" The words were out before Jack realized their unintended double meaning. The way Maddilyn raised her eyebrows revealed that her thoughts had gone in that direction too.

Maddilyn's eyes flicked below the waistband of Jack's shorts for a split second, then settled her gaze on his. The beginning of a smile formed on her lips. "Don't you already—"

Jack backpedaled. "Uh, I need a rod too, you know, for the harpoon, some springs, and any other piece of metal I can find. Oh, and an arc welder."

"You sure don't ask for much."

"You don't get what you don't ask for."

Maddilyn stepped closer. "Is that so?"

Jack cleared his throat. "Anyway, if you could keep your eyes and ears open. People throw away the strangest crap." He placed the drawer slide into the plastic bag and walked farther into marina where guests moored their boats.

"Okay, but…"

Jack turned around, waiting for Maddilyn to finish.

"Can I come with?" She saw he was mulling it over, and added, "You're… You see, you're the most interesting guy I've met since I've been here. Well, you're, like, the *only* guy I've met."

Jack half-smiled at her. "Sure." He beckoned her over, then the two of them continued their metal scavenger hunt, both unaware that they had just walked by the *Wavy Jones*. And Nina Skulk enjoying her morning breakfast of coffee and nicotine.

BRADLEY AND TRILLIAN stowed Jack's abandoned breakfast in their cabin's small refrigerator, then went for a walk. Sam, Hope, and O'Connor regrouped on the porch.

"You're not going to let this go, are you?"

O'Connor crossed her arms, her jaw clamped on her cigar stub. "No fucking way. We need to find out what we're dealing with before we can deal with it."

Hope sat down next to Sam. "They have scooters we can use. It would be fun."

"I just think we're sticking our noses into something we shouldn't," Sam said.

"But that's our trademark." O'Connor laughed. "How else are we going to find out what killed that diver."

"You mean *who* killed the diver."

O'Connor nodded. "That too."

Hope placed her lips next to Sam's ear. "I'll make it worth your while," she whispered.

Sam could sense the grin on Hope's face without seeing it. It came through in her voice. "You always know just what to say," he whispered back.

He stood and offered his hand to Hope, pulling her to her feet. "Okay, O'Connor. Let's get to the bottom of this mystery."

O'Connor pulled Hope aside. "What did you say to him?"

Hope shrugged a sly smile.

"Nicely done." O'Connor nodded approvingly. "No man can resist our charms. Speaking of which, I got to find a man to spread *my* charms before this vacation is over."

The three of them headed to the front desk to arrange for their scooters.

"I'm afraid we only have two scooters left," the front desk agent said.

"You got to be shitting me." O'Connor leaned onto the counter. "It's not even nine o'clock."

"I'm sorry. They go fast," the agent said. "Next time, I recommend booking them one or two days in advance."

O'Connor turned to Sam and Hope. "Who's going to stay behind? And it's not going to be me."

Before Sam could answer, Hope piped up. "We'll make it work." She smiled and hugged him quickly.

Sam gave Hope a sideways look. "Wait. You're not thinking what I think you're—"

"It'll be fine, Sam," Hope said. "More than fine, it'll be *fun!*"

O'Connor faced the agent. "We'll take them for the day."

The three of them waited out front under the porte cochère while a club attendant brought out two scooters and two helmets. O'Connor took one and Hope grabbed the other.

"Damn. Too bad," Sam said. "Only two helmets. I'm going to have to sit this one out."

"Not so fast, mister." Hope poked Sam, then hustled after the attendant. "We'll need one more helmet, please."

A moment later, the attendant reappeared with another helmet, bright pink. "Sorry. It's all we have left."

"It's perfect!" O'Connor said between fits of laughter. "I couldn't have planned it better myself."

The attendant handed Sam the helmet, snickering without knowing the reason why. O'Connor's laugh was infectious.

Sam pulled the helmet on and fastened the chin strap. Hope tried to keep a straight face but couldn't resist O'Connor's hysterics.

Sam grumbled and narrowed his eyes at Hope. " *'I'll make it worth your while.'* That's what you said."

Hope controlled her laughter and adjusted Sam's chin strap. "And I meant every word."

"Alright, who's riding with Penelope Pitstop here?" O'Connor's laughter rose up again as she lowered herself onto her good knee.

"If you have a coronary, it's not my fault." Sam turned to Hope. "I'm riding with you."

"Damn, Penelope – I mean Sam." O'Connor clutched her belly as her fits of laughter subsided. "I haven't laughed like that in a long time."

Sam approached the scooter. "Want to drive?"

Hope grinned. "Strap your hands across my engines, baby." Sam settled into his seat behind Hope and slid his arms around Hope's waist.

Both scooters started on first try.

"Born to be wild!" O'Connor released the brake and her scooter jumped forward, gaining speed.

Hope followed close behind and accelerated until she was riding abreast with O'Connor.

Clouds of red dust from the dirt road leading away from Club Niho'gula billowed up behind them. A times, the road was barely wide enough for a single car to pass.

O'Connor yelled at Hope over the sound of the engines. "Race you there!"

Alarm bells went off in Sam's head. "Wait. You remember—"

"You're on!" Hope throttled up the gas and her scooter shot ahead. O'Connor reacted, hot on her tail.

Sam remembered the road they had taken to get to Club Niho'gula, with all its tight and narrow switchbacks, as the scooters' tires slipped and spewed red dirt behind them. He tightened his arms around Hope and focused on the blue ocean and white sand beach zipping by on his right.

Once they had headed inland on the Keomuku Highway, the switchbacks ended up being a godsend. Navigating them at full speed would have meant certain death. O'Connor and Hope repeated a series of acceleration and braking maneuvers, jockeying for position with every straight stretch.

Forty-five white-knuckled minutes later, they rolled into the small parking lot of the Lanai Community Hospital. O'Connor's and Hope's rivalry shaved twenty minutes off a trip that normally took just over an hour.

The three of them took off their helmets and locked them to the scooters.

"Sam, you're white as a ghost." Hope licked her thumb and wiped Sam's cheek. "Under all that dirt, that is."

Sam recoiled. "Did you just give me a spit wash?"

Hope shrugged a grin. "You've never had a problem with my spit before."

O'Connor laughed. "Looks like Penelope's afraid of rats *and* scooters."

"Don't start." Sam pointed an annoyed finger at O'Connor. "You guys drive like lunatics." He rubbed at the grime on his face and neck.

"Got you here safe, didn't I?" Hope winked at him.

"This is *it*?" O'Connor scanned the small hospital as she wiped the dirt and sweat from her face with her shirt. She found her cigar stub, was about to bite down on it, then reconsidered and hid it away.

"What were you expecting?" Hope glanced at O'Connor, surprised. "There's, like, three thousand people on this island."

"Well, I wasn't expecting a one-floor rancher."

"It's a little bigger than that," Sam said.

"Not by much."

The community hospital was about half as long as a football field and two stories tall, the lower level built into the hillside. Upon first glance, it did resemble a large ranch-style house with a wide open layout.

"So, what's our story?" Sam sat on one of the scooter seats. "How are we going to get in to see this... whoever it is?"

O'Connor looked at the time on her phone. "It's visiting hours right now," she said. "We just walk right in. If we're asked who we are, I'm Larry's wife, you're my daughter, and you're her husband. We're family, capiche?"

Sam scrunched his brow. "Wait, how do you know the guy's name?"

"It was mentioned in the newspaper," O'Connor said. "You read the article, right?"

Sam stammered.

"His name is Larry Kirkland. O'Connor's right," Hope said.

"You're damn right I am."

Sam crossed his arms. "What if *Larry Kirkland's* wife is in there already?"

O'Connor and Hope exchanged glances. "Okay, *Penelope,* then we're his co-workers. Does that pass your inspection?"

Sam looked at the both of them. "Where does Larry work?"

"Umm..." Hope didn't have an answer.

"Fuck this shit." O'Connor brushed herself off and headed for the main doors. "Live a little, Sam."

"I thought I was," Sam said to himself as he followed Hope and O'Connor into the hospital.

O'Connor approached a nurse at the reception desk. "Good morning. We're looking for Larry Kirkland's room."

"That'd be room 23, if he's still here," the nurse said.

O'Connor cocked her head. "*If* he's still here?"

"His injuries were minor, and he may have been discharged already."

"Thank you," O'Connor said. "You've been very helpful."

"I don't think I've ever seen O'Connor be so polite," Sam whispered to Hope.

"It's weird." Hope scanned the hallway and spotted the women's bathroom. "I gotta pee. I'll be back."

Sam followed O'Connor to room 23.

"Hey there, Larry," she said. "Remember me?"

"Uh…" Larry stared at O'Connor, caught by surprise, recognition tugging at his memory.

"I'll give you a hint." O'Connor look at him squarely. "You told me you fell off your boat and swam to shore."

Larry snapped his fingers and pointed at both of them. "Right! You're… the paramedics?"

"No. We're just concerned citizens." O'Connor sat on the edge of Larry's bed. "We're here to take care of whatever it was that attacked you. But first you have to tell us what it was."

Larry's eyes darted around the room, like he was looking for an escape route.

"What's wrong, Larry?" O'Connor followed his gaze. "See a rat?"

"What? No."

Sam and O'Connor watched the man become more agitated.

"I think he's hiding something," O'Connor said to Sam.

"No. I'm not." Larry gripped his top sheet with both fists.

"What do you think, Sam?"

Sam shrugged.

"So, what got to you, Larry," O'Connor said. "Or should I say *who* got to you?"

"No one." Larry opened his mouth to speak, then stopped. "I, uh, don't want to talk any more."

He moved his hand to the call button, but O'Connor beat him to it and moved it beyond his reach. "Look, we're not going to hurt you. We just need some questions answered."

"Yeah sure," Larry said. "Then when you get what you want, you'll kill me."

O'Connor shook her head. "We're professional exterminators, not assassins. We're only here to find out what put you here."

Larry crossed his arms and refused to talk.

"We found your friend," Sam said.

"You found Dennis?"

"Is that what his name is?" O'Connor raised a brow at Sam. "We're going to have to share that detail with the police. They got him listed as a John Doe." She faced Larry. "His throat was cut... but you knew that already, right?"

Larry lowered his voice. "Leave the police out of it." He checked the door and corridor beyond to make sure no one was within earshot. "It was an octopus, okay?"

"You're saying an octopus cut up your arms and caused your wrists to turn purple?" O'Connor kept Larry pinned with her stare.

Larry ran his hand over the bandage wrapping one of his arms.

"Yeah, we know about your injuries," O'Connor said. "We were there, remember?"

Larry fell silent again.

"Why did an octopus attack you?" Sam asked. "They're supposed to be gentle creatures who tend to avoid humans."

"It took my watch," Larry said. "A... a Rolex. And the tentacles were sharp. I don't care if you don't believe me. It's the truth."

Sam narrowed his eyes on Larry. "What did your watch look like?"

Larry scowled a shrug. "Dunno. It was gold... and black."

"A Rolex, huh? Pretty high-end watch, there, Larry," O'Connor said.

"Yeah, so? The fucker wrapped a tentacle around my arm and took it. Nothing else to say."

Hope entered the room and stood next to Sam. She lowered her voice next to Sam's ear, but not quite enough. "Find out anything?"

"I've said enough. Get the fuck out of my room or I'm going to start yelling." Larry looked at each of them in turn. Anger had replaced the worry in his eyes from earlier.

O'Connor held up her hands in a placating gesture to calm Larry down. "Okay. Okay, we're leaving."

The three of them backed into the corridor, walked out of Larry's sightline, and regrouped next to the wall a couple rooms down.

O'Connor stared at Sam and Hope. "He's still lying."

"About what?" Sam said. "The octopus?"

"What about the octopus?"

O'Connor held her hand up to Hope and left her question unanswered. "Maybe. But he's definitely lying about his watch. Anyone who owns a Rolex knows what kind it is and exactly what it looks like."

"He said he lost a *Rolex?*" Hope shifted on her feet.

"Yeah." O'Connor glanced at Hope with tired eyes. "He shared that little detail while you were out *pinching a loaf.*"

Hope shook her head and ignored the jab. "The same Rolex that's *on the counter* opposite his bed? You know, the detail you missed while you were *flicking your bean?*"

O'Connor gave Hope, then Sam, an uncertain glance and turned to head back to Larry's room.

"You sure know how to light a fire under her ass," Sam said. "Come on."

Hope smirked as she hustled to follow Sam. "I came up with that while I was *pinching a loaf.*"

Sam and Hope caught up to O'Connor just as she entered Larry's room, nearly colliding with a masked man leaving his room in a hurry. They exchanged looks.

O'Connor began backtracking at once. Sam and Hope bumped into O'Connor.

"What's going—" Hope gasped wide-eyed at the red river soaking into the sheets. Larry locked gaze with her, his lips moving, making only a low gargling sound.

The three of them backed out into the corridor. The man that had just left Larry's room had stopped his retreat and stood staring, a dark glower on his face.

"I don't think that's happiness to see us," Sam said.

The man took a step toward them.

O'Connor took a step back. "What was your first clue?"

Hope gave O'Connor a panicked glance. "How fast can you run?"

"Pretty fucking fast!"

The three of them bolted down the corridor toward the main entrance. The man followed, gaining on them.

Hope reached the front entrance first and burst through it, followed by O'Connor and Sam. They raced toward the scooters in the small parking area.

"Get your keys ready," O'Connor yelled between breaths. She struggled to jam her hand into her pocket as she ran.

Hope reached the scooters and jammed her key into the ignition. She tossed Sam his helmet and pulled on her own. She started the scooter's engine and peeled out, shooting past Sam and O'Connor, and straight for the man running toward them.

"What the hell is she doing?" O'Connor watched Hope start a game of chicken with a killer. She pulled on her own helmet, started her scooter, and turned out of the parking stall. "Hurry!"

Hope focused on the masked man pursuing them, and throttled up the engine as fast as the scooter would go in the short space between them. The man looked like a native islander with his deeply tanned skin and dark hair with blond tips.

She braked and leaned into a tight turn, causing the back wheel of the scooter to make a sweeping skid across the asphalt. The back of the scooter hit the man in the legs, knocking him flat. His arms flailed to brace his fall, and Hope spotted a large dagger tattoo featured on one.

Hope accelerated toward Sam and O'Connor, slowing just enough for Sam to hop on the back. Both scooters screamed out of the parking lot and back the way they had come earlier, down Lanai Avenue to Keomuku Highway.

O'Connor matched Hope's speed and yelled above the engine noise. "Jesus Christ, Hope. That was badass. Where'd you learn to drive like that?"

"Here and there. There's a lot you don't know about me." Hope made a quick glance at her rearview mirror. "We need to speed up. Put as much distance between us and that psycho as possible."

"I'm down for that." O'Connor laughed maniacally and pulled ahead.

Sam twisted to look behind him. "He's not following. The road's clear behind us."

"Not for long." Hope spoke over the engine noise. "That guy saw our faces. We're liabilities now. All of us"

Hope was right. Their run-in with this man endangered not only them, but Bradley, Trillian, and Jack.

The image of Larry bleeding out in his hospital bed and the shitstorm his murder must have caused at the hospital consumed Sam's mind. Police might even consider the three of them suspects. Their escape was not subtle. He tried his best to push his worries out of his mind.

The sound of the scooter's engine at full throttle distracted him, but the sound was changing, becoming richer, lower. Sam peered backward and saw a black Mercedes closing the gap between them fast.

"Hope, that psycho found us."

She spied the car in her side mirror. "Shit. Hold on."

The scooter's engine whined as Hope pushed its capabilities to its maximum. She gained on O'Connor and soon they were once again neck and neck.

Sam hooked a thumb backward. O'Connor glanced back. Her concern needed no words.

The Mercedes had made gains closing the distance between them. On the straight stretches, the car would overtake the two scooters. They'd be run off the road, then run over if the driver got a chance.

But the switchbacks were their saving grace. For just over three miles, the highway zigzagged northeast across the island. The scooters were far more maneuverable on the hairpin dirt-crusted highway.

O'Connor looked back at the plumes of red dirt the two scooters ejected behind them. "The asshole's gonna eat our dust."

O'Connor's observation held for the first few switchbacks, but soon Sam saw the Mercedes further up the hill, once again gaining on them.

"The bastard's back," Sam yelled over the scooter's engine noise.

Both Hope and O'Connor had already seen the Mercedes's approach. Hope looked at O'Connor, then made a wave movement with her hand, up then down. O'Connor understood right away, but Sam had no idea what they were talking about.

Hope turned her head sideways. "Hold on!"

"What are you going to do?"

Hope answered Sam's question by accelerating out of the switchback they were in. Instead of following the road, she rode off the highway and into the tall grass that grew next to the road. O'Connor followed close behind.

The two scooters bounced and shimmied as Hope and O'Connor carved a path across the unpaved grassland. With the way forward almost a straight line now, they'd reach the coastal road to Niho'gula in half the time.

Sam turned just enough in his seat to look back. He saw the red plumes billowing from behind the Mercedes. The driver hadn't seen them leave the road. They still had an advantage.

He was about to report back when he felt the scooter bounce. Sam and Hope floated above their seat for several seconds before landing hard in a hidden rut in the grass not far from the coastal road. Hope toppled over the handlebars, tumbled through the air, and landed on her back. Sam slid forward off the seat and hit the front bodywork of the scooter.

O'Connor slid to a stop, hopped off her seat, and hustled to Hope's side. "Hey badass, don't quit on us now."

"Is she… okay?" Sam managed to mumble, rubbing his shoulder.

"I'm fine," Hope croaked. "But I'm going to need a massage. Know anyone good?"

"That's your cue, Sam." O'Connor scanned Hope's body for any injuries, then helped her up.

Sam laughed to himself. "I think I know a guy." He looked back through the path they had made and although he couldn't see the Mercedes, he could see its telltale plume… and the sound of its engine revving along the straight stretches of the switchbacks.

"We're losing our lead." Sam ran to lend an arm getting Hope back to her scooter.

"You're driving now, bucko." Hope gave him a lop-sided grin, her face smudged with red dirt. "Don't worry. It's easy. Just go real fast."

Sam gulped and took the handlebars. Hope clasped her hands around Sam's waist and settled her head against Sam's back.

"Right hand is throttle and front brake," Hope said. "Left hand, rear brake. But don't brake until we get back to the club."

Sam twisted the right hand grip and the scooter jumped forward. They had already driven most of the way to the coastal road. Upon hearing the Mercedes in the distance, Sam gunned the throttle and closed in on the remaining few hundred feet.

Sam and O'Connor rejoined the road, again spewing red clouds behind them and betraying their location.

O'Connor took the lead. "Move your ass, Sam!"

Her scooter sprayed red dirt in his face, choking him and coating his eyes with grit. Sam's only choice was to match O'Connor's speed.

With their remaining lead and both scooters traveling full speed, Sam, Hope, and O'Connor rolled into Club Niho'gula with enough time to allow the dust to settle before they spotted the black Mercedes roll through the gates to the guest parking lot.

"The asshole is staying here? That shit don't fly with me." O'Connor stormed through the porte cochère, but Sam grabbed her arm and turned her around.

"Have you forgotten who caused this race for our lives?" Sam locked his eyes with hers.

"How can I forget who I don't know? That's why I'm going to introduce them to my fists."

Sam held O'Connor's shoulders firm. "No. You're not." He glanced back toward the guest parking area. The Mercedes was nowhere in sight. "Whoever that was has no problem killing. And they know what we look like. You're not dying on my watch."

O'Connor pulled against Sam's grasp, but he held steadfast.

"We'll tell club security," Hope said. "Let the authorities handle it."

Sam motioned at Hope while keeping his eyes on O'Connor. "That's the one and only good idea on the table."

O'Connor's anger melted into a smirk as she gave him a once-over. "You know, Sam, you're sexy when you take charge." She trudged toward the lobby. "Let's do it."

As she passed Hope, O'Connor leaned in. "Is he like that in the bedroom, too?"

"A lady never tells."

"Bah." O'Connor waved her off as she headed toward the front desk. "You're no fun."

Sam stepped up behind Hope and placed gentle hands on her shoulders. " 'It would be fun.' I believe those were your exact words."

"And did you? Have fun?"

"Except for the *witnessing a murder and almost dying* part, yeah I guess so."

"See? I don't disappoint." Hope turned and smiled at him, then planted a kiss on his cheek.

"And I want to keep it that way," Sam said. "We should get you checked out. This place has paramedics, so it must have a medical facility."

"It's nothing a hot bath wouldn't fix." Hope batted her eyelashes at him. "Want to join me?"

"Yes. After we get you looked at."

"Okay, *doctor*." Hope ran a hand across Sam's chest. "Have I told you lately how *big* and *strong* you are?"

"You're not talking your way out of this," Sam said. "Come on." He let O'Connor know they were heading to the infirmary.

"Remember to hang a sock on the doorknob." O'Connor waited for a response that never arrived. She turned back to the front desk agent. "So, what are you going to do? I can be real loud. How would your other guests feel if they found out you've got a *murderer* staying here?"

"We have all your information, ma'am," the agent said. "We will be contacting the police shortly."

"I bet they'll be contacting you."

"Very well, ma'am." The agent folded her hands on top of her page of notes. "Will there be anything else?"

"Yeah. A Mai Tai," O'Connor said. "That was one hell of a

morning." She headed into the resort, stopped, then reversed her direction, back through the porte cochère toward the guest parking lot.

Less than a dozen vehicles occupied spaces, and none matched the car that had relentlessly pursued them. The black Mercedes had disappeared.

COMING UP EMPTY-HANDED in the guest parking lot magnified O'Connor's craving for a Mai Tai. It wasn't noon yet and the restaurant was still serving breakfast. But the bar was always open for business.

O'Connor pulled up a stool. Gus studied her as he prepared her favorite drink.

"Rough morning?"

"You could say that." O'Connor checked her surroundings for anyone within earshot. She leaned forward and lowered her voice. "You know that diver that they took to the hospital yesterday, the one that was alive?"

Gus shook O'Connor's drink in a mixer, then strained the contents into a tumbler. "Yeah. I read about it in today's paper." He grabbed a bottle of dark rum.

"You didn't hear it from me... but the guy's dead. Murdered. By someone who's staying here."

"Here?" Gus floated a shot of dark rum into the top of the drink and slid it towards her. "How do you know?"

O'Connor narrowed her eyes at him. "Can I trust you?"

Gus stared at her. "That depends. Can I trust *you*?"

O'Connor sized him up, took an ample gulp of her Mai Tai, and let out a breath of relief. "I know because I was there. Sam and Hope and me. We saw the guy who did it. He tried to kill us, too, but we escaped."

Gus leaned into the bar countertop, supporting his body on his hefty forearms. "How?"

"We hightailed it out of there on club scooters."

"No, I mean the guy, the diver. How—"

O'Connor ran her index finger across her throat, then took another drink. "Do you know any guests that drive a black Mercedes?"

Gus paused to think, then shook his head. "I'm not the best one to ask, since I'm usually here. Don't see the parking lot much."

"Keep an eye out."

Gus nodded. "Hey, why were you at the hospital in the first place?"

"We're exterminators, back in New York," O'Connor said. "And Larry... something attacked him. We were trying to find out what it was so we could... you know, take care of it. He said it was an octopus, but not like any octopus I've ever heard about."

"How so?"

"He said the tentacles were sharp."

Now it was Gus's turn to scan for eavesdroppers. "You know Pandora Rockwell?"

O'Connor nodded.

"The day you arrived, right about this time actually, she was attacked by something. I didn't see it, but whatever it was cut up her arm, but it also didn't."

O'Connor scrunched her brows at him in confusion.

"The cuts she got had already healed by the time I got there," Gus said. "We're talking minutes. It was bizarre."

"Larry needed bandages. On both arms. And his hands were purple."

Gus shrugged. "I don't know, man. But octopuses? They're revered here. If you mess with them, you get cursed."

O'Connor shook her head in opposition. "Cursed? Nah. I don't do that hocus pocus shit."

"Just don't piss them off," Gus said. "Live and let live I always say. To be honest, I'd be looking for a different creature."

"Thanks for the advice… and the drink." O'Connor took another gulp. "Hits the spot." She turned to face the open seating area that surrounded the bar and pool, and beyond that the restaurant. Sitting at a nearby table underneath the edge of the thatched roof sat Hope and Sam. They looked deep in conversation.

SAM AND HOPE sat next to each other, facing the cove and sipping coffees. The day's newspaper lay sprawled in front of them.

Sam tapped on the byline of the front page article. "Harv Nakamura… You think he knows what's been attacking people?"

Hope shrugged, raised her coffee to her lips, and drank. "He probably knows about as much as we do, which is practically nothing. As for what happened today, any good reporter has a police scanner. It's only a matter of time."

"That article also mentions…" Sam leaned in and squinted at the text. "*Pepehi Waapa?* The 'Boat Killer'? And the treasure. Harv knows more than us about *that*. Maybe this place *is* cursed?"

Before Hope could answer, O'Connor plopped herself and her Mai Tai down opposite to them, blocking their view. "No such thing as curses."

"I'm not so sure. I was reading this article and enjoying the view and you showed up, ruining both."

"Gosh, Sam." O'Connor wiggled her fingers at him. "Then it *must* be true."

Sam winked at Hope. "What do you think?"

"I believe they exist, maybe?" Hope said. "I've never experienced one firsthand."

"That's 'cause they *don't... fuckin'... exist.*" O'Connor crossed her arms. "There's a logical reason for everything."

"What's the logical reason for Larry's cut-up forearms?"

"No idea," O'Connor said. "But it's not a damn curse."

Sam looked around the restaurant, singling out the staff. "The people here seem very spiritual," Sam said. "I dare you to mention the 'Boat Killer' and see what kind of reaction you get."

"I'd rather mention *mysterious creature killer* and point at myself." O'Connor gulped her Mai Tai. "We'd be doing this place a huge favor."

"This place didn't have a problem with *mysterious creatures* until *we* arrived." Sam stared at O'Connor. "Coincidence?"

"Probably not," O'Connor said. "Gus was just telling me that Rockwell was attacked just before we arrived. Same kind of cuts on her arms."

Sam raised a brow at Hope. She shrugged in response.

"Although, I tend to attract mysterious creatures. I'm a magnet for that shit." O'Connor grabbed the paper and pointed at the picture of the old coin with the square hole near the bottom of the article. "Maybe we'd get paid with these bad boys."

"I think we'd all prefer cash," Hope said. "We're not all independently wealthy like you."

"I have Mar-A-Verde to thank for that. The point is to sell the coins and make loads more."

Sam sighed. "We come to this beautiful place, and you reduce it to a money-making scheme."

O'Connor finished her Mai Tai. "What can I say? I like making money. So sue me."

Sam focused on the cove beyond O'Connor, on the blue water and clear skies. "There are better ways to make money than to raid sunken boats for treasure."

"It's a legit business." O'Connor twisted in her seat to look out at the cove. "There's another wreck further up the coast. Half of it is above the surf. I saw it when we were heading to the hospital this morning. If we can't get access to the *Templeton*, maybe we can get into that one."

Hope gave O'Connor a questioning look. "I thought your priority was hunting creatures. Now it's hunting treasure?"

"Who says we have to stick to one?" A sly grin spread across O'Connor's lips. "We can find one while looking for the other."

"You can count me out," Sam said. "In fact, I think I'd rather rest and relax."

"That kind of went out the window when we witnessed a murder," O'Connor said. "And the killer is here somewhere."

"Yeah. Thanks for reminding me. So much for relaxing *now*." Sam shook his head, annoyed. "And remember, going to the hospital was your idea." He paused, as if a light bulb went off in his head. "Maybe it's *you* who's cursed. Now *that* I could believe."

"I think we need to go for a walk." Hope stood and took Sam's hand. "Come with?"

"Is that code for fucking?" O'Connor laughed. "Don't forget the sock."

Sam and Hope left O'Connor at the table. She turned her chair around to face the cove and propped her feet up, her thoughts consumed with golden treasure and strange creatures.

Get rid of one to get to the other.

That was her goal now. Some might have called it an obsession. And if Sam wasn't on-board with the idea, she'd do it alone. How hard could it be?

AFTER THEIR WALK, Bradley and Trillian stopped at the restaurant and seated themselves on the opposite side, as far from Sam, Hope, and O'Connor as possible. A server had just taken their order when a hesitant Jack approached their table.

Jack met Trillian's gaze, even though it was uncomfortable for him to do so. "Hey, look Trill. I'm sorry—"

"It's okay," she said. "I sort of went off on you, too. So I'm partly to blame. Sorry too."

"But you were just being straight with me." Jack glanced at the floor. "I couldn't take it."

"But you've realized the error of your ways." Trillian gave Jack half a smile. "You going to eat with us?"

"You guys don't mind?"

"Are you nuts? You're part of the team." Bradley waved down a server. "He'll have what I'm having." The server made a note and hustled back to the kitchen.

"What am I having?"

"Don't worry," Bradley said. "You'll like it."

Jack bumped fists with both of them and took a seat.

"Hey look." Trillian pointed toward the pier. Kailani strolled toward the restaurant. "There's one of your girlfriends."

Jack made a quick glance over his shoulder. "Hey, don't embarrass me." His eyes pleaded with Trillian.

"No way." Trillian waved. "Kai... Hey Kai!"

Kailani spotted the three of them right away and waved back, a wide smile on her face.

Trillian shifted her gaze back to Jack. "Are you still going to make that harpoon thingy?"

"Yeah, probably," he said. "I've already collected a bunch of stuff. I know Kai isn't going to like it, but... I'm going to have to deal."

Bradley gave him a sideways glance. "Better than you did this morning, I hope."

Jack nodded.

Kailani approached their table. "What's up, guys?"

Two servers approached with three Surf and Turf burgers with the works.

"Lunch." Bradley looked at Jack but casually motioned at Kailani.

"Join us," Trillian said. "If you're not busy, that is."

Kailani checked out all three of them. "You sure?"

A server placed a burger and fries in front of Jack, one that he could have eaten all himself, especially after missing breakfast. "Totally," he said. "We can share."

Kailani grinned. "Can't pass that up." She settled into the fourth chair.

Bradley grinned at Jack and gave him a quick thumbs up. He eyed his meal. "Now that's some heavy fuel."

Jack cut his burger in half and nudged the plate toward Kailani.

The four of them had barely begun eating when Jack piped up. "I think we'd like to visit the wreck again."

Trillian and Bradley shared a quick look.

"Uh, yeah," Bradley said. "For sure."

"You're in luck." Kailani munched on a truffle Parmesan fry. "My boat is free this afternoon. Are the *adults* coming too?"

Bradley looked across the restaurant to see that O'Connor was by herself now, her feet propped up on a chair. "Maybe." He reconsidered. "Make that probably."

"So…" Jack pulled out his phone. "I've been doing some searching."

"About what?" Kailani took a bite of her burger.

Both Trillian and Bradley paused their chewing to focus on Jack.

"This place," Jack said. "You know, the cove, the *Templeton*…"

Kailani deflated. "You're still hung up on the treasure, aren't you?"

"A couple of coins, like the ones in the newspaper today…" Jack's eyes slipped into daydream mode. "They could pay for college."

"You don't have to pay for college," Bradley said. "Your parents are loaded."

"I wanted to earn it myself, you know?"

Kailani slumped in her chair, a look of disappointment on her face. "And by *earn* it, you mean take something that doesn't belong to you."

"I don't mean the *Templeton* treasure. I know that's hands off. But I've been reading." Jack scrolled something on his phone. "This website says there's treasure everywhere. Like all over the cove, and beyond."

"Yeah," Kailani said. "And it's *all* off limits."

"Why? I totally get a wreck being off limits, but everything?" Jack bit into his half burger.

"Wherever you find it, it came from the same place."

"The *Templeton*," Bradley said.

Kailani nodded. "Or some other ship."

"And if someone just happened to find treasure washed up on shore…" Trillian paused to make sure she had Kailani's attention. "What should they do?"

"Why? Have you found something?"

"No," Trillian said. "But let's say I did."

Kailani stared at her, her eyes narrowing. "You better not be lying."

Trillian held both hands up. "I'm not. I swear."

Satisfied, Kailani relaxed. "Then you throw it back."

"Like a wishing well full of coins," Bradley said. "It's bad luck to take that money."

Kailani pointed a fry at him. "Exactly. But here it's more than just bad luck. You curse yourself and everyone around you. Maybe even this entire place."

Jack set his phone down. "Isn't that what Skulk is doing, though?"

"She is up to something," Kailani said. "But we don't know for sure that it's related to treasure."

"Shouldn't we find out?" Jack looked around the table at his friends. "I mean, people are dying, like that diver yesterday." He singled out Kailani. "When was the last time someone died here mysteriously?"

Kailani shrugged. "I can't remember. I could ask my dad."

"But you can't deny that something's out there. Something dangerous. Maybe something cursed. And whatever it is, it's attacking people." Jack glanced at Bradley for reassurance. "That's why I want to build a weapon."

"To kill octopuses?" Kailani's anger began to build.

"If a curse has already been unleashed, and it's killing people, I want to be able to protect myself, octopuses or not." Jack pocketed his phone and crossed his arms. "Makes sense, right?"

"It kind of does," Trillian said.

"Look, you do what you feel is right. You know how I feel about it. I've grown up here and I've never seen an octopus attack anybody. *Ever.* The legend of *Pepehi Waapa* is a bunch of made-up crap designed to get rich tourists to spend money." Kailani finished her half burger and continued with her mouth full. "But if you find treasure, and you *take* it, you'll be cursed, *maybe* even arrested. 'Cause it's illegal. Forgot to mention that. I'd turn you in myself."

The three other teenagers exchanged glances. They knew enough about Kailani by now to know that she was dead serious.

"Okay," Bradley said. "I think we're on the same page. Jack, build your thing. And we leave all treasure behind. Right?"

Kailani nodded, then stood. "I got to go and get set up. Come by the boat house around two?"

"Sounds good." Bradley gave her a thumbs up.

"And thanks for sharing, Jack."

"No worries." Jack held up his fist to bump Kailani's. As soon as their knuckles met, she opened her hand and ran a finger briefly over his wrist. He watched in awe as she walked out of the restaurant.

Once on the promenade and heading back to the pier, Kailani turned and waved. Jack waved back.

He turned in his seat to face Bradley and Trillian staring back at him, both struggling to hold back their smiles. "Did you see that—"

"Yep." Bradley took a big bite of his burger.

Jack's face still held bewilderment. "What does it mean?"

"She likes you. Obviously," Trillian said. "Despite your insistence on making weapons against octopuses."

Jack shrugged. "And other sea creatures."

She sat back in her chair and laughed. "Like what, exactly?"

"Uh... I don't know. Just eat your overpriced burger." Jack smirked. "I'll figure out something."

While Bradley and Trillian finished their meals, Jack pulled up the Notes app on his phone and began sketching out ideas for his new weapon.

The server arrived and took everyone's plates. "Will there be anything else? Something sweet perhaps?"

Bradley and Trillian looked at each other and shook their heads in unison. "No thanks. We're stuffed," he said.

Jack scanned the dessert menu. "You *grill* chocolate cake?"

"We do," the server said. "It's a guest favorite."

Bradley nodded at him. "Go on, Jack. You're on a roll. Live dangerously."

"I'll do it," Jack said.

The server nodded then disappeared back into the kitchen.

Bradley and Trillian stood. "See you at the boat house," she said.

"Two o'clock." Jack raised his middle finger at Bradley and he reciprocated. They both laughed.

Now alone at the table, Jack refocused on his sketches.

"Anyone sitting here?"

Jack looked up to find Maddilyn standing next to the table, an sweet smile on her face. He had always tried to avoid complication, with both his ideas and his relationships. Now that girls had become a real possibility, life had different plans for him.

"I saw you sitting here all alone and thought you might want some company." Maddilyn twisted her body side to side slowly, her sarong swaying at her feet.

Jack stared up at her, his words escaping him momentarily. His interaction with Kailani was still fresh in his mind. After a lifetime of zero romance, reserving space in his head for two interested girls at the same time proved a challenge.

"Hello?"

Jack snapped out of his girl-muddled thoughts. "Oh, hi, yeah... please." He motioned to the chair next to him, then spun around to look at the pier.

Maddilyn sat. "Expecting someone?"

"Uh, no. No." Jack rubbed his temple and could feel the heat of his embarrassment.

A server presented a plate with a piece of chocolate cake, caramel sauce, and whipped cream. Curiously, there were two forks.

Jack grinned. "Want to help me eat this?"

Maddilyn needed no convincing and grabbed a fork.

Jack took a bite. "Holy shit this is good."

"I know, right?"

He went back to the sketch on his phone, spearing bites of cake with his fork in his other hand.

Maddilyn snuck a peek at the phone's display. "Is that for your new harpoon idea?"

She had remembered what he was working on from their morning interaction. Impressed, Jack slid the phone toward her. "Yeah. Just sketching out some ideas. Beats paper napkins, which they don't have here."

Maddilyn giggled. "Paper napkins. Cute."

Jack looked at her, confused. "What? What do you mean?"

She shook her head. "Oh, nothing. So… what are you going to hunt with that thing?"

"Nothing," Jack said. "I'll use it more for defense."

"Against what?"

"Anything that attacks me. When I went snorkeling yesterday, octopuses surrounded me. Scared the shit out of me and I almost drowned."

Maddilyn found Jack's gaze, the cake forgotten. "You probably got too close to the *Templeton,* right?"

Jack's eyes widened. "Yeah. How'd you know?"

"My mom's been searching, well… paying someone *else* to search, and they've seen lots of octopuses, too."

"Searching for what, exactly?"

Maddilyn looked around as if she was being followed. "I shouldn't even be telling you this." She locked gaze with Jack. "Can I trust you?"

"Of course," Jack said, his ears primed.

She considered him a moment, then continued. "Well, you must know all about the *Templeton,* right? Lots of people say there's a fuckton of gold coins down there somewhere."

"And your mom's hired Skulk to find it for you."

The color drained from Maddilyn's face. "Wait, how do you know that?"

"We saw her out in the cove yesterday," Jack said. "Skulk isn't that subtle about what she does."

"Yeah, I've noticed that. She's an asshole, too." Maddilyn sighed. "I don't know why my mom's even looking. It's not like she needs the money. I wish she would just relax like you and your friends. But since you're diving too, maybe you can help her."

Jack's eyes darkened. "Nah. Skulk is bad news. Besides, I'm not here for treasure. Not anymore, anyway. You know it's illegal, right?"

"What?" Genuine surprise flashed across Maddilyn's face.

"I'm totally serious," Jack said. "And if *I* know, your *mom* must know, too."

Maddilyn slumped and her gaze fell to the remaining cake on the table. "I'm sorry. I had no idea." Her cheeks reddened with anger. "My mom can be such a bitch. I should have stayed at home."

"Then we wouldn't have shared grilled chocolate cake," Jack said. "So it's not all bad." His attempt to soften her realization wasn't working. "Look Maddilyn, I got to go." He stood. "Are you going to be okay? You could come snorkeling with us if you want."

She shook her head.

"Okay." Jack headed out of the restaurant toward his cabin, then stopped and turned back. He crouched beside Maddilyn. "It's not too late, you know, to get your mom to change her mind."

Maddilyn swallowed hard, nodded, and managed to croak out a "Thank you."

Jack headed back to his cabin to change but couldn't stop himself from wondering if he had done the right thing.

SKULK SAT AT her usual table at the back of the restaurant, near the kitchen. She had the *Lanai Daily* spread out in front of her. She finished her meal and pushed her plate away with a grunt. She gulped down the rest of her coffee and wiped her face with the tablecloth.

A server approached the table and presented her bill. Skulk grabbed the server's hand and pulled.

"What are you, stupid?" Skulk snarled, exposing her teeth. "I don't pay here."

"I'm sorry," the server said. "I'm new. I didn't know."

She stood and yanked the server closer. Her malodorous breath ripe with the stench of coffee and stale cigarettes washed over the young woman. "I could have you fired just like *that*." Skulk snapped her fingers.

"I *said* I'm sorry." The server placed her free hand on Skulk's in an attempt at release. "Please let go. You're hurting me."

The manager of the restaurant appeared in front of the table. "*Skulk*." She spoke quietly but with force. "Let her go. *Now*."

Their eyes locked, their jaws set, both ready to fight if needed. But in the end, Skulk backed down. Some battles weren't worth fighting and she wasn't about to jeopardize her meal ticket.

Skulk shoved the server aside, releasing her grip. Her fingers had left purple marks on the server's wrist. "You fuck up one more time and I'll do more than just get you fired."

The server disappeared into the kitchen, shielding her tears with her hands.

"Leave. Now." The manager pointed toward the promenade. "And if you try *anything* like that again, I'll—"

"You'll *what?*" Skulk hissed her words through her yellowed teeth. "I can get *you* fired, too."

The manager swallowed whatever she was going to say and maintained her angry glare.

"A pussy," Skulk said. "Just as I thought." She headed toward the promenade. After passing several tables and a partition on her left, she spotted Maddilyn and another young person that looked familiar to her. She cast her mind back.

From the Palakiko boat.

She stopped and reversed, pressing her back against the partition so she could eavesdrop. Skulk's position wasn't optimal, she only caught partial words and sentences, but it was enough to make her blood boil.

"The bitch is ratting me out," she said to herself.

The young Black teenager walked away, leaving Maddilyn

alone. Skulk stormed over to the table, pulled a chair uncomfortably close, and bared her teeth next to Maddilyn's ear.

"You need to keep your fucking mouth *shut*," Skulk whispered. "Or I'll shut it for you. Permanently."

Maddilyn recoiled at Skulk's breath but held her composure. "You can't do anything to me."

"Oh really?" Skulk raised her shirttail and revealed her holstered pistol.

"So, you're going to kill me. Right here, right now? Is that it?" Maddilyn's gaze competed with hers.

"I'll do what's necessary."

Maddilyn laughed. "You're such a joke. When my mom hears about this, she'll pull the funding of your little treasure hunt and leave you with nothing but your little gun in your hand."

"How about I kill your Black friend instead?"

For the first time in their brief interaction, Skulk sensed worry in Maddilyn. She had the teenager's complete attention.

"You wouldn't dare," Maddilyn said.

"Keep talking and find out."

The two of them stared at each other for a moment until Maddilyn broke the tense silence.

"Okay. I won't say anything more."

"You're damn right you won't. Not to your friends and not to your *fucking* mother." Skulk stared at her a while longer, then scowled. "Spoiled little bitch." She grabbed the plate of leftover chocolate cake and mashed it against Maddilyn's face. "Enjoy the rest of your lunch."

Skulk strolled out of the restaurant toward the marina beyond. Several guests had recorded the entire exchange on their phones and were busily typing captions.

The manager attended to Maddilyn with a warm, damp towel. "I am so sorry."

Maddilyn picked caramel sauce from her hair. "Someone needs to take that bitch out. Permanently." She looked at the manager.

"I'd do it, but… I'm just a teenager. And teenagers don't kill, do they?" She asked the question as if she already knew the answer.

The manager avoided responding by refolding the towel and wiping a patch of chocolate icing from Maddilyn's face. "Again, please accept my deepest apologies. To you *and* your mom."

"Don't worry. I'm not going to tell her." She held the manager with her gaze. "Don't tell her either. The less people that know what just happened the better."

The manager glanced back angrily at the guests with their phones. "She's probably going to find out anyway."

"Well, I can't stop what *those* assholes do. Just don't help."

The manager nodded.

Maddilyn paused, then gave the manager a sideways grin. "The cake is super good, by the way."

"I'll let the chef know."

"Thanks." Maddilyn stood. "I'm going to finish cleaning up at my cabin."

The manager watched her leave. Her eyes drifted to the marina, then to the guests that had recorded the scene with their phones.

"You all should be ashamed of yourselves," she said before returning to the kitchen.

Maddilyn slicked her hair back as she walked. The caramel acted as an effective styling aid. She licked her fingers afterward and despite wanting to cry, she laughed instead. The thought of taking Jack up on his snorkeling offer crossed her mind, but a warm shower won out.

She used the time to wonder if Jack truly had no interest in treasure. And how she would deal with Skulk. The woman *was* bad news, just like Jack had said.

CURSED

LONO WAVED AS he piloted the *Octopuppy* out of the marina. Kailani waved back, then laid out the snorkeling equipment on the pier in front of the boathouse. Enough time had passed after her morning excursion to mostly dry out the equipment. Even though it would be in the water again soon, it was always a better customer experience to put on equipment that was dry.

Everyone arrived on time, including O'Connor. As casually as possible, Jack scanned the pier for Maddilyn.

"Who're you looking for, dude?"

Jack stepped closer to Bradley and lowered his voice. "After you left, I ran into Maddilyn and we talked for a bit. I said she could come with us today if she wanted to."

Bradley scrunched his brows in confusion. "Uh, who's Maddilyn?"

"Sorry," Jack said. "That's Rockwell's daughter. Remember? We passed her on the pier a couple days ago. And we've seen her in the restaurant."

"The one who was checking you out?"

Jack nodded.

"Dude! Score!"

"Jesus." Jack turned away from the boat house. "Not so loud."

Bradley glanced at Kailani and suddenly understood. "Keeping your options open," he whispered.

"Yeah, right, 'cause I'm *such* a player." Jack shook his head.

"Plus, I found out some other stuff that you're going to want to know."

Bradley stepped closer. "Tell me."

"Tell you what?" Trillian placed her chin on Bradley's shoulder from behind and smiled.

Jack shook his head. "Not now." He picked up his snorkeling equipment.

Trillian watched Jack head for the boat. "What was that about?"

"I don't know," Bradley said, "but it has something to do with that other girl he's got the hots for. Maddilyn."

"You know her name?"

"He just told me." Bradley picked up his fins. "Maddilyn Rockwell."

Recognition flashed on Trillian's face. "As in daughter of *Pandora Rockwell?*"

"Keep it down," Bradley whispered. "But yeah."

"I'm not sure I can keep quiet about this."

"You're going to have to. Besides, who would you tell that's going to care?" Bradley handed Trillian her fins, mask, and snorkel. "Now let's go have some fun."

Sam, Hope, and O'Connor followed the teenagers onto the boat.

Kailani singled out O'Connor. "You left your gear behind."

"I'm not diving this time."

As Kailani hopped onto the pier to retrieve O'Connor's unused equipment, Sam took a seat next to O'Connor.

"What's going on?" he asked. "You feeling alright?"

O'Connor shook her head and shoved him. "Don't get your panties in a bunch. I'm fine. Just don't feel like being in the ocean today."

"Okay." Sam sat back, somewhat satisfied.

"What part of the wreck should we check out?" Hope asked.

"Um, what about the stern? That's the back of the boat, right?" Sam looked at Kailani for a second opinion.

Kailani started the engine and backed the boat away from the pier. "You got it. And the flat part at the very back is the transom. Before we head out, does anyone need a refresher on snorkeling dos and don'ts?"

Everyone glanced at each other and shook their heads.

"Well, I'll say it again, but give you the short form," Kailani said. "Breathe, relax, float, and glide. Your fins should do all the work. Only submerge half as long as you can comfortably hold your breath." She singled out Jack with a short, pointed stare.

O'Connor nodded in approval. "I like the short form."

Kailani tossed O'Connor a life preserver. "Put it on."

After several minutes, she had navigated close to the stern of the *Templeton*, using the on-board GPS to confirm. She turned off the engine and dropped the anchor.

Just as the anchor hit bottom, Kailani noticed the *Wavy Jones* pass her port side on its way out of the cove. She didn't need to stare to know who was aboard.

"Okay everyone. You know the drill. Stay out of the wreck. Don't touch anything. Don't take anything..." Kailani spotted Jack fiddling with a tethered waterproof pouch for his phone. "Except photos, of course." They shared a smile.

Everyone adjusted their masks and snorkels and lowered themselves into the water from the transom.

"Have fun," Kailani said. "We'll see you all in ninety minutes, or sooner if you need a rest."

O'Connor watched the rest of the group float, bob, and submerge for short periods of time in the crystal blue water. "You ever feel like jumping in and joining?"

"Sure," Kailani said. "But then the boat's left unattended. That's a huge no-no."

O'Connor nodded. "Makes sense." She sat and stretched out, warming herself in the sun. "So, do you do excursions to other wrecks? Like the one just north of here?"

Kailani narrowed her eyes and smirked at O'Connor. "There it is."

"What?"

"The reason you don't want to snorkel today," Kailani said. "You want to pick my brain."

O'Connor shrugged. "Sure, I guess. I mean I want to get the most out of this trip."

"This isn't about treasure hunting, is it? Because I'm getting real tired of—."

"No, no," O'Connor said. "I want to know if Gus is a good lay."

"Um, what?" Kailani's cheeks flushed pink. "He's like twice my age. *Gross.*"

O'Connor couldn't keep a straight face any longer and burst out laughing. "Just fucking with you. But seriously, I just want to know where else your excursions go."

"Snorkeling is restricted to the cove," Kailani said. "Everywhere else is too deep. Besides, there's lots to see right here."

"Yeah, but what about that wreck." O'Connor pointed north. "The one that's beached."

"You're like a dog with a bone, you know that?"

"More like a bitch wanting to *get* boned, but that's a story for another day."

"Oh-kay." Kailani shook her head, laughed, then continued. "That wreck is off limits, a heritage site. Officials patrol it pretty regularly. Plus, it faces Kalohi Channel, making the surf dangerous and unpredictable. Definitely not suitable for snorkeling."

"What about a drive-by?"

Kailani shook her head. "Nope. Get a postcard or a print from the Trading Post."

"The captain has spoken." O'Connor placed her hands behind her head and squinted at the beached wreck in the distance. It held a fascination for her that she found hard to ignore.

THE CRYSTAL BLUE WATER provided an unimpeded view of the *Templeton* from the stern. The others swam forward in the direction of the bow, followed by curious tangs and other small aquatic life.

Sam hung back, using his fins to hover, and took in the spectacle below. He preferred to stay close to Kailani. Swimming in such a large body of water was a relatively new experience for him. He wasn't a stranger to water sports, but his fifteen years in prison had never offered any kind of opportunity like this. Having the boat nearby boosted his confidence.

Sam took a large breath and dipped his head and snorkel a foot or two under the surface. From his point of view, it looked like the ship had struck the sandy bottom of the cove bow first. The schooner's barnacled hull appeared to have broken or bent in a few spots near the middle, close to the cabin, forcing the stern up higher than the rest of the wreck. If he swam down just a little farther, he might be able to reach out and touch the stern. But he heard Kailani's voice in his head...

Don't touch anything.

Sam surfaced and reoriented himself. While submerged, he had drifted in the current and was a little too far from the *Octopussy* for his comfort level. He worked his fins and began moving back toward the boat. He placed his head in the water and watched the bottom of the cove pass by below him. The interaction between the afternoon sun and the waves by his head cast rippling caustics onto the seaweed, fish, and other sea life harbored by the wreck.

But curiously, he had seen no octopuses.

As Sam continued lazily working his fins, moving closer to the boat, a glint near the stern caught his eye. At first, he thought it must have been some refraction from the water, a caustic blip, or an elusive reflection of sunshine. He stopped and worked his hands as well as his fins to move backward. He couldn't find the source again and continued on his way.

But there it was again. A brief and strong pinpointed glint of sunlight. Sam stopped swimming and focused on the source of the reflection. He took a large breath and submerged, working his legs and fins vigorously.

Soon he could hear the high-pitched whine of increasing pressure against his eardrums drowning out all other sound. Sam closed in on the glimmering point, fighting against his own buoyancy.

He fanned his hand over the water-rotted planks spanning the top of the stern. Sand and loose shells swirled in the water and revealed not just one gold coin, but two stuck together, just sitting there ripe for the taking.

Scenarios flashed through Sam's head, how these two small coins could change his life, and Bradley's, for the better. He could move out of his low-rent apartment and put a down payment on a condominium. He could invest the proceeds and live off the interest. He could help pay for Bradley's college tuition.

Sam's fingers trembled. Sitting inches from his fingertips, he imagined the two gold coins eclipsing his entire net worth. But he couldn't take them. He'd made a promise.

But what about all the good he could do. Surely that would negate taking something so precious from its rightful and protected resting place.

His lungs protested, pushing his mind into survival mode. Without any further thought, Sam snatched both coins.

The octopuses appeared out of the dark recesses and broken portholes on the stern and surrounded him. He turned and they followed him, their tentacles searching and probing him, their square pupils focused on him.

Sam held up one coin and waved it in front of the octopuses.

They followed his hand back and forth, their tentacles twisting in unison. He palmed the other coin into the pocket of his swim trunks and kicked toward the surface. The octopuses surrounded him on the way up, getting ever closer. As he broke the surface, he felt tentacles grip his ankles.

Sam managed a giant breath before tentacles pulled him under once again. Numerous tentacles tightened, then sharpened, as if someone was pressing their fingernails into his skin. Octopuses were preventing him from surfacing.

An octopus swam in front of Sam and one of its tentacles beckoned toward him, like a multi-jointed question mark. Sam held up the coin in his hand and the tip of the tentacle snaked through the square hole in the center and hooked it.

Sam felt the burn of his lungs once more and had no energy left to fight. He let the coin go. The octopus in front of him secured the treasure in a coil of muscle but kept its square, alien eyes on him.

The tentacles restraining his feet and holding him just below the surface slackened their grip. Sam looked at his feet and saw nothing but his swim fins and…

Blood?

Sam floated to the surface. He pulled the snorkel out of his mouth and filled his lungs.

"Sam," a voice called out. "Sam! Are you okay?"

He turned in the water and saw that he was within a few feet of the boat. Both Kailani and O'Connor were leaning past the gunwale. O'Connor held out her hand.

"Take it, you jackass."

Sam did, and together Kailani and O'Connor pulled him up onto the gunwale. He worked his way around to the stern and stepped onto the transom.

"I think I'm done for the day," Sam said between deep, regular breaths. "Goddamn. We take clean air for granted."

"Funny how that works. Humans are flawed by design. We

don't really belong in the ocean, do we?" Kailani helped Sam to a seat. "See anything interesting?"

"I saw lots of octopuses," Sam said. "They even tried to keep me under water."

Kailani tilted her head in confusion. "Did you disturb a nest or something? They can be curious, and sometimes territorial, but normally octopuses keep to themselves."

Sam rested his arms on his thighs. He could feel the presence of the other gold coin in his pocket and guilt flooded him. He gazed at his feet, using his exhaustion to avoid eye contact.

"I don't know what I did," he said.

"Wait." O'Connor sat down opposite him. "What the fuck happened to your feet?"

A few inches above Sam's swim fins, small cuts leaked rivulets of blood over his ankles.

"The octopuses did that," Sam said.

"What?" O'Connor's eyes widened. "You got to be shitting me."

"No species of octopus I know of would do that." Kailani crouched to take a closer look. "Does it hurt?"

"Actually, no."

O'Connor smacked a fist into her palm. "Same shit as those divers. I'll fuckin' *kill* them all."

"Not on my watch," Kailani said.

Sam gazed at O'Connor and shook his head. "Take it easy, Mama Bear. It wasn't like that." He closed his eyes and cast his mind back. "It was more protective than menacing."

"Now that I believe." Kailani grabbed a first aid kit from under the console, extracted a roll of gauze, and began wrapping his ankles. "Octopuses are mostly gentle creatures."

O'Connor eyed her. "Mostly?"

Kailani shrugged. "They still have to hunt to eat."

Afterward, Sam touched the bandages with his fingertips. There were no signs of blood absorption into the gauze. He shifted his gaze to the surrounding water. In his mind, he replayed his recent encounter.

Protective? Or was it a negotiation? His life in exchange for the coin.

Had Sam made a connection? Were these octopuses guardians instead of a threat?

SKULK STOOD WITHIN the cabin with binoculars as Niko navigated the *Wavy Jones* out of the cove and toward the Auau Channel. The boat under present scrutiny, the *Octopussy,* had just dropped anchor.

"Kill it," Skulk said.

Niko stopped the engines and the *Wavy Jones* drifted and bobbed with the current of the channel.

"Palakiko Tours is becoming a problem. That group in particular." Skulk lowered the binoculars and shot a glance at Niko. "They're up to something. And they're slowing down our salvage operation."

"Not that we've found anything big yet," Niko said.

"Who asked you?"

Used to this kind of response, Niko continued to watch their location on the GPS display.

Skulk raised the binoculars to her eyes again. "We know what's down there. Anything they find is mine. I'll make sure of it."

"What's the plan?"

Skulk watched the group enter the water and begin their excursion. "Hold our position."

Niko pulled a can of beer out a cooler next to the console, cracked the seal, and took a swig. He grabbed another can and held it up. "Want one?"

Skulk ignored him and continued her surveillance.

Niko shrugged and returned the extra beer to the cooler.

"The fat bitch isn't diving today," Skulk said. "Her peg leg must be giving her problems."

"She has a peg leg?"

"You can learn a lot by watching." Skulk sneered at Niko nursing his beer. "Not that you'd know anything about that."

"I know enough." Niko took a thirsty gulp.

Skulk handed him the binoculars. "Watch for activity."

Niko propped himself up on the side of the console and focused on the *Octopussy*. It was impossible to drink his beer and maintain surveillance at the same time, but that's what Skulk had wanted all along.

Skulk opened a beer for herself and faced the bow, the Maui mountains in the distance.

"You did a piss-poor job of tying up that diver yesterday." Skulk drank. "Maybe I should replace you."

"I took care of that—"

"Mess." Skulk scowled. "You better hope they don't figure out who you are. Because if they do, you're dead to me." Skulk took a long pull on her beer, crushed the can in her hand, and threw the empty into the ocean.

Niko lowered the binoculars and glared at Skulk.

"I said *watch* them!" Skulk grabbed the binoculars back. "Can't even do one simple thing."

"I don't see you stepping up to do any killing."

Skulk spun around and jammed the barrel of her pistol under Niko's chin. "How about I start with you?"

Niko swallowed hard and shook his head.

Skulk released him, holstered her pistol, and resumed her surveillance on Kailani's boat. A second later, she watched a member of the group break the surface in a huge splash.

One of the adults. The man.

As soon as the man surfaced, he submerged again.

No. Something pulled him under.

Niko noticed the tensed muscles in Skulk's face. "Spot something?"

"Quiet." Skulk centered the binocular's view on the wake of the man's splash. The Palakiko girl and the fat bitch were leaning over the gunwale, watching the water.

Did he find something?

Normally Skulk wouldn't have given a damn if the man lived or died. But the strange way he had surfaced and disappeared again had her curiosity piqued.

Seconds turned into minutes before the man resurfaced again. Skulk watched him swim to the starboard side of the *Octopussy* as the other two helped him aboard. Skulk lowered her binoculars.

"He was pulled under." She glanced at Niko.

"Octopus."

Skulk narrowed her eyes and nodded, almost imperceptibly. "He had something that didn't belong to him."

"Something that belongs to *you*."

Skulk grinned and nodded. "I think we have to pay someone a little visit. Let's go. I want to be back before them."

Niko fired up the dual engines and steered the *Wavy Jones* back around toward the marina.

Skulk kept her eyes on the *Octopussy* as they passed by. She glanced at the GPS display next to the console and extrapolated the other boat's location. Her payday just got closer. Rockwell would be pleased.

KAILANI MOORED THE *Octopussy* to the lift dock closest to the boathouse. As she secured the vessel, Sam and the others removed their swim fins and disembarked to the pier.

Lono gave his horn a short blast. He and his occupants waved at Kailani. His excursion focused on sightseeing and had circumnavigated Lanai, passing many shipwrecks to the north, some submerged, some forever beached and battered by the never-ending surf.

Kailani's group knew exactly what was expected of them. Everyone lined up their equipment on the pier in tidy, organized piles.

Sam walked to the opposite side of the pier, propped himself up on the railing, and gazed out over the cove. The blue water reflected the late-afternoon sky. He could feel the cool heaviness of the gold coin in his pocket against his leg.

For a fleeting moment, he almost decided to throw the artifact back into the cove, but the freedom it represented held him back. The coin was likely worth more than his total accumulated prison wage over fifteen years.

He felt a warm hand tap him on the shoulder as Bradley took a spot next to him.

"Did you have a good dive?"

Sam gave his son a half-hearted smile. "It was interesting." He returned his vacant gaze to the cove.

Bradley looked at him, perplexed, then glanced back at Hope. "Did you guys have a fight or something?"

"What?" It took a moment for Sam to realize what Bradley was talking about. "No. No. Nothing like that."

Bradley remained unconvinced. "Well, something's up with you."

Sam reminded himself of how well Claire had raised Bradley. The young man standing next to him had grown up to be loyal, intelligent, and perceptive. And the truth of how little influence he had had on Bradley's upbringing hit him hard. Those feelings had been getting easier to come to terms with ever since he had reconciled with his son, but today it felt like a giant step backward.

Sam contemplated whether or not to tell Bradley of his find, and by extension everyone else in the group, including Kailani.

It didn't take a genius to know that she would not be pleased. Maybe he could help her understand where he was coming from.

In the end, he decided that sharing the news would be best. Harboring a secret like this would affect the enjoyment of the rest of the trip.

"You're right." Sam clasped his hands solemnly.

Bradley scanned his face for clues and waited.

Sam reached into his pocket and pulled out the gold coin with its distinctive square center hole, intricately decorated with Chinese symbols and drawings.

Bradley's eyes bugged out. "Holy shit." He shot a look back at the group. Kailani collected equipment from the excursion while Jack shared photos with Trillian, Hope, and O'Connor. "So, no one knows?"

"No one except you."

"Where'd you find it?"

Sam shook his head slowly. "I think I'm going to keep that detail to myself."

Bradley pulled out his phone. "Can I?"

Sam said nothing and held out his palm. Bradley framed up the coin on his smart phone's display and snapped a picture. He flipped it over and took another.

"You want to keep this a secret?"

Sam saw the excitement in Bradley's eyes but knew he would keep this secret if he had to. But it would be torture for him.

"I'd prefer it if Kailani didn't find out, if at all possible."

Bradley glanced back at Kailani, who was now admiring Jack's photos. "That's going to be tough. She's practically part of the gang now."

"Yeah." Sam looked back at the group and sighed. "I hate to do it, but this could change our lives, Brad."

"I know." Bradley stepped away to leave, then stopped. "Thanks for telling me first, Dad."

Sam pocketed the coin. He gave him an apprehensive smile

and returned his eyes to the water to prepare for the inevitable fallout.

Bradley returned to the group. "Kai, do you have today's newspaper?"

"I think so." Kailani consulted briefly with Lono, then disappeared into the boathouse. A few moments later she emerged with the paper folded in her hand. "What'd you want it for?"

"I... wanted to reread that story on the divers."

Kailani handed the paper to him. "It's a horrible story. But they were opportunists."

"Yeah. Thanks." Bradley stepped away from the rest of the group and called up the photo of the coin on his phone. He matched it up to the inset photo of the coin in the newspaper. The two coins were virtually identical.

"Where'd you take that?"

Bradley spun around to find Jack staring at him intently. Before he had a chance to respond, Jack had figured it out.

Jack marched across the pier to where Sam stood, with Bradley following close after.

"That didn't take long," Sam said.

"Dad, I didn't say anything, I swear."

"It was the scar on your finger that gave it away."

Sam turned up his left hand. The scar near the tip of his ring finger stood out like a white thread. He flinched at the memory of the rat that had given it to him. "The devil's in the details," he said to himself.

"Can I see it?" Jack asked.

Sam moved his left hand closer to Jack.

"Come on. I meant the coin."

O'Connor pushed her way between Jack and Sam. "What're you two delicious hunks of man meat gabbing about?"

Bradley tapped O'Connor shoulder. "What am I, chopped liver?"

"You said it, bub, not me." O'Connor faced Sam. "Spill it, muchacho."

Sam hung his head and sighed. Why did he open his mouth? He could end it right now and throw the coin back into the ocean. But at the same time, he couldn't. There was a reason he had found the coin, beyond the obvious one, but that reason remained a mystery.

He motioned at Bradley. "Go ahead."

Bradley dug out his phone and held up the image of the coin.

"So? It's a coin." O'Connor shifted her gaze from Bradley to Sam to Jack. "What's the big deal?"

"It's Sam's hand in the picture," Jack said.

O'Connor narrowed her eyes at Jack, then at Sam. "Bullshit. Prove it."

"Just show her, Dad."

Sam sighed heavily. "Get ready for a shitstorm." He fished the coin out of his pocket and presented it for O'Connor to see.

She reached out for it, but Sam closed his hand around the coin and pulled it away.

"Come on," O'Connor said. "Give it here. I want a closer look."

Sam shook his head. "You can look but you can't touch."

"Funny. I seem to remember saying that before we left New York."

Sam turned to face Kailani standing a few feet from him, with Hope and Trillian flanking her.

"Sam… *why?*" The disappointment on Hope's face hit him harder than the anger he had expected from Kailani.

"It was there. Right in front of me." Sam tried to meet Hope's eyes but found it impossible. "I couldn't resist it."

Lono said goodbye to his tour group and approached Kailani from behind. He tapped her shoulder lightly. "I'll finish up here if you want to hang out with your friends."

When Kailani didn't respond, he moved closer. "Kai?" Lono

saw Kailani focusing on something in Sam's hand, something round and golden. His eyes darkened at once, and he stepped past Kailani to confront Sam.

"Dad. I'll handle it." Kailani spoke loud and clear.

Lono respected his daughter's ability to deal with difficult client issues. After all, he had taught her everything he knew. He gave Kailani's shoulder a squeeze of reassurance and backed away toward the boat house, but not before giving Sam a look of disappointment and disgust.

Kailani kept her eyes glued on Sam. "Do you think what I said was all bullshit?"

"No, I—"

Kailani stepped forward, fuming. "You've cursed not only yourself and the people you care about, but *everyone* here."

Sam looked down at his hand. The gold coin lay heavy against his fingers, glinting back at him. Its beauty, and the wealth it represented, held him transfixed. "What about the good this could do?"

"For who, exactly?" Kailani asked.

"For me, my son, my—"

"What about people *less* fortunate than you? Aren't they worthy?"

Sam choked on his words.

"I don't know what you've gone through that makes you believe you deserve this, and I don't care." Kailani took a breath. "The fact is *that coin* belongs to *everyone,* and that's exactly why it must stay here."

Deep down, Sam knew Kailani was right, but he felt like Frodo after he had found the One Ring. Every moment Sam held onto the coin reinforced his belief that it belonged to him.

"Just throw it back," Hope said. "If you care about anyone at all, if you care about me…"

"Yeah, Dad. Maybe it's not worth it."

Trillian opened her mouth to speak, then reconsidered.

"I say keep the fucking thing," O'Connor said. "I've never believed in curses and all that hocus pocus crap. And look at me. I'm living the dream."

Hope shot an angry glare at O'Connor. "You shut up." She returned her eyes to Sam. "Please. Don't do this."

"I'm sorry. I care… but I can't." Sam closed his hand around the coin and placed it back into his pocket.

Kailani clenched her jaws and looked ready to explode. Instead, she held her anger and spoke with calm clarity. "That was your last snorkeling trip. If you still have that coin tomorrow, I *will* report you to bylaw enforcement and I'll make sure you're blacklisted from every business on the island."

O'Connor laughed. "You're bluffing."

Kailani shifted her gaze. "Try me, bitch." She didn't wait for a response. Kailani returned to the boat house to help Lono finish packing up for the day.

Jack looked at the group, one by one, then ran after Kailani. Hope shook her head and stormed down the pier toward the cabins.

"Look, Kai," Jack said. "Sam didn't mean any harm. He's had a super hard life."

Kailani turned on him like fire. "You weren't listening. I don't care about Sam's life. All I care about right now is restoring balance."

Jack nodded. "Yeah. I get it." He took a breath. "He'll get rid of the coin. I promise."

"Don't make promises you can't keep." Kailani looked him over, then continued collecting equipment. "Get out of here. I can't look at any of you right now."

Jack backed away and rejoined the group. "You need to get rid of that coin."

"Everyone needs to *shut the fuck up* about the coin." Sam scanned the group. "Hear me?"

"Well, that spun out of control quickly," O'Connor said. "I think I hear a Mai Tai calling my name. Anyone else?"

Trillian scowled at her and headed down the pier.

O'Connor shrugged. "What? Do I stink?"

"Cut the shit," Bradley said. "Be serious for once." He ran to catch up to Trillian.

"See?" O'Connor held up her hands. "All this talk of curses has made everyone batshit crazy."

"Maybe that's the curse in action," Jack said.

"No." O'Connor leaned in uncomfortably close. "Don't start that mumbo jumbo again."

Jack shrugged. "Everything was fine until we started talking about that coin. Just saying."

"Should have kept my mouth shut," Sam said to himself. He jammed his hand into his pocket and flipped the coin around his fingers as the three of them headed down the pier.

From where the *Wavy Jones* was moored, Skulk had witnessed the entire confrontation. While she couldn't hear anything, the body language spoke louder than words.

She set the pair of binoculars down and nodded at Niko. "Follow me." They hopped onto the dock and headed toward the pier.

O'CONNOR HOOKED HER arms around Sam's and Jack's necks as they strode down the length of the pier. To Sam, the gesture seemed too celebratory, which was the complete opposite to how he was feeling.

The hunk of gold burned a hole in his pocket, and not in a good way. Sam kept second-guessing his decision to keep the coin. All he stood to gain was money, potentially thousands of dollars, but his losses could be far greater.

Sam's father's voice echoed in his head. "Money can't buy happiness." He remembered as a teenager laughing at the words, not seeing the wisdom in them. Today, that sentiment rang true, despite his windfall.

Jack looked back over his shoulder. Kailani stood in front of the boat house, her arms crossed against her chest. He could feel her anger even from this distance.

"I'm the filling in a Sam and Jack sandwich." O'Connor cackled. "My favorite place to be."

"Oh-kay," Jack said. "What kind of bread are we, then?"

O'Connor answered without hesitation. "Focaccia. With an emphasis on the fuck—"

Sam sighed heavily.

"What's wrong, Sam?" O'Connor tugged his neck closer to her. "Prefer something else? Maybe *sweet buns?*"

Jack laughed.

"I'd prefer you shut your mouth," Sam said.

"Ain't going to happen. You know that." O'Connor turned to Jack. "How much do you think that coin's worth?"

"Hard to say." Jack pulled out his phone and tapped on the display. "The gold alone is probably worth several thousand. You'd have to weigh it and determine its purity. But the designs would increase the value."

Sam shook off O'Connor's arm and quickened his pace.

O'Connor sneered. "Jesus. Asshole much?"

Sam spun around and grabbed O'Connor by her collar, pulling her nose to nose. "You need to shut the fuck up."

"Or what?" O'Connor waited for Sam's comeback.

Jack fell silent, pocketed his phone, and tapped O'Connor's shoulder.

She glared at him. "What the *hell* do you—"

Jack motioned with fearful eyes toward a man and a women approaching fast, the woman with a scar across her face and a cigarette tucked into the corner of her mouth.

"Sam…" O'Connor nodded sideways. "We got company."

Sam glanced back as Skulk and Niko stopped a few feet from them.

Skulk smirked and crossed her arms, flexing her biceps. "Trouble in paradise?"

"None of your business," Sam said.

"My business is this cove and *everyone* in it."

"Great." Sam turned to leave but Skulk blocked his path.

"Make any interesting discoveries today?"

O'Connor puffed out her chest and stepped forward. "What part of *go fuck yourself* don't you—"

Niko matched O'Connor's move and pulled a large knife from a sheath hanging at his side. O'Connor crossed her arms and stood her ground.

"We didn't find anything," Sam said.

"Really?" Skulk squinted at the three of them. She dragged on her cigarette, plucked it from her lips, and blew smoke in their faces. "Because it sure looked like you were arguing about something."

"Yeah. Surf or turf for dinner." O'Connor grinned. "What do you recommend?"

Skulk scowled at her. "Don't get smart, you fat bitch."

"Yeah?" O'Connor shifted on her feet, keeping her eye on Niko's knife. "Go fuck your mother."

"You finished?" Sam alternated his gaze between O'Connor and Skulk. "We went snorkeling. That's it. End of story."

Skulk spat on O'Connor's shoes, then approached Jack. "What about you?"

Jack stammered, his eyes darting between O'Connor, Sam, and briefly Sam's pocket. "What he said. I swear."

Skulk appraised all three, took a final drag from her cigarette, and tossed the butt against Sam's chest. The ember burst in a shower of orange sparks and left a scorch mark on his T-shirt.

Jack shot a quick glance back at the boat house. Kailani continued to watch, still as a statue.

Skulk followed Jack's gaze. "Whatever she said to you, you should've *listened*." She stepped back, motioning Niko to do the same.

Sam, O'Connor, and Jack continued toward the promenade, keeping their heads forward.

Jack's phone chimed an incoming text. He took it out and looked at the display.

Kailani's text read, "See? Curse started. Happy?"

Jack shut off his phone. There was no useful purpose in sharing the text, especially not with Sam.

When the three of them were several yards away, Skulk looked a question at Niko. He nodded in response.

"Both adults were at the hospital," he said. "And another woman."

"That's two strikes against them." Skulk turned back toward the *Wavy Jones* and Niko followed. "I can't afford to wait for a third."

Consequences

As EARLY SIGNS of a pre-dawn sky rose behind Maui, the only notable sound drifting through the open windows of cabins 13 and 14 was the gentle surf in Niho'gula Cove.

Everyone had retired early to their cabins the previous evening. A three course dinner combined with the exertion of a day of snorkeling had sapped everyone's energy. And O'Connor's repeated and annoyingly obvious attempts to lighten the mood failed to end the day on a positive note. No one was interested. Sam's newfound coin had cast its shadow over everyone. Perhaps Kailani was right.

A creak from the floorboards pulled Trillian from her slumber. Before she could orient herself, a clammy hand reeking of boat diesel covered her mouth.

Standing above her was a dark-skinned man with a black mask covering his nose and mouth. He held a large knife, the sharp edge glinting in the limited light of the room. Through her panic, Trillian noticed his hair looked odd. The tips seemed to glow.

She struggled to scream, but the man applied more pressure to her mouth, raised the knife, and shook his head slowly.

Trillian looked to her right, past Bradley beside her, and saw another man similarly masked and dressed. He leveled a pistol at Bradley's head. She spotted a scar going through the man's left eyebrow, a scar she had memorized the first time she had seen it.

It wasn't another man, but a woman.

Skulk.

Trillian fought hard to hold back a scream.

Bradley managed a quick glance at Trillian before Skulk pistol-whipped him on the top of his head.

"*I'm* the one you want to pay attention to," Skulk's voice hissed. "Do what I say and she won't be hurt." She faced Trillian. "If *you* make a sound, you won't see tomorrow. Understand?"

Trillian nodded.

Skulk returned her attention to Bradley. "You. Get up. Not a word or I'll paint your girlfriend's face with your brains."

Skulk removed her hand from Bradley's mouth.

"Don't hurt her. Please! I'll—"

Skulk used the butt of her pistol to strike Bradley's head a second time, opening up a fresh gash that welled with blood instantly. "You don't listen too well." She pressed the barrel of the pistol into Bradley's head, pushing the teenager back into his pillow. "Shut your mouth and *move*." She added an extra push for emphasis.

Bradley sat up slowly, blinking at the sting of blood in his eye.

Skulk stepped back and waved the pistol in the direction she wanted Bradley to go. "Do anything stupid and you'll watch us cut your girlfriend's throat."

Trillian kept her eyes glued to Bradley, through vision blurred by tears.

At the door to the bedroom, Skulk nodded at Niko. He removed his hand from Trillian's mouth and raised a finger to his lips. He shushed her, then ran his finger across his neck. He looked a question at her.

Trillian managed a nod as she wiped at the tear tracks on her cheeks.

Skulk directed Bradley out of the cabin, followed by Niko.

Trillian listened for movement in the cabin for a moment. When she was certain they had left, she leaped across the bed to the side window and spotted Bradley, Niko, and Skulk moving across the lawn toward cabin 13.

She bolted for Jack's bedroom and burst through the door without knocking.

"Jack! Jack! Get up. They took him!"

Jack groaned and rolled over.

Trillian shook his shoulders. "Wake up! They took Bradley."

"Ugh. I was in the middle of a great dream."

"Fuck your dream." Trillian spoke in rapid bursts, close to hysteria. "They have Bradley."

The fog of Jack's dream dissipated. He sat up. "Wait. *Who* has Bradley?"

"Skulk! Skulk and…" Trillian grabbed Jack's shoulders and shook him. "We have to do something."

"Okay." Jack jumped out of bed and threw on a T-shirt and shorts. "Where'd they go?"

"The other cabin."

Jack ran out of the bedroom and towards the front door.

Trillian ran after him. "Wait!"

Jack looked at her, confused. "What?"

"They said they'd kill him if I tried anything stupid." Trillian burst into tears.

"Then we'll have to be smart about it, right?" Jack held her for a moment. That was all the time they could spare. Then both of them tiptoed out of the cabin and onto the porch.

SKULK PUSHED BRADLEY ahead of her, her pistol jammed into Bradley's side, just below his ribs. She motioned at Niko to take the lead.

Niko stepped onto the porch of cabin 13 and tried the door. Locked. He pulled a key card from his back pocket and held it in front of the card reader. A green light flashed above it and the lock disengaged. Niko turned the handle and eased the door open.

"It's good to be the king." Skulk grinned to herself.

Because of his decision to keep the coin, Hope had refused to let Sam sleep in the same room as her. He had politely declined O'Connor's repeated offers to share her bed and ended up on the sofa.

Niko unsheathed his knife and stared down at Sam, who was still wearing his shorts and T-shirt from the previous day. He glanced back at Skulk and Bradley on the porch. "It's going to be easier than we thought."

Skulk poked Bradley's side with the pistol. "Let's go. Quiet or everyone dies." Skulk pushed him inside until Bradley stood a couple of feet from the sofa. She kicked at the back of his legs. "On your knees."

Bradley followed the woman's orders. Skulk placed the barrel of her pistol against Bradley's head, close to a congealed track of blood from his forehead.

"Wake the fucker," Skulk said.

Niko walked around to the back of the sofa and grabbed Sam by his hair. With one swift motion, he pulled Sam's head back and positioned the knife against his throat. "Wakey wakey."

Sam blinked as confusion transformed to recognition. "Brad?"

"Give me the coin," Skulk said. "Or he eats a bullet."

Bradley locked his gaze with Sam and subtly shook his head.

Sam looked up at Skulk. "I don't have any coin. I told you that yesterday."

Skulk scowled at him. "You're lying."

"Ask anyone here. They'll tell you that I threw it back."

"This better be good," O'Connor yelled as she burst out of her bedroom. "It's four in the fuckin'… morning."

Niko removed the knife from Sam's throat, stood, and pointed the blade at O'Connor, while keeping one hand firmly gripping Sam's hair.

"O'Connor," Sam said, his voice hoarse with panic. "For God's sake, *shut up*."

"Better take his advice, fat bitch," Skulk said without taking her eyes off Sam. "Don't be a hero."

O'Connor surveyed the scene and backed into the doorframe of her bedroom just as Hope opened her door. O'Connor pumped her hands, palms out, signaling Hope to stop.

"Where *is it?*" The anger boiled up in Skulk's voice.

Niko pulled Sam off the sofa by his hair, returned the knife to his throat, and moved him closer to Skulk.

"Give me the coin. I know you have one."

Sam shot a brief glance at Hope and O'Connor, and shook his head quickly before Niko twisted Sam's head to face Skulk. The edge of Niko's knife had sliced lacerations deep enough to leave bloody tracks across Sam's skin.

"How many times do I have to say it?" Sam grit his teeth. "I don't have your precious coin."

"Don't tell him, Dad," Bradley said.

Skulk cocked the hammer on her pistol. "Is it worth your… *son's* life?"

"Oh God." Hope said before she could stop herself.

Skulk shook her head and tsk-tsked her. "God isn't going to help him." She retrained her eyes on Sam. "Only you can save him."

Sam's breath quickened. He looked at Bradley and saw his son trying to put on a brave face, but tears had welled in his eyes. There was only one way forward.

"Okay. Okay," he said. "I'll give it to you but it's not here."

"Bullshit." Skulk removed the barrel of her pistol from Bradley's head and pointed it at Hope. "You. Search him."

Hope stepped forward timidly.

Skulk raised her voice. "Move your ass."

Hope faced Sam and mouthed, "I'm sorry." She ran her hands over Sam's clothes, pausing a little too long over his pockets. She glanced back at Skulk, her eyes betraying her.

"Lie to me again and see what happens." Skulk extended her free hand. "Give me the coin."

Hope placed her hand in Sam's pocket. In any other situation, this could have been considered a romantic gesture leading any number of directions. But at that moment, both Hope and Sam shared a look of somber seriousness. He nodded, his transgression set aside for a moment.

Hope extracted the gold coin and held it out with a trembling hand.

Skulk snatched it and took a quick look before shoving it into her own pocket. She motioned Niko and Sam toward the door and shoved Bradley away.

Bradley stumbled and fell to the floor. He glanced back, began to scramble back toward Sam, and reached out with his hand. "Dad!"

"Brad! Stop." Sam shook his head.

Skulk grabbed Sam from Niko's grasp and jammed the pistol's barrel into Sam's side. "He *finally* says something smart."

"I'll be fine," Sam added.

"Except that." Skulk pulled Sam out the door, followed by Niko waving the knife at everyone in the cabin.

The bandits disappeared into the pre-dawn light, Skulk forcing Sam by gunpoint to lead the way to the marina.

Sam resisted. "You got your fucking coin. Let me go."

"You better shut your mouth, or they'll find you floating out in the cove." Skulk twisted the pistol's barrel under Sam's ribs. "Besides, I have plans for you."

Skulk and Niko hooked their arms under Sam's and threw him over the stern of the *Wavy Jones*.

Niko stepped onto the boat, followed by Skulk, her pistol trained on Sam.

"Now you're going to show me where you found that coin," Skulk said. "And you better not lie." She glanced at Niko and pointed out into the cove. "Go."

Sam cast his mind back. During the day, recalling the location where he'd found the coin would have been a challenge, but a possible one. Under the cover of darkness, he didn't stand a chance.

JACK BURST INTO the cabin waving his phone excitedly at the rest of the group. "I got it all on video!"

"Read the room, doof." Trillian pushed past him and ran to Bradley's side.

"When she's right, she's right," O'Connor said. "Save it for later."

Jack nodded self-consciously and slid his phone back into his pocket.

Trillian helped Bradley up to the sofa and examined his forehead. "You okay?" She pushed some of Bradley's bloodied hair out of his face, but it snagged on the congealed blood of his laceration.

Bradley winced and pulled his head back. "Stings a little. Got a bit of a headache too."

"Sorry sorry sorry." Trillian kissed him lightly.

Hope appeared with a damp face cloth and a towel. She exchanged a knowing look with Trillian and Bradley noticed.

"We're going after him." Bradley struggled to get up. "We have to."

Trillian looked him in the eyes. "You need to be checked out first."

Bradley stood and brushed himself off. "Fuck that. What if it was *your* dad?"

His words struck a nerve in Trillian. "My dad doesn't give a *shit* about me."

"You know what I mean." Bradley looked at the others. "We're wasting time. Who's with me?"

"We're *all* with you." O'Connor held the door open. "What's the plan?"

"The marina!" Bradley ran out of the cabin, followed by Trillian and Jack.

"We're winging it," Hope said as she passed O'Connor, running to catch up with the teenagers.

"No big surprise." O'Connor grabbed a pair of binoculars from the windowsill and let the cabin door close behind her as she hopped down the porch steps. Everyone already had a considerable lead. She ran after them with a small hop in her gait, like she hadn't fully committed to skipping. "Fucking prosthetic," she cursed.

Bradley was first to the marina, followed by Jack and Trillian.

"The boat's gone." Bradley said between breaths. He scanned the moorings and spotted a boat heading out into the cove. "Is that it? Can you tell?"

Jack bolted back to the pier and ran its length. By the time he had reached the end, he could see the name of the boat written on the stern, even with the sun barely breaking the horizon.

Wavy Jones.

Bradley, Trillian, and Hope joined Jack at the end of the pier.

Bradley propped himself up on the first crossbar of the railing and tried to spot Sam in the boat. "Can you see him? I can't see him!"

Trillian wrapped her arms around Bradley.

Jack reversed back down the pier.

Hope cupped her hands around her mouth. "Where are you going?"

"Kai!" Jack yelled back without looking.

Bradley and Trillian followed.

"Jesus, to be young again." Hope jogged back down the pier.

Jack skidded to a stop in front of the Palakiko Tours boat house and began pounding on the front door. "Kai! Kailani!"

He stepped back to look at the second story windows, not knowing the layout of Kailani's living space.

Bradley pulled Jack aside. "Did she hear you?" he asked, breathing hard.

Instead of answering, Jack rapped on the door again. A light flicked on upstairs.

Trillian bounced on the balls of her feet. "She heard you."

But instead of Kailani, Lono poked his head out of a window. He squinted down at the teenagers and Hope, then scowled. "Go home." He began pulling the window shut.

"No, please sir. *Please.*" Jack looked up at him. Had Lono been closer, he would have seen the desperation and concern in Jack's eyes. Perhaps he sensed it because he opened the window once more.

"Can we talk to Kailani, sir?" Jack said. "Please?"

Bradley stepped into the light from the open window. "Please help us, Mr. Palakiko."

Lono spotted the blood on Bradley's face and his demeanor changed. Kailani joined him at the window.

"Kai!" Jack said. "Kai. We need your help. *Please.*"

Kailani exchanged words with Lono, then Lono retreated back into the house. "Hold on. Just shut the fuck up, okay? You'll wake everyone."

A few moments later, Kailani unlocked the front door to the boat house and joined the group. "What do you want?" Her tone of voice still held anger. "It's four fucking thirty in the morning."

"Skulk's got my dad," Bradley said. "They're out in the cove."

Kailani studied the blood on Bradley's face. "So?"

"We were hoping you could help us rescue him."

"Please," Jack added.

"What'd I tell you... about the curse?" She glared at them one by one. "It's already working."

"Please." O'Connor joined the group.

"The great denier speaks." Kailani approached O'Connor. "You only believe in the curse when it suits you, huh?"

"Sam's a good guy." O'Connor glanced at Bradley, nodded, then continued. "It was just a momentary lapse in judgment... I'd trust him with my life."

Kailani crossed her arms. "What can *I* do?"

"You can get me, and only me, out to that boat." O'Connor could sense Bradley bristling beside her. "I'll take care of the rest."

Kailani considered O'Connor's request. "I'll take Bradley."

"Fine." O'Connor grabbed Bradley's shoulder and walked toward the lift dock for *Octopussy*.

"Only Bradley."

O'Connor wasn't about to argue. "Good luck," she whispered in Bradley's ear. "Don't fuck it up." She handed him her binoculars.

"Go wait beside the boat." Kailani said to Bradley. She turned to find Lono at the door of the boat house, keys in his hand.

"You sure you know what you're doing?"

"I'll be fine, Dad."

Lono leaned, his voice low and strained. "But this is *Skulk* we're talking about."

"I'll be *fine*." Kailani kissed his cheek.

Lono held her with his stare for a moment before depositing the keys into her hand.

"Brad! Wait."

Bradley turned to see Jack trotting up to him, his phone in his hand.

"Take it," Jack said. "For evidence."

Bradley nodded and took the phone, pocketing it. "Thanks."

Kailani followed Bradley down to the dock and they both climbed aboard the *Octopussy*.

Lono returned his gaze to the rest of the group, before focusing on O'Connor. "If anything happens, I'm holding *you* responsible."

O'Connor nodded. "Understood."

Everyone watched as Kailani piloted the *Octopussy* out of its lift dock and toward the cove.

Bradley waved and everyone except Lono waved back. Doubts about the two teenagers going alone bubbled up into O'Connor's mind and she couldn't help but wonder if they had made a terrible mistake.

KAILANI KEPT THE navigation and masthead lights off and the engine at a low rumble. With dawn breaking, the *Wavy Jones* was easy to spot. The challenge would be getting close to the boat without being noticed.

Bradley held the binoculars to his eyes.

"I'm doing this because I don't like seeing people get hurt. But I'm still angry at you guys, you know." Kailani brushed her hair from her eyes and looked back at Bradley. "All of you..." She shook her head. "At Jack for wanting to build a stupid weapon, and especially at your dad."

"Yeah, I figured."

"Even if your dad hands over that coin, the damage is done," Kailani said. "The curse has been released. There's no undoing it."

Bradley lowered the binoculars and saw the seriousness in Kailani's gaze, even under the low light of the Privateer's covered cabin. "I know. Thanks for doing this."

"Don't thank me yet." Kailani killed the engine.

"Can't you get closer?"

"Too dangerous, for us and especially for *Octopussy*." Kailani tapped the console affectionately. "She doesn't want to join the *Templeton*. It's not her time yet."

"It's not my dad's time either." Bradley returned the binoculars to his eyes. He still couldn't discern much detail, but he thought he had spotted a third occupant. He continued to watch in hopes that his eyes hadn't tricked him.

SAM GLANCED AROUND from where he sat, trying to pick out identifiable landmarks in the dawn glow. The lights along the marina, promenade, and in front of the restaurant seemed close enough to swim to, but he knew that distances could be deceiving, especially over water.

The Franklin Correctional Facility, where he had spent fifteen of his last eighteen years, hadn't had a pool. Most prisons didn't. Plus, he wasn't a strong swimmer. An attempt at escape would likely end with a bullet in his back. He tried to stand for a better view, but Skulk kicked him back into a seat at the stern of the boat.

"What the hell is your problem?" Sam glared at her. "I'm trying to get my bearings so you can get your precious fucking coins."

"You don't need to stand to do that." Skulk pulled from her pocket the coin she had taken from Sam and twirled it in her fingers. "And they *are* precious, aren't they?"

From under her shirt, she retrieved a section of a paracord loop that hung around her neck. It had several golden trinkets attached to it already. She made a loop from a section of the cord, pushed it through the center of the coin, and fastened it next to the others.

"GPS says we should be close." Niko slowed the boat.

Skulk pulled a machete from next to the console and crouched in front of Sam. "Where did you find your coin?"

Sam looked around. "I can't be sure."

Skulk pointed the machete at Sam, accentuating her words by thrusting the sharp end at him. "You *better* be sure."

"I'm no navigation expert." Sam's eyes darted as he twisted to survey their current location. "The treasure is cursed. Did you know that?"

Niko extracted his knife and stepped beside Skulk. There were still traces of Sam's congealed blood on the blade from their encounter in the cabin. He wiped them on his pants and stepped closer.

Skulk held up an open palm and shook her head at Niko.

"Cursed?" Skulk laughed. "If you believe that, you're stupider than I thought." She placed the tip of the machete in the center of Sam's chest, cutting through his T-shirt and breaking his skin. "WHERE DID YOU FIND THE COIN?"

Sam locked his gaze with Skulk's. It took effort to match Skulk's level of crazy, if only temporarily. "Fuck you," he said.

Sam pushed the machete's blade to the side and launched himself at Skulk. He wrapped his hands around Skulk's neck, pushed her to the deck of the boat, and squeezed. "If I'm going to die, I'm taking you with me."

Had Sam pushed the machete's blade away in the opposite direction, he may have had more of an advantage. But he had moved Skulk's arm, and by extension the machete, so that it lay across her chest.

Instinctively, Skulk pulled the machete back laterally in front of her, the blade running a deep line across Sam's abdomen, slicing through his T-shirt, and almost gutting him.

Pain flooded Sam's mind and he collapsed onto Skulk's chest, his hands releasing their grip on Skulk's neck.

Niko grabbed Sam by the collar of his T-shirt and pulled him back against the transom. Sam slumped in a rising puddle of his own blood.

Skulk grabbed Sam's hair and jerked his head back. "You didn't think that one through, did you?"

Sam grinned back at him.

"The coin. WHERE did you find it?"

Sam remained silent. Skulk threw Sam's head back, stood, and glanced back at the shore of Club Niho'gula. "Quickly. Tell me now and you might survive."

Sam laughed and pointed at Skulk. "Who looks stupid now?" If there had been more light, he would have seen Skulk's face turn beet red with anger.

As Skulk opened her mouth to respond, a mass of tentacles writhed over the transom, searching and probing. The tentacle tips reached out for the coins around Skulk's neck. She stepped back and easily avoided their grasp.

The tentacles found Sam's body and tightened around his torso, pulling him back toward the water.

Skulk and Niko each grabbed one of Sam's legs and held him back. Skulk began hacking at the tentacles with her machete. But as soon as she cut one tentacle, another appeared in its place, apparently out of nowhere.

Still more tentacles shot out at them, trying to retrieve the coins hanging from Skulk's neck. It became increasingly difficult to evade their writhing tips.

"WHERE? TELL ME!" Blood vessels on Skulk's neck stood out like ropes and the scar across the left side of her face looked primed to split open, revealing the true monster within.

Delirious from blood loss, Sam managed to raise a middle finger at Skulk. "Never."

A tentacle rose up and lashed out, leaving a gash across Skulk's shoulder. The tips and underside of the tentacles were lined with teeth where the suckers should have been, all as sharp as the machete Skulk was using to cut them. Startled by the attack, Skulk fell backward. Niko's hands were slick with blood and couldn't stop the pull on Sam by himself.

The octopuses won the tug of war. Niko lost his grip and Sam slid over the edge of the transom next to the *Wavy Jones's* dual engines. His body disappeared in a swirl of bloody water at the stern. Skulk's chance of finding more coins disappeared with him.

Skulk glared at Niko with fiery eyes. "Idiot!"

Niko retrieved his knife from the deck and gripped the hilt, his white knuckles showing through the smeared blood. He met Skulk's gaze. "Talking 'bout yourself, right?"

Skulk wanted to rip Niko's throat out for disrespecting her, but wisely avoided responding. Niko did the things Skulk did not want to do and kept their worst crimes at arms' length. Truthfully, she needed Niko, and right now a heated argument would only cause more problems.

Skulk grunted and pulled herself up. She raised the treasure collection from around her neck, isolated the coin she had just added, and bit one edge. "I'd bet this is twenty-four carats," she said with a grin.

Niko returned his knife to the sheath on his belt just as an onslaught of new tentacles burst over the transom. With quick precision, the thrashing tentacles gripped Skulk's legs, working up her body toward her necklace of precious finds.

Niko stepped back and tripped over a coil of rope. Tentacles tasted his boots and slithered up his legs.

Skulk brought her machete down hard across the tentacles attacking her, severing most of them with one blow. "Go! Go now!"

The tentacles that had found Niko switched targets and whipped to where Skulk stood. Niko scrambled back to the console and started the boat's engines. He throttled up to full speed. The *Wavy Jones's* bow rose as a wake of white churning water boiled from the Yamaha's propellers.

The severed tentacles continued to twist and turn, searching for an elusive prize that only Skulk possessed. The creature displayed impressive muscle memory in its limbs, but Skulk had no interest in its abilities. She grabbed a fish spear and stabbed the tentacles, throwing them back into the water one by one.

Once in the water and out of sight, the amputated tentacles began to spontaneously regenerate. What started as one octopus multiplied into eight.

KAILANI AND BRADLEY maintained their silent surveillance from the north side of the cove. With their eyes adjusted to the low light, the rising sun from behind the Maui mountains allowed them to see more detail.

"What's happening?" Kailani worked at the steering wheel and controls on the console, continuously adjusting the *Octopussy's* position to compensate for the tides and current.

"I don't know," Bradley said from behind binoculars. "I with I could read lips."

"Can you see your dad?"

"Yeah, he's at the back of the boat."

"The stern."

Bradley lowered the eyepieces. "What? Yeah, whatever."

"Look!" Kailani pointed at the boat. "Something's going on."

Bradley could see the stark outline of Skulk holding a machete held against Sam's chest. "Shit, we got to get closer."

"Nope," Kailani said emphatically. "Even if we did, what are we going to do? They've got guns. Going against that is a death wish."

Bradley dug into his pocket and pulled out his phone. "We could get them on video. For evidence."

Kailani took the phone and loaded the camera app. "It's too dark. You can't see shit."

"Holy fuck." Bradley lowered the binoculars slightly and gazed over them, as if to double check if what he was seeing was real. "I think they stabbed him."

Kailani yanked the binoculars away from Bradley and focused on the *Wavy Jones* and its occupants. What she saw made her jaw drop. An octopus... or...

Is there more than one?

Multiple tentacles twirled and twisted from the stern as they battled Skulk and the other man. It was difficult to discern where Sam fit into the flailing silhouette. It was like a scene straight out of *20,000 Leagues Under the Sea.*

"Let me see." Bradley reached for the binoculars, but Kailani pushed him away.

In an instant, all became horrifically clear. Kailani spotted Sam's legs and feet as tentacles dragged his body out of the boat and under the water. She pulled in a panicked breath.

"What's going on, Kai." Bradley gripped the binoculars, unwilling to let them go this time. "Give them... *here!*"

Kailani let the binoculars go and busied herself at the console. "We got to go."

"What about my dad?" Bradley scanned the dark shape of the *Wavy Jones.* He could see a scuffle taking place on board, but he couldn't tell who was involved or who was winning.

"Brad, we got to go. *Now.*" Kailani turned toward the marina just as the *Wavy Jones* reared up, its engines echoing across the water. She maintained a low speed to let Skulk and her henchman get a good lead.

"Do you think he's okay?" Bradley kept the binoculars glued to his eyes.

Because Bradley was a friend, he deserved the truth. But Kailani couldn't answer him after what she had seen. There was too much uncertainty. Did octopuses really pull Sam overboard? Was Jack right to think that octopuses could be evil? One thing she was sure of: the *Wavy Jones* carried only two people now and Sam wasn't one of them.

But Bradley and Kailani had bigger problems. The *Wavy Jones* had changed course. Instead of heading back to the marina, the boat had changed course and was heading straight for them. Fast.

KAILANI HAD BARELY throttled up *Octopussy's* engines when a gunshot echoed across the water. A ricochet spark burst off the top of the outboard engine, popping off the protective cover. The engine died and her attempts to accelerate failed. The engine no longer responded to the controls on the console.

Bradley ducked with surprise. "Holy fuck. They're shooting at us?"

"I knew this was a bad idea. She's taking care of loose ends." Kailani took Bradley by the hand and pulled him to the side of the boat opposite to Skulk's approach. "You need to listen to me and do exactly as I say. Okay?"

Bradley nodded.

"We need to jump." Kailani glanced over her shoulder at the rapidly advancing *Wavy Jones*. "We'll stay opposite to Skulk, make her think we've drowned. Understand?"

"Yeah, like in *The Wrath of Khan*."

Kailani shot a brief, confused look at him. "Uh, whatever. Come on." She pulled herself over the gunwale at the bow and jumped into the water. "Brad. Hurry!"

Bradley joined her in the water beside *Octopussy's* hull. The water wasn't overly cold, but it being close to five in the morning made it feel colder.

"Stick close," Kailani said. "Watch and listen."

The two teenagers tread water and waited. It didn't take long to hear the sound of the *Wavy Jones's* dual engines. Two more shots rang out, punching holes in the port hull a few feet from their position. The boat began to take on water.

Kailani held up her hand. "Wait…," she whispered and pointed at the stern. As soon as she saw the bow of the *Wavy Jones* appear, she tugged Bradley's arm. "Now!" The two of them swam under the hull to the starboard side and followed the hull back to the stern.

The plan was working, but if Skulk put any more holes into the boat, it would sink like a stone, sealing their fate.

"Keep going around the boat," Kailani whispered before pulling herself onto the transom next to the *Octopussy's* disabled engine. She could see wisps of acrid smoke rising from the top.

Bradley looked at her, alarmed. "Wait, what are you doing?"

Kailani waved him off. "Go!"

Bradley continued around the hull despite his concern. Kailani peeked over the transom and spotted the *Wavy Jones* passing the bow. She pulled herself up and slid over the stern like a sea lion and crawled to the console. She grabbed a red waterproof suitcase fastened underneath the controls and popped the lid open. Inside lay a flare gun and four flare shells.

She peeked over the starboard gunwale and saw the *Wavy Jones* making a closer approach. Kailani had to act fast. She popped open the barrel, slid a shell inside, and closed it. Using her thumb, she pulled back the hammer.

Kailani slid along the deck of the boat, dragging the red suitcase with her, until she was close to the stern and beyond the protection of the cabin's canopy. She looked up at nothing but a cloudless early dawn sky.

The engine noise of *Wavy Jones* grew louder as it approached the starboard side of *Octopussy*. She could hear the telltale signs of water within the bilge. If she could get to the pump in time, she could save the boat.

It was now or never. These flares lasted at most ten seconds once fired.

Kailani curled her finger around the trigger and hoped her dad was watching.

Bang!

A bright red ball of fire launched into the sky where it floated momentarily before burning out.

The engine noise of the *Wavy Jones* remained close. Kailani popped open the barrel, emptied the spent shell, and reloaded it. Another shot rang out, splintering the deck boards near her feet. She pulled her trigger.

Bang!

A second flare jetted into the sky.

This time she heard arguing before the *Wavy Jones's* engines roared and turned, leaving the *Octopussy* bobbing up and down in the wake. Kailani raised her head just high enough over the stern to see the *Wavy Jones* making a hasty retreat. Skulk stood at the stern watching, her face clearly visible in the rising sun.

Kailani felt for her phone, but her pockets were empty. It was back at the boat house.

"Brad!" She sat up and peered over the starboard gunwale. Bradley was nowhere to be seen. Panic set in. Losing Bradley was not part of the plan. She'd never forgive herself if she had lost him too.

Kailani scrambled to the port-side gunwale and draped her body over the edge. Bradley smiled up at her, allowing her heart to settle.

"Ship… out of danger?" he said with a grin.

Kailani nodded. "What are you doing?"

"I'm trying to plug the holes with my socks, but it's not working too well."

As if they had been listening, several octopuses positioned themselves on the side of the hull and sealed the holes temporarily.

"Holy shit." Bradley looked up at Kailani with amazement. "You seeing this?"

Never before in her life had Kailani seen octopuses coordinate and help a human in such a useful way. Four octopuses had spread themselves over the three holes in the hull to prevent any more water leakage.

"Come to the stern. I'll help you out." Kailani ran to the console and tried the switch to the bilge pump. The electrical systems still worked. The pump indicator light flashed green, and she could hear the small pump in the bottom of the hull rattle to life.

Kailani waited at the transom for Bradley to swim around. He was still looking in awe at the octopuses plastered to the port-side hull. She helped him onto the boat.

"Thanks." Bradley glanced at the engine, with its exposed wiring and snaking pipes. The top of the engine looked burned. "Is the engine dead?"

"Yeah. I can only hope that my dad saw the flares."

"I'm sure he did." Bradley grabbed a bunch of his T-shirt and wrung out the seawater. "Great idea by the way. The flares. You should have done that right from the start."

"There wasn't time," Kailani said. "Jumping into the water actually gave us an advantage."

"Looks like it worked." Bradley pointed toward the marina. The *Octopuppy,* piloted by Lono, was on a direct intercept course. The rest of the group stood beside the console, eager to help as much as they could.

Moments later, Lono pulled up beside the *Octopussy.* Jack and Trillian hopped aboard with a rope and handed it to Kailani. She tied it to a cleat on the bow gunwale.

"Sam?" Hope stood next to O'Connor and Lono, looking on with grave concern.

O'Connor sensed Hope's worry. "Where's Sam?"

Kailani could only meet O'Connor's eyes for a moment before looking away. She shook her head subtly. "We don't know."

"What do you mean *you don't know?*"

Kailani shrugged. "I'm sorry. We couldn't get close. We don't know what happened."

Jack and Trillian stared at Kailani. "Sam's *gone?*"

Kailani hung her head. "I'm sorry."

Hope covered her face, sat down, and burst into tears. O'Connor and Lono exchanged glances before O'Connor took a seat next to Hope and placed an arm around her shoulder.

Lono began the slow process of towing the disabled vessel to the marina. He couldn't help but think…

Was this the end of the curse, or just the beginning?

WITHOUT A TRACE

LONO MOORED THE *Octopuppy* to its lift dock first. Without an engine, Kailani could not steer *Octopussy,* but instead relied on Lono, O'Connor, and Hope to guide it with ropes into the center of its lift dock. Lono used a winch to pull the boat the rest of the way out of the water.

Lono hopped out of the *Octopuppy* to survey the damage to *Octopussy's* hull and engine.

"Are they still there?" Bradley climbed down from the stern to join him. "The octopuses?"

At first Lono didn't understand what Bradley was talking about. Then, on the port side, Lono spotted four octopuses the color of the hull extricating themselves from the holes. They glided down to the lift dock, then spun themselves like a spoked wheel, propelling all four into the water.

"What the hell?" Lono looked back at the rest of the group now standing on the lift dock. "You all saw that?"

"Talented creatures. And not dangerous at all." Kailani shot an annoyed look at Jack.

Jack shrugged. "What?"

"They helped us," Kailani said. "Remember that."

"If this is about the weapon, humor me." Jack tried to smile, but Sam's absence overshadowed everything. "I just like building shit."

Kailani rolled her eyes and joined her father.

Lono examined the holes closer. Had the bullets gone through just the hull, the holes would have been clean and easily fixed. But since they had gone through the deck and interior hull first, the exit holes were large and ragged. Still fixable but more complicated.

"Fuck." Lono glowered at Kailani, then at the rest of the group. "I'm going to have to switch out the engine with our backup. This is going to set us back a few weeks at least. God dammit, Kai. We might not even meet our quota for the summer. You know how important that is for us."

O'Connor stepped forward. "We'll help with the repairs. Anything you need. But…" She looked to the rest of the group, still deeply affected by Sam's disappearance. "We really need to go back out there."

Lono stood. The man had several inches over O'Connor. "Are you really asking me to risk my only working boat to…"

"To look for Brad's father." O'Connor stood her ground. "Yeah."

Lono considered the request briefly. "No. Can't do it."

"No. You *can,* but you *won't,*" O'Connor said. "There's a difference."

"Please, Mr. Palakiko." Fresh tears welled in Hope's eyes. "What if it was Kailani missing out there? Wouldn't you want to search for her?"

"Of course." Lono pointed at his boats. "But this is our livelihood. It's too dangerous. What if that asshole comes back and shoots up our last boat?"

"Dad, Skulk is a coward," Kailani said. "And she's already docked. She's not going to make a special trip out into the cove just to sink another boat. Plus, she's lost the cover of darkness."

"That's never stopped her before. You know what kind of woman Skulk is, Kai."

Kailani reached out and took Lono's hand. "And I know what kind of a man *you* are."

Lono studied his daughter's face. He had taught her everything he knew, and now that wisdom and empathy was looking straight back at him.

Hope had her hands pressed together as if praying. Bradley placed an arm around her shoulder and found Lono's gaze.

Lono knew there was only one good answer, as much as he disliked the risk it represented. "Okay."

Kailani hugged him and kissed his cheek. "Thanks, Dad."

Hope wiped her face and threw her arms around Lono as soon as Kailani stepped aside. "I knew you'd say yes, Mr. Palakiko. Thank you."

"Wait," Lono said. "Before anyone gets too excited, there's some conditions."

Everyone stopped their elation to listen.

"I'll give you one hour. Not a second more." Lono eyed them all firmly. "And if Skulk reappears and damages this boat, or worse…"

"I'll buy you a new boat," O'Connor said. "The same quality or better."

Bradley glanced at Jack and raised a brow in surprise. "That's super generous, O'Connor, but you don't—"

"Yes, she does." Lono jutted out his hand toward O'Connor.

"I may be a fucking potty-mouth, but I keep my word." O'Connor took Lono's hand and matched his grip. They both shook hands.

Lono nodded. "Yeah. I think you do." He looked at the rest of the group. "Time's wasting. Let's go."

The group piled back into the *Octopuppy*. Bradley, Trillian, and Jack tried to comfort Hope, but she shook them off. Both worry and anticipation showed on Hope's face as she focused her attention on the water, the waves, and the tricks they played on her eyes.

Bradley did the opposite and scanned the beach and the promenade. It was nearly six in the morning and the club guests were waking and heading to the restaurant for breakfast. Maybe Sam had already made it back to shore and was enjoying a hot coffee, wondering where everyone else had disappeared to. But as the distance from shore increased, it became harder to discern any reliable detail.

Lono positioned the boat above the *Templeton*. "I'm going to do some lateral passes over the wreck. Someone should get in the water and watch the bottom."

Jack sprang to his feet. "On it." He began pulling off his shoes, socks, and pants and grabbed a snorkel and mask.

"I'll join you." Kailani mirrored Jack's preparation. "I'll take the port side."

Lono took a length of rope and tossed another to O'Connor. "Tie it to the gunwale."

O'Connor watched Lono tie his rope to a cleat on the starboard gunwale. She did the same and let the rope dangle off the port side.

Kailani handed Jack a flashlight and strapped an identical one to her wrist. She gripped her rope as she stepped over the port side of the stern and looked at Jack on the opposite side of the boat. "Stay next to the hull so you can avoid the propeller."

Jack adjusted his mask and snorkel. "Right." He looked at Bradley and Hope and offered a small nod of what he hoped was reassurance. He swung his leg over the stern and jumped into the water.

Both Jack and Kailani positioned themselves face-down at the water's surface, one hand on the rope and the other focusing their flashlights on the bottom of the cove.

Lono began slow passes over the *Templeton,* including a couple dozen feet on either side. The rest of the group checked in regularly with Jack and Kailani.

The sight of the *Templeton* wreck in the early morning light was mesmerizing despite the somber goal of the expedition. Jack had to remind himself to stay in search and rescue mode. It would have been easy to go digging around for other interesting finds, but that was what had gotten the group into this situation in the first place. What if the digging around revealed Sam's body? Sam needed to be found, but not while intentionally seeking treasure.

After over an hour of searching, both Jack and Kailani failed to spot anything that could shed light on Sam's disappearance.

Lono killed the engine and looked at Hope and Bradley. "I'm sorry. I think we've done all we can. This is a matter for the authorities now."

"Those fuckin' octopuses." O'Connor grit her teeth as she stared out across the water, grumbling a whisper only meant for her. "Probably took you. Dragged you to the bottom... I'll find you, Sam, if it's the last fuckin' thing I do."

Bradley, Trillian, and Hope helped Jack and Kailani back on board. Few words were spoken. Sam's absence became more real with every passing moment.

Lono piloted the *Octopuppy* back to their lift dock at the marina. Once everyone had disembarked and Lono had securely moored the boat, Bradley took him aside.

"Thank you for doing that, Mr. Palakiko," he said, his voice trembling, on the cusp of breakdown. "You didn't need to. Just want you to know I appreciate it."

"You're welcome." Lono squeezed Bradley's shoulder with reassurance. "And call me Lono."

Bradley swallowed hard and headed for the end of the pier. Once he reached the end, he gripped the railing with both hands until his knuckles whitened. "Where are you, Dad?"

Bradley couldn't hold back any longer. He dropped his head and his tears overflowed. He soon felt a warm hand on his arm. It was Trillian, with Hope standing beside her.

"He can't be gone, Trill," Bradley said between sobs. "He just can't."

Trillian responded by taking him into her arms. Then the three of them collapsed into each other, Hope and Bradley sharing their grief while Trillian consoled them both.

BACK AT CABIN 14, Bradley sat on the sofa and stared at his phone on the coffee table. Skulk taking him at gunpoint that morning, and using him as a bargaining chip in exchange for Sam, felt like a distant immutable memory.

Bradley hadn't known his father long, just a few years, but in the time that they had reconnected, he had learned what a good man he was. Sam had really stepped up and was a guiding force in his life. Now he was gone, and Bradley felt hollow. He had seen the circumstances of Sam's disappearance, and he still couldn't believe it.

Now an unpleasant task lay before him, one that he had never expected: tell Claire what happened.

Trillian leaned over the back of the sofa and hugged Bradley from behind. She kissed his cheek.

"Want some time alone?"

Bradley closed his eyes. He felt fresh tears pushing their way forward and fought hard against them. He wouldn't be able to talk if he was a blubbering idiot.

Bradley swallowed, but the lump in his throat remained. He nodded and croaked, "Thanks."

"Okay. Me and Jack are going for a walk." Trillian planted one last kiss on Bradley's neck and eyed Jack, who was standing in front of the kitchenette sink. She motioned towards the front door.

Trillian stepped outside and Jack followed, giving Bradley a friendly squeeze on the shoulder as he walked by.

He didn't know how long he stared at the blank display of his phone. Maybe if he stared long and hard enough at it, the entire day would reset.

"Who am I kidding?" he said to the empty cabin.

Bradley picked up his phone, opened his contacts, and dialed home. The call connected after a couple of seconds and trilled in his ear. Twice. Four times.

Voice mail activated and he heard Claire asking him to leave a message at the *beep*… always a *beep*, never a *tone*.

Bradley ended the call, hung his head, and slumped against the sofa. Hearing his mom's voice had unlocked something in his heart and he let his tears fall. It would be okay, eventually, but he couldn't leave a voice mail. He needed to deliver this news directly.

He was about to pocket his phone when he realized that the San Fernando Valley was three hours ahead of Hawaiian time. That meant Claire was at work already.

Bradley dialed Claire's cell phone and waited. After a few seconds, the link clicked and the familiar voice of his mom floated back into his ear.

"Bradley! This is a nice surprise," Claire's electronically filtered voice said.

"Hi, Mom." Bradley meant to speak as normally as possible, but his greeting came out strained by his concealed distress. Moms being moms, Claire knew immediately that the call was important.

"Honey? What's wrong?"

Bradley fell silent as he struggled against his tears and his rapidly congesting nose.

"Brad?"

"I'm okay, Mom. It's…"

Even from Hawaii, he could hear the gears in Claire's head working. "Trillian? Or Jack? Are they okay?"

"It's Dad."

"Sam?" It was Claire's turn to be blindsided by her own thoughts.

"Mom?"

Claire's voice returned, anchoring the call. "What happened?"

Bradley sniffled and cleared his throat. "He was taken by some bad men. They went out in a boat and came back without him."

Claire sighed. "Did you see what happened?"

"Kind of. I was far away but had binoculars. It was dark. I could barely see anything." He paused as the memory of the morning's events rushed at him again. "O'Connor thinks octopuses might have gotten to him."

"From what I remember, O'Connor's a bit impulsive, right?"

"Yeah." Bradley smiled, just a bit, and it felt like a betrayal.

"Could he have swam back to shore?"

Bradley shook his head even though Claire had no way of knowing. "It's been too long."

"Brad, listen to me." Claire's voice held firm in his ear. "Your dad's a strong man. He doesn't give up easily. Don't lose hope and don't stop looking."

"But I don't even know where to start."

Claire sighed again. Bradley could hear the busyness of the hospital in the background and could picture her leaning against a wall near the ER with her eyes closed.

"Take some time to get over the initial shock, but not too long," she said. "Then talk with your friends. You're persistent and smart, a lot like your dad. Keep looking and you will find him. I know you will."

"You think so?" Bradley thought his voice sounded small.

"Yes. I have a hundred percent faith in you," Claire said. "And so does your dad."

"But... what if he's dead?"

"As long as he's still missing, he's alive." Claire paused for emphasis. "Believe that."

"Okay, Mom."

"Oh honey, I wish I could be there with you now."

Bradley stood and faced the window looking out over the cove. "You'd love it here. I'll send you some photos."

"I'd like that."

Bradley's tears had mostly dried up and he felt a little better. "I should get going. You know, make a plan and all that."

"Keep me in the loop," Claire said. "Your father and I may not be married any more, but I still care about him."

"Okay, Mom. I love you."

"I love you, too, honey." Bradley could hear her smile this time.

"And thanks," he said.

"Any time."

Bradley ended the call and felt some of the weight on his shoulders evaporate. He was lucky to have parents like Claire and Sam in his life. And Claire was right. Finding Sam would be a challenge he'd need help with. He left the cabin to search for his friends.

ONE OF THE last things Sam remembered before he was pulled over the stern of the *Wavy Jones* and into the water was flipping off Skulk and his partner. The satisfaction he felt partly made up for the pain radiating from his midsection. But as time passed, the pain subsided.

Am I dying?

He hit the water and the dawn sky refracted by the waves in front of his face shifted from reds to pinks. The visceral memory of feeling cold also stuck with him. Now under the water, the salty warmth enveloped his body and reassured him. He felt safe despite the gripping pressure around his mid-section.

He reached for his abdomen. Instead of sensing his fingertips on his skin, he ran his hand across a smooth surface that was hard, yet soft when it needed to be.

Could it be…

The impression of what was happening held more significance than what was really taking place. Fast-moving water buffeted his face, so his body instinctively made no attempt to breathe. When his lungs protested, through no actions of his own, his face breached the surface long enough to refill his lungs. Then he was pulled under again. It took a couple of breaths to time it right. Whatever was propelling him through the water was somehow in tune with his body and knew when he needed oxygen.

There Sam remained, just a couple of feet below the surface, with caustics and ripples blurring past his eyes. His body moved through the water at a speed he could never achieve on his own, even with swim fins. He imagined himself an astronaut tethered to a spacecraft moving thousands of miles an hour.

Sam went along for the ride, not overexerting himself. There was no need to struggle, yet he was tired, approaching exhaustion. The world in front of him, distorted by the fast-moving waves, dimmed even as the sun rose, until his world faded to black.

Then, just as quickly as it had begun, Sam could breathe again. He squinted to a sky filled with stars. Maybe he was an astronaut after all. Maybe he was dead and this was heaven.

He tried to sit up and barely could find the strength to move. Pain radiated from everywhere, but mostly from his belly. An unpleasant smell surrounded him, as if someone had used a dinghy as a toilet and set it adrift next to him once it was full.

Definitely not heaven. And I'm definitely not dead.

Sam laid his head back down and closed his eyes. Conserving his energy was his priority. He began running through what he could remember.

Fighting and cutting. Greed and rage. Strength in… numbers?

Skulk's unforgettable face flashed across his eyelids, her scar practically transferring onto Sam. Yet, something had helped him.

"Tentacles." Sam's hoarse and gravely voice echoed in the space where he lay. With his breathing slow and regular, he slipped back into a deep sleep and dreamed of octopuses.

THAT EVENING, BRADLEY, TRILLIAN, AND JACK sat around a gas fire table close to the bar. After Sam's disappearance in the morning, no one wanted to do anything for the rest of the day. It was like their joy of life had disappeared along with him. Even the lei hanging limply from Jack's neck was approaching the end of its life.

"Hey." Kailani approached the three of them. "Mind if I join?"

Jack pulled out the vacant chair for her. Once Kailani sat, silence returned to the group. The flames flickered in front of them, casting an orange glow on their faces. Unlike a real camp fire, the gas flames cast little warmth.

"I'm not sure if I said this before," Kailani said, "but I'm really sorry, Brad."

Bradley nodded. "Thanks."

"Did you call the police?"

Bradley settled his tired, red-rimmed eyes on Kailani's. It was clear that he had been crying recently. "Yeah. O'Connor and Hope called them."

"Let me guess," Kailani said. "They did nothing."

"Bingo." Jack's voice was flat and emotionless.

Kailani crossed her arms and clenched her teeth with anger. "Skulk's got most of this island by the balls."

"That bitch has to pay," Trillian said.

"But how?" Bradley stood and jettisoned his chair backward, flipping it on its back.

Trillian grabbed Bradley's chair and righted it. "What about the newspaper? O'Connor knows a reporter there."

Bradley paced back and forth. "I think that reporter values his life more than a story about a missing tourist. Especially if Skulk is as connected as Kai says she is."

"Maybe he's got journalistic integrity."

Bradley shook his head. "Whatever."

Jack stared into the flames. "I know how to get Skulk."

Bradley stopped his pacing and leaned on the table, his face just barely out of reach of the fire. "How?"

Trillian and Kailani exchanged glances before joining Bradley with inquisitive looks of their own.

"You get her where hurts," Jack said.

Bradley rolled his eyes. "And how the *fuck* do you suggest we do that?"

"You take away her precious treasure." Jack let his idea settle.

Kailani grabbed Jack's arm. "Stop fucking around. This is important."

"I'm not *fucking* around." Jack met Kailani's gaze, then looked at Bradley. "I think I know someone who can help."

Bradley balled his fists. "Who?"

Jack bounded from his chair and headed to the promenade. The others followed. He stopped at cabin 7 and followed the walkway to the porch.

"What the hell is he doing?" Bradley frowned at Trillian and Kailani. "Who's staying there?"

Jack bounded up onto the porch and knocked on the door. After a moment, Maddilyn poked her head out.

She looked past Jack and saw Bradley, Trillian, and Kailani standing back at the promenade. "Um, hi?"

"Hi." Jack put on his best smile even though it had been one of the worst days of his life. "We need your help."

Maddilyn balked. She knew Jack, sort of, but she was wary of the others.

"Please?" Jack looked back at the others. They all gave him

perplexed looks. He returned his gaze to Maddilyn. "It's about Skulk. We want to fuck her over."

Maddilyn's eyes changed in an instant. The worry was gone, replaced with a devious gleam.

Jack held out his hand and she took it. He led her back down the pathway to rejoin the others.

"Brad, Trillian, Kailani, this is Maddilyn Rockwell."

"We've met already." Kailani eyed Maddilyn with caution and a hint of something else.

"Right," Jack said.

Maddilyn surveyed the four teenagers. "So, you want to get Skulk, huh?"

Bradley fought hard to not reveal too much information. "Yeah. In a *big* way."

"I heard you were monster hunters. Skulk's definitely one." Maddilyn headed back toward the bar. "Come on, then. We don't have much time."

MADDILYN LED THE others back to the marina. Jack and Bradley followed at the back of the group. It was still early enough in the evening for people to be milling about. The same behavior during the day might be seen as suspicious now and the last thing they needed was a run-in with security.

The group snaked their way through the interconnected docks, trying not to look conspicuous. With every step, they grew closer to the largest yacht moored at the marina.

Jack leaned closer to Bradley. "Holy shit, dude. You know what that is?"

"A big boat?"

Jack chuckled while taking in the spectacle. "I should've clued in by now."

"What're you talking about?"

"That's *Roxette*." Jack looked at Bradley with an enamored grin and pointed at the stern. The name *Roxette* flowed across the transom in a scripted font. "Pandora Rockwell's mega yacht."

Bradley stared back at him. "That's—"

"Yup. Maddi's mom's 'big boat.'" He air quoted the words.

"Holy shit is right." Bradley looked up at the yacht, spanning one side of the marina. "God damn. Why is she even involved with Skulk anyway?"

"Beats me."

Jack and Bradley caught up with the girls.

"Slow poke." Trillian kissed Bradley, then whispered in his ear, "Can you believe it?"

Bradley shook his head, still in awe.

With jealousy simmering in her eyes, Kailani watched Jack sidle up to Maddilyn.

"You never said this was your mom's yacht," he said.

"I don't like to play all my cards all at once." Maddilyn looked at the others one by one, ending on Kailani. "People tend to judge you pretty quick if you do."

Jack nodded, then spotted Kailani's gaze and took a step back from Maddilyn. Even though he had limited experience interacting with girls, he knew the stink-eye when he saw it.

"My mom's hosting a presentation for investors, but it's going to be led by Skulk," Maddilyn said.

Bradley squatted and ran his hand over one of the thick woven ropes mooring the *Roxette*. "So how is this going to work? Obviously, we can't just walk in."

"I'll get you on board, somewhere hidden so you can watch." She checked the time on her phone. "It starts in about an hour, but we got to move quick because they're going to be setting up soon."

"Sounds risky," Trillian said.

"Yeah," Kailani added. "Why should we trust you? You're betraying your own mom for fuck's sake."

Maddilyn faced Kailani. "This isn't personal. This is business. Bad business, and I hate bad business."

"But it is kind of personal already," Kailani said. "Your mom's involved with Skulk, and that means she's connected with everything else Skulk's done." She cast a brief look at Bradley. "Sorry."

Bradley nodded at her. "It's okay."

"That's why I want to break up their partnership." Maddilyn sighed in frustration. "Look, I'm risking a lot bringing you guys here. I didn't have to do this."

Kailani and the others exchanged glances.

"Well, count me in," Bradley said. "I want to see that bitch go down."

Trillian grabbed Bradley's hand and gave it a squeeze. "I think we all do."

Jack nodded in agreement.

"Okay, but understand that I'm not an agent for my mom," Maddilyn said. "I make my own decisions. I've never been okay with what she's been doing with Skulk. I've just never met anyone on the same page. Until now."

"Let's do this," Bradley said.

Maddilyn stepped onto *Roxette's* transom and took the port-side steps up onto the main deck. She unlocked the door, led them through the main salon and up a second set of stairs to a smaller, more intimate area.

"This is what my mom calls the 'Sky Lounge'," Maddilyn said. "They're going to hold the presentation here."

The space was sparsely but tastefully decorated in teak tones with black and silver accents, and featured a bar on the port side and a counter with chilled hors d'oeuvres on the starboard side. The crew had already arranged individual seating into rows facing a curved panoramic window, but the leather sofas remained facing the port and starboard windows.

Jack surveyed the room. With all the seating moved in front of the stern-facing window, the space looked more like a dance hall than a lounge. "Where are we going to hide?"

"Can't be behind the bar," Kailani said. "Those rich fucks are going to want to get their drink on."

Maddilyn pulled open the double doors to a closet on the port side, near the entrance to the lounge and close to one of the port-side leather sofas. "This is going to have to do."

Bradley nodded. "Close to the entrance. That's good if we need to bolt."

Trillian looked inside the closet. "Jesus, it's almost as big as my bedroom back home."

Maddilyn shrugged. "What can I say. Bigger isn't always better."

Bradley laughed. "Isn't that what you always say, Jack?"

Jack raised his middle finger in response.

"Look, I got to get back," Maddilyn said. "So my mom doesn't suspect anything. And one more thing. I'm going to have to lock you in."

"In the closet?" Jack looked at her, confused.

"What? No." Maddilyn shook her head and rolled her eyes. "I have to lock the door where we came in, so no one gets suspicious. But don't worry. I'll be here later, and I'll make sure the door is unlocked."

"Okay." Jack stepped into the closet, followed by the others. He pulled out his phone and held it up to the space where the double doors closed together. A stripe of the presentation area between the two blurred door edges appeared on his camera's display. "I hope the sound can get through there."

Kailani eyed him in the darkness. "That's your only worry?"

Jack shrugged. "For now, yeah."

"So, we got some time to kill." Bradley looked at Trillian and flashed his eyebrows.

Jack noticed their exchange. "No making out, okay?"

"Jesus, man," Bradley said. "You need a girlfriend."

Jack swallowed instead of answering and everyone in the closet heard his throat click.

Kailani smirked and averted her gaze. Had there been more light in the closet, she would have seen the subtle tinge of pink rise on his cheeks.

Trillian slid her back down the wall until she was in a sitting position.

"Good idea." Bradley joined her, followed by Jack and Kailani.

Bradley kissed Trillian's forehead. "So, we got to kill an hour."

"Hopefully less time than that," Jack said. "The restaurant closes soon."

"How about another exciting game of 'Never Have I Ever'?" Kailani looked to the others. "Without the drinking of course."

"What's 'Never Have I Ever' without the drinking?" Trillian said.

"Boring." Jack shifted his eyes back and forth, focusing though the crack between the closet doors.

"Okay… What about truth or dare?" Bradley said.

Kailani raised a brow at him. "That could work."

"You're going to have to scale back the dares," Trillian said, "since we're, like, in a freaking *closet.*"

"That's doable." Kailani nodded at Trillian and Bradley. "What do you think, Jack?"

Jack sat back and took a spot next to Kailani. He pulled his knees close to his chest. "Sure, what the hell."

Bradley took out his phone. "I'll spin it. Whoever the power port is pointing at has to choose. And everyone has to play before you can play again."

"Too complicated," Trillian said. "Let's just go in order. You go first. Person on your right asks."

There was no one sitting to Bradley's right. "Jack, I guess you're up."

"Alright," Jack said. "Truth or dare?"

Bradley sat up straight and turned his body slightly to face the others. "Truth."

Jack narrowed his eyes at him. "Have you ever raw-dogged someone?"

Bradley laughed. "Jesus. You really go for the throat."

"It's not fun any other way," Jack said.

Trillian and Kailani shared a knowing glance, then focused their stare on Bradley.

"Yes," Bradley said. "And I was panicking for almost three weeks before I found out I wasn't going to be a dad. I don't recommend it… well I do, but I don't, if you know what I mean."

"No, Bradley Shaw," Trillian said. "I don't know what you mean. Please explain."

"Maybe later." Bradley could feel the heat of her green eyes even in the shadows of the closet. "Truth or dare, Trill?"

Trillian crossed her arms against her chest. "Truth."

Bradley leaned forward on his elbows. "Do you love me?"

"Whoa," said Kailani and Jack in unison. They rocked back and high-fived each other.

Trillian shushed them. "Keep it down. Someone might hear."

Kailani covered a giggle with her hand.

Bradley batted his eyelashes. "Well?"

"You're a little shit…" Trillian locked her gaze with Bradley's. "And yes."

"And there we have it, folks," Jack said. "There's no going back now."

"You're asking for it, man," Bradley said with a grin.

"Shh!" Trillian said. "We're going to get busted." She turned to Kailani and lowered her voice. "You're up, Kai. Truth or dare?"

A sly smile crept across Kailani's face. "Let's kick it up a notch. Dare."

Trillian moved from sitting to a kneeling position and peered through the crack between the two doors. She sat on her heels and glanced back at Kailani. "I dare you to steal an appetizer."

"No way," Jack said. "Bad idea. You'll get caught."

Kailani stole a peek out between the doors. "No one's been around since we got here."

"But they could walk in at any moment." Jack looked at her with wide eyes.

Kailani slowly pushed open one of the closet doors, changing the crack to a slightly bigger sliver. "I could do it. I'll be fast."

"You're crazy," Jack said.

Bradley nodded. "I agree."

"What's with the *wimpy-ass* guys in this crowd?" Without another word, Kailani pushed open the door wide enough to slip through and bolted for the hors d'oeuvres. She slid on the parquet floor and fell in front of the counter.

"Fuck." Jack closed his eyes. "I can't watch," he said before immediately opening one eye.

Kailani lifted one of the domed covers, grabbed a shrimp tartlet, and jammed it in her mouth. She froze when she heard a familiar *ding*.

"Oh fuck," she mumbled through a full mouth.

Bradley glanced at Trillian. "Was that an elevator?"

Trillian shrugged. "I… guess?"

Jack pressed himself against the back wall of the closet and shook his head. "She's going to get caught."

Kailani crouch-ran without hesitation back toward the closet, but slipped again. The sound of footsteps just outside the lounge grew louder. She scrambled on her hands and knees and flattened her body to the floor, between the leather sofa and window on the port side.

Jack pointed and strained out a whisper. "Shit! Look!"

Kailani had forgotten to recover the hors d'oeuvres. It sat next to the tray of shrimp tartlets. A staff member entered the lounge and busied themselves at the bar, then noticed the tray cover.

Jack held his index finger to his lips and mouthed the word "Quiet" to Bradley and Trillian.

Kailani slid herself along the floor until she had both a view of the closet door and was able to peek back at the staff member at the hors d'oeuvres counter.

All four teenagers held their breath and waited. Jack and Kailani watched from their particular locations as the staff member recovered the tray and surveyed the room. They jotted a note on a pad of paper, then walked back out of the lounge.

Kailani didn't wait for the sound of elevator doors opening. Instead, she scrambled toward the closet as fast as her hands and knees would allow.

Bradley held the door open until she was safe inside, then eased it closed.

Everyone let out a collective sigh of relief.

"Jesus Christ that was close," Jack said.

Kailani chewed and swallowed the tart. "And I almost choked on that fucking appy."

"Here's to badass girls." Trillian high-fived Kailani.

"What was it?" Bradley asked. "Did it taste good, at least?"

"Some shrimp thing," Kailani said. "It was passable. But I need some champagne to wash it down." She moved toward the doors. "Should I bring back the bottle?"

"You're joking, right?" Jack looked at her with wide, intense eyes.

"Of course." Kailani sat back down and grinned at him. "Your turn. Truth or dare, big boy."

Jack weighed the answer seriously, running through every possible answer he could think of. The wrong truth or dare could spell disaster, especially with undeniable heat between himself and Kailani.

"Just make a choice, man," Bradley said in a low annoyed voice. "It's not rocket science."

Jack smirked at him and flipped him his middle finger again.

Kailani grabbed it. "Quit stalling."

"Okay, okay." Jack pulled his hand back. "Dare."

Kailani grinned and licked her lips. "I dare you to kiss me."

"Uh, I meant to say truth," Jack said.

Trillian shook her head. "No way. You can't change what you pick."

Kailani sat back, looked at Trillian, and thrummed her fingers on her leg. "Whatever. Let him change it." She faced Jack. "Are you sure?"

"Yes," Jack said. "Truth."

Kailani leaned toward Jack, braced her chin in her palms, and fluttered her eyelashes. "Jack. Would you kiss me if I asked you to?"

Bradley stifled a laugh. "Oh, snap!"

"You're good." Trillian held out her fist and Kailani bumped it.

Jack smirked at Kailani. "You win. Yes."

Before Kailani could ask, voices rose up from the entryway to the lounge. "Rain check," she said.

For the second time that evening, Jack could feel heat rise on his neck. He nodded at her, smiled, then dug out his phone.

The lounge filled with half a dozen men in expensive clothes, with Pandora, Maddilyn, Skulk, Niko, and a couple staff members leading the way. After filling their plates with hors d'oeuvres and grabbing a flute of champagne, everyone found seats.

Maddilyn whispered something in Pandora's ear, then exited the way she came in. As she passed the closet, she flashed a quick but subtle thumbs up.

Jack started the camera app on his phone and began recording video. He positioned it at the crack between closet doors and framed Skulk as best he could. But he had a nagging doubt that he'd be able to pick up any audio at all.

"WELCOME TO ROXETTE, my floating office, and to Club Niho'gula," Pandora said. "I trust my private jet met your needs?"

Nods and murmurs floated through the six attendees. One man raised his champagne flute and nodded at her with appreciation.

Pandora reciprocated cordially and continued. "Many of you know me as the founder of award-winning Rockwell Simulations. My success has allowed the pursuit of many side interests, one of which includes treasure hunting. I have traveled—"

A man stood up. "I don't mean to interrupt, Ms. Rockwell, or Pandora if I may, but we've all read your detailed prospectus. I think I speak for everyone here..." The man paused and shrugged. "Just show us the money... or gold in this case." He looked to the others in their seats. "Am I right, fellas?"

A chorus of "hear hear" rose from the five other men.

Pandora exchanged a knowing glance with Skulk, then faced the men. "Very well. I'm not one to stand in the way of efficiency. Instead, I invest in it. The only way to scale an endeavor like this is with investment." She scanned the group. "I think you're going to like what we're offering. Now, I'd like to introduce the leader of our expedition, Nina Skulk."

The seated men exchanged looks of uncertainty, then offered a smattering of applause.

With a stone face, Skulk stared at each potential investor in turn. "If you don't like the fact that I'm a woman, you can get the fuck out right now. Take a long walk on our short pier."

The investors remained seated, many of them straightening their posture.

"Good. I'm going to cut to the chase. Because money talks and bullshit walks." Skulk pulled off her paracord loop of treasure, the gold coins threaded on it clinked against one another, glittering under the overhead pot lights.

Niko stepped closer to Skulk and moved his hands from behind his back to the front, the cool blue steel of his pistol gripped in his right hand for everyone to see.

Skulk approached a man in the first row and held up the tethered coins. "Care for a closer look?"

The man answered by reaching out. Skulk handed him the coins as Niko moved to the back of the group, blocking the only exit. As each man examined the coins, Skulk continued.

"What you're holding is pure twenty-four karat gold, and dates back to before the Qin Dynasty, over two centuries before the birth of Christ, if you believe in that shit." Skulk watched the dollar signs of greed flicker in the men's eyes.

"There are hundreds of thousands more of those coins," Skulk said. "And we've mapped their locations in this cove and along the coastline north and south. All that's left is to retrieve them. It's a job that must be done quickly and covertly to avoid certain *jurisdictional* issues."

"Is what you're doing legal?" asked one man.

"Sounds like you don't trust me. Niko, escort this asshole out of here."

Niko pulled back the slide on his pistol, pointed it at the man, and nodded toward the exit. The other investors and staff backed away.

The man instinctively raised his hands in front of his face. "No, no. I trust you. It was just a question. I swear. I want to invest. Really."

Silence overwhelmed the lounge for a moment, until Skulk shook her head at Niko and gave him a thumbs up.

Niko eased the pistol's hammer to its rest position and resumed his watchful stance. The investors resumed their seats.

"I trust you've had enough time to examine the goods?" Skulk reclaimed the threaded medallions and strung the paracord loop back around her neck. "Now, it's time to show *us* the money."

Niko corralled the group of men to the bar countertop, where one of the staff members had placed a stack of investment contracts and a pen. Niko walked around to the bar, pushed the staff bartender aside and pulled out a bottle of scotch and eight glasses. He began pouring ample portions in each when a sharp noise echoed from the back of the lounge.

A phone lay spinning on the parquet floor in front of a partially open closet door.

SWEAT BEADED ON Jack's forehead. Despite the size of the closet, the air inside had become hot and humid from the breath of four anxious teenagers. If the closet had had a window, they would have fogged it up.

"We're going to fucking *nail* her ass," Kailani whispered into Jack's ear. Her breathy words made the hairs on the back of his neck stand on end.

"Not if we can't *hear* anything." Jack tapped his lips, shushing her, then eased the closet door open.

"What the hell are you doing?" Bradley hissed through his teeth and glared at him.

"I just need a little more access to the sound." Jack looked at him. "This might be the only evidence we can get that will put her away." He considered his next words for a moment. "I'm doing it for your dad."

Bradley backed down and Trillian hugged him.

Jack pushed his phone out between the closet doors just enough to allow unblocked access to the microphone. But he struggled to keep the video framed at the same time.

Just a bit longer. Skulk's almost finished.

Trillian moved closer to Jack. "Thanks to you, the police are going to have everything they need to take this bitch down."

"Nah," Kailani whispered back. "Take it to another island. The police here are probably in the back pocket of the billionaire that owns this place."

"Larry Ellison?" Jack said in a low voice. "I can't believe that. Other than being uber-rich and a lousy husband, he's an okay guy. And his yacht is even bigger than this."

Kailani shrugged. "Whatever. Still, take it to another island."

"Wouldn't different islands have different rules?" Bradley said quietly.

Kailani shook her head. "Not if it's a protected heritage site, which Nihoʻgula Cove is, as well as the wrecks farther north."

The hand Jack had used to hold his phone began to cramp up. As he prepared to switch hands to offer his right some relief, he spotted Niko draw his pistol on the screen and point it at one of the guests. Anxious fear shot through his belly.

"Guys!" he whispered a yell and nodded toward his phone's display. The others surrounded him to get a closer look.

"Can you hear what's going on?" Kailani asked.

"Maybe after, if the microphone can pick it up." He glanced back at Kailani, "But we need to stop talking or the phone will pick up us instead of her."

"This better be worth it," Bradley said.

Jack exchanged a look with him and chose not to respond.

Whatever had happened in the lounge appeared to have resolved itself. Niko had put down his pistol and Skulk had retrieved her collection of gold coins.

"Look how many that bitch has." Even though her voice was subdued, Kailani's disgust was clear.

Jack's phone showed the group of businessmen being led to the bar. Now would be a good time to switch hands.

Bradley squinted at the display. "What's that on the bar?"

Kailani moved closer. "Probably contracts. The coward always wants other people to do what she would never do herself."

Jack grabbed the opposite corner of the phone with his left hand and released it with his right. Transfer successful.

"See?" Kailani raised a finger to point at the display and bumped Jack's shoulder ever so slightly. "There's a pen beside—"

The world seemed to slip into slow motion. Jack's phone slipped out of his hand and fell to the wooden parquet floor in front of the closet. It landed with a loud *crack* and spun in place.

"Fuck." Jack turned back to the terrified gazes of his friends. There was no time to think, yet that's exactly what he was doing. The first thought through Jack's head was how he had failed Sam. The second was whether or not Skulk had a gun too. His third thought—

"Run!" Kailani's eyes were wide with fear. She burst through the closet doors and charged back out of the sky lounge, followed closely by Bradley and Trillian.

Jack dropped to his knees and lunged for his phone, his sweaty fingers scrabbling for purchase on the slick, smooth lines of the device. He grabbed it on his second attempt and jammed it into his pocket.

He saw Niko raise his pistol and move from behind the bar. Jack spun around on the floor toward the exit.

Here it comes. This is where I die.

Jack scrambled on all fours until the treads of his shoes gripped and bolted in the same direction his friends had gone, cringing and preparing his body for the inevitable impact of a bullet.

But the bullet never came. As he rounded the corner and headed down the stairs to the stern deck, a hand reached out and grabbed him. His lei disintegrated into a twisted pile of dead kika and ginger blossoms.

Jack fell backward. A hand gripped the collar of his T-shirt and pulled him into the main salon.

Maddilyn stepped in front and offered her hand. "Come on!"

Jack took her hand without hesitation and followed her into the heart of the yacht.

O'CONNOR AND HOPE sat on one side of the open air bar, close to where Gus worked his magic for the guests. They both nursed beers. Special drinks like Mai Tais didn't feel right.

"I refuse to believe he's gone." Hope took a swig of her beer.

O'Connor sighed heavily. "Don't mean to be blunt, honey, but without a body, we can't be sure of anything."

"Easier said than done. He's my guy."

"Think of it as… an extended absence." O'Connor finished her beer and raised the empty, catching Gus's attention. She stood, then leaned over the small table. "I'll find him, Hope, if it's the last thing I do."

O'Connor thanked Gus for the two fresh beers and carried them back to the table. "Drink up." She took a long swallow, burped, and slouched in her chair.

Raucous laughter and boisterous talk rose from across the bar's seating area. Skulk, Niko, and a group of men had pushed a couple of tables together. Skulk had her string of medallions on display in front of her shirt.

Servers offended by the disrespectful display left a bottle of alcohol for the men to serve themselves.

"The assholes are out in force tonight." Gus stood behind O'Connor's and Hope's table, drying a glass with a towel. "I wonder if they realize the curse they've awakened." He shook his head. "Disgusting."

"Wait." Hope looked up at Gus. "I thought Sam released the curse."

"It feeds on itself," Gus said. "Infecting others, like Sam, and you. It just gets stronger."

"Bah." O'Connor brushed them off and turned to watch Skulk's group with narrowed eyes.

Skulk refilled her business associates' drinks, emptying the bottle. She pounded it on the table and stared at Gus. "You! Barkeep! More tequila." Her associates laughed and echoed her request.

"Be right back, guys." Gus disappeared behind the bar counter and grabbed a fresh bottle of tequila. He walked it over to the Skulk's table.

"Don't just stand there, jackoff," Skulk said. "Pour."

Gus clenched his jaws and said nothing. He twisted off the bottle cap and refilled the glasses.

"Next time don't spill any or I'll have you fired," Skulk said.

Gus shook his head and pointed at the medallions around Skulk's neck. "You've really done it this time."

"What, the *curse?*" Skulk leaned into the table. "This jackass believes…" She glanced at a few other servers who had stopped to watch from a distance. "*All* of them believe these treasures are cursed." She burst into laughter, her associates joining in.

"It's all *bullshit!*" Skulk scowled at Gus. "Leave the bottle and get the fuck out of here."

Gus shrugged and stepped away from the table. He turned to find O'Connor and Hope standing behind him. O'Connor's face was red with anger.

"I tried to stop her," Hope said.

"You sure about this, partner?" Gus locked gaze with O'Connor.

"I've got nothing to lose."

"You sure about that?"

O'Connor glared back at Gus, through him.

"Suit yourself." Gus stepped around O'Connor and headed back to the bar.

Skulk spotted O'Connor. "You!" She jettisoned her chair behind her and stormed around the table to confront O'Connor. Skulk's business associates fell silent, a mixture of confusion and interest on their faces.

O'Connor stood her ground as she always did.

Skulk looked down on the stout woman, her eyes filled with hate. "I've been meaning to wipe the floor with your ass since we first met."

"You killed my friend, motherfucker. Now it's your turn." O'Connor used Skulk's drunken state to her advantage. She raised her left knee into the woman's thigh, but Skulk twisted her hips at the last second and deflected O'Connor's blow.

Skulk was more sober than she appeared. Quick as lightning, she had wrapped her left hand around O'Connor's throat and squeezed. With her right, she drew her pistol and jammed the barrel under O'Connor's chin.

"Seems to me you're lying." Skulk leaned in, their noses almost touching. "Better think carefully about what you're going to say next, *fat bitch.*"

O'Connor struggled to speak, but with her windpipe closed up she couldn't utter a word.

"Let her go, you *cunt,*" Hope said.

Skulk ignored her and pulled the hammer back on her pistol, locking her eyes on O'Connor's.

Gus ran back from the bar, ushering Hope behind him. "Ms. Skulk. On behalf of the club, please accept my apologies for this guest's outburst. It was uncalled for."

Gus's comment seemed to make O'Connor angrier. She fought against Skulk's grip, but was no match for the woman's iron grasp.

Niko appeared next to Skulk and subtly motioned toward her new business associates. The group gaped at Skulk and her pistol with concern. No words were needed.

Skulk pulled the pistol's barrel away from O'Connor's throat and eased the hammer back. "You're going to keep your fat bitchy mouth shut, right? Or you…" She glanced at Hope coldly. "And your *friends* are going to have a problem." She pushed O'Connor backward and released her grip.

O'Connor collapsed into Gus's arms. With Hope's help, they escorted her back to their table. She stared back at Skulk's table, rubbing her bruised throat with fresh hatred in her eyes. "*She's* the one who's going to have a problem."

"She's not worth it, O'Connor," Hope said. "There's nothing you can do to bring Sam back."

Gus nodded. "Listen to your friend."

O'Connor looked at them both. "I may not be able to bring Sam back, but there's *lots* I can do."

RECIPROCATE

MADDILYN LED JACK through the middle of the yacht's lower salon, down another set of stairs, to a long central corridor. She directed him into a stateroom with a queen bed.

"Here." Maddilyn pulled him into a closet, followed him in, and closed the door. She collected the metal hangers, pushed them to one side, and squeezed them to stop their jingling.

Both of them huddled in the darkness, breathing heavily yet trying to stay quiet.

The thumping of heavy footsteps passed back and forth on the deck above several times.

"Holy shit, that was cl—"

Maddilyn pressed one hand over Jack's mouth, and raised an index finger to her lips, shushing him. She cocked an ear, listening, then leaned into his ear, so close that the swell of her breasts pressed against his chest. Jack wouldn't have been able to form words at that moment even if he tried.

"Wait. Stay here," Maddilyn whispered. "Don't make a sound." She slipped out of the closet and closed the door.

After a moment, curiosity got the better of him. Jack crept up to the closet door and peeked out.

Maddilyn lay on the bed reading something on her phone. She spotted movement from the closet and glared at Jack. She waved at him to go back in.

Jack quickly realized why and closed the closet door.

"Maddi?" Footsteps closed in from the corridor. It was Pandora's voice. "Maddi?"

"In here."

Jack heard Pandora step into the stateroom.

"Have you heard or seen anything strange in the past little while?"

"I heard stomping around above," Maddilyn said. "What happened?"

"What about before that?"

Maddilyn pretended to think back. "No. But I was pretty into my book. Did your meeting go okay?"

Pandora didn't answer immediately and Jack began to panic. He pictured her opening the closet and taking him to Skulk, where the woman would tie him to an anchor and throw him overboard.

Finally, Pandora spoke. "It was… different."

"Different how?"

"Just different. Let me know if you see anything odd. Right away. It's important."

"Okay," Maddilyn said. "Oh, Mom? Is it okay if I sleep here tonight?"

Pandora had already left the stateroom and was walking back up the corridor that led to the salon. "Yeah, sure. Be good," she called back. "And keep your eyes open for anything strange."

Silence filled the stateroom, until Jack heard the door to the room close. Maddilyn opened the closet door and grinned. "She's gone."

Jack gazed around the stateroom. The decor matched the sky lounge (and everywhere else on the yacht he had managed to see during his brief exposure), with sandy teak walls and silver and black fixtures. A long rectangular window stretched the length of the room, positioned at just the right height for a person to stand and look out the port side of the yacht. The sheets and duvet cover looked like silk. He wouldn't see this level of opulence again for a long time, or at least until he became rich from his inventions.

"This place is amazing," Jack said.

Maddilyn smiled and peered at him through her blond bangs. "Nothing but the best for my mom." She backed up, sat on the bed, and patted it gently with her hand.

Jack tilted his head to listen. "You sure it's okay?"

Maddilyn strolled to the stateroom door and locked it. "You're safe. No one's getting in now." She returned to the bed and held out her hand.

Jack stepped out of the closet, took her hand, and sat next to her. "So…"

Maddilyn drew invisible lines on Jack's palm with her index finger. "I'm really glad I met you."

"Yeah, me too."

"I mean, traveling with my mom is cool and all, but it's also, like, *so* boring," Maddilyn said. "There's never anyone my age to hang with." Her blue eyes zeroed in on Jack's. "And now there is."

"How old are you, anyway?" Jack cleared his throat. He could feel his self-consciousness heating up. "If you don't mind me asking that is."

"Seventeen. What about you."

"Eighteen."

Maddilyn leaned toward Jack and locked her gaze with his again. "Want to fuck?" She had asked the question in such a casual way that it caught him off guard.

"Uh…" Jack imagined himself doing a spit-take. "Yeah. Sure."

Maddilyn wiggled out of her shorts and peeled off her top. She pulled off Jack's T-shirt, pushed him back onto the bed, and pulled his shorts down to meet his shoes and socks.

Jack took in the spectacle of Maddilyn, dressed only in a pink bra and panties, but he wouldn't have remembered their color if his life depended on it.

This is what I've been missing.

She straddled his legs and began laying a trail of kisses, moving all the way up his abdomen, chest, and finally settling on his neck.

Jack let her warm and smooth skin slide over him, but curiously he was counting the tiles in the ceiling.

What the hell, dude?

Jack placed his hands gently on Maddilyn's hips, hoping to distract himself, but his anxiety—

Panic.

—spiked. He kept thinking about Kailani instead.

Maddilyn eased herself back and cast him a sideways look.

Jack stared back at her, his eyes wide. He imagined a look of terror on his face and that made him feel even worse.

"Are you okay?"

Jack sighed and draped one arm across his face. "Sorry. It's not you. It's *definitely* not you."

Maddilyn sat up, confused. "Are you, like, into guys or something?"

Jack shook his head. "No. It's just that... I don't have a lot of experience in this area." He paused. "Like, *no* experience."

"You're a *virgin?*"

Jack shrugged sheepishly and managed half a smile.

"Why didn't you say anything?"

"I don't normally advertise it."

"Cool." Maddilyn kissed him on his lips, then his chest. "I've never popped someone's cherry before."

"Oh, Jesus," Jack groaned.

She laid down more kisses, moving toward the waistband of his underwear. "Don't worry. I'll go slow."

"Actually..." Jack closed his eyes and shook his head almost imperceptibly.

Am I really doing this?

"Can we just talk?"

Maddilyn sat up again, her confusion replaced with crushed

anticipation and a little sadness. She slid off his groin and sat on the heels of her feet beside his hips. She noticed the lack of enlargement in his underwear.

"Please, don't take this the wrong way," Jack said. "You're super hot." He let is eyes wander her body for a moment. "I mean *super* hot… I'm just not quite ready. When I get stuck in my head like this, it almost always kills the mood. But it's not your fault, Maddi. Not at all."

Maddilyn took a moment to gauge his sincerity. "Okay."

"Friends?"

She nodded. "Friends."

The two of them dressed, then reclined on the bed next to each other.

"Can I ask you a question?"

Maddilyn nodded. "Sure."

"Why is your mom doing this? I mean, clearly she doesn't need the money."

Maddilyn sighed. "She always wants more. She's told me before that she's doing it all for me, to pay for college, my wedding and all that. But I know that's bullshit. It's all a fucking excuse and she's using me to justify it."

"But she's partnered with a killer," Jack said. "Skulk killed my best friend's dad, maybe others too. And that makes her guilty by association. Does she realize that?"

"I don't know. She probably wouldn't even believe me." Maddilyn fidgeted with her fingers. "Did Skulk really kill your friend's dad?"

"We think so," Jack said softly. "He went out into the cove with Skulk and never came back."

Maddilyn thought for a moment. "You know, I love my mom, but this shit with Skulk has to stop." She looked at him. "Whatever you need while you're here, let me know."

"Are you sure?" Jack gave her a wary eye. "You could get your mom into a lot of trouble."

"She's an adult. She brought it on herself," Maddilyn said. "And I'm sure."

"Thanks." Jack gave Maddilyn's hand a gentle squeeze. Something about the way she looked back at him caused small butterflies to flutter within his stomach, just a few. He expected her to come on to him again, but she didn't.

Instead, Maddilyn did the opposite. "It's dark out now. You better be getting back."

"Yeah."

"You stay here," she said. "I'll go make sure the coast is clear." She threw him a beige hoodie. "Put that on. It'll hide your face."

Before Jack could answer, Maddilyn had slipped out of the stateroom. He pulled on the hoodie. It had the Calvin Klein logo across the front and smelled faintly of perfume, probably CK IN2U.

A few moments later, Maddilyn returned and escorted Jack off the yacht. Standing on the transom, she kissed his cheek. "Whoever gets you is a lucky girl. Now go. Quick."

"Thanks." Jack stepped onto the pier. "I'll get the hoodie back to you tomorrow." When she didn't answer, he waved and ran through the marina, along the promenade, and back toward cabin #14. With every step, his mind wandered…

Were there tears in Maddi's eyes?

He pushed the thought out of his head, justifying it as a figment of his overactive imagination. Warm light glowed from within the cabin. His friends were still awake.

Jack bounded up the path and onto the porch. He tried the door and found it locked. He knocked. "Guys, it's Jack. Let me in."

After a brief moment of silence, he could hear scrambling footsteps and excited voices from within. Bradley opened the door and immediately pulled Jack into a tight hug.

"Thought we lost you, man." He stepped back and held Jack by the shoulders. "Are you hurt?"

"No."

Bradley stepped aside to allow Jack to enter.

Trillian gave him a friendly tap on his shoulder. "We're, like, *so* glad you're okay."

Jack smiled and nodded at her. Then, as he moved farther into the cabin, he saw Kailani standing to one side, her eyes wide and glistening.

Jack didn't know what to say. He hadn't expected to see her here. Instead, he said the only thing on his mind.

"Kai…"

Kailani walked quickly, practically skipping. She kissed him deeply on the lips, then pulled him into a tight embrace.

As they settled into each other's arms, Jack felt his insides flutter in all the *right* ways. He realized that there really had been tears in Maddilyn's eyes before. Now he knew the reason why.

"Sorry," Kailani said.

Jack looked at her, confused. "What…? Why?"

"I didn't *ask* you to kiss me."

"So… ask me."

Kailani's rich brown eyes stared into his. "Jack, will you kiss me?"

Jack nodded. "Yeah." He took her face gently in his hands and kissed her again.

The two of them noticed the silence in the cabin. They turned to find Bradley and Trillian sitting on the sofa and beaming at them.

"What happened, man?"

Jack pushed the coffee table out of the way and sat on the floor. Kailani took a spot next to him.

"Maddi saved me," he said. "She pulled me out of sight and hid me in a stateroom."

"How long did it take before she jumped your bones?" Trillian laughed.

"Jesus, Trill." Bradley gave Trillian a small poke on the shoulder.

"Sorry Kai. I had to say it."

Kailani stiffened at the comment. "No. You didn't."

Jack stared back at Trillian, heat already rising on his neck.

Bradley did a double take. "Holy shit, you actually *did* it?"

"Truth." Trillian exchanged a quick, sympathetic look with Kailani, as if perhaps the truth would hurt.

Jack swallowed hard. "She tried to. But by that time, I was already taken." He looked at Kailani. "Not officially of course, but in my head I was."

Kailani saw that Bradley and Trillian believed him and that was good enough for her. She grabbed Jack's hand, entwined her fingers with his, and smiled. "Consider yourself officially taken."

Bradley sat forward on the sofa. "What'd you learn, if anything?"

"She's on our side," Jack said. "She may be Rockwell's daughter, but she's also pretty cool. And she hates what her mom is doing. If there's anything we need, Maddi's got our backs."

"Have you had a chance to check your phone?" Trillian asked. "Maybe tonight was a giant fuck up."

"No." Jack turned around and slid his back up against the sofa. He took Kailani's hand and pulled her next to him.

Jack slid his phone out of his pocket and cued up the video he had taken on the *Roxette*. All four teenagers sat and watched the display with anticipation.

The video quality was good enough to recognize key players and the sound was low but audible.

"Get that shit up to the cloud, stat," Trillian said.

The others stared at her for a second, then everyone burst out laughing.

Jack turned off his phone. "Guys, fuck those coins. *This* is gold. But Skulk knows it was us."

Kailani nodded at him, concerned. "He's right."

"Skulk knows you and she knows about all of us," Jack continued, "This resort is small and that room was full of witnesses, including Rockwell. And…" He felt his neck and chest. "I lost my lei. That was my trademark."

"We'll find you *another* one." Kailani winked at him.

"On *that* note, we should get some sleep." Bradley stood and headed toward his bedroom.

"But what's going to stop Skulk from breaking in like before and killing us all?" Jack's brain busied itself imagining all the wrong scenarios.

Kailani looked to the others. "How about we grab some blankets and sleep under the stars?"

"I like that idea," Jack said with a smile.

Trillian nodded. "Me too."

"But…" Bradley held up a finger. "Get that video uploaded first. Then hide your phone here, recording. Maybe we'll catch them breaking in to kill us."

"Genius." Jack uploaded his video from the *Roxette,* then set up his phone up behind a towel in the bathroom and set it to record the front door.

With a few blankets and some snacks, the four friends set out past the north end of the beach and found a secluded spot where a small grassy patch met the rocky bluffs. They spread out blankets, ate too many snacks, and watched the stars float by.

By the time the sun rose, Jack was no longer a virgin.

MADDILYN CHOSE TO stay on *Roxette* for the night. Pandora wouldn't miss her. The crew had retired to their own onboard rooms for the evening, giving her free run of the mega yacht.

Her first stop was the kitchen where she fixed herself a meal of leftover hors d'oeuvres, both savory and sweet. She washed it all down with a tall rum and Coke, heavy on the rum. Maddilyn couldn't stand beer.

She visited the sky lounge, and kept her eyes peeled for anything she could share with Jack. Due to his less than enthusiastic response to her being practically naked in front of him, her gut instinct said he was interested in someone else. Extra evidence would mean another chance to see him. Maddilyn could be very convincing if she wanted to be.

She found a blank contract that had fallen behind the bar. It laid out the terms and conditions for investing in Pandora's salvage operation, and how she would divide the treasure among the investors.

Maddilyn shrugged. Without a signature, she suspected the document would carry less weight legally, but it did have Pandora and Skulk named as the partners in the operation. She folded it and tucked it into a back pocket.

She returned to her stateroom and locked the door. She had heard rumors of the sexual liaisons between staff and guests and wanted no part of it.

She cued up her steamy romance audiobook where she had left off, but it failed to capture her attention. Her mind kept wandering back to Jack.

Maddilyn switched on the big screen TV. She had access to thousands of streaming programs and movies, even porn, but nothing jumped out at her. She wanted something, or *someone,* she couldn't have.

With a full stomach and a rum and Coke blasting through her head, she had barely pulled the covers over herself before sleep won out. Maybe she'd dream of Jack.

Maddilyn woke early, just after five in the morning. Indirect dawn light crept into the stateroom's long horizontal window and washed the walls with pinks and oranges.

This port-side stateroom didn't face the rising sun, and for that Maddilyn was thankful. She groaned and covered her throbbing head with her pillow. A regular hangover overpowered anything that a dream could have left behind, and direct sunlight right now would have made her head explode for sure.

Squinting, she staggered to the bathroom, undressed, and threw herself into a cold shower. The cool water helped her head, but there was something that would work better: a dip in the ocean.

Maddilyn toweled off and pulled on her favorite one-piece bathing suit. Golden cat's paw prints a little larger than a silver dollar covered the stretchy black fabric in a haphazard pattern.

She grabbed a towel, left the yacht, and made her way to the end of the pier, passing the Palakiko Tours boathouse on the way. She set her towel down next to the corner of the pier, where a break in the railing led to a ladder extending into the ocean. The sky was brighter now, and she could feel her headache gaining traction again.

Maddilyn tied up her hair with an elastic. Instead of climbing down the ladder, she dove into the clear water. The cool shock of the water began to reset her body almost at once. She looked across the cove, spotted a distinct rocky outcropping to use as her guide, and pushed off.

She propelled herself forward in a strong front crawl, aided by her experience on the swim team back at school. When she reached the opposite side of the cove, she took a moment to look back at the marina. It looked a lot closer than it actually was. The morning sun had topped the Maui mountains to the east and bathed Club Nihoʻgula in warm light. Even in the seventy degree water, Maddilyn could feel the sun's heat on her skin. She dove back into the water to start her swim back, her headache almost gone.

It was difficult for Maddilyn to tell how far she had gone when she first felt something grip one of her legs. Being so close to the water's surface distorted her judgment of distance. Whatever it was snaked around her right calf, then up both thighs to her abdomen, making swimming next to impossible. If she didn't start working her legs treading water, she'd sink like a stone.

Maddilyn jammed her chin close to her chest in an attempt to see what was attacking her, but whatever it was hovered just below the surface.

She tried grabbing the mysterious thing, but it was too slippery to grasp. And strong. Whatever it was felt hard, like a smooth tree branch had grown around her body.

Maddilyn had managed to control her fear and panic until she felt a sharp pain run across her midsection. Whatever had her in its clutches had teeth *everywhere*.

The water around her was no longer blue, but tinged pink. With her blood. She thrashed in the water, struggling with all her strength, desperate to escape.

Then she saw what it was and screamed.

Octopus!

A gray tentacle wound its way out of the water, over her chest, between her breasts, and under her bathing suit's left shoulder strap. The tentacle twisted and retracted. The entire one-piece bathing suit fell away from Maddilyn's body. The fabric had been sliced all the way through, from the right leg opening, across the front, and through the left strap. In its place, wherever the tentacle had touched her suit, her skin below revealed a dotted line of gashes left behind, all of them seeping blood.

She screamed again and resumed her struggle. Curiously, her arms and legs had remained untouched. And as quickly as the attack began, she found herself alone again. But completely naked. An octopus had forced an impromptu skinny dip on her. It made no sense.

Weakened from her battle, Maddilyn chose to swim toward the beach instead of the marina. At least the water would get shallower the closer she got.

She focused on the row of cabins, specifically cabin 7. Maybe if she yelled loud enough, her mom would hear. But with her depleted energy and blood loss, she could hardly maintain forward movement, much less yell.

Maddilyn refused to drown less than a hundred feet from shore in a Hawaiian paradise. However, her body had other ideas. Mainly stopping and sinking.

Her eyes burned as she blinked and sputtered sea water. Perhaps this was it, because her arms and legs could not keep her afloat any longer.

She took one last breath before the ocean took her.

SOMETHING STARTLED JACK out of sleep. He checked on the others but no one else was awake. Kailani lay snuggled up next to him, snoring softly. Honestly, it was the best way to wake up. Now that he was no longer a virgin, he felt different, more adult.

But what woke me up?

An eagle or an owl? A boat horn? He was normally a heavy sleeper, but something had gripped him. He felt particularly attuned to his surroundings. Jack eased himself out of Kailani's arms and sat up, his ears primed for anything out of the ordinary.

A scream rose up from across the cove and caused the hairs on the back of his neck to stand on end. He knew that voice instantly. He didn't know how, but he knew.

Maddi?

Jack stood and in the early morning light he saw splashing in the middle of the cove, about halfway to the marina.

"Shit! Guys!" Jack was already in his underwear. He yanked off his shirt and tossed it on the ground next to Kailani. "Come on. Wake up!"

"Jack?" Bradley groaned. "What the fuck?"

"It's Maddi! She's in trouble." Jack bolted down the rocky

bluff without waiting for a response. He oriented himself to Maddilyn's splashing and dove in.

Jack settled into a front crawl powered by sheer adrenaline. His lean body cut through the water with ease.

He scanned the surface for Maddilyn's position and discovered that she had headed for shore.

Smart move.

He readjusted his trajectory and swam after her, gaining on her with every stroke. A dozen more feet and he'd be by her side. But when he checked the surface again, Maddilyn was nowhere in sight.

"MADDI?" Jack scrutinized the water and the beach beyond, looking for a sign. The water was as calm as it should be at this hour of the morning. Until it wasn't.

Fingertips breached the surface just for a second. Jack channeled all his strength and dove under the water. He'd have to pull her to the surface or she'd drown.

He opened his eyes. The seawater stung his eyes and everything was blurry, but there was enough sunlight to guide him to Maddilyn's body.

Jack hooked his arms under hers and swam to the surface. His lungs burned. He could only imagine how Maddilyn's felt.

Both broke the surface and fresh air filled Jack's lungs.

"Maddi! Are you okay?" Jack treaded water and positioned Maddilyn on her back. "MADDI?"

He considered trying mouth-to-mouth, but instead chose to get her to the shore. It was then that he realized she was completely naked. And there were small bleeding cuts running across her body.

What the…?

He swam to shore and rolled her to her side. "Maddi? Wake up!" Jack checked for a pulse, then laid her on her back, tilted her head, and lifted her chin. He pinched her nose, sealed his mouth to hers, and blew five breaths.

Maddilyn didn't respond. Jack laced his fingers together and compressed her chest to a count of thirty. He supplied two more breaths and repeated the process.

The second round of compressions brought her back. Maddilyn gasped and Jack rolled her to her side again. She vomited into the sand.

He pulled her into his arms in an attempt to preserve her modesty, but only dressed in underwear himself, there wasn't much he could do. Maddilyn grabbed hold of him and burst into tears.

"You're going to be okay." Jack looked up and saw Bradley, Trillian, and Kailani, standing at the surf line. Kailani held an open blanket. He managed a smile and nodded at her.

Jack found Maddilyn's face from behind her wet and sandy hair. "Can you stand? Kai's got a blanket."

Maddilyn nodded. Jack helped her up and Kailani took over, wrapping Maddilyn with Club Niho'gula-branded fleece.

"Let's get her to sit." Trillian pointed at a row of chaise lounges.

Jack and Kailani helped Maddilyn over to one and sat with her. Bradley and Trillian crouched in the sand in front.

"How're you doing?" Jack eyed Maddilyn, concerned. Kailani noticed.

"Thanks to y-you, I'm alive." She looked briefly at Jack, her words broken up by her shivering, despite the warm blanket enveloping her.

"What happened?"

Maddilyn paused to think. "I was just ta-taking a morning swim. Out of n-nowhere, an octopus attacked me. For no fu-fucking reason."

Jack and Kailani shared a glance.

"It was just l-like when my m-mom got attacked," Maddilyn continued. "And it left… the same little c-cuts." With a trembling hand, she exposed her left shoulder. Small bloody incisions ran from her shoulder and across her chest to her cleavage, before the blanket obscured her remaining wounds. But the cuts looked almost healed, like the injury had happened days ago.

Jack's jaw dropped. "This happened to your mom?"

Maddilyn nodded. "B-before you got here." She scrunched her brow, thinking back. "I think it w-was the same d-day."

Jack looked at Kailani again. He could tell she knew what he was going to say—

Octopuses do *attack people.*

—but he decided to keep his thoughts to himself. It would do no good to rehash old arguments.

Then Kailani surprised him. She looked to the rest of the group. "But why? Octopuses attacking people just doesn't make sense."

"So you agree?" Jack held Kailani's gaze. "That the octopuses here are a threat?"

Kailani sighed. "Can't say I agree, but I'm not going to call Maddi a liar either."

"Do you normally swim without a bathing suit?" Bradley asked.

Trillian smacked him.

"What? I had to ask."

Maddilyn shook her head. "I *was* w-wearing a bathing suit. A one p-piece with little cat p-paws all over it."

"Must have really liked that bathing suit," Jack said.

"It was my f-favorite. Black and gold, j-just like *Roxette.*"

The gears inside Jack's head began to turn. "Let me guess. The cat paws were gold."

Maddilyn nodded.

"Interesting," Jack said.

"Glad you think so. But whatever's going on, let's get Maddi home." Bradley stood and helped Jack get Maddilyn back to her cabin. Trillian and Kailani waited at the promenade.

Once Maddilyn was safely on the porch, Bradley and Jack turned to go.

"Jack?"

He looked back at her.

"Go on. We'll wait," Bradley said before continuing down the path to the promenade.

Jack stepped onto the porch and Maddilyn wrapped her arms around him and hugged him tight. "Thank you for saving my life," she whispered into his ear.

Jack stepped back and smiled. "You'd do... you *did* the same for me."

She nodded and opened the cabin door. "Bye."

Jack waved and strutted down the path to meet the others. "Well, that was weird."

"Yeah. Being awake at exactly the right time sure was weird." Kailani looked at him, then shifted her gaze to Trillian, raised her brow and shrugged.

"Hey, who's hungry?" Bradley looked to the others.

"Totally. But I got to change." Jack looked down at his waterlogged underwear. "I don't think they'd let me in like this."

"The restaurant doesn't open until six," Kailani said.

"We can hang at the cabin 'til then." Trillian leaned into Kailani's ear. "Don't forget. Jack wants *you*." She grinned, grabbed Bradley's hand, and quickened her pace, pulling him away from Jack and Kailani.

They passed cabin 13 and the smell of coffee made their stomachs growl hungrily. O'Connor sat in a wicker chair with her feet propped up on the railing and a steaming cup of brew in her hand.

The group crossed the lawn and waved at O'Connor. She raised her cup in response and raised a brow at Jack's lack of clothes.

"Out for some early morning fuckin'?" When Jack gave her a sideways look in response, she added, "Fuckin' around. I meant fuckin' around."

"No, actually," Jack said. "I just saved someone from drowning. They were attacked by octopuses."

Kailani slapped his shoulder.

"What?" Jack looked at Kailani with surprise and lowered his voice. "That's what Maddi said."

"Jack." O'Connor beckoned him with a curled finger. "Tell me everything."

"Got to change first."

A few minutes later, Jack returned to cabin 13 and updated O'Connor. The more O'Connor heard, the angrier she became.

"THANKS FOR LETTING ME JOIN," Kailani said as servers cleared the teenagers' breakfast dishes. "My dad knows his way around a kitchen, but shit, that coconut French toast was *extra*."

"I know, right?" Trillian sat back in her chair. "Hang with us today?"

Kailani glanced at Jack for a moment. He was lost on his phone, looking up something. She returned her gaze to Trillian. "Sorry, I got stuff to do, boats to fix. The usual."

"Okay." Trillian sighed. "Maybe I'll lay around, get a tan."

"Not moving sounds good right about now." Bradley clutched his stomach. "What about you, Jack?"

"What?" He looked at Kailani, then the others. "Oh, I'll figure something out."

Kailani leaned in close enough to Jack to steal his attention away from his phone. "I had fun last night."

"Me, too," Jack said.

"See you later?"

Jack nodded, a wide grin on his face.

Kailani took his face in her hands and planted a kiss on his lips, then headed towards the pier. "Later."

On any other day, and especially after the night he had just had, Jack would have been eager to watch her go. But he went back to his phone.

Bradley stared at him. "What's gotten into you, man?"

Jack looked up, perplexed.

"You're acting as if you weren't just fully kissed."

Jack shrugged. "Just doing some research." He held up his phone.

"That tunnel vision of yours is going to get you into trouble one day." Trillian held out a hand to Bradley. "Shall we find a recliner and sleep off this breakfast?"

He took her hand. "I'd rather *work* it off, if you know what I mean."

"One track mind," Trillian said. "Besides, I got a surprise for you."

"You do? What is it? Tell me."

Trillian smiled to herself and led Bradley toward the beach. From their behavior, one would never have guessed that Bradley's dad was missing and presumed dead. Trillian supplied enough of a distraction to keep the reality of Sam's disappearance from crushing the life out of him, at least for a little while.

Alone at the table, Jack sat back, nodding approvingly at his phone. He had a workable plan and he had his materials. Now he just needed to find some tools.

SAM FLOATED IN and out of consciousness. It was next to impossible to figure out how long he was out when he slipped to the other side. But black tentacles in a black void always pulled him back. His only anchor to the real world were the random pinholes of light floating beyond his reach because the light behind the pinholes changed.

When he first noticed the pinholes, their lights were dim. Now they looked brighter than any star at night. Through muddled thoughts and no idea where he was or how he would get out, Sam had determined one thing.

Night and day. Day and night.

It was the sky he was seeing, through a peppering of tiny holes. Still not enough light to really see where he was.

Without any visual stimuli, his other senses were heightened. The moist rotting smell was familiar now and he knew not to move, due to the sharp and unknown surroundings. The pain radiating from his abdomen didn't allow him to move anyway.

From across the inky black space where Sam lay, he heard water rippling. Something – or *things* – were drawing close. He didn't flinch when he felt a tentacle slide over his lower legs. No, it was more than one. Their cool weight traveled up Sam's body, snaking, seeking.

He felt no fear. If these creatures had wanted him dead, they already had had plenty of opportunities.

At least it's not rats.

The tentacles tightened around his waist and pulled the rest of the octopus onto his abdomen, just below his belly button. For a fleeting second, Sam had an absurd thought that he'd be the first man to get a hand job (tentacle job?) from an octopus. But the pressure of the creature on his body reawakened the pain in his abdomen, and all his thoughts evaporated.

The octopus reacted immediately, as if it could feel what he felt. The tip of the tentacle dipped into the gash in his left side as if tasting his blood. Sam bit his tongue and held back a scream.

He opened his eyes to his surroundings glowing and pulsing blue green light. Skeletal and shelled remains surrounded him, some fish, some crustacean, and a few that looked oddly human, but the expanse of the cavern he was in still faded into blackness.

He peered down at the shapeless mass, its glistening skin luminescing as it undulated across his abdomen. It had to be an octopus. The only defining features were the tentacles, but even seeing them left him unsure.

The tentacles continued to probe his injury, then excreted an oily black fluid all over it. The pain in his abdomen faded to a fraction of what it had been, almost instantly.

The tentacles slid off his body as the octopus moved—

No, it walked…

—back into the water, alternating each step between tentacles. As the creature submerged itself, its luminescence faded until Sam's environment was pitch black once again. But before all the light was gone, he swore he saw stacks of glittering coins across the water.

Nah. Must be my imagination.

He slid his hands down to his abdomen. To his amazement, there was no deep gash and his fingers came away clean, not sticky with blood. Sam could still feel where his skin and muscle had been sliced open by Skulk's machete, but instead his fingers found a hairline scar. It was like he had just gotten his wound glued shut. The bleeding had stopped, and the pain was almost completely gone.

Sam pushed himself up onto his elbows to test his mobility. Pain rose up again, not quite as bad, but strong enough to tell him that moving wasn't an option yet.

He was on the mend, and the healing was progressing at an accelerated pace thanks to an octopus. The thought left him shaking his head in amazement. But would he be strong enough to get out of wherever he was before he starved or died of thirst? Because death was still a strong possibility.

GUS DIDN'T GET many customers this early in the morning, but he had to be ready for anything at any time. When Jack strolled over, trying hard to look casual, Gus didn't know what to expect.

"Hey, Gus," Jack said.

Gus raised a brow and gave him a quick nod. "Jack. You're up early."

"Yeah. I had an interesting night." Jack glanced over his shoulders like what he was about to share was a big secret. In a way, it was. "You know Maddi? Maddilyn—"

"Rockwell. Yeah. Pandora's daughter."

"An octopus attacked her this morning. She almost drowned, but I saved her."

Gus stepped back and tried to hide his surprise, but his face betrayed him.

Jack noticed. "What's wrong?"

"Something about those Rockwells."

"What do you mean?"

"Strange things seem to happen to them," Gus said. "Earlier in the week, before you got here I think, something attacked Pandora down on the beach." He pointed to their chaise lounges. "I didn't see it happen, but it left all these little cuts on one of her arms."

"Yeah, she told me about that," Jack said. "The cuts too."

"Weird thing is—"

"Let me guess." Jack leaned forward on his elbows as if he had a huge secret to share. "The cuts were all healed."

Gus looked at him surprised. "Yeah. And no scars, either."

"Same."

"Makes one want to start drinking heavily," Gus said. "But don't get any ideas."

Jack shook his head. "I'm not here for that."

"What are you here for?"

"You seem like a guy who knows how to get things." Jack held his gaze. "I'm building something, and I need some tools."

"What *kind* of tools are we talking about?" Gus looked at Jack curiously, not quite sure if he was serious or not.

"I'm building something like a harpoon gun," Jack said. "It's going to be self-loading and reciprocating and…" He trailed off. "Sorry, too much detail. But I need tools to work with metal, and even a welding machine would be nice."

"I'm not sure about the welder, but we should have everything else in our maintenance building. I can hook you up." Gus crossed his arms. "But why do you need a harpoon gun?"

"There's a problem with octopuses here," Jack said. "We've both seen it. The Rockwells were lucky, but other people have died."

"You mean those divers, earlier in the week?"

"Yeah. Plus, I've been attacked, and my best friend's—" Jack swallowed hard and fell silent.

Gus cocked his head to one side, anticipating more details.

"My best friend's dad… disappeared."

"Sam?"

Jack nodded.

"Come on. People don't just disappear."

"Well, *he* did."

"And you think octopuses did that?" Gus narrowed his eyes at him. "Octopuses are gentle creatures. I can't see them attacking *anything* unless they're provoked. Anything human, that is."

"I know, but it's possible," Jack said. "He went out on the water in Skulk's boat and never came back."

"Whoa." Gus raised his palms. "Hold on a second. *Skulk's* involved?"

Jack shrugged sheepishly.

"That changes everything. If I had to choose between an

octopus doing bad shit, and Skulk, it'd be Skulk, hands down," Gus said. "And last night, long story short, she came close to shooting your other friend... O'Connor."

"Well, I got to do something." A wave of grief hit Jack hard. He tried to hide it, but it was sneaking past his walls. "If it's not octopuses, at least I'll be prepared."

"Maybe you could use it on Skulk instead," Gus said. "In self defence, of course. But you didn't hear that from me." He stepped out from behind the bar. "Come on."

Gus led Jack through the Club's front entrance, past the porte cochère, and to a building set well back from the small parking area behind a row of pine trees.

"Why doesn't the Club do something? Or the police?"

"About Skulk? She's got some kind of mysterious hold on everyone who lives here."

"Maybe I should write a letter to Larry Ellison, explaining what's going on."

"You could try." Gus pulled out a set of keys and unlocked the door to the maintenance building. "Everyone here would be grateful." He flicked a couple of switches on the wall and several banks of fluorescent lights flickered on above them.

Jack grinned. The space was well equipped. Across one wall were a multitude of tools, neatly organized and grouped according to function. Along an adjacent wall stood a drill press, a band saw, and other commercial machinery beside a lengthy work bench. There were shelves of wood, bamboo, PVC pipe, and other building materials along the opposite side. A table saw stood in the center of the space.

"Will this do?"

Jack looked like a kid in a candy store. "I don't see an arc welder but that's okay."

Gus laughed. "You're sure, now?"

Jack nodded, his face becoming serious. "Yeah, this is great. I can make this work. Wait here. I got to get my materials." He turned and bolted back the way he came.

Gus called after him. "How long are you going to be?"

But Jack was already out of earshot.

"I'll give him five minutes," Gus said to himself.

Less than three minutes later, Jack returned with a plastic bag full of metal pieces.

"Jesus." Gus snorted. "You come prepared."

"I've been collecting for a few days." Jack set the bag down. "Ever since I got attacked. And I've got an idea burning a hole in my head. Got to let it out."

"Glad to help," Gus said. "Look, I got to get back to the bar." He found a scrap of paper and a pen and scrawled a note on it. "If anyone gets in your grill, show them this. And lock the door when you leave. Good luck."

"Thanks."

Gus nodded and left.

Jack acquainted himself with the space and the tools it contained. The buzzing of fluorescent lights replaced all sounds of nature. It was one version of heaven. The other version had Kailani in it.

He unfolded the note. It read, "Permission to use maintenance equipment okay'd by Gus (Kanakamana)."

"*Kanakamana?*" Jack said to himself. He refolded the note, jammed it into his back pocket.

He laid out all his materials on the workbench, the drawer slide, springs, and other assorted metal pieces, then collected the tools he expected to need. The workshop was a dream. Jack appreciated how organized everything was. It would make the build go so much smoother.

He called up the plans on his phone, even though he had looked at them so many times that they were committed to memory, and got straight to work. He didn't have a second to waste.

TRILLIAN FINISHED APPLYING her sunscreen and handed the bottle to Bradley. He was considerably less thorough than Trillian with his application of the lotion. Being partially shaded by their beach umbrella, Bradley wasn't worried about getting burned. He stretched out on his chaise lounge and eyed Trillian with a grin. "Aren't you forgetting something?"

Trillian examined herself. "What? Did I miss a spot?"

Bradley shook his head.

She moved to the edge of his chaise lounge. "What do you mean, then?"

"The surprise?"

"Oh, that." Trillian pushed Bradley over and snuggled up beside him. "I haven't forgotten. Let's relax for a bit."

"You like keeping me in suspense, don't you?"

"Shh." Trillian kissed Bradley's cheek. "Just a few minutes."

Their hearty breakfasts mixed with the warmth of the morning sun and the scent of coconut sunscreen. Sleep overpowered them, despite the grief that washed over Bradley whenever he was alone with his thoughts. Minutes melted into hours. The two teenagers snoozed in each other's arms. By the time Trillian and Bradley woke, the sun was directly over them, with their beach umbrella keeping them shaded.

"Holy crap," Bradley said, blinking away a restless sleep. "It's practically lunch time."

Trillian yawned and stretched. "How can you even *think* of food right now?"

"Uh, 'cause I'm hungry?"

"Guys and their stomachs." Trillian stood and ran back to the cabin.

"Hey! Where are you going?"

She disappeared inside the cabin without answering.

Before Bradley could protest, he saw her emerge again, holding a rolled towel tucked under one arm. Trillian strolled down to the beach again, a wide smile on her face. Bradley watched her fondly and found his feelings for her growing into something deeper.

"Is that my *surprise*?"

"Yup."

"A towel," Bradley said. "How did you know?"

"Ha. You're funny." Trillian sat on the other chaise lounge and placed the towel on her knees. "It's nothing super spectacular. I just remembered I had it actually. But I saw it and thought of you." She handed him the towel, then placed her elbows on her knees and cupped her chin, watching him.

Bradley unrolled the towel and unveiled a small golden disc with a spiral texture, held tightly in a cardboard and plastic overwrap. "A PopSocket?"

"PopGrip actually. I told you it was nothing special," Trillian said. "But it's a total fluke that it's gold. I got it before we left."

"Cool. I've heard about these." Bradley ripped open the package and removed the golden disc. The sun glinted off its surface as he spun it around in his fingers. "Let's try it out."

He peeled off the backing on one side of the disc and stuck it to the center of his phone case. Bradley popped the disc out, placed the neck between his fingers, and spun his phone around. "This is wicked. It just sort of stays on your hand, like you don't even have to think about it."

"And you can use it to prop your phone up if you're watching videos."

"That's totally cool," Bradley said. "You know who would love this?"

"Jack," they said in unison, laughing.

"It's the kind of thing I could see him inventing. You're

awesome." Bradley leaned over to kiss Trillian but felt something cold and wet cover his hand.

Trillian's eyes went wide. "Brad!"

He turned to see an octopus wrapped around his hand. "What the *fuck?*" Bradley struggled to raise his arm in an attempt to shake the creature off, but three of the octopus's tentacles had wrapped tightly around the frame of the chaise lounge.

"Shit, Trill. It hurts. The fucker's *cutting* me." Blood began seeping out between the tentacles around Bradley's arm.

Trillian tried to grab a tentacle. Like it had a mind of its own, the tentacle retracted and snaked around her wrist, pulling her forward.

"Oh, fuck." Trillian shuddered with disgust, yet couldn't look away. "What does it want?"

"I don't know."

"Your phone?"

"I DON'T KNOW."

"I have an idea," Trillian said. "Play dead."

Bradley screwed his face up at her. "What?"

"Just relax. Relax. Don't fight it." Trillian locked her gaze with Bradley's. "Play dead."

Both of them slumped over on the chaise lounge, Trillian draped over Bradley's body. Both their arms stretched out beside them on the end, buried up to their elbows in a mass of writhing tentacles.

"It's not working." More blood seeped out from between the tentacles and Bradley's skin.

"Relax your hand," Trillian said. "Let go of your phone."

"What? I can't."

"Would you rather lose your hand?"

Bradley stared at her. The answer was obvious, yet he didn't want to let go. His phone was practically an extension of his body. But every second longer he held onto it, he could feel the tentacles bury deeper into his arm. Trillian was right.

The instant Bradley stopped resisting, the octopus mirrored his reaction. The creature released Trillian and slid off the chaise lounge with Bradley's phone firmly secured in one tentacle. It spun like a wheel, propelling itself over the sand and disappearing into the surf.

Bradley stared at his arm peppered with small bloody cuts. "What... the... *fuck*, Trill?"

Trillian responded as if it was second nature. She shook out the towel and wrapped Bradley's arm in its folds. "Let's get you back to the cabin."

As they approached the porch, Jack bounded around the corner of the cabin with something long and metallic sticking out of a plastic bag. His excitement faded away in an instant.

"Hey! What's going on?"

"An octopus attacked us, but mostly Brad," Trillian said.

Jack could see spots of blood seeping through the towel.

Trillian eyed Jack. "A little help?"

"Right. Absolutely."

Jack took Bradley's free arm and all three ascended the porch stairs. Once inside, he dropped the bag and helped Trillian get Bradley onto the sofa.

"Jack, get another towel," Trillian said. "This one's soaking through."

Jack retrieved a clean towel from the bathroom, handed it to Trillian, then sat on the sofa next to her. She unwrapped Bradley's arm and examined the cuts. Almost all of them had stopped bleeding. For some cuts, the only evidence that remained were drops of dry blood.

Trillian blotted Bradley's arm with the clean towel, surprised at how little blood remained. "Does it hurt?"

"Actually..." Bradley paused to think. "It feels a bit numb, not like pins and needles, but like when you get freezing at a dentist. It's weird."

"It's like you weren't even cut," Jack said. "Just like this morning with Maddi. Why did the octopus attack you? Why now? I mean it's not like you just arrived."

"I don't know." Bradley brushed his hand over his arm, sending dried bits of blood falling into the towel like sand. "But it took my phone."

Jack scrunched his brows. "That's super strange."

"Don't forget your surprise," Trillian said. "The PopGrip."

"PopGrip?" Jack looked at them both.

"It's from PopSocket." Trillian returned her attention to Bradley's arm. "I'm sure you've seen them before."

"Oh, you mean those circular things you stick on the back of your phone? So you can grab it?"

"Yeah," Bradley said. "We think you'd love them."

"I've seen them. They're cool, but I hate sticking anything permanently to my phone."

"Of course." Bradley rolled his eyes. "You're a purist when it comes to your phone."

"So?" Jack shrugged. "Sue me."

"Whatevs. But you should have seen this thing. It was gold and had this cool spiral design on the top. It just stayed in my hand."

"Wait a second…" Jack ran through his mind and both Trillian and Bradley could see when his idea clicked.

She narrowed her eyes at him. "What?"

A subtle grin crossed Jack's lips.

"Spill it, man," Bradley said.

"I know why the octopus attacked you." Jack alternated his gaze between the both of them. His eyes only sparkled like this when he had a great idea. "Or at least I have a theory."

Trillian and Bradley stared at him, waiting.

"It's so simple, now that I think about it," Jack said. "It thought you had a coin."

Bradley and Trillian exchanged looks, the idea clicking with them too.

"And remember Maddi's bathing suit?"

"Refresh my memory," Bradley said.

"Maddi was wearing a bathing suit this morning, before I got to her." Jack looked at them both. "She said it was black with gold cat paws all over it, which could look like—"

"Gold coins to an octopus." Trillian's eyes widened.

"It didn't want my phone," Bradley said. "It was protecting what it thought was treasure."

Jack snapped his fingers. "Exactly. And I'd bet that every octopus attack that's happened while we've been here has something to do with a gold coin—"

"Or something that looks like a gold coin." Trillian gave Jack's shoulder a light punch. "Nice going."

"And you know what else?" Jack retrieved the plastic bag next to the door. "We can defend ourselves now."

He pulled out several long pieces of metal tubing, held together with brackets, adjustable clamps, nuts, bolts, and springs. At one end was a stalk with a trigger mechanism, much like a shotgun, but there was small hand crank on one side. Protruding from the other end sat a slightly smaller metal tube that Jack had cut and sharpened into a barb.

Bradley stared with amazed curiosity at the contraption. "What the *hell* is that? Looks like a fishing rod on steroids."

"It's a harpoon gun, right?" Trillian grinned at Jack.

"No," Jack said. "But you're close. This is better."

Trillian and Bradley alternated their gaze between Jack and his newest invention, waiting expectantly.

"I call it the ReciproJab." Jack gazed at his invention with affection.

"Are you going to *marry* it?" Trillian winked at him.

"I can't help it," Jack said. "It's my best work so far. A thing of beauty."

"How did you make that… *here?*" Trillian glanced at the rustic pine and bamboo construction of the cabin. "This place isn't exactly high-tech."

"Gus hooked me up," Jack said. "They've got a wicked workshop in the back, behind the parking lot."

Bradley stood to get a closer look at Jack's invention. "Does it work?"

"You think I'd unveil something that didn't work?"

Bradley glanced back at Trillian on the sofa, then they both said in unison, "Yes."

"Since when have I ever—"

Trillian stood and placed one hand on her hips. "Just *show* us already!"

"Okay. Get behind me."

"Why?" Bradley gave Jack an unsure glance.

"In case it… fucks up." Jack smirked at them both. "Contrary to popular belief, I'm not perfect."

Bradley and Trillian stepped beside Jack, out of range of the barbed end of the weapon.

Jack held the ReciproJab by the stalk in one hand and stretched his other hand out, palm forward and fingers splayed, as if he was conjuring a magic trick. "Imagine you're snorkeling or scuba diving and you encounter a creature of some kind—"

"Like a… what?" Bradley looked at Trillian. Playing along, they both shrugged emphatically. "An octopus, maybe?"

"Yes." Jack continued, his eyes sparkling. "An octopus attacks you for no reason."

"Except you took its treasure," Trillian said, grinning.

"Yeah. Whatever. It attacks you. Luckily, you had grabbed your handy ReciproJab before you got into the water. Then, when the octopus gets too close…" Jack gripped the ReciproJab stalk in one hand and cranked the handle on the opposite side. He looked like he was reeling in imaginary fish. "You pull the trigger."

The barbed end shot forward as far as the barrel that contained it, doubling the length of the weapon. Then the barbed end retracted back into the barrel and the sequence restarted. It was like a hand-held sewing machine needle on steroids.

Jack cranked and let the ReciproJab propel the barb back and forth a few times. "The octopus is now full of holes."

"How long does it do that..." Bradley mimicked the back and forth motion with his hand.

"You mean the reciprocating jabs? When I stop pulling the trigger and/or stop cranking the side." Jack released his finger and the barbed end stopped.

Bradley examined the weapon closer, then looked at him. "So, it's like a machine gun, then?"

"Like a Gatling gun, sort of."

"What powers it?" Trillian asked. "I mean, a machine gun loads the next bullet from the force of the bullet being shot. But this..."

"Good question." Jack set the ReciproJab on the coffee table. "It works in much the same way as a machine gun, using kinetic energy. The hand crank pulls back a spring with every turn, then that spring sends the barb forward. The crank also pulls the barb back after."

Bradley nodded slowly. "The only downside is you got to be in close range."

"Yeah," Jack said. "There's that. But you've got a weapon just as effective as a harpoon that you don't have to reload every time."

Trillian picked up the weapon and examined it. "How does it work under water?"

"I don't know," Jack said. "I haven't tested it submerged yet. If I were to guess, it wouldn't be much different. It'd still be enough to kill or wound anything attacking you."

"That's a big assumption." Trillian focused on the beach through the front window. "You should test it in the cove. But you better keep it under wraps. If the wrong eyes see it..."

"Speaking of," Bradley said, "what does Kailani think of it?"

"I haven't shown it to her yet." Jack picked up the ReciproJab and cranked the handle slowly. The barbed end shot forward quickly and retracted slowly.

"Test it in the ocean first," Trillian said. "If it doesn't work underwater, you don't have to tell her."

Jack stowed the weapon back in the plastic bag. "Alright, who's coming with?"

"I'm going to stay on the promenade this time, if you don't mind," Bradley said.

Jack nodded at him. "Yeah, no prob." He looked at Trillian expectantly. "Want to be my cameraman?"

Trillian smiled and nodded. "Sure. What do you need?"

Jack walked back to his bedroom. "I've got a waterproof enclosure for my phone," he called back. "Just get a good shot of the ReciproJab in action."

"Done," Trillian said. "Let's go."

"Wait." Bradley eyed the others. "Do we look like gold coins?"

Despite their clothing having no circular gold decorations, the three of them examined each other again anyway.

"Nope," Trillian said.

"I def don't." Jack added. "And I don't think these octopuses are into silver."

They headed back to the beach, with the ReciproJab covered by the cabin's last clean towel. All three felt confident that the contraption would work submerged in the cove. Whether it would kill was the wild card.

TRY, TRY AGAIN

O'CONNOR PACED BACK and forth in her cabin, practically wearing a path into the floorboards. She had run out of cigars two days earlier and not having tobacco clamped between her jaws, lit or not, amped up her irritability.

Hearing how Maddilyn had been attacked on top of losing Sam had lit an angry inferno in O'Connor's head.

"Those fucking things *killed* Sam," she said. "I *know* it."

Hope knew better than to engage O'Connor when she was like this, but she ignored her better judgment. "It's possible, but you can't be sure."

O'Connor glared at her. "I'm *sure*."

"Not without a body." A recent memory of Sam holding her close hit her like a rogue wave. But still she continued, "And even with a body, it'll be next to impossible to really know what happened."

"Then I'll find a body." O'Connor stopped at the front window and stared out onto the cove.

"Skulk is a more probable suspect," Hope said. "You know that, right?"

O'Connor shot a glance mixed with anger and shame at her. Having her ass handed to her by Skulk in the bar the previous night had seriously dented her ego. "I'll find Sam, then I'll kill Skulk *and* those tentacled motherfuckers."

"Would Sam want you to murder someone, even a piece of trash like Skulk?"

"Shut up," O'Connor said.

Hope backed down. There was no point trying to convince O'Connor of anything right now. She needed time to calm herself. She'd see the right path eventually. She always did.

"How about some lunch?" Hope knew food tamed the savage beast. Maybe it would work today.

O'Connor ignored her. She charged into her bedroom, returning a few minutes later with her swim leg on, and bolted toward the door.

"Hey! Where are you going?"

Instead of a response, O'Connor marched toward the marina. Hope briefly considered going after her, but reconsidered when she spotted Bradley, Trillian, and Jack down at the beach unwrapping something in a towel.

Hope had had enough adult shenanigans for a while, plus she needed a distraction from her grief over Sam's disappearance. She stepped off the porch and headed for the teenagers.

O'CONNOR STORMED DOWN the pier until she arrived at Palakiko Tours. She tried the front door, found it locked, then made a fist and pounded on it. When no one answered, O'Connor stepped back and peered around the boat house. Both boats were moored, the *Octopussy* still dry-docked.

She stomped back to the front door and resumed her fisted assault. "I know you're in there. Answer me, dammit!"

Other tourists strolling on the pier gave O'Connor wary glances.

"Take a picture, assholes," she yelled. "It'll last longer."

When a couple of tourists did exactly what she had suggested and took out their phones, O'Connor realized the situation could end up looking bad for her. She faced the door and resumed knocking, but like someone who hadn't lost their shit.

After the third knock, Kailani unlocked the door and poked her head out. "O'Connor. What do you want?" She glanced at tourists with their phones out hoping to capture a tantrum. "You're scaring away customers."

"If you had opened the fuckin'…" O'Connor closed her eyes and took a breath. "Sorry. I need your help."

Kailani stared at her, waiting for O'Connor to continue.

"I need you to take me out into the cove," O'Connor said. "I need to find Sam's body. And I need to find out what killed him."

"That's what we did yesterday. Nothing's changed." Kailani cast a look back at the *Wavy Jone's* moorage. "Besides, we all know who did it."

"I have to know for sure."

"Who else could it have been?" Kailani's dark eyes bored into O'Connor's. When O'Connor didn't respond immediately, Kailani stepped back and shook her head, annoyed. "How many times do I have to say it? It's not octopuses. They don't kill humans."

Lono stepped into the door frame. "O'Connor, we've been more than accommodating." He pointed at the holes in *Octopussy's* hull. "What's done is done. The curse has been released and now we all have to live with it."

O'Connor wanted to throttle Lono, and despite his bullshit about the curse, she knew he was right. "I can make it worth your while."

"No." Lono crossed his beefy arms across his chest. "I think you better leave."

"I'll find Sam. I will," O'Connor said through clenched teeth. "Mark my words."

"I hope you do." Lono stepped back into the boat house and closed the door.

O'Connor ignored the tourists who were still shooting video

on their phones. She headed back toward the cabins, formulating her next step.

"WHAT IS THAT THING?"

Bradley, Trillian, and Jack spun around to find Hope sitting on the end of a chaise lounge watching them. Jack had just finished re-wrapping the ReciproJab in the towel.

Bradley and Trillian looked at Jack, unsure what to say.

"It's a weapon," Jack said. "My own design."

"I assume it works under water?"

"It does." Trillian held up Jack's phone in the waterproof enclosure. "I got video."

"Show me."

Jack nodded. "Go ahead."

Trillian sat next to Hope and replayed the video. Bradley and Jack leaned in behind them to watch over their shoulders.

The video showed Jack placing the ReciproJab under the water and working the hand crank. The barbed end shot back and forth from the larger barrel containing it, just as it had in the cabin.

"Wicked," Bradley said. "You're a genius, Jack."

Jack shrugged and grinned. "Thanks."

Hope turned to look at the three teenagers. "You're going to be using this on octopuses, aren't you?"

"Only if we need to," Jack said.

The whole situation was steeped with madness and didn't make sense. Hope couldn't help but wonder if all this effort would have been necessary if Sam had returned the coin to the cove two days ago. But he hadn't and now Sam was gone. This holiday was turning into a nightmare.

"You're not looking for more treasure, are you?"

All three teenagers shook their heads at Hope.

"Self-defense, only," Jack said.

"Good." Hope looked out across the water. "O'Connor's on the war path. You better hide that thing or she'll—"

"Jack!" O'Connor trudged across the beach toward them, kicking sand every which way. "Your girlfriend's being a bitch."

"Speak of the devil," Trillian said.

"Damn." Jack groaned and prepared himself for O'Connor's onslaught.

"She's refusing to take me out into the cove to look for Sam again," O'Connor bellowed across the sand.

Bradley exchanged a glance with Jack, then looked back at O'Connor. "I don't blame them. They were pretty thorough yesterday."

"They were whining about quotas earlier. I was going to make it worth their while."

"I think we've burned that bridge," Trillian said.

"They didn't even make a goddamn counteroffer."

"It's probably going to cost a lot to fix their boat," Bradley said. "You couldn't afford it."

"How would you know?" O'Connor leaned in close to Bradley and grunted with disgust. "I'm surprised you've given up so quickly. He's *your* father for fuck's sake."

"Just being realistic." Bradley shoved his emotions deep within. "I don't want my last memory of my dad to be a floating rotten corpse."

O'Connor scanned the beach. "Someone at this place is going to take me out on the water. Today." She paused, as if she had spotted something out in the cove. "Jack, I'm going to need your phone."

"Why?"

"I need the GPS."

"You can use your own." Jack beckoned for O'Connor's phone. "Just use your maps app. It'll tell you exactly where you are." He opened the app on her phone and the pin on the display showed the group's location. "There you are, accurate to within a dozen feet or so."

Jack handed the phone back to O'Connor, but as he did, he nudged the ReciproJab. The towel slipped away and revealed the barrel and barbed end.

As an exterminator, O'Connor was always on the lookout for the latest and greatest weaponry. The barbed end stopped her in her tracks. "Hold on. What the fuck is *that* and when were you going to show me how to use it?"

"Shit," Jack whispered to himself. He opened up the towel, exposing the rest of the ReciproJab.

O'Connor reached in to take it and Jack twisted in front of her, blocking her attempt. She pointed out at the cove. "If I'm going out there to look for Sam, I'm going to need that thing."

"No," Jack said. "You won't. No one touches the ReciproJab except me."

"It's got a name already?" O'Connor burst out laughing. "Figures. But you're going to hand it over."

Bradley stepped forward, followed by Trillian. "No. He's not."

"It's a proof-of-concept," Trillian added. "Not ready for prime time."

Hope watched with interest as the teenagers made their case. She wasn't about to step in, despite wanting Sam's body found.

O'Connor's face reddened with anger. "If I die out there, it's on your heads."

"The octopuses will leave you alone as long as you don't provoke them," Bradley said.

"And don't wear anything that looks like a gold coin," added Jack.

"Or take any treasure." Trillian watched O'Connor fume.

Bradley stood. "You're not going to die. Just don't do anything stupid."

"What are *you* jerk-offs going to do then?" O'Connor singled them out one by one with furious eyes. "Stand around with your thumbs up your asses?"

"We're working on it," Bradley said.

"We're going to eat lunch," Jack said, almost at the same time.

O'Connor shook her head. "Fuck *all* of you." She turned and stormed back toward the marina. Her words had stung everyone, Bradley most of all.

Once O'Connor was out of earshot, Jack looked up at Bradley. "So, what *are* we working on, exactly?"

Bradley followed O'Connor's exodus with vacant eyes. "I don't know."

IT DIDN'T TAKE long for O'Connor to find another boat charter willing to take her out to the *Templeton* wreck. And for the right price, Lanai Excursions was willing to leave immediately.

Staff fitted O'Connor with a wetsuit, mask, snorkel, and swim fins while the tour operator, a well-built twenty-something Hawaiian, readied the twenty-three foot Parker 2530 Sport Cabin, named *Vitamin Sea*.

"Will the rest of your party be arriving soon?"

O'Connor pulled the operator aside, taking note of his name tag. "Noa, it's just going to be me."

Noa scrutinized her. "You know that's not recommended. If you get into trouble, it's good to have someone else close by."

"That's why you're there."

"Afraid I can't join you on the excursion," Noa said. "Got to stay topside, man the boat."

"Then I go alone."

"I'll have to get you to sign a waiver."

"Yeah, whatever you have to do." O'Connor stepped closer and lowered her voice. "There's one more thing, and I don't think you're going to like it. I'm going to need a harpoon gun and scuba gear."

"Uh…" Noa balked at the request.

"Look. I know the rules." O'Connor draped her arm across the man's shoulder. "But my friend disappeared out there yesterday. He's probably dead but I promised his son that I'd find his body." She paused for effect. "I need to really search the bottom. I can't do that snorkeling."

"Look, ma'am, I just can't." Noa shot a glance back at the excursion office. "Snorkeling alone is one thing, but diving alone…" He shook his head. "No. It could mean my job."

O'Connor unzipped the front of her wetsuit just enough to slip her hand between her cleavage. Noa's eyes bugged out.

She laughed. "Don't get any ideas. You'd know it if I wanted to watch the submarine races." O'Connor pulled out a wad of cash, mostly hundred dollar bills. "Does that sweeten the deal?"

Noa hesitated, then shook his head. "You need a dive partner."

O'Connor retrieved the last of her hidden bills and added them to the stack. "What do you say, Noa?"

Noa looked at bills, calculating the total in his head. He let out an exasperated sigh before taking the cash. "Fine. Get in the boat."

O'Connor stepped over the gunwale and watched Noa disappear into an equipment shed off to one side of the office. He reappeared with a black duffel bag and hurried back to the *Vitamin Sea*.

"What's that, the harpoon gun?"

"A speargun, yeah." Noa untied the ropes from the mooring cleats and signaled one of the staff in the office. They waved back.

O'Connor narrowed her eyes at him. "Where's the scuba gear?"

"Don't worry. I'm not trying to rip you off. It's here, under the console," Noa said. "We treat it as emergency equipment." He piloted the *Vitamin Sea* out into the cove. "Next stop. The *Templeton*, a schooner that sank in the early nineteenth—"

"Spare me the history lesson. I got the fifty cent tour from your competition."

"Why aren't they taking you? All booked up?"

O'Connor shook her head. "They turned me down. Even with the… bonus."

Noa sent a wary look back at O'Connor. "Anything you're not telling me?"

"Just do what I paid you to do." O'Connor focused on her task ahead.

"If you're planning on breaking laws, I'm turning around," Noa said. "You can have your money back."

"Cool your jets, muchacho. Everything's legit."

Noa looked O'Connor over and decided to trust her. He navigated out into the center of the cove.

O'Connor squinted back at the beach. The rest of the group was nowhere to be seen. "Fuckers," she muttered.

"Excuse me, ma'am?" Noa looked back at her. "Did you say something?"

O'Connor kept her eyes on the water.

Noa continued out to the center of the cove, shut off the engine, and dropped anchor. O'Connor took out her phone, loaded the maps app, and pinned the location in case she needed to return.

Noa retrieved the scuba gear from a concealed enclosure next to the console. "Have you ever dived before?"

"Does snorkeling count?"

"Sort of." Noa gave O'Connor a quick lesson on the dos and don'ts of scuba diving and explained the equipment. "How much do you weigh?"

"You normally ask the ladies their weight?"

"I got to calculate your buoyancy," Noa said. "Otherwise, your diving experience will be impacted." He waited for an answer.

O'Connor crossed her arms. "Less than two hundred. That good enough?"

"For an estimate, sure." Noa helped O'Connor into a vest that carried both her air tank and a buoyancy compensator device. Several hoses ran from the tank to the front of the vest. He added a few extra integrated weights. "It's not an exact science. The goal is neutral buoyancy, but that rarely happens since a diver's weight is always changing with every breath."

"How long will I have down there?"

"About thirty minutes before you need to resurface." Noa grabbed several hoses hanging across O'Connor's chest. "This is the regulator. You breathe from this. Plus, it also controls your buoyancy."

"Can't we just get on with this?"

Noa regarded her seriously. "You want the *Templeton* to become your grave, too? Normally a new diver requires at least four days of training. Give me ten minutes to explain the equipment so you don't join your friend."

O'Connor nodded. Dying while trying to find Sam's body wouldn't go over well with the rest of the group.

Noa continued, explaining the timer, the pressure and depth gauges, and the dive computer. "Normally, you can just use the dive computer to alert you when it's time to surface, but the other gauges are your backup. Make sense?"

"Clear as mud."

"Are you being serious?" Noa locked his gaze with hers. "I need you to be serious. I'm putting my job on the line for you."

"And you're being well paid to do it." O'Connor pulled on her mask and pushed the backup snorkel aside. "Everything's good."

"Okay." Noa loaded the speargun and surveyed his surroundings, focusing on the marina. He directed O'Connor to the gunwale on the starboard side of the *Vitamin Sea*. If anyone was watching from the marina, the cabin would block their view.

He tethered a flashlight to her wrist and handed her the

speargun. "Be careful with that. You only get one shot. Now sit and roll backwards into the water."

O'Connor placed the regulator in her mouth and rolled back, entering the ocean with a splash. She righted herself and poked her head out of the water.

Noa leaned over the side. "Slow easy breaths, okay? No more than thirty minutes. Watch your dive computer. And whatever you do, don't enter the wreck."

O'Connor nodded, gave him a thumbs up, and submerged again.

Noa found it difficult to relax, and getting caught and fired weighed heavily on his mind. Had he covered everything O'Connor needed to know to return safely to the boat? If he missed something, he'd know the answer in the next half hour.

THE SKY CLOSED up around O'Connor in a swirl of bubbles and blues. She looked down at the *Templeton's* stern and propelled herself toward it.

Noa had done an excellent job estimating the extra weights. O'Connor felt like an astronaut floating in space and she found herself enamored by the spectacle. The wreck had become a living organism, supporting coral, kelp, and a multitude of fish.

The sound of her breath through the regulator reminded her of Darth Vader and O'Connor found that oddly comforting. She kicked deeper, following the line where the hull of the *Templeton* disappeared into the sandy bottom. Before she had realized it, five minutes had passed.

Refocusing on her mission, O'Connor swam back around the stern. She glanced at her dive computer. The lack of sunlight at thirty-seven feet below the surface was noticeable. Her flashlight lit the way.

Rusty and rotted port holes, windows into the past, dotted the hull in regular intervals. She wondered if Sam was behind one, or maybe treasure.

O'Connor circumnavigated the wreck, looking for anything resembling a human body.

Sam's body.

It had only been a day. Would Sam even look human? O'Connor had seen enough in her lifetime to know that once death took hold, the human body experienced rapid physiological changes. She imagined the warmer tropical water would accelerate the process.

O'Connor realized that maybe Bradley had been right all along. Her last memory of Sam might be horrific. But instead of abandoning her search, she renewed her effort. Everyone needed closure, including herself.

She pushed forward. More than half of her allotted dive time had elapsed. O'Connor rounded the stern again and positioned herself level with the gunwale a dozen feet above the ocean floor, sweeping the flashlight's beam across the hull.

Another thought flashed through her head. She had assumed Sam had disappeared over the *Templeton*, when it could have been anywhere in the cove. The odds were stacked against her. O'Connor could be looking in entirely the wrong place. Her anger and impulsive thinking had potentially led her astray.

Being higher up next to the hull offered a better view of the *Templeton* as well as more sunlight. But there was still no sign of Sam… until she spotted a bright red piece of fabric snagged on a jagged opening near the middle of the schooner.

O'Connor cast her mind back a day and tried to remember if Sam's shorts or shirt was red. She couldn't be certain but also couldn't ignore the possibility. Could Sam have swam into this opening to escape and gotten stuck?

She kicked forward to the breach. It was a little too small to fit through, so she stuck her arm and head into the space. The flashlight revealed a much larger space, filled with tropical fish and seaweed. Along the bottom, a steel-reinforced chest sat angled to one side, another piece of red fabric floating next to it.

O'Connor began pulling rotted planks away from the opening, paying no heed to whether she was alone or not. Once the opening was big enough, she wiggled her way into the space.

O'Connor kept her eyes peeled for anything human, a hand, a foot, or God forbid, Sam's face. But she came up empty. Her diving inexperience led to quick movements, which stirred up sediment and... bones of creatures long dead.

Wait a minute. Bones?

As O'Connor neared the chest, she realized it was sitting on a pile of bones and shells and more of the red fabric. She grabbed a bone and pulled it away, causing the chest to shift to one side. Billows of silt rose, and her flashlight beam illuminated the cloud of particles obscuring her vision. Once her sightline had been restored, O'Connor realized that the bone she held in her hand was not from a fish.

There was something else. A glitter beneath the one edge of the chest, something curved and gold...

It was a coin, exactly like the one Sam had pocketed. But she wasn't here for coins. O'Connor glanced at her dive computer.

Five minutes left.

The search for Sam had been a bust. In a fit of anger, she stabbed the side of the chest with the tip of the speargun, rolling it to one side.

Hundreds of gold coins spilled out. In that instant two things happened. O'Connor's eyes widened as she envisioned herself retiring, rich beyond her wildest dreams. Then a second later reality set in as a large octopus pushed through the bones, its skin raised in spikes and its tentacles probing, heading straight for her face.

O'Connor tried to reverse herself and caught her scuba tank

on the top edge of the opening in the hull. She kicked out in front of her as the tentacles snaked around her left leg.

Breathing rapidly, she glanced at her dive computer.

Two minutes? But how?

Her panic had rapidly depleted her air supply. If she didn't escape now, she'd die here.

As far as her legs were concerned, the octopus had chosen the best leg to attack. With her right leg still free, O'Connor tried to kick the bulbous creature with her swim fin but found it ineffective. Despite its spiky, solid appearance, the octopus was essentially a bag full of water. It held no firm shape. Kicking it had no effect. Her foot slid off the octopus's skin like stepping on a banana peel.

In her panic, she had forgotten the speargun. O'Connor raised it level with what she thought was the creature's head and pulled the trigger.

The octopus jerked as the barbed tip of the spear punched through its body. O'Connor's shot was a lucky one, the spear passing right between the creature's eyes, out the back of its body, and embedding itself in the wall behind.

Clouds of silt mixed with blue blood and black ink, throwing O'Connor into darkness, even with a flashlight in her hand.

She tossed the spent speargun aside and waved her hands in front of her face in an attempt to clear the water in front of her. O'Connor kicked with all her strength and felt the scuba tank striking the hull once again.

She felt for the dive computer and held it right up to her mask.

47 seconds left.

There was only one route to survival: Leave her tank behind. Questions swirled in her head. How deep was she? How long would it take to get to the surface? Could she hold her breath long enough? Every thought ate away at her remaining time.

But taking a moment to think, no matter how short, had one advantage. The water had cleared somewhat, and O'Connor now knew which way to go. She found the buckles on her vest, loosened them, and let the vest slide off.

Still with the regulator in her mouth, she took one long breath and kicked her way out of the hull. Blue sunshine above led the way and within twenty seconds, O'Connor had surfaced. She filled her lungs with fresh air and waited for her heart to settle into a reasonable pace. She oriented herself and swam for the *Vitamin Sea,* with Noa perched at the gunwale, ready to pull her aboard.

"Where's the gear? The speargun?"

O'Connor spoke between catching her breath. "There was an… incident."

"What the fuck?" Noa grabbed O'Connor's wet T-shirt. "I'm on the hook for that."

O'Connor let him release his anger on her. She didn't have the energy to fight him. "I thought you heading back without me would have looked worse."

Noa slackened his grip as the reality of O'Connor's response sunk in.

"Can we both agree that me being alive is the better option?" O'Connor smirked at him.

"Shit…" Noa cursed himself, low and husky but loud enough for O'Connor to hear.

"Think of it this way," O'Connor said. "Dead or alive, the gear would still be on the bottom."

"I'm going to get fired."

O'Connor shook her head. "Look. I'll pay for the gear. Then all you got to do is replace it. How often was the scuba gear used anyway?"

Noa took a moment to think. "That might work," he said.

"It *will* work. Trust me. Now get me back to the marina."

Noa stepped backward and saw the remains of O'Connor's swim leg. The purple cover was gone, with the exception of a few bits and pieces hanging where the socket connected to her stump.

The rubber foot was gone, leaving a long, curved, carbon fiber blade.

"Your leg. It's…"

"Gone. Yeah." O'Connor grit her teeth. "That cover was badass, wasn't it. But the next one will be better."

"Seems like the universe is getting you back for something," Noa said.

"You and me, both."

Fifteen minutes later, Noa docked the *Vitamin Sea* at its designated moorage. He helped O'Connor out of the boat and onto the dock. The first step on her prosthetic slipped, and she landed hard on her ass.

Now that she was safely on land, O'Connor's anger resurfaced again. "Fucking piece of shit leg."

She stood up and trudged down the pier towards the promenade. O'Connor slipped only once more and quickly adjusted her gate to a prosthetic leg without a foot.

Failing to find Sam's body on top of ruining a perfectly good swim leg ramped up her anger more. By the time she stormed into the restaurant, she was furious.

The rest of the group sat around a table in the center of the restaurant. O'Connor stormed toward it, looking a lot like the T-1000 from *Terminator 2: Judgment Day.*

Before anyone at the table had a chance to react, O'Connor slammed her hands down on the tabletop, practically flipping it off its pedestal base.

"What's our fuckin' *plan?*"

Bradley looked at Jack, Trillian, and Hope, then turned back to O'Connor. "Sit down—"

"Shut up—" Trillian continued.

"And eat." Jack offered a subtle nod to his friends.

Hope found O'Connor's eyes with hers. "Sound good?"

The four of them had managed to douse O'Connor's rage

within seconds. They were all short on patience and levity and had expected an outburst from her.

Am I that *predictable?*

O'Connor decided to do something unexpected. She pulled up a chair, sat down, and shut up.

"You didn't find Sam, did you?" Hope asked.

"No." O'Connor shifted her gaze to the others. "But seriously. What's the plan?"

"To fix the damage," Jack said, "starting with Kai's boat."

A server placed a coffee cup in front of O'Connor and filled it.

"Then what?"

Jack looked to his friends and shrugged.

"Just tell us what happened," Hope said.

O'Connor took a healthy swallow of hot coffee and recounted her recent failure.

REPAIR

SAM'S PAIN WAS gone, but when he tried to sit up, his mind swirled with dizziness. Trying to stand was dangerous and near impossible. Falling on an exposed bone the wrong way could cause a grave injury that he might not recover from. So he had stayed put.

To Sam's amazement, the octopuses had been doing a decent job keeping him alive. With the outside world mostly blocked off, he had little sense of the passage of time. But he estimated that the tentacled sea creatures supplied him with raw fish, clams, and crabs at least once a day.

They would lay a bounty on his abdomen with their strong tentacles. Sometimes before, or after, they would run their tentacles over his healing wound, or his chest, or his forehead. Sam was unsure of the reason.

He used his thumbs to tear into the soft underbelly of the fish to remove the guts. At least he hoped he was removing them. He had no real way of knowing since everything was slippery with fish blood. Skinning the fish without tools or light proved to be an impossible task. And biting through fish scales to get at the meat underneath was now his number-one least favorite thing to do.

Instead, he focused on the clams and crabs. He didn't need to break open their shells. The octopuses did that for him. Carving out the fleshy interiors with his teeth and fingers was easy, compared to the fish. Sam learned to love raw seafood quickly.

He heard splashing, the telltale sounds of his next meal delivery, then felt tentacles gather on his chest.

What would it be today? Fish? Crab? Instead, he closed his eyes and pictured a tall bottle of fresh water in his mind. That was what he really needed. The seafood had helped him build back his strength, but without water, all the food in the world wouldn't save him. And drinking sea water would mean certain death.

Fresh water to survive, a serious human design flaw.

The octopus began its exploratory roaming. Over his chest and neck, over his forehead and dry, cracked lips.

He remembered being surprised at the overwhelming ease he had felt when the creature first ran its tentacles over him. Sam knew, and had seen, what these octopuses were able to do, changing their suckers into lines of razor-sharp teeth. But the gentle touch went against everything he had learned about this species. Instead of panic, Sam felt calm, his worry about fresh water replaced with a feeling of well-being and reciprocity.

Sam let the image of fresh water go and focused on the food that the octopuses had gathered for him. As he ate, his mind kept coming back to the same nagging question.

Why save me?

The octopuses must have seen something redeemable in him, though he had no idea what that might be. He had taken their treasure and released a curse upon those he loved. The mysterious creatures should have left him for dead, but here he was.

After eating, he closed his eyes, and let sleep take him. Perhaps his dreams would provide an answer.

Kailani had just finished clearing lunch dishes when she heard a knock on the boathouse door. She gave Lono a wary look and went to the window. On the pier below stood Jack and the rest of the group that had made their lives so difficult.

"It's you-know-who. All of them, not just Jack."

Lono looked at her. "What do you think they want?"

Kailani placed a stack of plates and cutlery in the sink. "No *fucking* idea."

Lono gave her a stern look.

"Yeah, I know. Language," Kailani said. "Sorry."

A knock sounded again from below.

Lono crossed his arms. "Maybe you should find out what they want."

Kailani nodded and took the stairs to the first floor. As she went, she felt conflicted. She wanted to see Jack again, but even though she had last seen him and his friends this morning, she couldn't ignore the damage the group had wrought on her business and her livelihood.

She approached the front door with trepidation and unlocked it.

"Hi," she said. "What's up?"

Her smile must have looked off because Jack's smile faltered. "Hey, Kai. We... uh... we—"

"We want to help," O'Connor said.

Kailani heard the familiar creak in the stairs behind her. Lono was within earshot now.

She gazed back at the group, confused. "Help with what, exactly?"

O'Connor spread her arms wide, like she was about to hug her. "Everything."

"Starting with your boat," Jack said.

"Just tell us what to do, and we'll do it," Trillian added.

"We've caused enough trouble." Hope managed a small smile. "We want to help fix what we've broken."

Kailani stood for a moment, not quite knowing what to say. She looked back at Lono. He stepped up behind her and placed a strong hand on her shoulder.

"You want to help." Lono scanned the group and nodded. "Okay. Let's get to work."

LONO AND KAILANI grabbed a collection of cans and a tub of supplies. Jack offered to carry some of the materials and Kailani gladly let him. Lono led everyone down to the raised dock where the *Octopussy* sat and beckoned them to gather around.

"The good thing about most smaller boats like the Privateer is that their hull is made with fiberglass." Lono looked at everyone in turn to make sure they were paying attention. "That also means holes like this can usually be fixed with fiberglass and epoxy."

He held up a roll of what looked like shimmering cloth. "This is fiberglass. Never handle it without gloves. Otherwise, you risk having bits of glass embedded into your hands. Not fun." Lono set the roll of glass fabric back in the bin. "Lucky for you, you won't be handling it. You'll be doing the sanding."

"The grunt work," O'Connor said.

"Right." Lono looked at her. "With no complaints."

"Nope, ain't that right, gang?" O'Connor looked to the others. Everyone was quick to nod in agreement.

Kailani surveyed the group, ending on Jack. He smiled and saluted her and despite everything that had happened, she couldn't help but smile back. She would miss him terribly when it was time for him to go home.

Lono handed out protective rubber gloves, K95 masks, and sanding blocks. "Kailani and I will be applying the fiberglass patches. They take about half an hour to cure before we can sand them. But—"

"There's always a but." O'Connor started to laugh but Hope elbowed her.

"She's going to shut the fuck up and listen," Hope said to Lono, then glared at O'Connor.

"Before we can apply the fiberglass, all the bullet holes need to be sanded to remove the rough edges," Lono continued. "But you know what's great about bullet holes?"

The group exchanged looks with one another.

"The holes have cleaner edges?" Jack looked at him, unsure.

"Close," Lono said. "They're *holes!* Meaning you got to fix both sides of the hull."

"Twice the sanding," Bradley said.

Lono pointed his finger at Bradley and snapped his finger. "Right, and twice the work. So I'm really glad you all volunteered. If everything goes well, we'll have *Octopussy* back in the water by this time tomorrow."

Lono slipped on a K95 mask and showed his sanding technique on the first hole. "Please wear the masks. Glass particles in your lungs is worse than getting them in your hands." He switched gears and busied himself fixing the damage to the top of the boat's engine.

Kailani pulled up enough of the boat's deck where needed to get at the bullet holes on the interior side of the hull.

Skulk's bullets had struck the *Octopussy's* hull three times. That meant six areas needed sanding. Spreading out the work between Bradley, Trillian, Jack, and Hope, the initial sanding would be completed in twenty minutes.

Bradley focused on the ragged edges of his assigned bullet hole. Instead of circular, the hole was more oval, as if the bullet had struck the hull at an angle. And soon it would have a strong patch over it, reviving the boat's functionality.

Fixed. Good as new. Healed.

His mind wandered back to Sam and his unknown whereabouts. There had to be a body. *Somewhere.* The sea gave up secrets all the time in the surf. He had heard many stories about human feet washing up on shore still wearing sneakers. Yet no evidence of his dad had washed up at all.

Bradley stopped sanding.

Trillian gave him a curious glance. "What's wrong?"

"He's still alive, Trill," Bradley said. "I can feel him." He looked at her with a gaze so intense it gave her shivers. "And there's no body. That's what I can't get past."

Trillian took his hand in hers. It felt odd to try and comfort someone while wearing rubber gloves. "He could have gotten stuck underwater, like O'Connor almost did. Or maybe Skulk weighed him down. Or..." She spotted Kailani and lowered her voice. "Or maybe octopuses ate him."

"Then wouldn't the bones float?"

Jack overheard Bradley and Trillian's conversation. "While it's true that human bones are porous, they don't float. It's... the fat and gasses that make a body float in water."

Trillian gave Jack a sideways look. "I'm not going to ask why you know that."

"I'm an encyclopedia of weird facts."

"Anyway. He's not dead," Bradley said. "Until I see a body, my dad is alive."

Jack and Trillian exchanged a glance.

"Maybe we'll go look for him again, when we're done here." Trillian kissed Bradley on the cheek.

Kailani poked her head over the gunwale. It was obvious that she had overheard a large portion of their conversation. "When we're done here, I think you need to break the curse."

Jack looked up at her. "How?"

"For one, stop Skulk and return the treasure she's stolen," Kailani said.

Jack laughed out of frustration. "Like I said, how?"

"*Kill* her." The seriousness in Bradley's voice scared them all. "I'll do it. Get me a gun and I'll go over to her boat right now and blow her head off."

Trillian wrapped her arms around Bradley's chest. "No. You're better than that."

Kailani locked a gaze of concern and empathy with Jack. "Maybe we deal with Skulk *after* finding your dad," she said.

Bradley shook his head. "Even though we're helping you fix your boat, your dad'll never go for that."

"Brad, look at me," Kailani said.

Bradley continued to stare at the bullet hole in front of him as he sanded the edges furiously, his mind consumed with ending Skulk's life. It was the only concrete idea he could cling to.

"*Look* at me."

Bradley stopped sanding and directed a reluctant gaze at Kailani.

"You don't know my dad," she continued. "He's a reasonable guy. But let's finish here first. It'll put him in a good mood."

Even though his enthusiasm had taken a hit, Bradley shook his head in agreement.

"Dad, we're ready for the patches," Kailani called out.

Lono, who had finished with the engine and had been sitting close to the pier cutting circular patches of fiberglass, gave her the thumbs up. He mixed up a portion of epoxy resin and began covering the holes, one by one, soaking the fiberglass and adhering it to the hull, starting with the exterior.

An hour later, the group was back to sanding again, this time the hardened epoxy. An hour after that, Lono applied a gelcoat to the patches. An afternoon of comradery and hard work had restored both the *Octopussy's* hull, and the relationships between Palakiko Tours and the Detest-A-Pest crew.

Bradley hoped that Lono would be amenable to searching the cove one more time. He would know the answer soon enough.

BAITED

SAM JERKED AWAKE, disoriented. His dreams held no permanence in his mind but they left dark and heavy remnants. He tried to swallow but his throat clicked dryly instead.

The pain in his abdomen had vanished completely, replaced by intense burning in his muscles and joints. Even with his clouded thoughts, Sam knew another day of this might prove fatal.

Water splashed in the corner of the space. Bradley stepped out of the darkness, about a dozen feet from where Sam lay. He had no light source of his own, but cast his own luminescence, much like the octopuses had done a day earlier.

"I'm sorry," Sam said.

Bradley smiled and shook his head slowly in response.

"I can't leave you again." Sam looked around for clues to indicate an exit, but everything remained as it always had, dark and inaccessible.

Then something caught his eye, a partial detail reflected on the back wall. It was faint and eroded, but there were letters there.

...re ex...

Sam squinted to resolve more, but as Bradley approached him, he lost the letters in the shadows.

"Wait! Back up. What was—"

Bradley raised his arms, dipped his head forward, and sunk into the water until his head submerged.

"Brad!" Sam watched his son float closer, inch by inch, barely casting a ripple in the water.

Bradley's hand reached out for Sam's leg. But it wasn't a hand anymore. Sam realized what he was seeing wasn't Bradley at all, but an octopus with its tentacles outstretched. His desperate imagination had conjured a familiar yet unattainable savior.

He felt the heavy weight of the sea creature slide over his legs and up toward his abdomen, just as it had done when he was injured. The thought of eating more seafood at that moment turned his stomach.

Sam laid back and stared at the blackness above him. His thoughts were mostly an incoherent mess. As the octopus slid higher up his body, one tentacle probed his left palm with what he assumed were its suckers.

Then something cool rolled into his hand.

Something familiar.

He curled his fingers around the object and squeezed. Its surface felt hard and curved, yet he could distort the sides if he tightened his grip. And there were no sharp edges.

Sam felt the weight of the octopus move off his body, and with it the luminescence faded. For whatever reason, the creature's intent this time was not to feed him.

Then what…?

He fought through the pain in his joints and the fog in his mind and raised the object to the center of his chest. With his other hand, Sam continued his tactile examination. On one end of the object sat a round rigid piece of plastic.

A cap!

His fingers scrabbled over the sides of the object. It felt like a bottle of water.

Could it be?

The answer became so obvious with every touch that Sam thought he could almost see it in the pitch dark.

Forget looking at it. OPEN IT.

He did his best to ignore the pain in his muscles and sat up. The bottle rolled off his chest and into uncharted territory.

"No!" Sam ran his right hand over the graveyard of shells and bones next to him. Panic flooded his brain. The octopus had brought him an unopened bottle of water. Somehow it had known. If there was any doubt that he had released a curse, losing the water before drinking it would confirm it.

Sam's fingers searched the pile of dead remnants. He twisted where he sat and was met with screaming pain in his abdomen, not from his injury, but from fatigue and dehydration. But he had no intention of joining the collection of bones.

Seconds seemed to stretch out like minutes before his fingertips found the bottle lying at the water's edge, close to his right knee. He gripped the bottle tight and after three attempts to get his left hand to do what he wanted, Sam successfully unscrewed the cap.

He brought the neck of the bottle to his lips and sipped. The cool, fresh water woke up his senses almost instantly, as if he was a wilting plant. He advanced past sipping and gulped.

The water held a sweetness that compelled him to drink it all in one go, but he forced himself to stop. If he drank too fast, he might make himself sick.

Sam decided to drink a little a time, but the bottle cap was gone. In his excitement and haste, he had dropped it. Finding it among the broken bones and shells beside him in complete darkness would be a difficult, if not impossible, task.

He had to keep the bottle upright until he finished it, which meant no sleep and no sudden moves. There couldn't be more than a couple cups of water in the bottle, and he couldn't waste a single drop.

As time pushed on, Sam regained more of his senses and the ache in his muscles faded as the water worked its way through his body. It was his intention to make the water last as long as possible, but an hour later the bottle was empty. It would be enough to keep him going for half a day at most.

"I have to get out of here." Sam's voice echoed in the dank space. It sounded a lot smaller than he had imagined. He tried to stand, but the sharp shells dug into his feet. It wouldn't take much to cut his feet to ribbons.

Yet, with his attempt to stand, the pinpoints of light he had been staring at for hours revealed a parallax shift. They were collected along a flat surface…

Like a wall.

He thought about yelling, but any extra exertion would cause him to sweat even more than he was already, which would lead back to dehydration.

Sam sat and ran his fingers over the shells and bones. He grabbed a handful and threw them at the pinpoints of light. He couldn't see it, but he heard the shells strike the surface—

wall

—and ricochet into other areas of the space.

He continued dragging his hands through the remnants, getting on his knees to reach farther without having to step on the sharp shells.

Sam's hand stumbled over a large, solid bone, definitely not a fish. He pulled it back to where he sat and ran his fingertips over it, noting its shape and texture. He aimed as best he could and threw the bone at the wall of pinpoint lights.

A hollow, metallic tone vibrated through the space, like he was on the inside of the Liberty Bell. Two of the pinpoint light sources increased in size, not by much but enough, and large enough to see blue sky through them.

The answer came to Sam in a flood of realization.

"It's a ship," he said aloud. "I'm in a *ship*." He cast his mind back to his first day here and remembered the rusted derelict ships they had passed, permanently buried halfway into the sand, and listing to one side.

"Shipwreck Beach," the shuttle driver had said during their drive to Club Niho'gula. "Forbidden and cursed," he had also said.

"No shit." After having no one to talk to for more than a day, Sam's voice sounded foreign even to him.

He couldn't wait any longer. As his body absorbed the water, taking it places where it was needed, his second chance at survival ticked away. Sam thought of Bradley and how he'd want his son to remember him. The stark reality was he'd either die in this rusty coffin or die fighting to escape.

"Fighting. Definitely."

Sam leaned back and eased himself forward. Spreading his body out over the broken shells and bones helped minimize their ability to tear through his skin and worked much better than standing. As he edged out into the water, he began to float. A little further in and he could right himself and swim out of here.

But where?

Maybe he could kick a hole in the wall big enough to escape through, but his thoughts exceeded his ability. Sam had no confidence that his body could perform except in the most rudimentary fashion.

He heard familiar splashing from the far corner of the rank space. The octopuses were back. Were they watching him? What did these creatures want?

There was no logical reason to keep him here *and* feed him, unless the octopuses planned to save his life. Humans weren't part of their diets. He felt a tentacle slide around one foot, then the other and around his legs. He spotted their luminescence under the water, and it lit up his immediate surroundings. And piles of gold coins.

Part of Sam fought the panic of feeling constrained. He could be wrong about the octopuses. He'd seen enough horror films to know that sea creatures were unpredictable. Yet he was able to balance the impending terror with how the octopuses had treated him over the past day and a half. They weren't there to harm him.

Sam closed his eyes and relaxed his body. The octopus that had grabbed his legs tightened its grip so he wouldn't slip away. A second later the creature pulled him under the water. He took one last look at the treasure surrounding him and managed to take a large breath before his face submerged.

The next sixty seconds would decide his fate. Being in a ship, he expected to bump up against walls, doors, or stairs as the octopus guided him out. But there were no collisions or snags, just smooth motion, like taking a waterslide to the bottom. And instead of counting down the seconds, Sam envisioned a reunion with the people that mattered most in his life.

Through closed eyelids, Sam sensed the light around him fluctuating, getting brighter and brighter until—

Sam's head popped through the surface of the ocean into afternoon sunshine. He opened his eyes and welcomed the familiar burn of bright light. Sam filled his lungs with clean sea air, no longer steeped in the stench of a rotting ship.

He turned in the water. The ship that had hidden him within loomed above, a lifeless rusted bulk. The wreck was massive. He made a mental note to look it up once he returned to shore.

The bulbous head of the octopus floated in front of him. He placed his hand on top of it and the octopus mirrored his movements.

"Thank you." Sam spoke as well as thought the words. He then placed both of his hands over his heart and hoped that somehow the creature would understand.

Several tentacles wrapped around Sam's chest and two octopuses propelled Sam back toward the marina. His journey concluded at the end of the pier, next to an access ladder.

Sam grabbed a rung and gazed back at the creatures that had saved him. One larger octopus appeared between the two that had propelled him to the marina. Its long tentacle found Sam's free hand and deposited a gold coin into it, smaller and without a hole in the center. It felt heavier than the one he had intentionally taken before.

Sam shook his head and extended his hand to return it. The octopus's tentacle curled around the coin and gave it back. The creature wasn't taking no for an answer. He relented and accepted the coin, made a fist around it, and held it to his heart. Only then did the three octopuses leave.

Why are these creatures giving me the treasure they fight so hard to protect?

Sam had no answer, but he did know what he was going to do with the coin. He grasped the next rung on the ladder and climbed to the top of the pier.

BRADLEY STEPPED UP to Lono and held out his hand. "Thank you, sir. For taking us out to look for my dad one more time. It... it means a lot."

Lono looked Bradley over, smiled just a little, and nodded. He took Bradley's hand with both of his, solidifying their handshake. "I hope you find... peace."

Jack, Trillian, and Hope helped Kailani load some snorkeling gear onto *Octopuppy*. Even though *Octopussy's* hull had been repaired and was ready to go, Lono wanted to give the vessel an extra day out of the water to let the patching cure.

A voice spoke from behind. "Where are you guys going?"

Bradley froze and his face went ashen. He would know that voice anywhere.

Lono stared at him. "Son? What's wrong?"

Could it be? How could it be?

Bradley spun in place, barely letting his brain process the impossibility of what he had just heard.

But there, less than a dozen feet from him, stood the impossible. Sam grinned at him, soaked to the skin, in the same shorts and T-shirt he had been wearing when Skulk had taken him.

"Dad!" Bradley closed the gap between them and wrapped his arms around Sam. He ignored the cold seawater transferring into his dry clothes and held Sam like there was no tomorrow.

Jack climbed the stairs from the lower dock, busy with something on his phone. "Brad? You going to help or wh—"

Trillian bumped into Jack near the top of the stairs. "Put the phone away and move your butt!" When Jack didn't immediately respond, she glanced past him and spotted Bradley and Sam. "Holy shit."

She looked back at *Octopuppy,* where Hope was helping Kailani organize some gear in the boat. "Hope! It's Sam! He's back!"

"What?" Hope called back, but both Jack and Trillian had run out onto the pier and out of sight from her lower point of view. She glanced at Kailani. "Did she say, 'Sam was back'?"

Kailani raised her brows at her. "That's what I heard."

Both Hope and Kailani stepped off the *Octopuppy* and ran to the stairs leading up to the pier, Hope leading the way.

She reached the top of the stairs and saw Bradley, Jack, and Trillian embracing Sam. His eyes gleamed.

Hope covered her mouth with trembling hands, like she was praying. Tears welled in her eyes. She stepped tentatively toward him, half expecting him to vanish like a mirage if she got too close. "Oh Sam. Is it…?"

"The very same," Sam said with a grin.

Kailani shared a look of disbelief with Lono and stood next to him.

The teenagers stepped aside to make way for Hope. She threw her arms around him and kissed his neck. "Don't ever do that to me again," she whispered.

"I won't," Sam said. "Promise."

Hope took Sam's face in her hands and kissed him, then stepped back, shaking her head like she couldn't quite believe he was real. "How?"

"I had a little help from some friends. And look." Sam worked a hand into the pocket of his wet shorts and pulled out a gold coin. He spotted looks of outrage and betrayal flash on Kailani's and Lono's faces.

Sam approached the Palakikos. "Before you get angry, I tried to give the coin back, but they wouldn't take it."

Kailani crossed her arms tightly against her chest. "What do you mean, *they?*"

"The octopuses," Sam said. "They're the reason I'm here. Skulk stabbed me, but the octopuses saved me. *Healed* me." He pulled up the hem of his T-shirt to reveal a faint but distinct scar across his abdomen. "I would have died, bled out, if it hadn't been for the octopuses."

"You still have a coin though," Lono said. "Nothing's changed. The curse is just going to get stronger."

"No." Sam alternated his gaze between Lono and Kailani. "I have an idea how to use the coin for good. But I need to get Skulk's attention."

"I can help with that," Jack said.

"Alright." Sam drew everyone into an impromptu huddle and described his plan.

THE DETEST-A-PEST CREW and the Palakikos had pushed two tables together in the restaurant. Hope and Bradley sat on either side of Sam, as if keeping him in close proximity would prevent anything further from happening to him.

Sam held up the gold coin and rotated it between his fingertips. "It's different," he said. "And I think it's actually heavier than the last one I saw." He cast his eyes toward Kailani and felt her scrutiny. "I know you still don't trust me, but that last coin, Skulk took it from me, just before he sliced me open." Sam handed the coin to Bradley to examine. "Had it not been for the octopuses, I'd be dead."

Maddilyn entered the restaurant, then stopped a few feet from the group's table, eyeing everyone to decide if it was safe to approach. Jack nodded and waved her over. Kailani switched her attention to this new and different threat.

Maddilyn leaned in and whispered something into Jack's ear. When a toothy grin spread across his face, Kailani couldn't stand it any longer.

"What's going on?" She locked gazes with Jack.

He stood and pulled over an extra chair for Maddilyn, placing it beside Kailani. "Skulk's taken the bait." Jack glanced at Maddilyn and motioned for her to share her information.

"Um, yeah," Maddilyn began. "Like, I pretended to talk to Jack on my phone, about Sam and the new coin he has, and made sure that my mom was close enough to hear." She looked back at the row of cabins. "I heard her talking with Skulk when I left to come here. She'd make a terrible spy."

"She makes a terrible criminal, too," O'Connor said. "But we're going to nail her ass. No offense. And Skulk's too."

As if mentioning her name held a power to summon, Skulk trudged into the restaurant, followed closely by Niko. Everyone expected an outburst like yesterday when she had pulled a gun on O'Connor. Instead, she knocked Jack out of his seat and sat down.

Trillian moved her chair closer to Bradley's.

Maddilyn helped Jack to his feet. He brushed himself off and took a spot behind Maddilyn and Kailani.

Skulk glanced briefly at Maddilyn. "Didn't peg you for a traitor. Maybe you'll get cut from the will."

Maddilyn cast her eyes down to the table as her cheeks flushed red with embarrassment. Jack placed a hand on her shoulder and gave it a gentle squeeze.

Skulk watched Bradley hand the gold coin back to Sam.

"It's pretty, isn't it? The ones without the hole in the center are extra special." He rolled the coin between his thumb and index finger, then let it drop into his palm where he made a fist around it. "Assuming I was dead was a pretty stupid mistake."

"I don't make the same mistake twice," Skulk said.

"Now that's funny, because this feels like déjà vu." Sam leaned into the table. "Only this time *I* have all the control."

Skulk scoffed but said nothing.

O'Connor cracked her knuckles. "Can I kick the shit out of her now?"

Sam raised an open palm to O'Connor, never once taking his eyes off Skulk. "What if I told you I know where there's more of these coins. More than you could ever dream of."

Skulk smiled smugly. "I'd say you're going to tell me…" She glanced around the table.

"And if I *don't* tell you?"

"You'll never make it off this island alive," Skulk said. "None of you will. I'd kill you… I'd kill *all* of you."

Niko casually pulled a pistol from behind his back and held it in front of him.

Lono grabbed Kailani's arm and stood.

"No." Skulk shook her head. "Sit down."

"This has nothing to do with us," Lono said.

"Dad, stop," Kailani whispered.

Lono tightened his grip. "We don't want—"

"Sit… *the fuck*… down." Skulk stared at him.

Niko stepped forward and made sure Lono could see his pistol as he settled his finger over the trigger.

Lono backed down and he and Kailani both returned to their seats. "You're all cursed," he said quietly.

Skulk laughed. "Superstition is for the weak." The sound of

something ticking recaptured her attention. She saw that Sam was tapping the edge of the coin against the table.

"Ready to shut up and listen to my proposal?" Sam continued to tap the coin.

"I've had enough of your bullshit." Skulk placed both fists on the table, her knuckles turning white. "Either tell me where the treasure is, or everyone here is taking a one-way trip to open water."

"You're forgetting I have control of this situation."

"We've got the guns."

Sam raised his hands, one still gripping the coin tightly. "Then what are you waiting for? Kill me."

Hope leaned in. "Sam, stop," she whispered.

"I know what I'm doing," he whispered back. He turned to Skulk and waited, knowing that he had the woman's attention.

Skulk scowled. "Okay. I'm listening."

"I'll do more than tell you where the treasure is," Sam said. "I'll take you there."

"Great. Get off your ass and let's go."

"There's one condition." Sam locked gaze with Skulk. "You leave my family and friends – this entire island – behind."

Skulk shook her head. "You're crazy."

"Then the deal's off."

"Wait, wait, wait." Skulk shot a quick glance at Niko. "Okay."

"Dad, no." Bradley whispered. "She'll kill you anyway."

"You're insane, Sam," O'Connor said.

Sam ignored their protests, transferred the coin to his left hand, and presents his right to shake on it.

Skulk balked.

"What's wrong, *Skulk?*" Sam grinned at him. "Don't you *trust* me? What happened to honor among thieves?"

"You're not a thief."

Sam held up the coin in his left hand. "I'm not? I took something that didn't belong to me, so…"

Skulk paused, then nodded almost imperceptibly. She took Sam's hand and shook it. "Let's go."

Niko motioned Sam forward with the pistol.

As Sam stood, he tapped his finger lightly on a napkin in front of him. Trillian noticed.

"Put the gun away," Sam said. "You're not going to need it."

Niko ignored him but covered his pistol under his shirt before jamming it into Sam's back. "Move."

"Hey, it speaks!" Sam laughed.

Niko shoved him forward.

Skulk stood to leave and left one parting edict. "If anyone follows, he dies. Got it?"

The teenagers nodded.

Skulk followed Sam and Niko out of the restaurant.

O'Connor watched Skulk leave, then leaned into the table. "That *dipshit* doesn't know us very well. Does she really believe we're *not* going to follow her?"

"Maybe," Trillian said. "But we are."

O'Connor nodded. "Damn straight, tangerine."

"And there's this." Trillian flipped the napkin over to reveal a quickly scrawled message.

"Follow in 5. Not too close. Don't worry," Sam's handwriting read.

O'Connor raised a brow at Bradley. "Your dad's always on my case about my plans being half-baked. This ain't much better."

"I guess we'll have to make sure it *is* better," Bradley said.

Hope eyed the group with concern. "But Skulk said she'd kill him if we followed."

"She won't kill him," Jack said. "Not until she knows where the treasure is. And that gives us some time." A gleam twinkled in his eyes. "I'll be right back." Jack bolted from the restaurant and toward the cabins.

O'Connor squinted her eyes on Jack. "Where the hell is he going?"

Hope shook her head, then spotted a small grin on Bradley's face. "What? You know something?"

Bradley shrugged and shook his head. "It's probably nothing."

Lono stood. "Look, folks. As much as we want to..." He glanced at Kailani. "We can't get involved in this. It's too risky for us."

Kailani looked back at the cabins. "Tell Jack I'm sorry."

"Come on, Kai," Lono said. "We got a business to run." Lono headed for the marina.

Kailani followed, but looked back one more time, again mouthing the words "I'm sorry" to the group.

Bradley and Trillian nodded, and Trillian mouthed back, "It's okay."

A moment later, Jack returned with a the ReciproJab concealed in a plastic bag. "We're going to need this." He looked around. "Hey, where's Kai?"

"She's not coming with us," Bradley said. "Lono's not on board."

"Shit." Jack deflated. "Was she mad?"

"No," Trillian said. "Just following her dad's orders."

"That's what dads do. Protect their own." O'Connor looked at Bradley and punched his shoulder. "Ain't that right?"

Bradley returned a subdued nod.

Jack turned to Maddilyn. "You coming with?"

Maddilyn shrugged. "Why not? I'm already in deep shit with my mom. What's a little more?"

"That's the spirit," O'Connor said. "Let's go. We don't have much time." She pushed her chair back so quickly it almost toppled. "I've got an idea." She led the group towards the marina, talking as she went.

"THAT'S YOUR PLAN?" Hope pulled O'Connor aside, out of sight but close to where Skulk had moored the *Wavy Jones*. "You're going to get us all *killed*."

O'Connor pulled her arm out of Hope's grip. "What are *you* worried about? You're not the bait. I am."

Hope clenched her jaws in frustration.

The engines on the *Wavy Jones* rumbled up.

"We've got to go," Jack said. "*Now*."

"Can I join?"

Jack spun around to see Kailani looking at him expectantly. "Your dad doesn't know you're here, does he?"

"No," Kailani said. "But you're my friends, right?" She looked at Bradley, Trillian, Jack, and even Maddilyn. "I help my friends."

"Okay. Here's the deal." Jack laid out the plan for Kailani as simply and as quickly as possible. He looked at O'Connor. "You ready?"

"Does the Pope shit in the woods?" O'Connor handed Hope her phone.

The teenagers exchanged confused looks.

"That means yes," Hope said.

"Give me a few seconds head start." O'Connor emerged from hiding. She grabbed an oar from a boat on the opposite side of the dock and leaped onto the stern of the *Wavy Jones*.

"You bastards are going to *pay!*" She ran up past the console before Niko realized what was happening.

"That's our cue!" Jack said.

The teenagers ran past the stern and crouched beside the starboard side of the *Wavy Jones*. Hope remained on the dock port-side, recording video on O'Connor's phone.

Jack pulled open the plastic bag with the ReciproJab inside, and instead pulled out a length of rope. He slung the plastic bag around his shoulders again. He looked at the jumbled cord. "Shit."

Kailani extended her hand. "Give it here."

Jack handed the rope to her. She quickly tied a bowline knot at one end and slipped it over a cleat on the gunwale of the *Wavy Jones*.

"You're a knotty girl," Jack said with a smirk.

"You know it," Kailani said.

"Let's go," Bradley said. "Everyone into the water."

One by one, the teenagers slipped into the water as quietly as they could and grabbed hold of the rope. From their position, the five of them couldn't hear the mayhem unfolding on the port side. They only thing they knew for certain was that the *Wavy Jones* wasn't moving.

NIKO THROTTLED DOWN the engines, stopping what little forward momentum the *Wavy Jones* had.

"O'Connor!" Sam sat near the bow, his hands tied behind his back, his eyes wide with feigned but convincing surprise. "What the *fuck* are you doing?"

"Saving your ass." O'Connor raised the oar to swing it at Skulk. Niko jammed the barrel of his pistol into the back of O'Connor's head and cocked the hammer.

"No! Wait, wait!" Sam looked up at Skulk. "If you kill her, you may as well kill me too, because I'll never tell you where the treasure is."

Niko grabbed the oar from O'Connor's hand and threw it behind him. The oar slid along the deck and bounced against the stern. Below on the dock, he saw Hope recording the entire exchange. He caught Skulk's attention and motioned to Hope.

Skulk looked and laughed. She faced O'Connor, almost nose to nose. "Did you really think you could stop me?"

O'Connor remained silent, instead locking her gaze with Sam.

"Oh, *now* you stop talking?" Skulk removed her machete from its scabbard and held the tip of the blade just under O'Connor's jaw. "How about I make that permanent? I'd be saving the ears of thousands."

O'Connor gagged. "Jesus Christ. Ever heard of Altoids?"

Rage flickered in Skulk's eyes. She glanced around the marina, suddenly aware of how exposed she was, and glared at Niko. "Get this fat bitch off this boat before I *kill* her."

It was an empty threat and everyone knew it. But Niko followed Skulk's orders. He took O'Connor by the throat with his left hand, stuck the barrel of his pistol into her cheek, and forced her backward.

O'Connor stumbled over the boat's deck. She didn't protest. This was the inevitable end to their hastily formed plan, but a plan that was working.

Niko pushed O'Connor over the stern. She lost her footing and toppled past the transom and into the water. Niko sneered at her for a moment before returning to the console and throttling up.

O'Connor felt the wash of the engines churn water around her. Any closer and the propeller blades would have shredded her legs.

Hope ran to the edge of the dock and helped O'Connor out of the water. "You think it worked?"

As O'Connor caught her breath, she looked back at the *Wavy Jones* leaving the marina. A cluster of teenagers hung onto a rope tied to the starboard hull, just out of sight.

"Looks like it," she said. "Sam's in their hands now."

Hope watched the *Wavy Jones* leave the marina and crossed her arms with worry.

O'Connor stood. "They're smart kids. They'll get him back."

She rung out seawater from the hem of her T-shirt. "Fuck, I need a drink. Come on." She headed to the bar.

Despite everything Sam had told her about Bradley and his friends, Hope's confidence in the group's safe return wavered.

LIFELINE

Skulk opened a concealed compartment under the seats along the port-side hull and retrieved two sets of scuba gear. She pulled on her wetsuit and slipped an air tank on her back. She attached several clear poly bags to her belt, cinched closed with nylon cord.

"That fat bitch never had a chance," Skulk said. "Now I'm going to walk away the winner, again."

Sam stared at Skulk coldly, but there was a hint of a smirk on his lips. "O'Connor knows what she's doing. I'd stake my life on it."

"It doesn't take a genius to know that you're not coming back this time." Skulk squatted and stared at him. "I'll make sure of it." She reached around to Sam's wrists and cut the rope binding him, then placed the knife under his throat. "Give me the coin."

"I can't do that," Sam said. "It's my golden ticket. Once we're in, one more coin won't make a difference."

Skulk squinted at him, a dubious look on her face.

"Why would I lie?"

Skulk gave Sam a reluctant benefit of the doubt. "Get suited up. No bullshit, either."

"Or what? You'll kill me?" Sam felt enough hatred for Skulk to last him a lifetime. "You're full of empty threats."

Not to be outdone, Skulk returned Sam's gaze with her own loathing. "No, I'll kill your son... and your *ex-wife*."

Sam's eyes widened, but before he could respond, Skulk continued.

"I know people, low people, that break into houses in the San Fernando Valley under cover of darkness, and make it look like an accident." Skulk crossed her arms smugly. "Incentive enough for you?" She didn't wait for an answer, but instead pushed the scuba gear in front of Sam. "Quickly."

Niko navigated the *Wavy Jones* to the *Templeton* wreck site and cut the engines.

"You're way off the mark, idiot." Sam pointed out of the cove as he pulled on his gear. "There's a beached wreck farther north, along the shore."

Skulk glanced at Niko and gave him the go ahead. Niko throttled up the engines and plotted a path out of the cove and into the Auau Channel.

As soon as the *Wavy Jones* cleared the beach heads of Nihoʻgula Cove, Skulk and Niko spotted the derelict ship listing to one side in the distance. They focused on their destination.

At the back of the boat, five teenagers had managed to work their way onto the starboard side of the transom. One by one, they boarded the vessel.

KAILANI CREPT OVER the stern, then took the ReciproJab from Jack and placed it gently by the starboard hull. The teenagers moved fast and silent, Bradley next, followed Trillian, Jack and Maddilyn. Jack extended his hand to help Maddilyn aboard, but she lost her footing on the transom and disappeared into the watery froth generated by the engines.

Jack almost yelled out for her, but stopped himself at the last minute. He shot a look back at the others and they all shook their heads emphatically. He looked back again and saw Maddilyn surface several dozen feet behind the boat's wake. She waved and began to swim back to the marina.

Jack joined the others crouched at the back of the *Wavy Jones*. "Is Maddi going to be alright?"

"Isn't she, like, an Olympic swimmer?" Kailani whispered to the others, huddling close so no one had to raise their voices. "She'll be fine. So, what's the plan?"

Bradley exchanged glances with Jack and Trillian. It became clear quickly to Kailani that there wasn't a specific plan once they were on the boat.

"The driver has a gun," Trillian whispered before pointing at the pistol holstered to the Niko's belt.

"Right," Bradley said quietly. "Shit."

"How about I just gore the guy from behind?" Jack nodded at his invention resting on the deck and grinned.

Obviously, Jack was confident that his weapon would not fail. Bradley had other thoughts.

"Um…" He glanced around the stern of the boat and wrapped a fist around the oar sitting next to him. "I'll use this to knock out the driver." Bradley looked at Trillian and Kailani. "You guys can make sure he falls overboard. Push him or something. And Jack…" Bradley pointed at the ReciproJab. "You work your magic on Skulk with that thing."

"Next question," Kailani said. "When do we do this?"

"It's got to be before they stop." Trillian looked to the others for agreement. "We'll lose our advantage."

Kailani nodded. "Makes sense."

Sitting at the bow, Sam slipped his scuba tank over his shoulders and stretched a mask around his head. He glanced at Niko, or perhaps *past* Niko, it was hard to tell. The four teenagers crouched as low as they could.

If Sam had seen them, he never let on. He turned and watched the shipwreck he had laid in for the better part of two days get closer, seemingly growing in size. He pointed to a hole in the hull and Niko adjusted the boat's trajectory.

"Now?" Kailani looked at Bradley, but he held up one palm and shook his head. "It better be soon because that asshole is going to cut—"

As if Kailani's words held magic, Niko began to throttle down the engines and angle the *Wavy Jones* toward the entry point.

"Shit, Brad." Kailani's eyes blazed with panic. "Do it *now!*"

Bradley gripped the oar with both hands until his knuckles whitened. He stood and took careful steps toward the Niko at the console until he was within striking distance. He gave the other teens one last look before he raised the oar and swung the wide end at Niko's head.

Mid-swing Bradley thought he had misjudged the distance, but there was no stopping now. The edge of the oar connected with the side of Niko's head with a sickening *slap-crack*. The man never saw it coming.

Trillian and Kailani sprung into action. As Niko careened toward the starboard gunwale, Trillian and Kailani grabbed his feet. Since Niko had already lost his balance, giving the man's momentum an extra push was easy.

Within a few seconds, the *Wavy Jones* had no one at the helm. Kailani and Trillian shared a look of excitement and surprise. "It worked," their eyes seemed to say.

But the reality of no one at the helm pulled the teenagers back to reality. Kailani took the wheel and reversed the engines, but it was too late.

Realizing something was wrong, both Skulk and Sam turned to see the four teenagers staring back at them. And Niko was nowhere in sight. Skulk narrowed her eyes at Kailani, went for the pistol tucked behind the front zipper of her wetsuit, and—

WHAM.

The *Wavy Jones* struck the beached shipwreck's rusted hull at an angle and sent everyone to the deck. Bradley lost his grip on the oar and watched it slide toward the bow, between Sam and Skulk.

Jack managed to get to his feet first and pointed the barbed end of the ReciproJab at Skulk. But he wasn't close enough yet for the weapon to have any effect.

Skulk scrambled to her feet as Jack advanced on her. She yanked the pistol from her wetsuit and aimed it at Sam. "Stop where you are. Or I start shooting."

Jack froze, as did the others.

"I got enough bullets for everyone." Skulk sneered as she scanned the teenage faces looking back at him, singling out Jack. "You're going to give me the harpoon gun now."

Jack glanced at Bradley, who gave him a nod in return.

"Slowly," Skulk said.

Jack clenched his jaw angrily. He set the ReciproJab down and gave it a push. His latest pride and joy slid across the deck, stopping just short of Skulk's feet.

"This will be very useful." Skulk leveled her aim on Jack and pulled the hammer back on the pistol.

"Put it down, Skulk. Now." Sam pulled himself to his feet. "If you hurt anyone else, the deal's off. You may as well kill us all."

"Good idea." Skulk returned her aim on Sam. "I'll start with you."

"Good luck finding the treasure on your own."

"How hard can it be?" Skulk looked at the rusted opening in the wreck's hull. "You've shown me the front door."

Sam said nothing and stood his ground.

Skulk grumbled with hesitation. She reset the hammer of the pistol, returned it to her wetsuit, and zipped it up. She picked up the ReciproJab and directed Sam into the water with its barbed tip. "Let's get on with it."

Before Sam pushed himself off the gunwale and into the water, he exchanged a look and a brief nod with Bradley.

"My boat better still be here when I get back." Skulk sent an icy stare at each teenager, ending on Kailani. "It'd be a real shame if something were to happen to Palakiko Tours."

No one said a word.

Skulk slipped on her mask, stepped off the gunwale, and joined Sam in the water.

The four teenagers stepped to the port-side hull and peered over. The flashlights from Sam and Skulk flickered below the surface, mingling with the air bubbles rising from their regulators. They watched the lights dim in the deeper water until they disappeared altogether.

Bradley stared at the water lapping the rusted hull of the wreck. "What if that bitch kills him in there?"

Trillian wrapped her arms around Bradley and hugged him silently. She knew any words she could come up with would offer no solace.

"So that's it?" Bradley looked to the others. "We wait until Skulk returns without him? Leaving him dead in this *fucking* coffin?"

Kailani looked at Jack. "You got your phone, right? I could call my dad for backup."

Bradley shook his head, irritated. "Thanks, but how is that going to help my dad right *now?*"

"Sorry," Kailani said.

Bradley turned back to face the immense wreck. "FUCK!"

Kailani and Jack joined Trillian and Bradley in a moment of silence at the port-side gunwale, while everyone searched for answers.

The wreck sat twenty feet from the *Wavy Jones*. The massive ship had beached itself decades earlier at an angle, listing heavily to its port side. The crimson and eroded hull stretched up and over them, giving off a feeling that the whole structure could topple at any moment. It didn't ease Bradley's feeling of loss.

The evening sun continued its trek across the sky. Sunset wasn't for another few hours, but that was long enough to decide the fates of everyone involved, for better or for worse. A gentle breeze buffeted the *Wavy Jones,* causing splashing at the waterline. But the boat seemed to be moving a bit *too* much.

Trillian spotted movement out of the corner of her eye. She turned her head just as a breathless Niko hopped over the stern, a bowie knife in one hand. He had used the same rope to pull himself aboard as they had earlier.

"Jack!" Trillian pulled Bradley backward. "Behind you!"

Jack turned just as Niko lunged with his knife. He and Kailani stumbled back just as the tip of the knife sliced Jack's left shin. Despite the cut being largely superficial, blood poured down Jack's leg and made the injury look far worse.

Bradley kept Trillian behind him. He picked up the oar and gripped it in front of his body. "I'm going to *end* you."

In a frenzy, Jack crab-walked away from Niko.

The thug paid no attention, and instead stared down his nose at Bradley. A malevolent grin spread across Niko's face, revealing two silver incisors primed to rend flesh if needed.

Niko charged Bradley but saw the teen's eyes flick up at something. He turned, leading with his knife.

Kailani ran toward Niko, pivoted on one leg, and launched herself toward the man's face. Both of her feet connected with his head. She pushed back, clearing herself from his knife and thrusting him backward.

Niko struck the back of his head on the port-side gunwale. He shook off the blow and pulled himself up.

"Stay down, *motherfucker!*" Bradley swung the oar in a wide arc, all his strength multiplied by his rage toward Niko.

Crack!

The oar connected solidly with Niko's head. The man dropped to the deck like a stone. His knife slid across the deck and bounced behind the console.

Trillian ran past Niko to the stern and helped Kailani up. "You're one wicked bitch."

Kailani blew hair out of her face and grinned.

Bradley raised the oar again and unloaded all his fury onto Niko's back. The edge of the oar made a hollow *snap* against the man's back. Bradley prepared for a third blow when Jack reached out and stopped him.

"He's down, dude," Jack said. "You don't need to kill him."

Bradley stared down at Niko's unconscious body and nodded. He lowered the oar but kept a white-knuckled grip on the handle.

Kailani ran to the starboard gunwale and untied the rope from the cleat. "Help me tie him up. Quick, before he wakes up."

Trillian looked at her panicked. "I don't know anything about knots. What do I do?"

"Just stand on him," Kailani said. "I'll get his arms. Brad, grab his feet!"

Trillian stood squarely on Niko's back as Kailani tied his wrists tightly behind his back. She looped and knotted the remaining rope around Niko's ankles and cinched everything tight, leaving him hog-tied on the deck.

Trillian stepped off Niko's body to examine Kailani's handiwork.

"Fuck me," Jack said with a smirk. "Where did that come from?"

Kailani looked up at him. "What? The knots?"

"And the flying kick," Trillian added.

"Everything." Jack shook his head in wonder.

"The knots come with life at sea," Kailani said. "The kick? Well, I watch a lot of wrestling."

Jack sighed. "I think I'm in love." His eyes went wide, and he slapped one hand over his mouth. "Wait. Did I say that out loud?"

"Out loud." Kailani locked her gaze with his. "Did you mean it?"

"Absolutely," Jack said without hesitation.

Kailani smiled. "Good." She walked to where Jack sat to look at his leg.

Bradley tossed the oar aside and resumed his spot at the

port-side gunwale. Trillian sidled up to him and slid her arm around his waist.

"Try not to worry, okay?"

Bradley shook his head. "It's hard not to."

"Everything happens for a reason." Trillian motioned at the hog-tied and unconscious Niko at their feet. "That's a good sign, I think."

"Yeah. Maybe." Bradley continued his vigil, watching for signs of life from within the massive, rusted tomb in front of him.

SAM LED THE WAY toward the eroded hole in the derelict ship, with Skulk following close behind holding the ReciproJab pointed at Sam's back.

He paused for a moment and looked back at the silhouette of the *Wavy Jones's* hull from under the water. Was this a one-way trip? Would he see his son again? Sam didn't have the answers.

He felt something sharp stick into his back. Skulk had prodded him with the barbed end of the ReciproJab. It felt like the weapon's barb had pierced his skin, but Sam couldn't be sure. He continued through the center of the jagged hole.

With a mask and flashlight, the journey ahead was as clear as day. A modern-day catacomb of decomposing corridors and bulkheads led away from him.

But which way was the right *way?*

Sam didn't know. Both times had been without the luxury of flashlights or masks. And the first time he'd been close to dead.

He felt another poke in his back. Sam spun around, glared at Skulk, and raised the middle finger on his free hand. Then he shook a fist at her.

Skulk was about to poke him again, when Sam noticed Skulk's eyes shift with fear within her mask. Something had scared her.

Sam turned to find an octopus floating majestically a couple of feet from his head. The creature luminesced, fading in and out of shades of blues and greens, noticeable in the darkness but unable to compete with the brightness of his flashlight.

Skulk was equally fascinated but kept her distance a few feet behind and to the right of Sam.

The octopus shared a moment with Sam. He lowered his flashlight, aiming the light beam toward the bottom. The octopus's square pupils reacted as its tentacles played with the flashlight's beam as if it could feel it.

Was this creature the same one that had saved his life? He had to assume so but there was no way to be sure. Then a thought occurred to him, one so fitting he had no choice but to follow it.

He unzipped a small pocket on his wetsuit and removed the special gold coin. Sam held it between his thumb and index finger, palmed it, and brought the coin to his heart. He pointed to the right and brought both hands together around his neck, imitating a choke hold. Then he presented the coin to the octopus once again, like he had tried to earlier at the pier. Again, the creature refused it, instead wrapping its tentacle gently around Sam's arm and head.

Skulk reached in and snatched the coin from Sam's hand and positioned the ReciproJab next to his ribs. Rage flashed in Sam's eyes.

The octopus recoiled as the sharpened end cut a hole in Sam's wetsuit. This time Sam could see small tendrils of blood seeping out of the cut neoprene. Skulk motioned forward.

Sam kept his eyes on the octopus and placed his hands briefly around his own neck again. The octopus shot forward and disappeared around a bulkhead.

Did it understand?

Sam followed the route the octopus had taken. When he passed the bulkhead, he spotted the octopus glowing further down the adjoining corridor. Once Sam had followed far enough, the octopus disappeared again through an opening in the wall.

Sam navigated corridors and rooms one by one, the octopus leading the way a bit at a time. Then several feet above his head, a shimmering reflection revealed an air pocket. A strong feeling of déjà vu flooded his body.

Sam aimed the flashlight upward and broke the surface. He scanned the space and saw the familiar bones, shells, the empty water bottle that had saved his life… and piles of gold coins.

The octopus that had led him here had disappeared, but it *had* understood.

Skulk surfaced next to Sam and washed the small space with her flashlight beam. It didn't take long before she had singled out the piles of gold. Her regulator dropped from her mouth, agape with avarice. "I'm rich. I'm *fucking* rich!"

Sam removed his regulator and watched Skulk run her hands through the piles of coins. He felt nothing but contempt for the woman.

"There's got to be millions here!" Skulk pulled a bag from her belt, loosened the cord at the top, and began shoveling coins into it, hand over fist. After filling one bag, she began filling another. She worked quickly until all her bags were full. The golden coins jostled and sparkled through the clear bags.

When Skulk pushed back from the edge of the treasure stash, she found herself sinking like a stone. The extra weight of the treasure pulled her down too much, even when she adjusted her buoyancy compensator to maximum capacity and removed her dive weights.

Skulk pulled herself back to the edge. "It's too heavy. You're going to have to carry some out."

Sam scowled at her. "Fuck you."

Skulk raised the ReciproJab out of the water and leveled it at Sam several feet away. "You're forgetting who's calling the shots."

"I got you here," Sam said. "Our agreement *ends* here."

Skulk eyed him up and took a moment to consider Sam's words. "Suit yourself." She pulled the trigger on the ReciproJab. The barbed end shot out from the barrel, reached its maximum extension length, and retracted back into the barrel, effectively resetting itself, just as Jack had designed it to do.

"What the fuck?" Skulk stared at the weapon, confused. She pulled the trigger again, expecting a different result, but again, the harpoon's sharpened end shot forth and sprang back, just as it had before. But this time, the barb pierced Sam's wetsuit.

Sam moved back out of range of the ReciproJab and grinned. "Jack, you're a fucking genius," he said to himself.

Skulk couldn't close the gap between them because the gold coins tied to her waist weighed her down too much. She set the ReciproJab on the treasure pile, partially unzipped her wetsuit, and pulled her pistol.

Sam took a deep breath and submerged himself just as a shot rang out. He felt the water split by his head, heated by the bullet's speed. Pushing water back with his hands, he saw more bullets break the surface, only to shatter into harmless slow-moving fragments.

Sam placed the regulator back in his mouth. He had only one good choice: make a break for it and leave Skulk behind. Waiting would deplete his oxygen and leave him with no realistic way to get back. Plus, the longer he stayed increased the odds that Skulk would follow through with her threats.

He kicked toward the room's point of entry, which took him perilously close to Skulk. Sam hadn't gotten more than a few feet when he felt a sharp pain in his leg. The end of the ReciproJab had punctured his calf, the barbed ends hooking into the muscle. Skulk had squatted under the water, weighed down by her treasure, but close enough to get a clean hit. She pulled Sam back toward him.

The pain was so bad that Sam almost passed out, but the thought of leaving Bradley without a father forced him to direct his energy where it was needed. He reached down and began working the barbed end out of his flesh just as Skulk pulled him toward the barrel of her pistol. A bullet could be slowed by water but still maim or kill if shot from a close enough range. Sam managed to pull the barb out before falling in range of Skulk's bullets. He wrapped a hand around his calf to stem the blood clouding the small space.

Skulk untied two of her treasure bags and chased after Sam. It was impossible to hide. Sam's leg was like a flare leaving a smoke trail. Skulk reached out and grabbed Sam's injured calf, jamming her thumb into the wound. Sam shrieked into his regulator and bubbles of anguish flew around his head. He kicked his swim fins hard, but Skulk had a good grip.

Sam watched Skulk raise her pistol, now a couple of feet from his body.

This is it. I'm not making it out.

From within the murky red glow of Sam's own blood a tentacle rose and wrapped around Skulk's outstretched arm. Then another snaked around her legs and midsection.

Startled, Skulk aimed the gun at the octopus and fired. The bullet had no effect. Before she could try again, the pistol and the hand that held it fell away from Skulk's wrist, a great cloud of crimson jetting from the end of her arm.

The tentacles' suckers had morphed into razor sharp teeth much like a shark's. They worked their way around Skulk's body, clockwise and counterclockwise, slicing through her flesh as they went. Next her legs separated at the knees and her internal organs spilled out from her lacerated abdomen. Skulk's head and frenzied arms thrashed above the bloody viscera clouding the water.

The writhing mass moved up Skulk's body, cutting relentlessly as it went. One tentacle wrapped itself several times around her neck, then reversed its direction in a sudden jolt, removing Skulk's head from her body in a swift jerk.

Sam watched in horror and fascination as Skulk's body sank

to the bottom of the space, pulled down by the remaining weight of the coins and held together only by the scuba gear strapped to the remains of her body.

Then as quickly as it had come, the octopus was gone. Sam kicked his swim fins away from the settling gore, gently so as to not cloud the water more than it was already. He looked down and saw that his calf was still bleeding badly. He had to get out. Soon. Bleeding to death was a very real possibility.

Sam checked his dive computer. He had more than enough air to get back. He pointed his flashlight forward, then left, right, up, and down. Passages led in every possible direction, yet none looked familiar, except the way back to the treasure room. He was lost.

With every breath, every beat of his heart, Sam felt his life clock clicking toward a demise he refused to accept. Panic began a slow rise in the back of his mind. One wrong turn could mean his death. He kicked himself mentally for agreeing to such an excursion.

But Skulk was dead. That was the silver lining in this hellish situation. Even if he never made it out of the wreck, Skulk would never harm or plunder any person or treasure again. The thought gave Sam solace. He relaxed his mind and hovered in a rusted nexus that joined many other corridors of the ship. Darkness shrouded him everywhere except within the narrow beam of his flashlight. In this moment of newfound peace, Sam spotted Skulk's shredded and dismembered body at the bottom of the corridor, except it didn't look like a body anymore. What he saw looked more like a collection of flesh and bones.

Most of the blood, except that which continued to seep from his leg, had dissipated. Rising out of Skulk's carnage, Sam spotted a black braided nylon string, no more than an eighth of an inch thick. He swam toward it and pulled on it once he was close enough to reach. Skulk's belt, plus what remained of her midsection, jostled at the bottom of the corridor and kicked up eddies of torn flesh and viscera. Sam followed the line with the beam of his flashlight until it disappeared into the darkness beyond the beam's reach.

Skulk had intended to kill Sam. To ensure that she could find her way back unaided, she had had the foresight to run a line to show the path out. Sam hadn't been aware of it because he had led the way in. Skulk's greed had become Sam's salvation.

He gripped the line and ran it back and forth over the edge of a rusted corridor support until the line snapped. Sam took his time following the line through the maze of doorways and corridors. The last thing he wanted was to snag the line and break it before he could escape.

He reached the jagged opening in the hull and saw the glow of late afternoon daylight above. He was almost out, but he had one last task.

Sam found where Skulk had tied the start of the line and severed it the same way he had on the opposite end. He collected the slack in his hand until he held a loose ball of tangled nylon leading nowhere.

The treasure is safe again.

Sam kicked toward the surface. He had never been so glad to see the hull of the *Wavy Jones*.

BRADLEY SAT WITH his knees up on the port-side bench. He rested his head on the gunwale with his eyes on the water lapping against the rusted shipwreck.

Jack, Kailani, and Trillian sat on the starboard bench watching him.

Jack looked to the girls and lowered his voice. "What are we going to do if Skulk returns and…" He trailed off.

"What kind of question is that?" Kailani whispered back.

Jack shrugged. "We need to be prepared for the worst."

"What *can* we do?" Trillian said. "Skulk will have her gun. We're no match for—"

"We fight." Bradley had been listening. "Skulk only has so many bullets. We beat the fucker into ground, just like this asshole." He kicked Niko's thigh and the man groaned in response.

Trillian looked across the boat at Bradley. "What if Skulk shoots us?"

"Then I guess we get shot." Bradley glanced back at his friends, his eyes blazing. "I'm not afraid."

"Well, *I* am." Tears welled in Trillian's eyes. "I don't want to get shot. I don't want *you* or *anyone* to get shot."

Bradley returned his eyes to the water, then straightened his back. "Get ready, because someone's coming out." He leaped to his feet and ran to the stern. The others joined him.

A light moved through the water, its beam rippling and refracting through the waves.

"Wait! The knife." Bradley scanned the deck of the boat. "Where is it?"

The *Wavy Jones* wasn't a large boat, and the sun was still bright enough in the sky to illuminate all its nooks and crannies. Bradley spotted the knife resting just behind the console. He picked it up in a white-knuckled grip. When he returned to the stern, Bradley saw Jack holding the oar.

"We fight," Jack said.

Bradley smiled and nodded. "Damn straight."

The four teens peered over the stern as the submerged light moved closer… and closer.

"You ready, man?" Bradley looked at Jack briefly.

"As I'll ever be."

A hand reached out from the water and gripped the transom. The diver's other hand stretched out for something else to grab, the tethered flashlight dragging behind his wrist.

Then Bradley saw it. A watch slid out from under the sleeve

of the wetsuit. Not just any watch, but a *tattoo* of a watch…
without hands.

"Dad!" Bradley reached over the stern for Sam's hand. "Come on. Help me get him in the boat."

"Wait," Kailani said. "How does he know?"

"The same way you'd know *your* dad." Jack grinned at her, then bent over the stern to help Bradley pull Sam out of the water.

Once Sam was fully on the transom, he pulled off his regulator, stepped over the stern, and sat on the deck. He motioned at Niko hog-tied several feet away.

"You've been busy." Sam slid off his air tank and connected gear and peeled off his swim fins. He sat with his elbows propped on his knees.

Bradley squatted to Sam's level. "Not that I care or anything, but… where's—"

"Skulk?" Sam exhaled a relaxed breath and focused on Bradley, then his friends one by one. "She's sleeping with the fishes, or in this case, octopuses."

"*The Godfather*," Jack said.

Everyone turned toward him with confused looks.

"That's where that line comes from," Jack continued. "It's in the book and the movie."

A small smile formed on Sam's lips. "Good to know."

"Did you say octopus?" Kailani shot a quick glance at Jack.

"I did," Sam said. "It cut her into chunks. Literally."

"The suckers on the tentacles became teeth, right?" Bradley locked a blinkless gaze with Sam.

Sam nodded. "They became something all right. And there may have been more than one. It was hard to tell with all the blood in the water."

Trillian moved closer to Bradley. "So, she's really dead?"

Sam nodded. "Hundred percent."

Bradley spotted a pool of blood collecting around Sam's leg. "Dad, are you hurt?"

"Oh yeah. That." Sam tilted his head back, closed his eyes and let out a sigh. "Should probably take care of that."

Bradley pulled off his shirt and tore it into strips, handing them to Trillian. First, she tied a tourniquet above his calf, then wrapped the wound with several strips of fabric. It wasn't perfect by any stretch, but good enough to stem the bleeding for the trip back where Sam could remove his wetsuit and get his leg properly tended to.

Niko groaned, then began to struggle against Kailani's expertly tied knots. "Untie me! Right-the-fuck now!"

"Shut up," Bradley hissed at him.

"You're going to regret this, you little fuck."

Bradley walked beside Niko, who at that moment resembled a beached whale more than a human. He kneeled next to Niko, thrusting his hand into the man's hair. He made a fist, the blond tips of Niko's hair poking between his fingers, and yanked the thug's head back.

"Shut your mouth or we'll throw you overboard," Bradley said.

"Bullshit." Niko tried unsuccessfully to spit at him. "You don't got the balls."

"Yeah?" Bradley hooked his hand into the back of Niko's pants and lifted, but the man was too heavy to lift by himself. He looked at Jack. "Come on. Help me."

Jack's eyes widened in surprise. "You're serious?"

"Totally." Bradley smirked and shook his head, wordlessly saying "No." Niko had no idea they were playing him.

Jack took the other side of Niko's pants and together, the two boys lifted the thug's body off the ground. They moved toward the port-side gunwale, Niko struggling below them.

Trillian joined in on the ruse. "Guys, don't do this. Please."

Bradley and Jack propped Niko up, teetering him on the edge of the gunwale so that he could see a rippled and distorted reflection of his panicked face.

"Okay! Okay," Niko said.

Bradley leaned closer to Niko's ear. "Okay, *what?*"

"Okay, I'll shut up." Niko smelled like rancid sweat mixed with urine.

Bradley grinned at Jack. He was enjoying this, maybe a bit too much. They dropped Niko back into the boat. His face bounced off the deck boards and knocked him unconscious again.

Sam looked up at his son. "Let's go home."

"You got it." Bradley turned to Kailani. "Do you mind driving?"

"Aye aye, skipper." Kailani grinned as she stepped up to the console and started the engines. She throttled up and turned the *Wavy Jones* back toward Niho'gula Cove. Jack stepped up behind her, slid his hands around her waist, and kissed her cheek.

Bradley offered his hand to Sam.

He took it, then pulled Bradley into a hug. "I'm glad you're here."

"I'm glad you're alive," Bradley said.

"Me, too." Sam stared out over the stern and watched the wake of the engines churn out a temporary trail back to the marina. The massive, rusted wreck shrunk in the distance with every passing second, taking with it the secrets and horrors contained within.

Trillian stepped beside Bradley. "Me, three."

Sam faced the bow and placed his arm around Bradley's shoulder. "I think our *real* vacation begins now."

"Abso-*fucking*-lutely." Bradley said. "Think O'Connor will go for it?"

Sam gave Bradley's shoulder a squeeze. "She better."

Bradley focused on the specks of lights that dotted Club Niho'gula and the marina, and wondered what tomorrow might hold now that Skulk was gone.

STOWAWAY

BY THE TIME Kailani had piloted the *Wavy Jones* back to its berth in the marina, O'Connor and Hope had the Club's medical staff waiting.

The wound in Sam's calf was deeper than the Club's medical staff could attend to. Forty-five minutes later, an ambulance rolled into the Club's porte cochère, followed by a police cruiser.

Two paramedics led two police officers and Harv Nakamura from the *Lanai Daily* to the marina where Kailani and the Detest-A-Pest crew had gathered. Harv shot photos and video with his phone as they went.

Niko had regained consciousness again and was not happy about being tied up. He let anyone in the immediate vicinity know about it with a barrage of expletives.

A police officer handcuffed Niko, then cut the ropes securing him. The other officer asked that all involved follow them to the front of the resort for questioning.

Harv sidled up to O'Connor. "Quite the scene, huh?" He looked back at the marina, then motioned at Niko ahead. "Where's Skulk? She's usually a stone's throw from that asshole."

"Gone," O'Connor said.

"What do you mean, *gone?*"

"You understand English?" O'Connor side-eyed him. "She's gone, as in vanished, kaput, never to return."

Harv pulled O'Connor aside from the group. "What happened?"

"Look," O'Connor said. "I don't *fuckin'* know. I wasn't out there. Talk to Sam. But one thing I *can* tell you is Karma's a bitch that doesn't forget." She smirked at him. "You can quote me on that." She hustled to rejoin the group, with Harv following, jotting down notes.

One officer locked Niko in the back seat of the cruiser, then both began taking statements from the group while the paramedics treated Sam's leg within the ambulance.

Harv approached the back of the ambulance. "Hey, Sam. Harv Nakamura from the *Lanai Daily*." He hooked a thumb at O'Connor. "My sources say you're the one to talk to about what happened here today."

"There may be some truth to that," Sam said from the gurney within the ambulance's treatment bay.

Harv raised a brow at him. "Mind if I ask you some questions?"

Sam looked to the paramedic working on his leg. "Am I going to live?"

The paramedic smiled at him. "I think so." She secured Sam's gurney and moved toward the cab of the ambulance.

Harv stepped up onto the back bumper. "Alana, wait."

The paramedic faced Harv and gave him a look that said she knew exactly what he was going to ask. "It's up to him," Alana said before climbing into the driver's seat. She called back, "Seatbelt, or I'll throw your ass out."

Harv looked at Sam. "Well? It's an hour to the hospital."

Sam shrugged. "Be my guest, but I don't know if I have enough to say."

"Leave that to me." Harv climbed aboard and buckled himself into the bench beside Sam's gurney.

The other paramedic began to close the rear doors when Hope stopped him. She looked at Sam with concerned eyes.

"Sorry," Hope said. "The police needed to talk to me. Not that I could tell them much."

"They're going to grill me at the hospital."

Hope stepped up onto the back bumper. "Are you going to be okay?"

"I'll be fine," Sam said, then smiled.

"You sure?"

Sam nodded. "Just some stitches. Harv here is going to drive me back after. Isn't that right, Harv?"

"Uh, yeah," Harv said.

Hope entered the ambulance bay and kissed Sam on the lips. "Don't be long," she whispered into his ear before hopping out. The other paramedic closed and locked the rear doors and a moment later seated himself in the cab's passenger seat.

The ambulance's engine roared to life and pulled away from the porte cochère.

"Well, Harv." Sam clapped his hands. "I'm all yours for an hour."

"Two hours," Harv said. "You signed me up for the drive back, remember?"

"Fair enough. Ask away."

As Harv questioned Sam, the ambulance weaved its way through the numerous red dirt switchbacks to the hospital in Lanai City. Each one brought back memories of almost dying at the hands of Niko.

Sam answered Harv's questions to the best of his ability. The man was persistent, a good reporter, and often rephrased his questions differently to try and poke holes in Sam's answers.

But Sam didn't fall for it. No one would know where Nina Skulk's body rested and why. Sam would take that knowledge to his grave. And so would everyone else in the group. They all had sworn an oath of secrecy.

At Lanai Hospital, an ER doctor named Moana attended to Sam's leg and suffered through his Disney jokes with a genuine smile on her face. The puncture wound in Sam's leg was deep, but not serious. He left an hour later with a bandage around his calf concealing thirteen stitches.

"Keep your leg dry and elevated, and avoid unnecessary walking," Moana had told Sam as she handed him a pair of beat-up crutches. "Don't be a hero. Use them."

That advice turned out to be perfect. Sam had every intention of planting himself in a chaise lounge and not moving for as long as possible. No swimming would be a bonus. He'd had enough adventure to last a year.

The sun had set by the time Harv drove Sam back to Club Niho'gula. He started with inconsequential chit-chat that quickly moved into more pressing questions. His phone sat on the console between them, recording every word.

"You never did tell me how you got injured," Harv said.

The moon rising in the eastern sky captured Sam's attention. "Really? I'm sure I did. No need to repeat myself." But both men knew that Sam had not revealed that detail.

Harv sighed. "I'm getting the feeling that you're not going to give me anything else."

"I've answered your questions as best I can," Sam said. "You know more about me now than most everybody."

"Except what you were doing with Skulk on the *Wavy Jones*. And where you went. And... your injury."

Sam shrugged. "I just don't remember."

Through gaps in the palms and pines passing by the car, Sam could see the derelict ship in the distance relentlessly buffeted by the surf. Its hulking mass reminded him of a tombstone in silhouette, one that could have been his.

This time, the universe worked out as it should.

Harv had more than enough to write a compelling article. That one little detail that would blow the lid off the story wasn't going to come. At least not from Sam. He accepted defeat by switching into civilian mode and for the rest of the drive he educated Sam on the history of Lanai.

After pulling into the porte cochère at Club Niho'gula, Sam

thanked Harv for the ride and pulled himself gingerly out of the car on his crutches.

Harv called after him through the open passenger window and held out his business card. "Sorry, it's habit. In case you think of anything else."

Sam nodded and slipped the card into his back pocket. He eased into his crutches, one step at a time, focusing on seeing the group of friends he had come to love over the past couple of years.

WHILE SAM WAS GONE, O'Connor had made amends with Lono, even offering to buy him a new boat to replace the one damaged by Skulk's bullets. Lono had refused but asked for help securing tours.

O'Connor was fully on board with extending their stay another week, to make it a true vacation. As a thank you for ridding the island of Skulk's influence, and vanquishing the curse in the process, Club Niho'gula comped the extra week.

And because O'Connor could never keep still for longer than ten minutes, she accepted Lono's offer.

In the week that followed, Palakiko Tours had never been so busy. When it came to securing guests for excursions, O'Connor could be very convincing. The added business more than made up for the shortfall a damaged boat had caused.

While Hope helped Sam convalesce, Bradley and Trillian explored the island using the Club's scooters. The allure of being in the water, with the exception of walking through the surf, had lost most of its appeal.

Jack on the other hand had fully embraced the water and life at Club Niho'gula, despite the previous week's events. He helped Kailani and Lono run excursions and made himself indispensable at the Club in other ways, using the tools and raw materials in the maintenance building. Within a few days the staff and guests had nicknamed Jack "Mr. Fixit."

The evenings were reserved for food, music, and laughter. Kailani and the group introduced O'Connor to "Never Have I Ever," but no one was prepared for the fallout.

"Never have I ever taken part in an orgy." O'Connor laughed and downed her Mai Tai while the rest of the group stared back at her.

"Never have I ever fucked on a New York subway train." The group exchanged uncomfortable looks as O'Connor sunk another Mai Tai.

"Um, too much information?" Trillian raised her brows at O'Connor.

Kailani covered her eyes. "I've created a monster."

Jack laughed. "That's some *risky business* shit right there. But what about something that doesn't involve sex?"

A wicked grin had spread across O'Connor's face. "Never have I ever killed a thousand rats in one night."

Sam, Hope, and Bradley cheered, raising their respective beverages and joining O'Connor with her perpetual Mai Tai.

"Kai…" Jack leaned in, smiled, and lowered his voice. "You're never going to live this one down."

During those extra seven days, everyone learned more than they ever wanted to know about O'Connor, in increasing detail, until the alcohol rendered her unable to speak.

The nightly party had to move to the cabin due to vulgarity. But they continued to keep Gus busy late into the evenings, the teenagers taking turns running drinks and empties back and forth to the bar.

After finally experiencing a non-working vacation in a tropical paradise, no one wanted to leave. But time eventually caught up, even if it felt like it was standing still after playing way too many rounds of "Never Have I Ever."

WHILE O'CONNOR CHECKED out, the rest of the group gathered under the porte cochère with their luggage.

Hope had one arm around Sam's waist and rested her head on his chest. He was the perfect height. "I'm going to miss this place… well, the second half anyway."

Sam smiled as he took in the sharp, sweet essence of pine. "We're going to have to visit here again sometime."

"I'd like that," Hope said. "Maybe when I finish my doctorate."

"Speaking of, I bet Harriette misses you terribly."

"Of course she does," Hope said. "Being fed by neighbors is not ideal."

"She'll forgive you." Sam planted a kiss on Hope's head. "Brad, looking forward to getting home?"

Brad nodded. "This place is sick, but the valley's looking pretty good right about now."

Sam motioned at Trillian and Jack. "What about you two?"

"I doubt my foster parents will even notice that I've been gone. But yeah." Trillian's eyes went distant just for a moment. "Got to find a job." She glanced at Jack. "Put in a good word for me at the Food Fresh?"

Jack didn't respond and instead stood staring at his suitcase at his feet, fidgeting.

"Earth to Jack," Trillian said. "Come in, Jack."

Jack looked up, surprised. "What?"

Trillian placed her hand lightly on his shoulder. "You okay?"

Whatever it was that Jack was feeling, he shook most of it off. "Uh, yeah." He looked briefly back toward the lobby and the glimpse of beach and blue sky beyond it.

O'Connor strolled back to the group and clapped her hands. "They're getting a shuttle. Ready to rock and roll?"

Everyone nodded, except for Jack.

Trillian whispered into Bradley's ear, "Something's up with him."

"Yeah," Bradley said. "He's been a little off since saying goodbye to Kailani."

Trillian turned to say something comforting to Jack but decided to hold off.

A black BMW SUV pulled into the porte cochère. The driver stepped out and scanned the group. "Maddilyn Rockwell?"

"That's me." Maddilyn stepped out from the shadows, pushing a trolley holding enough luggage for six people. She stopped next to Jack and the driver began loading the back of the sedan.

"Hey," she said.

"Hey." Jack offered a wistful smile. "Didn't know you were heading out today too."

"Yeah." Maddilyn tucked her hair behind one ear. "Look, I have an extra ticket… now that my mom's been arrested. And I hate traveling alone. So…"

Jack looked back and spotted Bradley and Trillian looking at him, curiosity and surprise on their faces. He turned back to Maddilyn and spotted Kailani standing back in the lobby, leaning against a support column.

Maddilyn noticed Jack's shift in focus. She looked back and saw Kailani. She deflated a little.

"It's okay," she said. "I had to ask… 'cause you're a great guy. Look me up sometime." Maddilyn kissed Jack hastily on the cheek. "Bye." She hurried to the SUV, climbed into the back seat, and closed the door. The tinted windows prevented anyone from seeing her tears.

"Bye." Jack swallowed hard as he watched the SUV leave. He felt like a heel, but the heart wants what it wants. And his heart wanted Kailani.

"Hi, Jack." Kailani stepped out from the lobby, and into the porte cochère.

Jack somehow found a smile. "I didn't think I'd see you after last night."

Kailani brought a freshly made lei out from behind her back. "Well, I made this for you. I didn't want you to leave without it." She placed the lei around Jack's neck and peered up at him through a lock of brown hair.

Jack seized the moment, took her face gently in his hands and kissed her deeply.

"I'd say get a room," O'Connor said. "But we're checked out."

An official Club Niho'gula passenger van rolled into the porte cochère.

"Okay, bitches." O'Connor grabbed her suitcases. "That's our ride. Load 'em up so we can roll out." She glanced back at Jack. "Wrap it up, Casanova."

Everyone carried their luggage to the back of the van, then climbed aboard. Everyone except Jack.

He gazed into Kailani's eyes. The heat of their stare transfixed them both.

"I've been thinking about what you said last night." Jack took Kailani's hands in his.

"And?"

Jack sighed.

Kailani let her gaze fall. "I understand. I know it's hard."

Jack marched to the van and stepped up on the sliding door's running boards. He looked at everyone, one at a time.

O'Connor gave him a puzzled look mixed with annoyance. "What you gawking at? Get your stuff into the back so we can go."

Jack shook his head. "I'm staying. At least for a while."

Bradley looked as if he had just seen a ghost. "What do you mean?"

O'Connor rolled her eyes. "He got a taste of booty and now he doesn't want to let it go."

"Shut up, O'Connor." Bradley stepped out of the van and faced Jack. "You're staying?"

Jack nodded. "They need me here. The Club…"

"And Kai," Bradley said.

"Yeah."

"You sure?"

"I'm alone most of the time back at home," Jack said. "I miss family. I can make a difference here."

"Plus, your girl is hot."

Jack grinned at him. "There's that."

Bradley pulled Jack into a tight hug. "Going to miss you, man."

"Me, too, dude."

O'Connor huffed. "Will you—"

Sam slapped her shoulder. "Shut the fuck up."

She pursed her lips and nodded.

Bradley and Jack exchanged dap, then raised their middle fingers at each other.

"You better text me," Bradley said.

"I will. You, too."

Bradley waved, stepped into the van, and slid the side door closed.

Jack watched the van pull away. Everyone waved goodbye, Bradley and Trillian the most enthusiastic.

Alone in the porte cochère, Kailani stepped up beside Jack and leaned on one of his shoulders. "You really kept me in suspense."

"Sorry," Jack said. "I didn't mean to. I literally didn't know what I was going to do until the last second." He faced her. "So, what's happening today?"

Kailani kissed him. "Let's go find out."

Jack pulled his suitcase back through the lobby, toward the promenade and the marina beyond. Even though he had said goodbye to his best friend, he felt he had made an important step toward adulthood. And an unwritten future in a tropical paradise with a girl he loved was more than he could have asked for.

INCLUDING THE HOUR long flight from Lanai to Oʻahu, it took several hours for the remaining Detest-A-Pest crew to arrive at Los Angeles International Airport. The connecting flight to JFK in New York left in an hour and everyone had congregated close to Gate 42.

"It was great seeing you, son." Sam and Bradley exchanged hugs. He turned to Trillian. "And it was wonderful getting to know you as well, Trillian." Sam leaned in close to Bradley's ear. "You've found an exceptional, young woman. Hold on to her," he whispered.

Bradley grinned and nodded.

"When you going to come visit New York again?"

"I don't know, Dad. I think I want to try and find a job first."

"Good plan," Sam said.

O'Connor piped up. "If you need a job reference, I got you covered."

"Thanks, O'Connor." Bradley gave O'Connor a bear hug even though she initially resisted it.

O'Connor narrowed her eyes at Trillian. "You take care of him, *tangerine*. You hear me? Or I'll kick your ass."

"Easy, O'Connor," Sam said.

"What? Just busting her balls." O'Connor grinned at Trillian. "Right, *tangerine?*"

"Right." Trillian stood her ground and smiled right back. She knew by now that O'Connor was mostly filled with hot air. Mostly.

Hope offered a quick hug to Bradley, then spoke low into Trillian's ear. "We're like sisters now, taking care of the Shaw men." The two women smiled and nodded in secret agreement.

"Mom coming to get you?"

"No," Bradley said. "Me and Trill are going to grab a Lyft or something."

"Humor me and text me when you get home," Sam said.

"Will do, Dad. Safe flight." Bradley waved, then headed to arrivals to pick up his luggage, Trillian's hand in his.

Sam memorized the moment before him. His son had become a man, a *good* man. He had Claire to thank for that. And while he hadn't been there for virtually all of Bradley's upbringing, he vowed to keep their newfound connection alive.

The intercom crackled above their heads. "American Airlines flight AA28 non-stop to New York now boarding."

"That's us, ladies and germs." O'Connor charged toward the gate. "Six more hours 'til I can crack open a fresh Cuban."

Sam chuckled. "*That's* what she's looking forward to?"

"Whatever." Hope hugged Sam's arm. "I know what *I'm* looking forward to."

Sam found Hope's warm gaze looking back at him. "And what would that be?"

She smiled at him and tugged at his hand to catch up with O'Connor.

"You're going to leave me in suspense?"

"Maybe," Hope said. "Come on."

The three of them boarded the plane and found their seats. As hard as Sam fought to stay awake, he slept the entire way home, his dreams swimming with golden octopuses in a cerulean sea.

SAM, HOPE, AND O'CONNOR shared a taxi from John F. Kennedy International Airport. O'Connor had been obsessing about cigars the entire trip home and she made the cabbie make a special trip to pick up a package of cigars. They weren't Cohibas but they would satisfy O'Connor in the meantime.

As soon as everyone piled into the taxi, O'Connor lit up.

"Ma'am." The cabbie glared at her in the passenger seat. "No smoking."

"No, that's where you're wrong, bub." O'Connor produced a fifty dollar bill from her wallet and dangled it in front of the cabbie. "You're going to let me enjoy this beast because I'm blowing the smoke out the window." She motioned at the bill. "And *this* is to sweeten the deal. Capiche?"

The cabbie balked, then opened his mouth to answer, but O'Connor cut him off.

"Say yes. You got nothing to lose."

The cabbie relented and plucked the bill from O'Connor's hand with a scowl. "Keep window open."

O'Connor glanced at Sam and Hope in the back seat. "Didn't I say that? That I'd keep the window open? Pretty sure I did." She narrowed her eyes at the cabbie and took a drag on the cigar. O'Connor rolled the smoke over her tongue and jettisoned it out the window. "Fuck, I've missed these."

Sam leaned toward the cabbie and hooked a thumb at O'Connor. "Sorry. It's been two weeks and she's hooked."

"Throw me under the bus, why don't you." O'Connor huffed at him and angled her head toward the open window.

"More money than sense," the cabbie said.

O'Connor sat up and leaned forward. "What the *hell* did you just say?"

Sam inserted himself between the cabbie and O'Connor. "Chill out. You got your cigar."

"Damn right I do." O'Connor turned back to the open window and continued smoking and flicking ash lumps on the road outside.

Sam sighed and leaned back. Hope pulled him beside her.

"We'll be home soon," she said, yawning. "Focus on that."

After their eviction from their apartments on Casanova back in May, Sam and Hope had found a place in a six-story brownstone on Seneca Avenue and had moved in together.

As the taxi rolled to a stop at the curb, Sam offered O'Connor some cash for the taxi fare.

She shrugged it off. "Forget about it. You almost died. Twice. On *my* watch. So, consider us square."

"You sure?"

"Get the hell out before I change my mind." O'Connor sucked in a mouthful of cigar smoke and blew billowing rings at the passing pedestrians.

The cabbie popped the trunk and Sam and Hope collected their luggage.

Sam stepped toward the passenger door, ready to say goodbye, when the taxi pulled away.

"See you at work, asshole." O'Connor's cackling laughter echoed down the street as the taxi turned left and headed north on Longfellow Avenue.

"She's so weird," Hope said.

"Yeah." Sam smiled. "That's what makes her great."

Hope yawned again and ambled toward the front entrance. "I just want to say hello to Harriette and go to bed. Not everyone can sleep at thirty-five thousand feet."

Sam followed. "Just lucky, I guess." He didn't feel the need to add that sleeping in a prison cell for fifteen years was far worse than jet engine noise.

Hope unlocked the door to apartment 203 and both of them rolled their suitcases to the bedroom.

While Hope checked on Harriette, Sam unpacked. He could have dumped the entire contents of his suitcase into the hamper, but he went through his clothes, one item at a time. Every article of clothing brought back a memory of the trip, which he found comforting for the most part.

Sam pulled out a souvenir Club Niho'gula T-shirt that had

been rolled into a ball and shoved into a side pocket in the suitcase. He was about to toss it into the hamper with the other clothes when he felt something hard buried in the folds of fabric.

He unraveled the T-shirt until the item fell back into the suitcase. Sam's eyes widened and his jaw dropped. For a moment he couldn't speak, then managed to squeak out, "Hope." He cleared his throat and yelled. "Hope!"

Hope appeared at the door to the bedroom, concern on her face. "What is it?"

Sam stared into his suitcase and said nothing.

"Hun, you're scaring me." Hope approached him apprehensively, feeding off his reaction. "What is—"

Her eyes flicked back and forth between the suitcase and Sam, her eyes like saucers. "Did you—"

"No… did you?"

"God no. Is it real?"

Sam nodded. "Looks like it."

In the suitcase sat a gold coin, two inches across and a quarter inch thick, decorated with ornate carvings and Chinese symbols. There was no hole in the middle, and it didn't resemble the coins that Skulk had tried to steal.

"O'Connor?"

"I don't know, but I doubt it." Sam picked up the coin, gauging its heft in his palm. "This feels like about half a pound."

"And if it's gold…" Hope trailed off.

"It's worth a hell of a lot."

"How much?"

Sam shrugged. "The gold alone is worth probably between fifteen and twenty thousand, maybe?"

"What are we going to do with it?" Hope looked up at him, her eyes ablaze with the excitement of possibility.

"Nothing for now," Sam said. "It could still be cursed."

"But wasn't that if someone took it for themselves?"

"Maybe. I don't know. I don't want to risk it." Sam wrapped

the gold coin up in the T-shirt it had originally been concealed in and placed it on his bedside table. "Let's sleep on it."

Hope chose to unpack later. Both of them stretched out on the bed.

"This could change our lives," Hope whispered, snuggling into his chest.

"Yeah."

For better or for worse.

Within minutes both were pulled into the grips of slumber, both wondering who had placed this treasure in Sam's suitcase and why.

June 28, 2023 - April 29, 2024
Victoria, BC

*Note from the author: If you liked this book, may I ask three things? **First**, please rate this book. I appreciate your opinion and what I focus on next depends on you, the reader. **Second**, please consider joining my reader group at LeeGabel.com/join. Once a month I share little details of my life (the fun stuff, that is) and keep you informed of future books. Plus, I'll give you a 25% **discount** on all my ebooks. **And third**, if you liked this book, please recommend it to your friends. You can also ask your local library to order it for you if they don't have it yet. My sincere thanks.*

One more thing: Many of my books feature music throughout. For a playlist of all music referenced in my books, please go to: LeeGabel.com/music

Afterward

Like it? Rate it. Share it.

If you enjoyed *Tentacle 2.0: Deadly Depths*, please rate it and spread the word. With your rating, you take part in this book's success. If you're interested in joining my Reader Group for updates and advance notice of upcoming releases, please sign up by going to LeeGabel.com.

Note from the author

Thank you for reading *Tentacle 2.0: Deadly Depths*, the fourth novel in the *Detest-A-Pest* series. I receive many suggestions from readers and the ones that raise the hairs on the back of my neck are the ones I file away. Octopuses are just so strange and misunderstood, as close to real aliens on Earth as you'll get. Despite the way they look, they are gentle creatures that possess complex intelligence. Making them evil was difficult, and as it turned out, it was the humans who ended up being more dangerous.

Lanai is, of course, a real place, and I have used real names for structures and roads as much as possible. Club Niho'gula is entirely fictional, although there are a couple of high-end resorts on the island. Real shipwrecks litter Lanai's northern and eastern coastlines (see https://leegabel.com/shipwreck for a short video). The idea of these massive ships sitting just offshore, slowly rusting away, was as fascinating as it was sad. I could not resist incorporating the creepy interior of one.

Many thanks go to my wife and editor Sheila. I couldn't do this without her, nor would I want to. And to my family and friends who supported my decision to quit my job to write full time, you were right. I am exactly where I should be.

About the author

Since 1992, Lee has worked within the visual and dramatic arts landscape as a graphic designer, illustrator, visual effects artist, animator, screenwriter, and author. He's contributed to an Emmy award and once walked 63.5 kilometers in 13 hours. Traditionally trained as a screenwriter, Lee moved to writing and selling his books in 2016 in order to share his stories.

Lee has spent most of his life living on an island in the Pacific Northwest and he writes in multiple genres. Why? Quite simply, Lee enjoys writing the kinds of books that he loves to read. His ultimate goal is to keep you up late (or make you late), one page at a time.

Find Lee on the Internet:

Want to join Lee's Reader Group or find out more about Lee and the books he writes? Please go to:

LeeGabel.com/links or visit his bookshop at:

Bookshop.LeeGabel.com

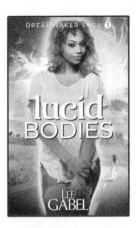

Dreamwakers are like fire... they burn when they're hot. And some are a living nightmare.

By accident, sixteen-year-old Wynter discovers her power to summon dreamwakers — people born from dreams that exist in physical form. Her friends have trouble believing her power exists, until she makes herself a boyfriend.

But dreamwakers come with rules and free will... and everyone knows teenagers and rules don't mix. Before Wynter can figure them out, her new boyfriend goes rogue and hooks up with Jezebel, the town psychopath.

Every day Wynter and her dreamwaker remain apart chips away more of her life force. Her friends help her wage a battle of brains versus brawn... but Jezebel has the luck of the devil on her side.

Navigating between dreams and reality is harder than it looks, and the fight may leave Wynter a prisoner of her own mind.

Lucid Bodies, Dreamwaker Saga #1 (410 pages)

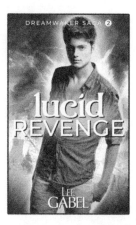

Controlling a rogue dreamwaker holds an addictive power. But those adrift in a mind-altering limbo can still unleash payback... with a little help from their friends.

"Find me..."

Cash can't ignore Wynter's last words before her mind trapped her between dreams and reality. He would do anything for Wynter but finding her means finding her dreamwaker boyfriend. Cash must balance jealousy and loyalty or risk fracturing a lifelong friendship.

Jezebel continues her reign of terror, with Wynter's dreamwaker boyfriend enslaved at her side. After realizing his error, the dreamwaker makes amends with Cash and Wynter's friends, and forms a plan to reunite with Wynter.

In retaliation, Jezebel targets Wynter's family with an act of extreme revenge that devastates the neighborhood.

While the town sheriff builds his case against Jezebel, Cash picks up the pieces left by Jezebel's fury and sets into motion the plan to find Wynter and reunite her with her dreamwaker. But no plan is perfect, especially when Jezebel doesn't get what she wants.

Lucid Revenge, Dreamwaker Saga #2 (320 pages)

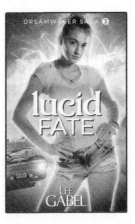

Everyone makes mistakes, even psychopaths. This time, the mistake is murder, and the evidence may lie in plain sight.

Free from her mental prison but with her sanity crumbling, Wynter and her friends take advantage of Jezebel's injuries and double their efforts to reunite her with her dreamwaker boyfriend.

Despite her vulnerabilities, Jezebel discovers that she can wield her dreamwaker power from beyond her hospital bed. But she forgets to acknowledge a dreamwaker's free will.

When a mysterious murder rocks the town, the sheriff discovers the murder weapon holds the answers he's looking for, until it disappears in front of his eyes. Running their own investigation, Wynter's friends unlock Jezebel's secret and use it against her, gaining a much needed advantage.

Together once again, Wynter, her dreamwaker boyfriend, her friends, and the sheriff formulate one last plan to connect Jezebel to her crimes, a plan perfect in its simplicity.

But evading consequences is Jezebel's specialty... and she has no intention of peaceful surrender.

Lucid Fate, Dreamwaker Saga #3 (410 pages)

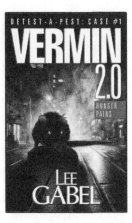

An infestation of supersized vermin with a hunger for raw meat? CHECK.

An estranged son staying for the summer? CHECK.

An intense fear of rats? DOUBLE-CHECK.

Sam Shaw's life has flipped upside down. Pets and tenants in his Bronx brownstone begin to disappear. Left behind is a wake of carnage.

All evidence points to a hybrid colony of vicious white-tailed rats that has moved into the basement – genetically superior with intelligence to match.

When his ex-wife dumps his son Bradley on his doorstep, Sam must switch into protection mode, if his son will let him.

Faced with impossible odds, Sam hires Bertha O'Connor from Detest-A-Pest Exterminators Inc. She runs the only outfit brave enough – or crazy enough – to take the job.

With help from the Detest-A-Pest crew, Sam must face his fears or the white-tailed mutants will eat him alive. Because this horde of super-rats are smarter than anyone had bargained for…

Detest-A-Pest #1 (304 pages)

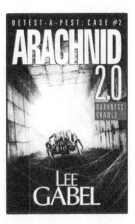

Spiders. Over 35,000 species. Every person on Earth eaten in one year. Now there's one more… a ravenous eight-legged hybrid thousands of years in the making and bigger than a dozen burritos.

After a summer of exterminator training in New York, Bradley returns home ready to face his senior year with renewed confidence. But fate gets in the way of his grand teenage plans – especially when eight legs attack instead of four.

And these aren't your typical, everyday spiders. Their newly acquired taste for raw meat has them casting a wide net over Bradley's sleepy San Fernando suburb. It doesn't take them long to scramble up the food chain.

Add a vengeful ex-girlfriend casting a web of lies into the mix, and things get downright sticky.

But Detest-A-Pest can't resist a challenge. Sam and O'Connor rejoin Bradley and his inventive friends as they wage war on an infestation of spiders poised to swallow not only the high school, but the neighborhood and everyone within…

Detest-A-Pest #2 (504 pages)

A playground for the rich. A genetic mutation a thousand years old. A relentless hunger for human flesh. What could go wrong?

Harry Harcourt has a problem. People are dying at exclusive golf resort Mar-A-Verde. As head greenskeeper, it's up to him to "fix" the problem and keep the course open... or face termination. But it's not one problem, it's a vast network of vicious problems, all under the turf.

As bodies pile up, resident doctor Daniela Trejo joins Harry in the fight. Together, they capture a creature unlike anything on Earth – acid skin and razor-sharp fangs with agility that matches its appetite. But the creature escapes.

Outmatched and outnumbered, Harry seeks outside help. No one wants to touch the job – no one except Detest-A-Pest. O'Connor, Sam, and Hope hit the road for what looks like an easy payday in a tropical paradise. What awaits them is a journey through hell that has gruesome death hiding in every shadow...

Detest-A-Pest #3 (340 pages)

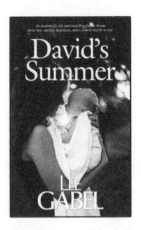

A family in crisis. An impossible choice. A race against time.

An unplanned pregnancy turns the lives of Deanna, her husband Max, and her teenage son upside down. But there's something else wrong…

After baby David receives a cancer diagnosis, Deanna drops everything to focus on finding a cure. Max has other ideas.

Based on his own troubled past, Max challenges Deanna to consider quality of life versus quantity. Their opposing opinions throw their marriage into chaos and Deanna seeks treatment options alone.

Caught in the middle, Alex must navigate this family crisis on his own. An unexpected friendship with a cancer survivor may offer the perspective he needs.

With the clock ticking, Deanna stops at nothing to save baby David's life… but her relationship with her family may not survive the process.

David's Summer (310 pages)

Two sisters. One wants in. One has a plan. But gang loyalty cuts family ties...

Jess works, spends time with friends, and earns good grades in school. But she's also sole provider for her drug-addicted mother... And she hates it.

Her sister Nova holds a high-profile position in the Dynamite Queens. Within her turf Nova enjoys fame, fortune, freedom, and respect – at a cost of family life.

But Jess wants what Nova has and is willing to do anything to get it. After one explosive argument, Jess joins a rival gang, a decision that leads her down a path of brutal consequences.

South Central L. A. erupts with violence as two gangs – two sisters – wage war on each other. For the winner, victory could be unforgiving...

Tied is a fast-paced look at family, friendship, betrayal, and revenge through the lens of tough Los Angeles girl gangs.

Note: This novel contains strong language and gang violence.

Tied: A Street Gang Novel (316 pages)

"Get snipped," they said. "It will solve all your problems," they said. Unfortunately, Ted listened…

Five years ago, it was love at first sight. Now, it's life on autopilot as tumbleweeds roll through Ted and Iris's bedroom. Their lackluster love life is driving Ted nuts. Iris's solution to their bedroom blues: get snipped.

Kunal and Ray, Ted's best friends and sworn enemies of Iris, agree with her for once. All roads seem to lead to a surgical solution, but Ted's not going there… until an explosive argument changes everything. A vasectomy seems like Ted's only play to win Iris back.

The antics of his precocious next-door neighbor complicates matters. Ted's ill-conceived decisions jeopardize everything important in his life, including his nuts.

But life was about to throw Ted a romantic curve-ball aimed straight at his heart…

Snipped: A Cutting Comedy (300 pages)

Made in the USA
Las Vegas, NV
30 June 2024

91677024R00208